"You should always wear your hair thus."

"I would look like a half-mad hoyden."

"You can be a hoyden tonight. You can be anything you want with me, Anne."

"What a terrifying offer." She sighed, closing her eyes as he bent to kiss her again, his mouth demanding a little more this time. His tongue teased her lips, coaxing, and she parted for him, allowing him access to the innermost recesses of her mouth, allowing him to fill her with heat, to tease, to mate with her as he would.

His hand moved between them, slowly undoing the laces of her vest. . . .

By Susan Carroll
Published by Fawcett Books:

THE LADY WHO HATED SHAKESPEARE
THE BISHOP'S DAUGHTER
THE WOOING OF MISS MASTERS
MISTRESS MISCHIEF
CHRISTMAS BELLES
MISS PRENTISS AND THE YANKEE
THE VALENTINE'S DAY BALL
BRIGHTON ROAD/THE SUGAR ROSE

THE
PAINTED
VEIL

Susan Carroll

FAWCETT CREST • NEW YORK

To my most esteemed patroness and friend,
Marilyn Sue Lemmon,
a good and gracious lady

A Fawcett Crest Book
Published by Ballantine Books
Copyright © 1995 by Susan Coppula

Library of Congress Catalog Card Number: TK

ISBN 0-449-14962-5

Manufactured in the United States of America

First Edition: October 1995

10 9 8 7 6 5 4 3 2 1

Prologue

❧⟨∞⟩❧

"Nine of the clock and a foggy night."

The ancient charley's voice rang out with cheerful assurance. The only other sound disrupting the stillness was a carriage rattling by, its team of horses clopping along the rain-wet cobblestones.

The old watchman stepped with confidence along Clarion Way, the street so serene it might have been no more than an architect's sketch of fashionable London. At the head of the square stood the Countess Sumner's brick mansion, the oldest house in the district. It loomed like an imposing matriach over the row of recently built townhouses. With their gleaming colonnades and brass door knockers, the modern structures appeared almost smug in their prosperity, candleshine spilling through the windows into the murky street below.

Most of the occupants had likely dined by now and were in the process of attiring themselves for the evening. Soon the street would become a hive of noise and activity, doors opening and closing, coaches coming and going, gentlemen and ladies dressed in their silks whisking away to some round of entertainment: a rout, a ball, or the theatre.

But for now, the old watchman paused to savor the quiet. Obadiah set down his lantern upon the pavement, flexing his gnarled fingers. Only a few hours more and he could go home to his mutton and pint of porter. He would be mighty glad of it, too. He was more tired than usual this evening, feeling his years, he supposed.

It was unseasonably warm for an early April evening, the

1

sudden shift in temperature causing mists to rise from the pavement. The far end of the square was all but lost in fog, the faint glow of the gas lamps providing little illumination.

The damp settled into Obadiah's bones, aggravating his rheumatism, but other than that, he scarce minded the haze blanketing the street like a gauzy coverlet. Far better fog than rain.

There were some as might think it made his task of patrolling the streets more dangerous. But whatever happened amiss on Clarion Way? Perhaps there was the occasional attempt at housebreaking or bout of fisticuffs between a footman and some pert delivery boy. But for the most part the square remained as orderly and dignified as the facades of the houses. Obadiah had little to do but call out the passing of the hours and the state of the weather, his watchman's rattle for summoning aid mostly unused.

Now it would be a far different tale tonight in Bethnal Green or that tumbledown area behind Westminister. The fog would bring the pickpockets, the thieves, and the footpads in droves. Obadiah did not envy his fellow charleys who patrolled those areas, especially poor old Adam Nash working the streets of Cheapside. They'd been having a spot of trouble there of late with one notorious cutpurse, known only as the Hook.

More daring and swift of foot than the rest, no one had ever gotten a proper look at the villain, other than to note he had only one hand, the other sleeve ending in a wicked bit of curving steel. The rascal grew bolder every day. Most recently, he'd robbed a plump baronet bare yards from the houses of Parliament. When that gentleman had objected to parting with his purse, the Hook had spiked his victim's shoulder like a butcher cleaving into a fat haunch of mutton.

Obadiah shuddered at the mere thought of it. Picking up his lantern, he shuffled along again, feeling fortunate to be far removed from the vicinity of the Hook and other suchlike murderous fiends. His most hazardous duty lay in checking the locks and windows of Number 32. The house hadn't been let this season and might offer a great temptation to some knowledgeable cracksman.

By the time Obadiah had completed his circuit around the dark, silent house, the traffic on the street had picked up some. Gentlemen who had chosen to dine at their clubs returned home to change their attire.

Obadiah watched as a hackney cab set down Nicholas Drummond, a congenial young gentleman with an arresting smile. Mr. Drummond wore a coat with several shoulder capes and a high-crowned beaver hat perched upon waves of tawny hair. He often called in the square to visit his married sister, or his cousin who lived several doors down.

After paying off the cabbie, Drummond strode away whistling a tuneless song. Upon spying Obadiah, he nodded by way of friendly greeting.

"Evening, Obadiah."

Obadiah swiftly doffed his own soft-brimmed cap.

"Good evening, sir."

"How goes it tonight?"

"All's quiet, sir. Naught to complain of except the damp."

"Indeed, the fog does seem to be getting worse. Well, have a care for yourself, Obadiah."

With another wave, Drummond sprinted up the steps and was admitted into his sister's house. The exchange had been brief, but Obadiah felt as warmed by it as if he'd taken a nip of rum. A real kindly gentleman was Master Nick. There weren't many like him. Few of the Quality would take any heed of a lowly watchman, let alone bid one to take care of oneself.

Certainly not Mr. Drummond's cousin, the marquis of Mandell, who lived at the farthest end of the street. Very high in the instep was the marquis. His lordship took no more notice of Obadiah than he did the gatepost. But perhaps that was just as well. Obadiah almost trembled at the thought of Mandell's gaze turning his way. Very hard intent eyes had the marquis of Mandell.

Obadiah supposed it was not his place to be studying the ways and characteristics of the Quality on his street, but the tedium of his job often left him little else to do. He trudged

down the length of the pavement, going so far as the next
square, then turned to come back again.

It was nearly quarter till ten and Mr. Drummond had
been correct. The fog did seem to be getting worse. When
the door to Number 17 opened, Obadiah was far enough
away that he could scarce make out the figures of two gentlemen stepping down into the mist. But he did not need to.
He knew full well who lived there.

Mr. Albert Glossop was the bane of the old charley's existence. Unlike Master Nick, Mr. Glossop displayed no
kindness or polished manners. A high-spirited youth, he and
his cronies derived some of their chief amusement from tormenting the watch, especially when Mr. Glossop had had a
touch too much brandy, which was not infrequent.

Obadiah had lost count of the number of dead cats that
had been flung in his path, buckets of slops tossed on his
head, hot coals shoved down his back. With vivid recollection of such past encounters, Obadiah hung back, waiting
until he was sure the two men coming out of Number 17
had gone well on their way.

By the time they reached the pavement, he was certain
one of them was indeed Mr. Glossop. There was no mistaking that familiar peacock blue redingote or the jaunty tilt of
his *chapeau bras*. The gentleman with him was obscured
by a dark cloak and a wide, floppy-brimmed hat pulled low
over his eyes. It was a plumed hat like Obadiah had once
seen in an old painting of one of those cavalier fellows.
Lord, who would wear a thing like that nowadays? But Mr.
Glossop had been entertaining some foreigners of late and
it was well known how queer those Frenchies could be.

The gentlemen summoned neither carriage nor hackney,
but walked off down the street. When the stranger turned,
Obadiah thought he caught a flash of something like the silver head of a walking stick. He gave it little consideration,
feeling only too relieved to have escaped the notice of Mr.
Glossop and his companion.

Only after the two men vanished into the mist did Obadiah resume his rounds. The fog-bound silence of the street
began to seem a little oppressive and he would be glad

when Clarion Way clattered with its usual nighttime activity.

Obadiah consulted his timepiece and started to sing out, "Ten of the clock and—"

His words were cut off by a cry that chilled his blood. It was like nothing human, an animal howling in pain. Obadiah whipped around, trying to still the pounding of his heart. What in the name of God had that been? Perhaps someone's dog crunched under the wheels of a carriage?

But Obadiah saw no coach, no sign of a dog or beast of any kind. There was nothing—only the relentless mist.

Then a voice rang out. "Help! Sweet Jesus! Someone please help me!"

Obadiah froze, making no move to dash to the rescue. That had sounded too much like Mr. Glossop. Likely this was only another of Master Bertie's tricks, Obadiah told himself. He was not about to go rushing forward simply to fall prey to a nasty bit of Glossop's humor.

But there came another shriek too convincing to be faked. Sweat beaded on Obadiah's brow despite the chill night air. Every instinct he possessed told him to flee in the opposite direction. But he forced himself to go forward, his lantern held high in his trembling hand. He had not taken many steps when a shadow rose up from the pavement before him, melting out of the mist, a figure garbed all in black.

"You there! What are you about? Halt!" Obadiah attempted to shout, but his voice came in wheezing gasps. The hooded phantom paid him no heed. In a swirl of dark cloak, the man vaulted over a wrought iron fence and vanished behind the marquis of Mandell's house. Obadiah fancied he heard a demonic laugh.

The Hook was the first thought that popped into the watchman's panicked brain, but he babbled, reassuring himself, "No, no! Not here on Clarion Way."

Perhaps he should seek to pursue the apparition. The marquis would not take kindly to a caped spectre creeping about beneath his windows and laughing. But Obadiah convinced himself that it was more his duty to see who had been calling for help.

There was no evidence of any other living soul, but something had been left abandoned on the pavement, like a bundle of clothes. As Obadiah crept closer and the haze parted, he saw that it was the form of a man, crumpled upon the paving stones. A man wearing a peacock blue coat.

"Nay, Mr. Glossop," Obadiah quavered, "Please don't be playing any more jests upon me."

He knew with desperate certainty that at any moment Bert Glossop was going to leap up, startling him out of his wits with a bloodcurdling cry or a box to his ear. Indeed, he prayed Master Bert would do just that, do anything but lie there, so still.

Standing over Glossop, Obadiah raised his lantern. He had to make himself glance down at the young man. Bert Glossop stared back at him, glassy eyed, his mouth hanging open.

It made him look rather stupid. It made him look dead. Obadiah's knees buckled beneath him, but he managed to kneel down. He had some vague notion he ought to check for a pulse. But when he got up enough nerve to touch the man, Obadiah's hand came away sticky with blood oozing from a hole torn in Glossop's throat.

Numb with shock, scarce knowing what he did, Obadiah tried to wipe his fingers off on the front of Glossop's coat, but another pool of crimson splashed over the folds of peacock blue.

A moan escaped Obadiah. He staggered back. His stomach heaving, he was violently ill. But even with his scrawny frame wracked by spasms, he groped for the handle of his watchman's rattle.

Obadiah sounded it harder than he ever had in his life.

Chapter 1

Moonlight poured through the long windows and spilled over the four-poster bed where the marquis of Mandell lay entangled in the sheets with his mistress. Even sleep failed to soften the hauteur of his features, his face all hard angles from his high cheekbones to the sharp outline of his nose and jaw. Waves of rich sable-colored hair tumbled over a lordly brow.

But as his dark head tossed upon the pillow, his full sensual lips were twisted with a torment he would never have revealed in his waking hours.

The dream had him in its grip again and once more he experienced that sensation of terror and helplessness. He could feel his tall, powerful frame dwindling into that of a sickly boy. He was back in the *apartement* in Paris and the police were hammering at the door.

Open! Open in the name of the tribunal of the revolution!

Mandell moaned, struggling against the sheets. He could feel himself being lifted from the bed into his mother's arms. Her face seemed to be lost in mist, but he could see the sheen of her golden hair, sense her fear in the thudding of her heart.

She was thrusting him into the coffinlike narrowness of the cupboard. A sob tore from Mandell's throat.

Hush! Hush, my little one. You must be very quiet.
Maman!

He tried to clutch at her, but the door was already closing, locking him into the suffocating darkness, leaving him prey to the terrors of the distant sounds. Wood splintering, tromping boots, harsh voices, his mother's scream . . .

Then the dream shifted and he was a full-grown man, a man burning with pain and frustrated rage. His hand gripped the hilt of his sword and he swung it wildly, hacking at the wood, breaking his way out of the cupboard.

But instead of the bedchamber, he emerged into the murky half-light of a street, crowded with faceless phantoms, the stench of their tattered, filthy clothes as rank as the scent of blood.

You murdering bastards! he screamed.

He charged at them, raising his sword, but they scattered like brittle leaves before a powerful wind, the street echoing with their mocking laughter.

And Mandell realized that it was not a weapon of steel he wielded at all, but wood. A child's toy.

Someone threw something at his feet. He glanced down at the object, all golden and bright, sticky red. His mother's head . . .

"No!" Mandell sat up in bed with a jerk, his heart thundering. It took a moment for the haze to clear from his eyes, to realize where he was. Breathing hard, he stared wildly about him until the room came into focus.

Not Paris, but London, the familiar feminine surroundings of Sara Palmer's bedchamber. With a shuddering sigh, Mandell sagged back onto his elbows.

He had only been dreaming, and more humiliating still, crying out like a child in his sleep.

"Mandell?" Sara's voice came from beside him, soft, questioning.

Mandell nearly cursed aloud to find he had awakened her with his thrashings. She sat bolt upright, regarding him with wide green eyes, her long, dusky hair falling over the lush swell of her breasts.

"What is it, Mandell? What is wrong?" She risked a tentative touch to his shoulder.

He realized suddenly that his flesh was bathed in a sheen of cold sweat. It glistened over the muscles of his chest, the matting of dark hair. He flung himself away from Sara, swinging his legs over the side of the bed.

"Was it a nightmare?" she persisted.

He didn't answer, and merely located the breeches he had discarded earlier. He rammed his legs into the close-fitting garment, then stood easing the fabric up over his hips. As he fumbled with the buttons on the flap, he walked to the window.

The night beyond seemed vast, cool, and soothing. He stood staring into its emptiness until he was certain he had recovered his composure, and relegated the dream to the dark corner of his mind where it belonged. He said at last, "It was only a nightmare, nothing of any consequence. I am sorry I disturbed you."

"That is quite all right, my lord," Sara replied. "I am sure I do not blame you. I have not slept easy myself since the report of that killing the other night. Every time I close my eyes, I see some murderous fiend with a hook coming after me."

"I doubt *you* would have anything to fear, madam." A reluctant smile creased Mandell's lips. He felt restored enough to face her again. The dark-haired beauty sat propped up against the pillows, clutching the coverlet over her breasts. She looked almost helpless, swallowed up in the vastness of that great bed, but only a fool would have mistaken Sara Palmer for other than what she was; a most formidable woman.

"Besides," he continued, "there is nothing even to connect this Hook to the crime except for the babblings of a hysterical old watchman. Bert Glossop was the kind of fool to inspire any number of people with a desire to kill him."

"Yes, he was—" Sara started to agree wholeheartedly, but she brought herself up short, assuming a prim expression. "Of course, one must not speak ill of the dead."

"Why not? Glossop was a perfect ass. I cannot imagine that death did anything to improve him." Mandell arched one brow in mocking fashion. "You had best take care, my Sara. You are starting to sound as hypocritical as any of my set. And heretofore, I have always found you so wonderfully refreshing."

"I still am," she murmured, flinging back the covers from his side of the bed, patting the mattress. There was a sparkle in her eyes, her lips parting in invitation.

He made no move to rejoin her. He had banished the nightmare, but the painful emotions it had aroused left him feeling wearied and not in the least amorous.

"I beg your pardon, my dear," he said, "but I fear I must leave you. It is nearly midnight, and if I am going to put in any appearance at the Countess Sumner's ball, I must go back to my house and change."

She took his rejection in good part, with only a tiny pout. He had half expected her to make more of an effort to change his mind, which led him to suppose Sara was not really in the mood, either. As he reached for his shirt, she rose languidly from the bed, stretching her arms over her head, making no attempt to shield her nakedness. She had no modesty, but then, Mandell thought, there was no reason why she should. The full curves of her body could have served as a model for a sculptor depicting Venus.

Sara enveloped herself in one of those filmy wrappers she favored, the pink tint of her flesh shimmering through the sheer white silk. While Mandell shrugged into his shirt, she lounged against the wall, watching him through the thickness of her lashes.

"I don't suppose," she said, "that you would consider taking me with you tonight?"

"To Lily Rosemoor's ball? I doubt you would find it very interesting."

"Why don't you give me chance to find out?"

"We have been through this before, Sara," he said, shooting her an impatient glance. "There are certain times and places that a man does not flaunt his mistress."

"But I have heard that the countess is very open-minded, not so particular as some about whom she admits into her house."

"The decision in this instance is mine, not Lily's, my dear."

A flicker of annoyance crossed Sara's features. "You express such contempt for your society, yet you are so careful to follow the niceties of its code. Sometimes I think it is you who is the hypocrite, my lord."

"I never pretended to be otherwise," he drawled, but with a slightly bitter set of his lips. He stepped in front of the oval mirror that hung over her dressing table, in order to achieve what he could with a neckcloth that had become rumpled during their earlier loveplay.

Sara was one of the few women he had ever known who did not load her dressing table down with bottles, jars of scent, and other useless paraphernalia. The cherrywood surface was bare except for a silver-handled brush and the vial of laudanum Sara took for her headaches.

As he leaned closer to the mirror, folding the cravat, he attempted to mollify his refusal to take her to the ball. "I only mean to stay at Lily's an hour or more. I could return then, if you like."

"I fear I won't be here. Not tonight. Nor tomorrow. Nor any other night."

The words were pronounced without rancor, in a tone that was merely matter-of-fact. Mandell glanced up to see her arms folded across her breasts, her face steeled with determination.

Her announcement was not entirely unexpected to Mandell. After the briefest pause, he went on tying his cravat.

"So I am to understand the arrangements I have made for you are no longer satisfactory?"

"Oh, as to that, Mandell, you have been generous with your money. And with other things. . . ." She touched him, her fingertips running up his arm, the caress light, suggestive.

Then she sighed, dropping her hand back to her side. "But I have realized for some time now that the thing I want most you are never going to give me."

"And that is?"

"Your name."

"I believe I made that clear from the outset—"

"You did," she interrupted. "Abundantly clear. You could

never marry a woman of such dubious social background. Although my father was a gentleman, a sea captain, and my late husband a man of good family and property in Yorkshire."

Mandell said nothing. He had never believed in the existence of the sea captain or the dead husband. He had no idea where Sara had really come from and he had never cared. She was entitled to her secrets. The devil knew, he had plenty of his own.

"There is no way of making you understand, Sara," he said. "I possess few scruples, but I do have some sense of what I owe to my grandfather, the honor of his house. I would have to be madly in love with you to forget all that."

"Which you never will be. You and I, my dear Mandell, are practical people. We are not the kind to fall madly in love with anyone."

"That is precisely why we are so well suited to one another."

"We would be, were I not so ambitious. I know that there are plenty of other titled fools out there who would not be troubled by your scruples." A spark lit Sara's eyes, like the green fire of an emerald. "I want to be 'my lady somebody.' I want to take my place in your world, the society you so scorn. I want to attend all those routs, balls, receive vouchers to Almack's, perhaps even make my curtsy to the king."

"The king is as mad as you are."

"Well, the Prince Regent then! Go ahead and sneer if you like, Mandell. But this is what I want."

"I was not sneering at you, my dear. You may well achieve your ambition. I don't doubt but what you are clever enough to do so. But after you have it all, the title, Almack's, a place in society, I wonder if you are going to want it. You have a certain freedom now that you don't quite appreciate, unlike myself, a prisoner to all the trappings of an ancient family name."

"From where I stand, the gilt bars of your prison look mighty good."

He smiled and shook his head, but he made no effort to sway her decision. In truth, when he had begun the liaison with Sara, he had known it would end this way. No recriminations, no repinings, a blazing affair that had burnt itself out like so many others. To give Sara her due, she was a little better than the rest, not quite in the common way.

He finished knotting his cravat. It was a shambles but it would do to see him home. Searching for his boots, he completed his dressing in silence.

Rubbing her arms and shivering, Sara rustled over to the hearth. She put another log on the fire, then poked at the embers to stir up the flames.

When he had eased himself into his frock coat, Mandell turned to her. He held out his arms and quoted, "Since there's no help, come let us kiss and part."

She might have been justified in flinging the next line of Drayton's sonnet at him, *Nay, I have done, you get no more of me.*

But Sara never read poetry. Dusting off her hands, she moved into his embrace, raising her mouth to his. Even now her lips were generous, her tongue fiery hot against his. Drawing back, she gazed up at him, her eyes soft.

"You have been my lover all these weeks, and I suddenly realize I don't even know your Christian name."

"I don't have one," Mandell said. A memory intruded upon him—the lordly figure of his grandfather looming over him, a shivering child of ten, the old duke of Windermere flinging the certificate of Mandell's baptism and his French passport into the fire.

And so dies the past, boy. You have but one thing to remember now and that is that you are the marquis of Mandell, my heir.

And the flames had leapt up, consuming the papers in one greedy lick. If only memories could be burnt away as easily.

Shaking off the troubling reminiscence, Mandell pulled Sara close for one last kiss, then eased her out of his arms.

"Farewell, my dear. If the respectable life is what you want so much, I hope you find it."

She stroked his cheek, an unusually tender gesture for Sara. "And you, Mandell. My wish for you is that just once in your life, you desire something strong enough to risk everything for it—your life, your soul, even the honor of your precious family name."

"Regrettably, madam, I cannot think of anything I would ever want that badly." Upturning her hand, he brushed his lips against her palm.

Releasing her, he moved toward the door with his usual pantherlike grace. Sara stared at him, taking one last look at that tautly honed male form she had known so intimately. One last look at the darkness, the danger to be found in that lean face whose latent sensuality never failed to arouse her.

She felt a curling of heat, a mad impulse to call him back to her bed one last time. But if she did so, it would only be harder to let Mandell go while her dreams drifted further away.

So she remained where she was until the door clicked behind him. The she heaved a deep sigh at her own folly. She must be mad to fling off her protector, possibly the most magnificent lover she had ever had, and this while she was still uncertain of what she meant to do next. She had no immediate prospects, only vague ambitions.

Yet she could not summon the energy to do any more thinking tonight. Pressing her hand to her brow, she could already feel the nigglings of one of her infamous headaches. She wanted to flop back into bed, but the tangled sheets were a reminder of Mandell, redolent with his musky scent. She would find no repose there until she called Agnes to change the linens.

But Sara had no need to summon her maid, for the next moment the woman, in her starched apron and cap, burst into the room. The tidings Agnes brought drove all thoughts of Mandell out of Sara's head.

"Oh, madam, *he* is here," the flustered maid squeaked. "Round by the back door."

Sara did not have to ask whom the woman meant. Her heart gave a sick thud of fear and anger.

"I will be down at once," Sara said grimly. She had a great deal to say to that brother of hers.

She paused only long enough to change her wrapper for

another dressing gown less revealing. Flinging a shawl about her shoulders, she crept through the house to the cold and silent kitchen, only glowing ashes left on the hearth of the massive bake oven.

Gideon Palmer lounged just inside the doorway. Despite the jagged scar that creased his chin, he was a handsome young man in scarlet regimentals. His rakish smile had been more than one poor maid's undoing.

"Sara," he said, with a lazy grin. "My dear sister."

But she was not about to be charmed by him, not this time. She launched into him without preamble.

"Albert Glossop is dead!" she hissed. "Damn it, Gideon! What *have* you been doing?"

Mandell had the hackney cab set him down at the end of Clarion Way. With such a press of carriages depositing people at the Countess Sumner's door, the entire thoroughfare was clogged. Mandell found it far easier to proceed on foot.

He had no intention of stepping round to Sumner House himself until he had changed his attire. Fortunately his own townhouse lay just at the end of the street.

Lily's ball was certainly gaining the lion's share of the attention tonight, for the rest of Clarion Way remained shadowed and silent. As Mandell progressed farther along the pavement, he felt as though he had stepped out of a circle of light and confusion into the soothing quiet that night was meant to be.

Not even a footman was to be seen lingering about the square, not since Glossop's murder. Away from the excitement at the opposite end of Clarion Way, Mandell was quite alone, except for the cloaked individual who stood outside of his house.

Mandell tensed and might have reached for the swordstick hidden in the handle of his walking cane, except that hooded figure was slight, obviously a woman.

She leaned up against his wrought iron fence, blocking the short path that led up to the stairs of the house. As Mandell drew closer, he saw the woman shudder and heard a muffled sob.

He rolled his eyes. He never had much patience for a weeping female, certainly not one who chose to snuffle over his fence at this time of night.

Stalking up behind her, he said, "I beg your pardon, madam."

He had spoken quietly, but even that caused her to gasp. She whirled around, clutching her hand to the region of her heart.

Mandell had entertained the notion that this must be some maid from one of the houses, likely disappointed in a rendezvous with a lover. But the richness of the woman's satin cloak dispelled that idea.

She was clearly a lady. But what the deuce was she doing in the street at this hour, and why did she have to be doing it upon his doorstep?·

As she recovered her breath, she said, "Oh, it is you, Lord Mandell. You startled me."

So she knew him. But he didn't think he knew her. The voice was not familiar. As she took a wary step back, her hood fell back a little revealing a pale, heart-shaped face, and delicate features that conveyed an impression of haunting sadness.

She was young, but not a chit just out of the schoolroom. She might have been pretty, but it was difficult to tell, her eyes being so swollen with her tears. Her hair certainly was beautiful, tumbling to her shoulders in a cascade of honey gold. There was something vaguely familiar about her, but Mandell could not quite place it.

After assessing her appearance, he asked, "Have we met before, madam? You are . . ."

He waited for her to fill in the blank, but she only retreated deeper into the shelter of her hood.

"That is none of your concern, my lord. Be pleased to pass on your way."

"Well, my Lady Sorrow, I would be happy to do so," he said drily, "but that is a little difficult when you bar my path, rusting out my gatepost with your tears."

"Your gate?" she faltered. "You live here?"

"To the best of my recollection."

She choked on a bitter laugh. "Is this not typical of my fortune? I do not even have the right house."

She mopped at her eyes with the back of her hand. Even in the dim light of the street, Mandell could see that her eyes were very blue, like violets from those long ago springtimes he had spent in the country instead of walled up in the stone and grit of London.

"Do forgive me, my lord, for being such a fool."

She tried to rush on, but this time Mandell blocked her way. He never sought to burden himself with anyone else's misery and he was not about to do so now. All the same he felt curiously loathe just to let her go.

"You shouldn't be wandering about alone at night, milady. It is not safe." He was not about to bring up the murder. If there was a chance she had not heard of Bert Glossop's death, there was no sense in terrifying her. Instead he concluded, "Even here on Clarion Way, there is a danger of—er—footpads."

"But I have nothing left of value for anyone to steal."

She ducked past him and moved off rapidly down the street, never glancing back. Mandell stood by his gate, watching her go. There might have been a time in his more hot-blooded youth when he would have been intrigued enough to follow her, discover the secret of her tears, perhaps the sweeter secrets still she kept concealed beneath that cloak.

But he was far too jaded and cynical now to go pursuing mysterious young women through the streets. As he observed that proud slender shape vanish into the darkness, for a fleeting moment Mandell was sorry that this was so.

Chapter 2

It was well past midnight by the time the marquis of Mandell arrived at the Countess Sumner's ball. He permitted a servant to remove the black cloak from his broad shoulders. Without glancing around, Mandell handed off his gloves, high-crowned hat, and gold-tipped cane to another pasty-faced footman. Then, straightening his cuffs, the marquis passed between twin marble pillars into the main drawing room.

It was a long chamber done up with gilt mirrors and hung with red damask like some opulent Italian palazzo. Mandell presented a stark contrast in the severe style of his evening clothes, the unrelenting black relieved only by the snowy folds of his cravat.

The gallery was already thronged with the countess's guests. Mandell observed the assembled company through cynical eyes. Apparently Glossop's murder had done little to discourage any of the haute ton from venturing abroad in search of their pleasures. If anything, it added a certain titillation to the hum of gossip. The well-bred voices could be heard even above the scrape of the violins.

"My dear, positively too dreadful."

"That murderous footpad, the Hook . . ."

"Mr. Glossop's throat pierced quite through."

"And it happened right here on the corner of Clarion Way."

Mandell's lip curled with contempt and he wondered why he had come. He might have done better to have appeased Sara, lingering in her bed, except that he had been troubled with a restlessness of late that not even she could satisfy. Sometimes he felt as hollow, as empty as this roomful of chattering fools.

The hour was advanced enough that Lily was no longer receiving latecomers. Mandell waved aside the servant who would have announced him. He strolled into the drawing room, but he had not taken many steps when he was accosted by Sir Lancelot Briggs.

The man came scrambling to Mandell's side like a bumbling puppy. Briggs was plump, with shirt collars worn too high, his hair curled too tight. His eyes lit up with joy at the sight of Mandell and he clutched at the marquis's sleeve.

"Mandell! Oh, thank God! Thank God you are unharmed."

"Which is more than can be said for my coat," Mandell complained, prying Briggs's fingers away.

"I am sorry. But I have been so anxious about you, what with that fiend the Hook still roaming abroad."

"Oh? Have you seen him tonight?"

"Well—well, no, but one knows he is still out there, lurking. After what happened to poor Bertie Glossop, I fear none of us are safe until that villain is captured." Briggs added shyly, "I looked for you at the club earlier. When you did not come to dine, I confess I was worried."

Mandell eyed Briggs with distaste. The man trailed after him so much he was becoming known as "Mandell's toady." Perhaps that did not affront Briggs's pride, but it certainly did Mandell's.

"Your solicitude is touching," the marquis said coldly, "but I trust I may alter my schedule without it becoming a matter of public concern."

Briggs turned a bright red. "Yes, of course. That is, I am sorry. I only . . ." He allowed his words to trail away, his cowlike brown eyes welling with hurt. He walked off, looking crestfallen.

"Why, Mandell? Why must you always be so cutting?"

The quiet voice might have been his conscience except that Mandell did not believe he possessed one. Turning, he discovered that his cousin Nicholas Drummond had come up behind him.

Nick's sartorial magnificence was almost blinding. He wore a mauve frock coat, lace spilling from his cuffs, his neckcloth folded in an intricate arrangement. It amused Mandell that Nick, intensely serious about everything else, should be so frivolous in matters of dress, loading himself down with fobs and diamond stickpins. Mandell, on the other hand, who accounted nothing to be of great importance, wore no jewelry save his gold signet ring.

Nick asked, "Why do you always treat poor Briggs so shabbily? He is your friend."

"I was not aware that I had any friends," Mandell replied.

"Briggs apparently thinks otherwise. The man is devoted to you."

"So would a dog be, if I had one." Mandell drew forth an enameled snuffbox and flicked open the lid with a careless but practiced gesture. "I don't entertain sycophants."

"No, you are the last man anyone could accuse of that. That is why I don't understand what possessed Briggs to attach himself to you."

Mandell helped himself to a pinch of snuff, then returned the box to his pocket. "That is my own fault. We were both at a gaming hell once and a Captain Sharp was fleecing Briggs at cards. When Briggs was foolish enough to object, the fellow threatened him with a pistol. I felt compelled to intervene."

"Did you, by God!" Nick's eyes warmed with admiration, but Mandell would have none of it.

"I don't know what comes over me," he drawled. "I am beset by these beneficent impulses from time to time like a recurrent bout of the brain fever. It is the one great flaw in my character."

"Well, flawed or not, I am deuced glad to see you. I thought you would be otherwise engaged this evening. Have you tired of the charms of your latest mistress so soon?"

"Why? Would you like me to introduce you to her?"

"No, thank you," Nick said, laughing. "I am far too occupied with my work for such a diversion. I have been meaning to call upon you. I have a favor to ask."

Mandell cast his cousin a pained glance. "Not to second you in another duel! My dear fellow, this is becoming a tiresome habit. I can sympathize with you in some measure. There are a good many people I would like to shoot myself, but not over politics. Now it would be another matter if you fought over a woman or because someone's waistcoat offended you."

Mandell flicked his fingers against Nick's own silk garment, a pattern of bright mauve stripes.

"Damn your eyes, Mandell," Nick growled, "there is nothing wrong with my waistcoat, and no, I am not about to fight another duel. I am still recovering from the effects of my last meeting with Beresford."

He rubbed the back of his left hand, which bore a recent scar from a pistol ball. Mandell had only been thankful that Beresford, who was a crack shot, had been content to aim for Nick's hand rather than his hot head.

"It is something else entirely I need to ask you about," Nick said. "But perhaps we had better find someplace more quiet where we will not be interrupted."

"If you insist, though it is not my habit to steal off into secluded alcoves with politicians."

Nick grinned. "And do not all the mamas in this room know it! As soon as you appeared on the threshold, Lady Ormsby gathered her girls about her like a flustered hen. I believe she has sent out for their chastity belts."

"An unnecessary precaution," Mandell murmured. "I have seen her daughters."

After which quip he permitted Nick to lead the way through the drawing room. This was not an easy feat, for the gallery was packed. Couples performing a quadrille had scarce enough room to pace off their steps. More than one lady present had recourse to use her fan, the blazing lights of the chamber's four chandeliers being over brilliant.

The curtained alcove seemed cool and quiet by comparison. Nick flung himself down at once upon a claw foot sofa, but Mandell chose to remain standing.

"Is it my imagination," he said, "or are the voices of the ladies a little more shrill tonight?"

"Oh, I suppose there is still a deal of excitement owing to Bertie Glossop's death." Nick shrugged. "Mind you, I would not have wished Glossop any harm, but in a queer way, his murder has turned out to be a good thing. I had hoped that the activities of the Hook might have done so sooner, but it seems to have taken something this grim to shake certain people out of their complacency."

The more Nick warmed to his subject, the more heated his voice became. "Now perhaps the good citizens of Mayfair will understand some of the terrors the West End poor have faced for years. Parliament will understand the need to do away with our outmoded police force. The time has come to organize one efficient central unit—"

"My dear Nick," Mandell interrupted as soon as he could get a word in. "If you are going to start addressing me as though I were a public meeting, I fear I will be obliged to eschew the pleasure of your company."

"But—"

"And besides, you know I am the last person likely to sympathize with your notion of an efficient police."

Their eyes locked and Nick apparently took his meaning, for he spoke in milder tones. "What happened to your mother in Paris took place a very long time ago, Mandell, and it was a different thing altogether."

"Was it?" Mandell said, his voice going cold and hard. He was on the verge of leaving when Nick flung up one hand.

"No, I am sorry. Come back. I promise I have done with my speeches about the police. This was not what I wanted to talk to you about anyway."

Mandell returned, but he eyed his cousin with wariness, wondering about the nature of the favor Nick required. Nick was not often beforehand with the world, yet he seldom asked to borrow money, at least not for himself.

Mandell had a dread that Nick's forthcoming request must have something to do with one of his infernal causes.

Nick cleared his throat, a bad sign. "Of course, you know John Hastings," he began.

"No, I cannot say that I do."

"He is my footman, the one who usually answers the front door."

Mandell's brows rose a fraction. "I have a vague recollection of some burly youth, but I have not as yet had opportunity to strike up an intimacy with him."

"Don't go all haughty on me, Mandell," Nick implored. "The thing is, John wants to marry Emily."

Mandell regarded him blankly.

"*Emily*, your downstairs maid."

"I was not aware that I had a downstairs maid, let alone one named Emily, but I will take your word for it," Mandell said. "Now what is all of this to do with me? I am not the girl's father to be giving my blessing."

"No, but it would be much more convenient for John to be part of the same household as his bride. Alas, I am not in a financial position to take on any more servants. So I thought, that is I hoped, you might be persuaded to employ John."

Mandell frowned. "Sometimes, Nicholas, the interest you take in the affairs of your servants borders on madness."

"Then you refuse?"

Mandell knew he certainly should. He kept only a small staff at his London house. Nor did he think that Nick's tendency to meddle with the lower orders should be encouraged. This incident was a minor one, but as a member of the House of Commons, Nick was forever pressing for reforms to alleviate what he deemed the misery of the working class.

"What the boy does not understand," Mandell's grandfather would frequently growl, "is that reform only leads to idleness and dissatisfaction amongst the poor. From there it is but a step away to revolution."

The danger of revolution was one of the few points that Mandell and the Duke of Windermere agreed upon, born of

a shared pain. The old man grieved for the loss of a beloved daughter, Mandell for the mother he had barely
known.

Mandell started to refuse Nick's request, but his cousin
looked so hopeful. It seemed churlish to disappoint Nick
over such a trivial thing. The fate of the nation could hardly
be affected by permitting the marriage of one insignificant
servant.

Mandell vented an exasperated sigh. "Oh, the devil!
What is another footman more or less?"

Nick brightened. He leapt up to shake Mandell's hand.
"Damme, Mandell. You're a capital fellow."

"Now is there anything else you think I should do?"
Mandell grumbled. "Perhaps arrange a wedding breakfast
for the happy couple?"

"You needn't go as far as that, but a small gift might be
nice."

At Mandell's dark look, Nick grinned. "Only jesting," he
said.

Their business concluded, Mandell and he stepped past
the curtain, returning to the ballroom. If anything, the gallery seemed more crowded than before.

"What a damned crush this is," Mandell said. "Is there
anyone interesting present tonight?"

"The Prince Regent is here, and your grandfather."

"I said *interesting*."

"Oh, you mean ladies," Nick chuckled. "Well, the Beau-
fort heiress is here and the Countess Sumner's sister is back
in town, having set aside her mourning at last."

"And who might she be?"

"You remember. Lady Anne Fairhaven, Sir Gerald's
widow."

Mandell grimaced. "Oh, yes, the deadly proper Sir Gerald Fairhaven. I did not even know that he was dead, but
given how dull he was, it would have been difficult to tell."

"You knew his brother Lucien had inherited the baron-
etcy. How did you think he got it if Sir Gerald was still
alive?"

"I did not give the matter much consideration. Sir Lucien

is not exactly one of my bosom companions. None of the Fairhavens have ever interested me much. As I recall, the lady Anne seemed not much livelier than her late husband."

"Lady Fairhaven is certainly quiet, but I never thought her dull," Nick said. "In fact there is something quite appealing about her. She has the most remarkable sad eyes."

"I wouldn't know. The lady never let me get close enough to her to find out. I rather think she has a strong disapproval of men with libertine propensities."

"Certainly Lady Fairhaven is a woman of great virtue."

"Indeed? I suppose that could be an amusing way to spend an evening, trying to discover exactly how unassailable that virtue might be."

"Leave Lady Fairhaven alone, Mandell. She does not need you tormenting her. I hear she has come through a bad time of it since her husband died."

"All the more reason she might welcome a little diversion," Mandell said. "Perhaps I shall seek her out, unless, of course, you've a mind to try your own luck with the lady."

"No! You know I am not in the market for a wife."

"Neither am I."

"That is exactly my objection," Nick said hotly. "Lady Fairhaven may no longer be a debutante, but I don't think she knows much of the world, certainly nothing of the sort of sport you seek. There is still an innocence about her."

"Ah, but that is the trouble with innocence," Mandell mocked. "For most of us, it is such a temporary state."

Not giving his cousin a chance to retort, Mandell sauntered off, leaving Nick glowering after him. But far from harboring any thoughts of seduction, Mandell intended only to pay his respects to his hostess, then escape this den of heat and noise as soon as possible.

Skirting the edge of the gallery in his search for the countess, Mandell collided with the corpulent form of the Prince Regent. His Majesty's frock coat glittered, overdecorated with the jeweled ribbons of far too many orders. He stared at Mandell, the prince's florid features turning even redder.

"My apologies, Your Highness," Mandell murmured. He stepped back a pace and sketched a bow that was correct but still lacking in deference.

The prince's jowls quivered and he stared straight through Mandell. He ambled past without a word of acknowledgment. The cut was unmistakable, but Mandell's lips creased into a smile. He knew that he had never been a favorite with the Prince of Wales, not since the time George had been named regent due to his father's madness. So many others had crowded around the vain prince, flattering and offering their congratulations, that Mandell had been unable to resist expressing his condolences instead, along with a wish for the old king's speedy recovery. In the midst of his triumph, George had been obliged to look a little ashamed at rejoicing over his father's misfortune. The prince had never forgiven Mandell for that.

The greeting Mandell received from Lily, the Countess Sumner, was far warmer. Traversing the length of the room, Mandell spotted her, hovering over some young woman seated on a silk-covered chair.

At the sight of Mandell, Lily closed the distance between them with outstretched hands. A fading beauty, she made far too free use of the paintpots, but her figure retained a voluptuous charm.

"Mandell," she cried. "You came after all. I vow you are a most welcome sight."

"Am I? I had begun to wonder." He carried her fingertips to his lips.

She laughed. "Oh, you mean your reception from the Prince Regent. Aye, I saw it all. You must not mind His Grace. The poor man is sadly put out. He was the focus of attention amongst the ladies until you walked in. You must have a dance with me later. I have all manner of interesting gossip to share with you."

"Not about Bert Glossop, I trust. I have heard more than enough on that score."

"Oh, no, something far more interesting." She leaned forward to whisper behind her painted chicken-skin fan. "The Prince Regent has left off wearing his stays."

"And just how would you be knowing that, my lady?" Mandell asked.

"Because one can no longer hear him creak when he walks. How else should I know it, you naughty man?" She closed up her fan and rapped his wrist.

A laugh escaped Mandell, one of genuine amusement. The rest of London might be in an uproar over murder, but trust Lily Rosemoor to be more interested in the regent's stays. Mandell had always been more at ease with the countess than with other women. He liked his mistresses younger and not quite so giddy. She preferred her lovers blonde and more poetic. So their relationship had never been hampered by any sexual tension.

With the ease of long acquaintance, Lily linked her arm through his. "Come, Mandell, there is someone you must make your leg to. You will never guess who has returned to London. Anne, my darling little sister."

She tugged Mandell over to the chair where the young woman sat, staring pensively down at the floor tiles. Mandell had never taken much notice of Anne Fairhaven, but she appeared as he remembered her, pale and prim, her fair hair done up in a crown of braids. The style was perhaps a little too severe, but it drew attention to the slender column of her neck. Clad in a high-waisted lavender gown, she was like a fine pastel lost amidst the brightness of more garish oil paintings.

"Anne," Lily called gaily. "Do but look who has arrived."

Lady Fairhaven glanced up. Mandell experienced the shock of more recent recognition as the candleshine played fully over her delicate features. Impossible that it should be so, but Anne Fairhaven was the woman who had been weeping by his gate. She had been half lost in shadow then. Her hair tumbling free had made quite a difference from her usual prim style. But there was no mistaking those violet-hued eyes. They were clear now, only the shadows beneath bearing testimony to her former unhappiness.

Before Mandell could move or speak, Anne shot to her feet, a blush staining her cheeks.

"My lord," Lily said. "You do remember my sister, I trust?"

"Of course," he said, managing to gain possession of Anne's hand. "The virtuous Lady Fairhaven."

"The wicked Lord Mandell," Anne countered, snatching her fingers free of his grasp. "Excuse me, Lily, my lord. I was on the verge of retiring to the card room. There is someone I must speak to."

For the second time that night, she fled from Mandell without a backward glance. Her gown, demure as it was, clung to the willowy curves of her hips. She moved with a grace that was somehow far more alluring than the exaggerated sway of bolder women.

"I declare," Lily exclaimed. "Whatever got into her? Mandell, what have you done to frighten my poor Anne?"

"Nothing." Mandell smiled. *"Yet."*

The countess wagged her finger at him. "I dislike that gleam in your eye, my lord. You must form no designs upon my little sister. It would do her a world of good to take a lover. But you are far too wicked for her, I fear."

"Do you know," Mandell said pleasantly, "I have been warned away from the lady enough times, it is beginning to rouse the devil in me."

Lily clucked her tongue at him and would have said more, but her attention was caught by the arrival of some other latecomers. She fluttered away to greet them like the distractible butterfly that she was.

That left Mandell free to wonder about Anne Fairhaven's strange behavior. What had induced such a proper lady to roam the streets unescorted, weeping as though her heart would break? Mandell's curiosity was aroused enough this time to pursue her—at least as far as the next room.

She had ducked into a small adjoining parlor set aside for those wishing for cards instead of dancing. When Mandell crossed the threshold, he found her standing near the hearth, observing the play at one table. Mandell saw nothing in this particular foursome to attract her interest.

The group consisted in part of a callow youth and Sir Lancelot Briggs. Briggs gave Mandell a hopeful smile, but

Mandell ignored him, more struck by the other two players. One was the Lady Anne's brother-in-law, Sir Lucien Fairhaven. A large man with sun-streaked blond hair, his face was deeply carved with lines of dissipation.

But most surprising was the fourth man at the table, Mandell's grandfather, the august duke of Windermere. His Grace rarely tolerated the company of fools, so it was a mystery to Mandell why he would play at whist with any of these men. His white hair swept back in a queue, his close-set eyes were shadowed beneath bushy brows. He acknowledged Mandell's presence with a curt nod.

Although Anne did not look Mandell's way, she was obviously aware of his approach. She stiffened as he came up to her.

"How fortunate," he said in low tones. "It would seem we meet again, my Lady Sorrow."

"Don't call me that," she whispered, trying to sidle away. "I had hoped you would not recognize me."

"I would have had to have been drunk not to. I liked your hair better down. It looked more golden in the moonlight."

"Do go away," she hissed. "I am trying to concentrate on the game."

Mandell glanced idly at the table, when suddenly he realized what held her attention. Someone at the table was cheating and doing it badly. The card being dealt by the youth was scratched, a botched attempt to mark the deck. It must come to the notice of the entire table in a moment.

The question was who was responsible. Briggs? No, the fellow lacked the wit to be other than honest. The spotted youth? He had obviously been losing badly, trickles of sweat mingling with the blemishes on his brow. As for the jaded Sir Lucien, he had accumulated an impressive pile of paper and coins in front of him.

Whoever was guilty, Mandell knew his grandfather would not take kindly to the discovery he was playing with a cheat. Disgrace for one of these men was imminent. The marked card had been shuffled his grandfather's way. The old man's eyes were far too keen to miss it. But just as the duke reached for the card, Anne suddenly overturned a glass of wine perched on the table. The gesture was awkward, and Mandell could tell, quite deliberate.

The wine splattered in a splash of dark purple across the table and over the cards. Three of the men jerked back, only the duke remaining unperturbed.

Sir Lucien cursed, sopping at the mess with his handkerchief while one of Lily's efficient footmen hastened over with a napkin.

"Anne!" Sir Lucien spluttered, giving her a vicious glare. "You clumsy little—"

Mandell felt something cold and lethal stir inside him. Sir Lucien had an ugly voice. Mandell did not think he quite liked the tone of it.

But before he could do or say anything, his grandfather stepped into the breach.

"It was not Lady Fairhaven's fault," the duke said. "I fear I jarred her hand. Certainly there is no need for such an ill-bred display of temper, Sir Lucien. I think you should beg the lady's pardon."

The man had not been born whom the old duke could not browbeat. Sir Lucien flushed and looked like a sulky schoolboy, but he muttered, "I am sorry, Anne. But must you keep hovering there behind me? You are putting me off my game."

The duke rose to his feet, making a bow to the flustered Lady Fairhaven. Mandell had to give the old devil his due. No one could behave in more courtly fashion to a woman.

"It must be very tedious here for you, my lady," the duke said. "Allow me to provide you with some amusement. Here is my grandson. Mandell, take Lady Fairhaven in to dance."

"Oh, no. No!" Anne protested, but Mandell stepped forward swiftly.

"With the greatest of pleasure," he said.

"Always so obedient," the duke said with great irony. For a moment his gaze locked on Mandell's, their eyes clashing with old antagonisms. Then His Grace stepped back to permit Mandell to approach Anne.

She shrank away, turning in appeal to Sir Lucien, her expression akin to despair. "Forgive me, Lucien. But you know I have been hoping to speak with you. If you could spare me but a moment—"

"Later," Sir Lucien snapped. He was already shuffling a new deck of cards.

Mandell observed this byplay between the two with interest and he wondered if Anne would yield. She had little choice. The incident had already focused every eye in the room upon them. After another hesitation, she permitted Mandell to take her arm.

As he led her toward the door, he bent down to speak softly in Anne's ear. "I hope he appreciates it."

"Who?" she asked.

"Whomever you just saved by that little accident."

Then you noticed—" She stopped, biting down upon her lip. "Of course. *You* would."

"I saw the marked card, not who authored it. Sir Lucien perhaps?"

"No," she made haste to disclaim. "It was the boy. He is far too young. He should not even be permitted to play."

Mandell was not certain he believed her, but all he said was, "I trust your intervention will give the *boy* pause to reconsider the wisdom of his actions."

"I hope so, too."

When they passed into the drawing room, Anne tried to wriggle free. "Your grandfather was terribly kind, but of course, you are not obliged to dance with me."

"Good. I hate dancing unless it is the waltz."

"How unfortunate. The orchestra is playing a reel, my lord." Her gaze skated back toward the card room. Mandell wondered about the nature of her interest in Sir Lucien Fairhaven. He usually had no difficulty in thinking the worst of people. But the suspicion that Anne Fairhaven might be carrying on an intrigue with that underbred oaf was strangely unwelcome. "There is little use your lingering about here," Mandell told her. "That card game will likely not break up for hours."

"I know," she said. She looked very tired. It was strange.

Signs of fatigue rendered most women rather hag-ridden. Anne only appeared younger, more vulnerable.

"Perhaps you had better let me take you in to supper," Mandell said in a gentle tone he rarely used. "You appear as though you need some nourishment."

"I am not at all hungry, my lord." She pressed one hand to her brow. " 'Tis only the heat, the noise. I fear it is giving me a headache. I am sure I shall feel better if I step outside for a moment. Pray excuse me."

She took a step toward the tall French doors that opened onto the terrace leading to the countess's garden. She halted when Mandell moved to accompany her, casting him a look of dismay.

"There is not the least need for you to accompany me, my lord."

"No?" Her wariness amused Mandell. "I begin to get the feeling, Lady Sorrow, you would as soon dispense with my company."

"That I would. You are far too likely to plague me with a deal of questions I don't wish to answer."

"Then you may tell me to mind my own business. You have already done so once tonight."

"But I don't think it would be proper being alone with you in the garden. Not proper or—or . . ." She hesitated, biting down on her lip.

"Or?" he prompted.

"Or safe!"

Mandell's lips curved into a slow, wicked smile. He raised her hand lightly to his lips, feeling her fingertips quiver at his caress. "Safe? Decidedly not. But do you truly wish to be?"

Giving her no chance to protest further, he slipped his arm about her shoulders. Gently, inexorably, he swept her through the doors and into the night.

Chapter 3

✺

Lily's garden looked different by moonlight. By day, it was a place of serenity, sunlit walks, a springtime wilderness of budding flowers. By night, it was a place of seclusion, seductive fragrances, and threatening shadows that seemed to echo Mandell's words.

Safe? Decidedly not. But do you truly wish to be?

Anne Fairhaven shivered. Yes, she wanted to cry out. That was exactly what she longed for, to be safe back in Norfolk, her little daughter Norrie cradled in her arms, to return to the security that had vanished when Gerald had died.

Only dire necessity had forced her back to London, amidst the glittering society she had always hated, thrusting herself into scenes and situations where she did not belong. Never before had she dared steal away from the bright lights of a ballroom to take a midnight stroll. But she found herself doing many things she had never done these past few months, reckless things, frightening things. Desperation did that to one.

But she was still mistress of herself enough to know she did not want to be in a moonlit garden with any man, especially one as dangerous as the marquis of Mandell. She scarcely exchanged a word with him before tonight, but she knew him well by his reputation, winning fortunes at the gaming tables, winning ladies to his bed, appearing to place no value on either prize. A hard, cruel man, he was reputed to have crippled another man in a duel when Mandell was but sixteen.

He stood out at any assemblage he attended, his eyes of-

ten dark with contempt as he regarded the company. Yet
Anne had noted he was always welcome, especially by the
foolish women. They clustered in groups, whispering.

Mandell. Handsome as ever.

*Aye, and never showing a sign of his age. You know, he
must be past thirty-five and not a hint of grey in that glossy
hair. I swear he must be in league with the devil.*

My dear, he is the devil.

And though she had never taken any part in this gossip,
Anne thought so, too. What was she doing out here alone
with him? She was not the sort of woman to draw upon
herself the attentions of such a libertine and she could only
marvel that she had done so now. Let this be a lesson to her
to take greater care in future whose gate she wept upon.

The ridiculous notion almost caused her to smile, and
God knows she had had little enough to smile about since
Gerald had died. She rarely entertained such frivolous
thoughts and decided Mandell must be to blame.

The man made her so nervous with his silk-soft voice.
His presence seemed to fill the night, dark, overpowering,
and undeniably male. She was relieved that he had at least
taken his hand away from her shoulder. Yet somehow she
still felt his touch, as cool and caressing as the breeze tickling her hair.

Rubbing her arms, she announced in what she hoped was
a firm tone, "There. I am feeling better now. That was all
I needed, just a few breaths of air."

"Indeed?" Mandell drawled. "I had the impression that
you have scarce drawn breath since we came out here."

Anne was annoyed to realize he was right. She was holding her breath even now as he stalked closer. She expelled
it in a long sigh.

"Small wonder if I am a little edgy," she said. "All this
talk of the Hook and murder. One scarce feels safe venturing into one's own garden."

"So you prefer wandering through the streets instead?"

"I did not know *you* were going to be there," she retorted
without thinking, then stammered, "I—I am sorry. I did not
mean—"

"Don't apologize. I enjoy a woman who is honest. Now if I could only persuade you to be equally as truthful about why I found you wailing by my gate."

"I was distressed because I had become lost in the dark. I ended up at your doorstep by mistake and now I wish you would simply forget you ever saw me there. I assure you, I was doing nothing wrong."

"I never supposed that you were, Lady Sorrow."

"Good. That's settled then. We may go back to the house."

She started to slip past him, but he caught her wrist. His grip was light but she still had the panicky sensation of some woodland creature hopelessly ensnared.

"Why are you in such a hurry, my lady? Do I frighten you so much?"

"Yes! No. That is . . ." She faltered, struggling for possession of her hand.

"Alas, my black reputation. Tell me. What sort of dreadful gossip have you heard?"

"Nothing. It is not the gossip so much as my own impression of you."

"Which is?"

"That you are a man who has made a career out of wickedness and enjoys it very much," Anne blurted out, then winced. Excessive candor. Her mother had always said it was her worst fault and the years had done little to cure it.

But Mandell appeared amused rather than offended. "A career of wickedness," he mused. "Well, you must admit that is far more diverting than politics or going into the army."

"I admit nothing except that it is shameful for a man to waste his time in such a sinful fashion."

"Some sins, my lady, are never a waste of time." He raised her hand to his lips, barely whispering a kiss across her fingertips. The sensation caused her heart to pound. The intensity of his eyes held her spellbound even as she struggled to be free.

To her surprise, he released her. She stepped back,

clutching her hand to her as though it were a treasure he meant to steal.

"Flee then, if you must, my virtuous Anne. But are you really sure you want to go back there?" He gestured toward the bright lights of the ballroom. "Back to paste on a smile when your heart is aching, to exchange insincere greetings with people who don't care a whit about you, to allow no hint of your private pain to escape you lest it be reduced to a source of gossip?

"Nay, Sorrow, you would do far better to linger here in the darkness with a rogue like me. I, at least, would expect nothing of you."

"Wouldn't you?"

"I would even give you my assurance, for the moment, that you will be safe. I'll make no further effort to pry into your secrets."

Anne hesitated, stealing a glance back toward the security of the ballroom, the harsh lights spilling through the French doors. Mandell's uncanny perception unnerved her. How could he possibly understand her feelings so well? Her face ached from smiling and uttering commonplaces, struggling to pretend that nothing was wrong when nothing was right. And all the while she waited upon tenterhooks for her chance to confront Lucien.

Her brother-in-law was unlikely to leave the card table for hours. The strain of continuing to hide her anxiety was driving her mad. The garden, by contrast, was dark and soothing, the rustling shadows seeming designed for concealment, a place to go with all her misery, her fears, her despairing hope that Lucien might at last be brought to see reason.

The garden would have been perfect if not for Mandell. And yet at the moment he did not appear so threatening. He seemed almost kind. The subtle mockery that shaded his features was missing, the expression in his eyes merely thoughtful.

"Well," she said at last, "I suppose I might walk with you as far as the gate and back."

A ghost of a smile touched his lips. With a courtly bow,

he offered her his arm. After the barest hesitation, Anne took it, resting her fingers on the crisp fabric of his sleeve.

He led her along the gravel walkway in silence, the glitter and noise of the ballroom fading into insignificance. From the way he escorted her, with such an air of distant politeness, they might have been taking a very proper stroll through St. James's Park at the fashionable hour.

Anne could only marvel at the situation she found herself in, going for a midnight walk with one of the most notorious rakes in London. Her late husband would have been scandalized. So would her mother.

What was it Mama had always said? "Lily has beauty, Camilla has wit, but you, my Anne, have neither. That is why you must always strive to be a perfect lady, correct in all things. The gentlemen will never come flocking to your side, but at least you may obtain a worthy husband."

And Mama had been right—to a certain degree. Anne's proper manner had won for her marriage to the handsome and estimable Sir Gerald Fairhaven. But being good and meek had not been enough to secure her future. Not enough to prevent her world from shattering, not enough to keep her from losing what she treasured most. *Norrie* . . .

Anne was roused from her unhappy musings by a tickling sensation against her cheek. Startled, she glanced up to discover Mandell staring down at her. He had plucked a white blossom and brushed it against her face, to regain her attention.

"For you, milady," he said, offering her the flower with a gesture of exaggerated gallantry. "This—er—whatever it is. I am afraid that, beyond roses, I cannot identify one bloom from another."

Anne accepted the blossom, but it discomfited her to think that he must have been studying her face while she had been lost in her gloom-ridden thoughts. Those intense eyes of his saw far too much. To cover her unease, she rushed into breathless speech.

"I cannot identify all of Lily's flowers, either. She has so many strange ones. Her garden is quite exotic."

"Rather like the countess herself."

"I would have planted only primroses or marigolds. So unimaginative." Anne plucked at the blossom he had given her, sending a shower of petals cascading to her feet. "Do you have a garden, my lord?"

"Oh, yes. Just what you would expect. Weeds, thorns, briars, some deadly nightshade."

"Perhaps you should engage a new gardener," Anne began seriously, then caught the twitch of his lips and realized he was teasing her. She almost relaxed enough to return his smile.

Moonlight bathed his proud aristocratic features, accenting the planes and hollows beneath his high cheekbones. Anne eyed him with fascination. She felt rather like a moth, risking a flutter near a bright flame, but keeping back far enough so there was no danger of singeing her wings.

She had always sworn to Lily that she did not perceive the attraction of the rakish marquis, but Anne saw it well enough. He was handsome, despite his look of a man who had experienced far too much of the world.

A fallen angel, the romantic Lily would sigh. But the term did not fit. No, Mandell had never been cast out, Anne decided. He had with deliberate arrogance turned his back on heaven.

"If you keep staring at me like that," Mandell said, "you will put me to the blush, my lady."

"Oh! I'm sorry." Anne lowered her eyes, aware that she was the one who was blushing. "It is just that we have never been well acquainted before. I never had the opportunity to—to—"

"To study wickedness up so close?"

"No. That is, you are not the only wicked man I have ever known. There is also my brother-in-law, Lucien," she added dully.

"Lucien? You wound me by the comparison, Sorrow. Your esteemed brother-in-law, and you will forgive my saying so, is an underbred boor. He is taking himself to the brink of ruin and doing it with no originality. Whereas I flatter myself that at least I am going to the devil with a little style."

"Are you?" Anne regarded him with grave curiosity. She had spent so many of her days striving always to do what was right, what was proper. She could not help but be intrigued by someone who lived as he pleased, not giving a damn for the consequences or the world's opinion.

"Surely you cannot be satisfied with your life," she said. "Pursuing such a reckless course. Has it made you happy?"

"Ah, now I have the feeling you are trying to learn my secrets, my lady. You would not like them." He was still smiling but his voice held an edge of warning.

"I did not mean to pry. It is only that I have noticed you before at other gatherings. You seem solitary, alone even in the midst of a crowd."

"So you have noticed me before? I am flattered. I wish I could return the compliment, but I feel as though tonight I am seeing you for the first time."

"You are not. I was always there." Anne was surprised by the trace of bitterness in her voice. Yes, she had always been there, fading into the woodwork. "I daresay you just don't remember me very well. I have not been to London for the past two years."

"Two years? Has it been as long as that? I never really knew you before. But you have changed. You are not nearly as mild as I recalled."

"I suppose I am different. It is owing in some part to being widowed."

"You miss your husband a great deal?"

"Naturally." Anne moved automatically into the expected response. She had had enough times to perform it since Gerald's funeral. "Of course one would. Miss one's husband or—or any close acquaintance. Any death diminishes one. 'Never send to know for whom the bell tolls. It tolls for thee.' "

"Then you were not in love with him?"

Anne started to protest, but he silenced her, saying, "My dear Lady Fairhaven. A grieving widow usually does not wax so cheerfully philosophical, nor does she quote Donne."

He did not sound shocked, merely amused. All the same, Anne hung her head. She had the feeling the moonlight revealed her face too cruelly, those less than perfect feelings she sought to keep tucked away.

She was startled to feel his fingers beneath her chin. Slowly, he tipped up her head, forcing her to look at him. His expression astonished her. She would never have thought Mandell's smile could ever be quite that gentle.

"You have nothing to be ashamed of," he said. "I would have thought worse of you if you had esteemed Sir Gerald. He was a pompous, narrow-minded prig, full of his own self consequence."

As a dutiful wife, Anne knew she ought to defend her husband's memory, but that shocking voice that piped up inside of her from time to time whispered that Mandell was right.

It scarce mattered for she could not speak anyway, not with Mandell standing so close, holding her prisoner with his eyes. They were as dark and relentless as a night with no stars.

He continued, "And I no more approve your choice in poets than I do husbands. I have never been that fond of Donne. My tastes run to something more like . . . 'Say what strange motive, Goddess! could compel a well-bred lord to assault a gentle belle? O say what stranger cause, yet unexplored, could make a gentle belle reject a lord?' "

He caressed a tendril that had strayed loose from her braids. The back of his hand grazed against her cheek.

"I—I am afraid I don't recognize that passage," she said.

"It is by Alexander Pope. *The Rape of the Lock.*"

"Oh!"

He twined the strand around one of his long slender fingers. "You are fortunate I have no scissors or I would be tempted to do a little theft myself. Your hair is like spun gold in the moonlight."

Anne flushed, reaching up to rescue her curl. She was not accustomed to such compliments. Lily would have known some light response to make, Camilla some clever retort. But she was not Lily or Camilla. She was only Anne.

She summoned up her most prim expression. "Is it possible, my lord, for you to hold a conversation with a woman without attempting to flirt with her?"

"I don't know. I have never tried."

"I wish you would do so. At least with me."

"Why? If ever there was a woman in need of a little flirtation, I have a notion it is you."

"What I need most," she said sadly, "I fear *you* cannot give me."

"Faith, milady! For the heaven you promise me with those lips, I would be more than willing to attempt it."

"You—you should not say such things to me."

"And you should not purse up your mouth that way. It might give a man the notion you want to be kissed."

"If any man ever tried it," she said fiercely, "he would fast realize his mistake."

But as soon as the words were out of her mouth, Anne realized the mistake had been hers. A rake like Mandell could regard such a statement as nothing other than a challenge.

Before she could move, he closed the distance between them, slipping his arms about her waist. Anne's pulse leapt with alarm. She splayed her hands against his chest in an effort to hold him at bay.

"You—you promised," she faltered. "You said for the moment I was safe with you."

His dark eyes mocked her. "That was then. This is now."

"You tricked me!"

"Lured you down the garden path? I fear that I did." He whipped her arms behind her back, pinioning her wrists in a steely grip. "But then you already knew what a reprehensible fellow I am, my virtuous Anne."

"Don't . . . don't call me that," she said. Her struggles were futile as he drew her against him, the softness of her breasts crushed against the unyielding wall of his chest. Beneath his silken garments, she could sense his muscles tensed like iron. The layers of clothing that separated her from his hard masculinity seemed far too flimsy a barrier.

"Why should I not call you virtuous?" he asked. Resting

his cheek alongside her temple, he breathed a kiss against her hair. "Aren't you?"

"No. Yes, but—but—" Unable to escape, she tried to remain rigid, but the heat of his mouth caressed the sensitive skin behind her ear, causing her to tremble. "You make it sound like a mockery."

"Forgive me, but I have never been any great respecter of virtue." He drew back, and she tensed knowing that he meant to have his kiss.

"Please," she whispered. His eyes glinted in the darkness. They held no mercy, only a fire that caused her heart to pound with a strange mixture of fear and excitement.

His mouth came down to cover hers. She had steeled herself for one final, furious resistance, but the softness of his lips took her by surprise. She had been braced for something far more hot, ruthless, not this gentle questing, this coaxing caress.

She could not prevent a sigh from escaping her. Her mouth parted slightly beneath his. The pressure of his kiss became more demanding and he eased his tongue between her lips.

Anne stiffened. The shock of a contact more intimate than she had ever known reverberated through her entire body. His mouth teased, tasted, plundered, his tongue mating with hers. Disturbing sensations of heat rushed through her, making her knees grow weak.

She held herself still against him, but deep within some dark secret place in her heart something stirred, just a brief flickering of that passionate part of herself she had learned to deny.

She did not respond to Mandell's embrace, but briefly, achingly, shamefully, she wanted to. When he released her at last, she was thoroughly shaken.

The kiss that left her so shattered showed few visible signs of affecting him except for a peculiar gleam in his eyes, his breath coming light and quick.

"That is much better," he murmured. "With a little more

such effort, we might erase that primness which spoils your mouth entirely."

Anne touched one trembling finger to her lips, bruised and moist from the force of Mandell's embrace. A hot flood of mortification coursed into her cheeks. She had not responded to Mandell's improper advances, but she had not put up a life-and-death struggle either.

Mandell glanced down at her with a slight frown. "You are not going to weep or swoon on me, are you?"

Anne shook her head.

"Good. Would you like to hit me?"

Anne shook her head again. She felt too stunned, groping her way through the confused haze of her own emotions to do anything. She released a great shuddering breath.

"You—you must be quite mad. Why did you want to do that to me?"

"Why did I want to kiss you?" Mandell's voice was laced with amused incredulity. "My dear Lady Fairhaven, your education has been sadly lacking."

"Yes, but I mean, why me? I am not at all the sort that—" Anne stumbled on, miserably aware she was making no sense. "You have been kissing the wrong woman."

"Oh, I don't think so. Unlike you, my dear, I never get lost in the dark."

He reached for her again, but this time she managed to evade his grasp. Whirling, she stumbled down the path. Her legs so unsteady beneath her, she was never sure how she made it back to the terrace.

It did not occur to her that Mandell was not pursuing until she had actually breached the threshold of the French doors. When the darkness behind her remained still, she drew up short, panting with relief, striving to regain her composure.

For once she blessed the fact that her presence attracted so little notice in a crowded ballroom. The only one who seemed to observe her precipitate return was Mr. Nicholas Drummond. He regarded her with a frown of concern. But his stare did not bother so much as another's might have

done. She was sure Mr. Drummond was too polite a gentleman to indulge in any speculation or gossip.

Though she scarce felt in control of herself, she forced
herself to step away from the windows. It astonished her
that more people were not glancing her way. Mandell's kiss
must have left some indelible mark upon her.

Managing to make her way past a flock of chattering
dowagers, Anne regarded herself in one of Lily's opulent
gilt mirrors. She was both reassured and disturbed to see
she looked much the same as ever. The same pale, dull old
Anne. Her cheeks were a little more flushed perhaps, but
that could be attributed to the heat of the ballroom. And her
mouth? Her lips were composed into that familiar prim line
that Mandell teased her about. Only when she moistened
them could she seem to taste the heated fury of Mandell's
kiss.

How could she have been such a fool to have trusted
him, to have allowed him to lead her so deep into the gardens? She should have known better. A wolf, no matter
how benign he might seem, was still by nature a wolf.

She supposed she had felt safe simply by virtue of her
own propriety, her lack of beauty. She was hardly the kind
of woman to inspire a man to unbridled passion. When Lily
and Camilla had been on the verge of coming out, Anne
knew that her mother had taken them both aside, warned
them of the dangers of rakehells, how to handle the company of such men. She had never felt it necessary to have
such a talk with Anne.

So how should she have best reacted to Mandell? With
icy dignity? With furious scorn? Anne had no idea. She
only knew what she should not have done, and that was to
have stood there meekly letting him kiss her, trembling like
a frightened doe. She could not begin to fathom his motives, why he had singled her out for his attentions. Perhaps
he had simply been bored, found it amusing to see if he
could fluster the "virtuous Anne." He had made no attempt
to come after her. Likely he lingered in the garden, laughing at the way she had run from him.

That thought cut her deeply, hurting Anne more than she

would have believed possible. She felt the stinging of tears in her eyes, and swiped at them with the back of her hand. That would be all she needed to make her humiliation complete. She remembered that Mandell had asked her if she wanted to weep. He had not sounded mocking then, only a little alarmed at that prospect.

"That is what you could have done," Anne told herself sarcastically. "You could have blubbered all over him. *That* would have taught him a lesson."

Angered by her own weakness, she gritted her teeth and tensed her hands into fists. She found some solace at the thought of teaching Mandell a lesson of a far different sort. The next time he was ever so brash as to offer to let her hit him . . .

But there was not going to be any next time. She did not intend to let Mandell come within a dozen yards of her again. And she doubted that he would try. He had already had his diversion.

It had been a distressing incident, nothing more. She would be wise not to make too much of it. She had other worries at the moment, a far greater torment than Mandell to contend with.

Lucien.

It was three in the morning before Sir Lucien Fairhaven left the Countess Sumner's ball. He strode down the curving stair into the entry hall, haughtily snatching his cloak from one of the footmen before Anne realized her brother-in-law was on the brink of departure.

Anne rushed to the door of the small parlor where she had hid herself away since her walk in the garden with Mandell. Regardless of the curious stares of Lily's servants, Anne called out, "Lucien! Wait!"

She was certain he heard her, but he did not once look back, stalking through the massive front doors into the night. Anne felt the familiar despair tighten in her chest, and cursed herself for the inattentiveness that had allowed Lucien to escape.

She had retreated to the small downstairs parlor for most

of the evening, leaving the door ajar so that she could observe all departures without running the risk of encountering Mandell again. But the strain of too many sleepless nights and an exhaustion of spirit had finally taken their toll. She must have nodded off, for how long she did not know. Only the clock chiming three had startled her awake in time to see Lucien making his exit. A minute more and she would have been too late. Perhaps she still was.

Refusing to accept that, Anne raced across the hall toward the front door. Lily's elderly butler attempted to intercept her flight. "My lady, wait. At least allow me to fetch your shawl."

But Anne brushed past him, all but stumbling in her haste to clear the stone steps, the short span of walkway leading to the pavement. She halted, gazing frantically about her. The cobblestones yet rang with the clatter of cabriolets and carriages pulled by smart-looking teams of horses. This accursed city never seemed to sleep.

Anne feared that Lucien was already on his way to his next round of entertainment. But no! There was his elegant brougham pulled up to the curb at the corner. One of Lily's own footmen had darted out to hold open the door.

"Lucien!" Anne cried, striving to be heard above the rumble of a passing vehicle. Lifting her skirts, she propelled herself forward with a desperate burst of speed.

Lucien affected not to hear her, but the footman touched his sleeve, respectfully indicating Anne's approach.

Lucien paused with one foot mounted upon the step of his carriage. With obvious reluctance, he turned to face her. The street lamp shone full on his blond hair and the harsh planes of his once handsome countenance. The sullen set of his mouth offered Anne no encouragement.

"What is amiss, Anne?" he snapped as Anne drew up beside him. "Did I forget my gloves or something?"

Anne placed one hand over the region of her heart, attempting to recover her breath. "No. You forgot—that is, you know I wished to speak to you."

"Another time, perhaps. The night is still young. I have other engagements."

"No, now!" Her voice sounded almost shrill. Anne forced herself to speak in milder, more placating tones. "I have been waiting so long."

"To no purpose. You and I have little to say to each other."

"We have a great deal to talk about. That is the sole reason Lily invited you tonight, so that we would have a chance to heal our differences."

Lucien's face washed a dull red. "The countess might have spared herself the invitation. She certainly did me no favor. An evening of cards with whelps and old men. And you, hanging upon my sleeve, like some Covent Garden doxy seeking a night's work."

Anne flinched at his insulting words, aware that Lucien's coachman leaned forward to listen with undisguised interest. The young footman, holding the door, shuffled his feet with embarrassment, pretending not to hear.

"Please, Lucien," Anne said, striving to keep calm and reasonable. "Come back into the house. We cannot discuss this in the street."

"We cannot discuss this at all, Anne. Now, if you will excuse me, I have more important matters to attend."

"Nothing is more important than this."

Lucien turned as though he would mount into the carriage, but Anne clutched at his arm, clinging with a strength she scarce knew she possessed.

"For the love of God, Lucien. You have my daughter. You brought her here to London. One of Lily's servants saw a little girl exactly like Norrie being carried into one of the houses nearby. You cannot deny it."

"Why should I?" Lucien's mouth curved into a hard ugly line. "I will tell you exactly where she is. I leased number twenty-six, a most elegant house. You need not worry about Eleanor. I have been giving her the best of everything."

"You must let me see her!"

"Haven't you got enough else to amuse you in London at the height of the season? You always have been a most strange creature, my dear sister Anne."

"You have kept Norrie away from me for three months.

Most of that time I have not even known where she was. You have no right."

"I have every right. She is my ward. Gerald left guardianship of the girl to me."

"He never meant for you to separate us in this cruel fashion."

"Gerald's intentions hardly matter now. Poor Anne. That is the price you pay for choosing the wrong brother." His gloating smile only emphasized the coarse heaviness of his features, the dark rings beneath his eyes. It was difficult for Anne to remember that this man was actually younger than she and that she had once harbored more gentle feelings toward him.

"Is that what this is all about then?" she asked. "A revenge against me because I wed Gerald instead of you?"

"I always told you that you would be sorry one day."

So he had, but Anne had taken it for nothing more than the rantings of a wild, passionate boy. She had already been betrothed to Gerald when she had first met his younger brother. So at odds with the rest of the stolid Fairhavens, Lucien was either reviled or ignored by his family. Anne had felt sorry for him, had only thought to be kind. Never had she dreamed the youth would fancy himself in love with her and propose a mad scheme for their elopement. He had taken Anne's rejection most bitterly. She had done her best to reason with the boy.

And now, although she knew it was hopeless, she attempted to reason with the man. "Lucien, that all happened over eight years ago. You were not really in love with me. If you are honest, you will admit you only wanted me because I was Gerald's bride."

"And now I have everything that belonged to my esteemed older brother—his title, his lands, his daughter. I could even have you now." Lucien's gloved hand stroked her cheek in a gesture that sent a chill down Anne's spine. "Except that I don't want you anymore."

"You cannot possibly want Norrie, either. At least allow me to see her. Surely that is not too much to ask."

"Really, Anne! Most women gladly farm their children

out to servants or to wet nurses. There is something un-
wholesome about this sickly attachment of yours to the girl.
I think it would be in the best interests of my niece if I sent
her off to school, perhaps abroad somewhere."

Although Lucien mimicked Gerald's sanctimonious tone
almost to perfection, there was no disguising the hint of
malice that played about the corners of his mouth. Anne
could feel the blood drain from her face.

"You know Norrie is not strong enough for anything like
that. Her health has always been delicate and she is only six
years old."

"Seven," he mocked. "Did you forget your beloved
daughter had a birthday last month? She had a lovely day.
I gave her a pony and six new frocks. Your absence was
hardly noted. I vow the child has forgotten you already."

Anne could not trust herself to reply. She had spent the
day in the bleak emptiness of the nursery, the presents she
had bought for Norrie stacked unopened upon the table
while she set stitches into the gown she was making for
Norrie's favorite doll, trying not to water the silk with her
tears, trying not to drive herself mad wondering where her
daughter was, praying that Norrie was not too frightened or
unhappy.

Anne began hoarsely, "Lucien, you were my friend
once—"

"Before you married Gerald."

"If I hurt you, I am sorry. But there must be something
I can do to make amends, to make you change your mind."

"You have never begged."

"What?" Anne felt as though she had done nothing but
beg these past months, cajoling, pleading through letters,
through her solicitor, through repeated attempts to see
Lucien.

"You have never asked me nicely enough. You have
never begged for the return of your daughter."

Wearily, Anne pressed one hand to her brow. "Please,"
she whispered.

"No!" Lucien regarded her through hard, bright eyes.
"On your knees. Here. Now. In the gutter."

The young footman made a muffled sound of protest and Anne stared at Lucien in horror. He could not possibly mean it. But the lines of his face were implacable and she saw that it would take nothing less than her complete and abject humiliation to appease his wounded pride.

Anne swallowed hard, closed her eyes, and thought of Norrie. That was all that it took to sweep the last of her dignity aside. Stiffly, she lowered herself to a kneeling position on the pavement, feeling the cold and damp seep through the thin material of her gown. Raising her hands in supplicating fashion, she said, "Please, Lucien. I beg of you."

The moment seemed to stretch into hours. Dimly, Anne was aware of the restive movement of the coach horses, the fact that tears were trickling down the young footman's cheeks.

But her focus never wavered from the tall blond man looming over her. Something softened in Lucien's eyes and he reached out as though to stroke her hair. A wild surge of hope rushed through Anne.

Then he turned his back on her, saying coldly, "Get up, Anne. You are making a spectacle of yourself."

As Lucien vaulted into the carriage, something snapped inside of Anne, all the ache of too many nights spent hovering over Norrie's empty bed, too many pleas that had fallen upon deaf ears. A rage of despair tore through her, racking her entire frame.

"Damn you!" she cried.

She scrambled to her feet and launched herself at the coach, managing to prevent the footman from closing the door. Glaring up at Lucien, she said, "Give me my daughter back."

"When hell freezes over, madam."

"Give me Norrie or I vow I will kill you, Lucien."

With a snarl, he lashed out, dealing Anne a shove that nearly sent her sprawling onto the pavement.

Before she could recover her balance, Lucien slammed the carriage door himself, roaring out a command to his coachman. With a crack of a whip, the team started into movement, the brougham lumbering away from the curve.

"No!" With a choked cry, Anne rushed forward, only restrained from racing after the coach by the young footman grasping her shoulders.

"Let me go!" Anne gasped. "I have to—have to make him—"

"Milady, please," the youth pleaded. "You will only get hurt."

Anne scarce knew what brought her back to her senses, the footman's wide frightened eyes or the sight of Lucien's carriage vanishing into the darkness. The terrifying rage drained out of her as suddenly as it had come. As she stared into the yawning emptiness that was the street, she ceased her struggles. With a murmur of apology, the footman released her.

She wrapped her arms about herself to still her trembling, aware that she had behaved like a wild woman. She could yet hear the echo of her own shocking words.

I vow I will kill you, Lucien.

Never in her life had she felt such hatred of anyone, but Lucien had driven her to it. She knew beyond all doubt there was no hope of ever persuading him to return Norrie. Rubbing her arms, she waited for the familiar despair to wash over her, a despair blacker than any she had yet known. But it did not come. Rather, she felt a cold weight of determination settle over her heart.

The threat she had uttered shocked her all the more, for she realized she had meant it. She turned, wending her way back to Lily's house, scarce seeing where she went.

"I will have my daughter back," she vowed. "Whatever it takes! I swear to God I will."

Chapter 4

~~~~~~~~~~

The prospect of a murder occasioned barely a whisper from those overhearing the plot. But the famed actor Edmund Kean no longer created the same sensation as he had upon his arrival in London years ago. The theatre at Drury Lane was only half full tonight. Although his performance as Macbeth was as mesmerizing as ever, the audience seemed more concerned with turning their attention toward a late arrival.

Mandell slipped unobtrusively into his box, yet a ripple of murmurs went through the crowd, the disturbance audible enough to carry past the floats to where the actors paced out their steps.

"Is this a dagger which I see before me?" Kean ground out, though no one was certain whether he wanted most to use it on Macbeth's erstwhile king or Mandell, who took his time, swirling his black cape from his shoulders and assuming his seat.

The marquis stripped off his gloves at a leisurely pace, oblivious to the irritation he was causing the actor. Mandell never troubled himself to arrive on time. Prompt attendance at the theatre only subjected one to the horrors of the musical interlude. Some misbegotten fellow in the orchestra was bound not to have prepared properly. Mandell's keen ear could detect an instrument even slightly out of tune and the sound was a torment akin to having hot spikes shoved under his nails.

He settled back into his seat and the audience subsided as well. Kean succeeded in despatching the king and now lamented over his bloodstained hands. It was a stirring performance, but the theatre had long ago lost all magic for Mandell.

He could still remember the first time he had visited Drury Lane. He had been but twelve, on holiday from school when his grandfather had brought him to a matinee production of *Romeo and Juliet*. Mandell had been held spellbound, moved to tears by the plight of the young lovers.

It had disturbed the old duke to hear his grandson expressing such emotion over the conjuring of a set of lowly players. When the play had ended, the duke had taken him backstage, forced him to observe how tawdry the costumes actually were, the glittering jewels only paste. When seen up close, the performers looked common, garish in their lead paint makeup. Romeo was no more than a drunken sot with a foul mouth, the dewy-eyed Juliet a harlot who serviced half the male cast in her dressing room.

The theatre was illusion, nothing more, and while Mandell might permit himself a certain restrained enjoyment, he should never become utterly taken in by it. Mandell had taken strict heed of his grandfather's words. It was a mistake he rarely made again, the cherishing of illusions. Now he no longer had any.

Below him, Macbeth went through the torments of the damned, tortured by his conscience. Mandell saw only a vain little man strutting about in a preposterous imitation of Scottish plaid. The marquis stirred impatiently, his gaze skating past the players, past the pit to the tiers of boxes. He found more diversion off the stage, within the interior of the theatre.

His eyes rested upon the box he usually occupied. Sara was there, as lovely as ever and with a companion. It did not surprise Mandell that his former mistress had found a replacement for him so soon, but her choice did. Lounging behind the dark-haired beauty was a raffish young soldier. Sara would hardly realize her ambition courting the attention of some half-pay officer, but Mandell supposed she knew what she was doing. No one knew her own interests better than Sara did.

Mandell's scrutiny moved on, remarking other acquaintances, dismissing them until he found the box he wanted. Just opposite him on the first tier sat a pale woman garbed all in white, the short puffed sleeves of her gown exposing the slender grace of her arms.

So Anne Fairhaven was still alive and well. She had not gone off into a decline over the assault upon her virtue by the wicked Lord Mandell. Mandell had to admit he had been curious to see her again, wondering if he would experience the same strange tug of attraction that had beset him that night at the countess's ball.

But moonlit gardens could weave illusions as well. The heady scent of roses, like an opiate, could cause a man to fancy there was something different about Anne from other women, a sorrowing angel whose gentle touch might be capable of curing the darkness in a lost soul.

Absolute nonsense, of course. Gazing at her across the theatre, he could see now that she was an ordinary mortal, only a little more solemn than the sort of lady who usually struck his fancy. She shared the box with her sister Lily and two of the countess's long-term admirers, the Honorable Mr. Adam Barnhart and Lord Douglas Cecil. The trio laughed heartily as the drunken porter staggered onstage to offer some comic relief, but Anne seemed set apart from the others, untouched by the laughter, alone as Mandell often felt himself to be.

Just an ordinary woman, yet he could not seem to tear his eyes away from her. She fingered the pearls at her neck, her décolletage more daring than the gown she had worn to Lily's ball three evenings ago. Mandell's gaze traveled over the soft rise of her bosom, the ivory column of her throat, the way her hair had been pulled up into a chignon of curls that glinted gold in the light cast up from the stage. The style left her face mercilessly exposed, vulnerable. It made him want to pull her into his arms and—

Mandell caught his breath, experiencing a familiar quickening of the blood. So he desired the lady. That was all it was. When he had kissed her, her lithe frame had felt good pressed against him, her mouth hot, moist, and inviting.

He wanted her. Then the solution was simple. He would have her. Fill some of his empty nights with the sweet pleasures of her body. And in having her, he would put an end to any . . . illusions.

And how readily would the virtuous Anne agree to these plans of his? A hard smile touched Mandell's lips. The lady's willingness did not overly concern him. When he had kissed her, he had tasted desire upon her lips, felt the brief tremor of passion course through her. A passion she had been quick to suppress. The next time he would not permit her to do so.

He had released her that night, fully expecting the usual reaction; tears, accusations, all the trappings of outraged virtue. He had to admit she had surprised him. Her only response had been that sorrowful bewilderment that he should even have wanted to kiss her. Could it be the lady truly did not realize how desirable she was? He would take great delight in teaching her otherwise.

He had permitted her to flee him once. The marquis of Mandell did not chase women across ballrooms. He bided his time. Stretching back in his seat, he steepled his fingers in front of him, content for the moment to watch her from the shadows of his own box, imagining how her honey gold fall of hair would look tumbled across his pillow, her prim mouth well kissed to a state of compliance.

These agreeable reflections were interrupted by the sound of a footfall behind him. Irritated to have his solitude intruded upon, Mandell turned to see who had the temerity to step into his box unasked.

His brows rose a fraction when he saw that it was his cousin Nick. Who else would wear such a horror of a flowered waistcoat and a frock coat—Mandell could not tell the exact hue, but he had a distasteful notion it might actually be purple.

Nick stumbled forward. Banging up against the empty seat he muttered a soft curse. Mandell had the impression that he was rather out of breath, but Nick's voice sounded steady enough when he spoke. "Halloa, Mandell. There you are. I had the deuce of a time locating you."

"Why were you even looking for me?" Mandell asked. "What are you doing here?"

"I came to join you. You invited me to."

"Did I? I must have been in a singularly mellow mood or else I believed you would be too busy to accept."

"Ah, well, the debates finished earlier than usual tonight," Nick said cheerfully, taking little trouble to keep his voice down. This earned him a few giggles and some shushes from the neighboring boxes.

Nick peered down at the stage, complaining. "Damme. They are still on the main bill. I had hoped they would have reached the farce by now."

"You are providing the farce, coz," Mandell drawled. "Do sit down."

"What? Oh!" Nick sank down onto his seat, only slightly abashed by another chorus of titters. He leaned forward, attempting to concentrate on the play, allowing Mandell the leisure to study his unexpected guest.

His memory might be faulty, but Mandell doubted he had invited Nick to join him tonight. There could be no worse theatre companion than his cousin. Nick fidgeted, drummed his fingers along the box rail, voiced loud asides. Mandell supposed it was the politician in Nick, unable to bear listening to anyone else declaim while he was forced to remain silent.

Nick did not chatter, but he seemed more restless than usual tonight, an aura of suppressed excitement about him. He clearly had no more interest in the play than he ever did. His cousin must want something of him, Mandell decided. With a sigh of resignation, he wondered what servant's marriage Nick might be arranging now, what widows' and orphans' fund he must be collecting for.

The first act finished and Kean stepped forward to take his bow to an enthusiastic applause. Mandell's attention was drawn back to the Countess Sumner's party. Lily was sweeping a reluctant Anne and the two gentlemen from her box to flit about greeting acquaintances.

Mandell remained where he was. He had no desire to address Anne in the company of a crowded theatre foyer. When next he spoke to the lady, he meant to be alone with her.

Besides, he might as well find out what the blazes Nick wanted now. Then perhaps he would be left in peace. He turned to his cousin, who stretched.

"Entertaining fellow, Shakespeare," Nick said with a mighty yawn. "But why couldn't he have written his plays in plain English?"

"It's called Elizabethan poetry, cousin." For the first time, Mandell took full note of Nick's appearance. The coat, alas, was indeed purple, and rather disheveled for the dapper Nicholas. His ash-blond hair was disarranged as well, swept to one side in a clumsy effort to conceal the bruise darkening on his temple.

"What the devil happened to you?" Mandell demanded.

"Oh, the debates became a little heated tonight. Someone shied a book at my head."

"Tories can be so impetuous."

"Actually it was one of my fellow Whigs. I seem to be getting too radical for everyone's tastes." Nick touched his fingers gingerly to the bruise and winced. "Does it look very dreadful?"

"No, it matches your coat beautifully. What sedition have you been espousing now to rouse such passions?"

Nick's mouth set into a bitter line. "I have not been doing anything but trying to convince those blockheads that this city is crying out for an organized police force. Instead of supporting the notion, everyone treats me as though I were a second Cromwell attempting to organize a military state."

"Take heart, coz," Mandell said. "Perhaps our good friend the Hook will oblige you with another murder. That should stir things up in your favor."

To Mandell's surprise, this offhand bit of raillery caused Nick to go white.

"That's not amusing, Mandell," Nick said tersely. "There is nothing laughable about murder."

"Isn't there?" Mandell murmured. "I have often wondered whether death might not prove the greatest diversion of all."

Nick regarded him for a moment with troubled eyes, then said, "I have had enough of debates for one night. Let us talk of something else. We are going to have to leave the theatre early. I for one do not care to face our grandfather's temper if we are late."

"I have no plans for calling upon His Grace tonight."

"Mandell, you cannot have forgotten. We have all been bidden to attend a late supper. Even Mama and my sisters will be there."

"Give them my regards."

"But the supper is to honor you—your birthday."

"It is not my birthday. It is the anniversary of the day my grandfather adopted me as his heir." Mandell's tone was one of indifference, but it masked the bleak feeling that always stole over him at the memory of that day. The day he had been re-created as the marquis of Mandell, the day that he had utterly lost all sense of another identity.

He added, "I don't even know when my real birthday is."

"I have always found that hard to understand. I know our grandfather was bitter over what happened to your mother but—to blot out all traces of your youth, your connection to your father's family!"

"My damnable French blood," Mandell said drily. "There no longer is any connection. My father and all his family may be dead for all I know."

"If it distresses you so much, there must be a way that you could find out."

"Who said that it distressed me?" Mandell asked with a haughty lift of his brow.

"Surely you must want to know, at least what happened to your own father."

Mandell turned away, suddenly disturbed by a memory of himself as a child, staring up at a laughing young man with hair and eyes as dark as Mandell's own. He lifted

Mandell up to the pianoforte, patiently guiding his small fingers over the keys.

Mandell sucked in his breath, blotting out the memory, replacing it with one of his mother's blood staining the pavement.

"Very likely, my father is dead," he said. "I hope he is, and burning in hell."

"Perhaps he is, but I don't believe you will ever know any peace until you find out for certain. You ought to go back to France, Mandell."

"Leave it alone, Nick," Mandell growled.

Nick subsided. Neither of them said anything and tension filled the air until Nick broke it with a shaky laugh.

"Since it is not in truth your birthday, then I suppose I need not feel obliged to spout for a gift. My pockets are rather to let at the moment."

"Your pockets are always to let." Mandell turned back to face his cousin, feeling enough in command of his feelings to assume his usual dry tone. "Besides, I have already received a gift."

He drew forth a gaudy gilt-trimmed snuffbox, the sides decorated with jade dragons, their eyes gleaming with the fire of red rubies.

"Good lord!" Nick said. "Where did you get that awful thing? I can scarce believe that our grandfather would—"

"Nay, the old duke is not that sentimental. I received it from my dear friend Lancelot Briggs."

"I am surprised that you accepted it."

"So am I. I was sampling a fine madeira at the time and feeling unusually gracious." Mandell stared at the snuffbox with a slight frown. The scene had been embarrassing. He had been trying to enjoy his dinner at White's in peace when Briggs had entered the club and plunked down at Mandell's table. Mumbling something unintelligible, Briggs had blushed as shyly as a maid and shoved the snuffbox at Mandell.

Briggs's lips had trembled with a wistful smile, his eyes full of that doglike adoration. Such a simple man. Such an irritating one. For the life of him, Mandell did not know why he put up with Briggs or why he had pocketed the snuffbox.

But now, as he sat turning the absurd thing in his hands, his mouth creased into an expression that was half smile, half grimace. He mused aloud to Nick, "You know, it does tend to grow on one. I may actually learn to like it."

"There is no accounting for tastes."

"No, there isn't." Mandell angled a pointed glance at Nick's waistcoat, then returned the snuffbox to his pocket.

Nick cleared his throat. "Now about that dinner tonight—"

Mandell gave vent to a weary sigh. He hoped that they had worn that subject out, but Nick rushed on doggedly, "I know you and Grandfather have become estranged in recent years."

"That is scarce possible. We were never close to begin with."

"The old duke can be very autocratic and gruff, but beneath it all, Mandell, I believe that he truly loves you."

"Likely he does, but if you ever brought your head out of your law books, you might learn what a burden love can be. Your efforts at peacemaking have been duly noted, cousin. But you should stick with your politics and leave the diplomacy alone."

"You could not at least make an appearance at the dinner tonight?" Nick pleaded.

"No. I have other plans." Mandell allowed his gaze to drift across the theatre to where the Countess Sumner's party returned to the box. Anne was on the verge of taking her seat when she glanced up. Her eyes locked with Mandell's. Even from such a distance, he could see her face register both shock and dismay.

He bent slightly, favoring her with an ironic bow. She acknowledged the gesture by looking fixedly in the opposite direction. Her knees appeared to give out beneath her and she sank into her seat.

Behind him, Mandell heard Nick's soft groan. "Oh, no, Mandell! You are not still bent upon tormenting Anne

Fairhaven. I hoped that after what happened at the Countess Sumner's ball you would leave her alone."

"And what would you know of that?" Mandell turned to stare at his cousin. "Have you been spying upon me?"

Nick looked a little uncomfortable. "No, but I did see you escort her into the garden. I don't know what you did to upset her, but when she returned, she was flustered, blushing."

"The woman needs to blush occasionally. She is far too pale."

Nick swore softly. "Mandell, you've got that look in your eye. I know it well. You have set your sights upon seducing Anne Fairhaven. Why, Mandell? Out of all the willing trollops in London, why must you tamper with a lady like her? Sometimes I don't understand you at all."

"That is hardly surprising. I rarely understand myself." Mandell scarce knew what devil prompted him to goad his cousin even further. Plucking an imaginary piece of lint upon his sleeve, he said casually, "By the by, I am indebted to you for drawing my attention to the lady that night at Lily's. I might not have noticed her otherwise. You were quite right about the lady's eyes. They are a most haunting blue."

Nick's eyes flashed with the beginnings of his infamous temper. "Curse you, Mandell. The lady is obviously already suffering from some sort of heartbreak."

"Women's hearts rarely break. The gentler sex is far more resilient than you would suppose. I will admit there is something troubling Anne, but I daresay it will prove to be quite mundane. She will recover in my arms."

"You are damned confident, but there is the possibility the lady will have none of you. I despise gossip, but there has been talk that there may be something between Lady Fairhaven and her brother-in-law Lucien."

Mandell's jaw tightened for a moment, even the suggestion of such a thing enough to send a strange feeling coursing through his veins that was both ice and fire. He forced himself to shrug. "And so? I have ousted far better rivals than Sir Lucien."

"And what if I were to appoint myself the lady's champion?"

"Oh, I don't believe you would do that. You have more entertaining causes to fight for than a lady's virtue."

Nick jerked to his feet, his hands clenching into fists. Mandell remained as he was, leaning indolently back in his chair. His eyes held Nick's steadily until the young man looked away.

Nick slowly relaxed his hands and drew in a cleansing breath. "Damn it, Mandell, why do you do this to me? You know my lamentable temper. I . . . I would never want us to come to blows."

"We won't. At least not over a lady's honor. Your choice of waistcoats perhaps, but never anything so insignificant as a woman."

Nick shook his head darkly. "Talking to you is as much a waste of time as addressing Parliament." He bent to retrieve his hat.

"Leaving so soon?" Mandell inquired amicably. "Ah, I forgot. Your distaste for murder, and I fear *Macbeth* is only getting started."

Nick sketched him a tight-lipped bow. "Your servant, sir," he said, and stalked out of the box just as the next act was about to begin.

Mandell experienced a flicker of regret. If he valued any man's good opinion, he supposed it was Nick's. Some ten years his junior, his cousin was like the brother he had never had and perhaps the closest thing he had to a friend. But Nick's head was stuffed full of ideals; a belief in the possibility of a perfect world, that eventually reason would triumph and all men attain a level of goodness, even Mandell. Mandell could not allow his cousin to entertain such mistaken notions.

It was astonishing that Nick did not resent him. Mandell would not have blamed Nick if he had, and for reasons other than Mandell's penchant for goading him. If not for Mandell, Nick might have been the favored grandson of the Duke of Windermere.

Of course, when his grandfather had rescued Mandell

from France and adopted him as his heir, Nick had not even been born. But the fact remained. Mandell's arrival in England had cut Nick out of a considerable inheritance. Nick had never shown any sign that he minded. Despite his hot temper, he really was a good-natured fellow.

It rather surprised Mandell that Nick should wax so fierce in Lady Fairhaven's defense. He had never known his cousin to take particular notice of any woman before. But if there ever was a lady calculated to rouse a man's protective instincts, it was Anne. Faith, there was something about the lady that even stirred some noble feelings within him.

But not very many, Mandell conceded. The second act was well in progress, but once again all the drama he desired came from the box opposite.

Anne kept her gaze forward, but Mandell sensed she was taking in no more of the performance than he. Her hands fluttered from her lap to her pearls and back again. She appeared almost . . . frightened.

Of what? Mandell supposed that he did not have to look far to seek the cause. He wished he were seated beside her now, to still her hand and raise it to his lips, tell her there was no need for that much distress.

He wanted to inspire many emotions within her, but fear was not one of them. He could remain content just to hold her, until she was soothed, reassured—

Mandell abruptly checked these peculiar thoughts. He had to stop and remind himself of just who he was. Certainly not the romantic hero of this particular farce.

No, never the hero, he thought with a grimace. Always the villain.

While Macbeth schemed to make himself king, Anne Fairhaven's mind reeled with plots of her own. The sounds of the players' voices and the murmurs of the audience all faded to nothing. She was conscious of little more than the unsteady beating of her own pulse and the pistol tucked inside her reticule.

She clutched the silk purse against the folds of her gown,

the concealed weapon a disturbing weight upon her lap.
The pistol had been purchased only that afternoon when she
had pawned her jewels in a little shop in Bethnal Green.

Hiring a coach to escape from London, bribing servants,
and buying the weapon all required a deal of money. With
Lucien controlling the purse strings of her inheritance from
Gerald, Anne had had no choice but to part with her jewelry. While the old pawnbroker had pawed over her trea-
sures with his gnarled fingers, Anne had examined the
array of pistols he had laid out for her inspection upon the
dusty countertop.

The weapons had all terrified her, but at last she had
dared pick up the smallest one with the pearl handle.

"Ah, an excellent choice, milady," the pawnbroker had
said. "Just the right fit for a woman's hand."

"It seems rather small," Anne ventured.

"Oh, 'tis big enough all right. You'd be surprised at how
little it takes to kill a man."

How little it takes to kill a man. The old man's leering
words kept echoing through Anne's head. She was
wrenched back to her present surroundings by a light touch
upon her hand. Starting half out of her chair, she glanced
up and was dismayed to find Lily staring at her and not the
stage.

Had Lily finally noticed something, read some of Anne's
thoughts in her face? Perhaps the outline of the pistol was
even visible through the silk. It had been foolish to bring
the thing to the theatre tonight, but that had seemed far
safer than leaving the weapon lying about her bedchamber
where her maid or some other servant might find it.

Anne closed her hands over the purse. But Lily only
smiled and whispered, "Is not Mr. Kean as wonderful as I
promised? Are you not glad you came after all?"

"What? Oh. Oh, yes," Anne stammered. She scarce
dared breathe until Lily turned back to the stage. Her sister's obtuseness astonished her as did that of everyone else
she met this evening. Anne was certain no one could be
weaving such desperate plans as she without revealing it by

her expression. There must surely be a wildness about her eyes tonight.

Yet Lily had noticed nothing except that Anne was wearing her second-best pearls. As for Lily's two gentlemen friends, they paid her little heed. Anne supposed people saw only what they expected to see.

It had been thus all her life. When anyone looked at her, they had always thought, "There goes meek, proper little Anne."

Only one man had ever perceived anything different. Mandell.

Anne shuddered. She had been trying not to glance his way all evening. She had hoped to be gone from London without ever having to encounter him again. His presence in the box opposite made her wish she had followed her first instinct and pleaded a headache so that she could remain at home. But she had been doing her best these past few days to avoid drawing Lily's attention to herself, to behave as normal and complacent as possible.

Mandell's unexpected appearance had all but shattered what remained of her calm facade. Anne thought she had recovered from that episode in the garden, but one sight of that lean, aristocratic profile was enough to bring it all back with an overwhelming intensity—the moonlight and rustling shadows, the fragrance of the flowers, Mandell's mouth hot against her own.

What perverse fate had brought him to the theatre tonight of all nights? If anyone could guess there was something amiss with her, it would be Mandell with that uncanny way of his. She fancied him staring at her across the theatre, that dark gaze closing the distance between them, stripping her to the soul. She could feel his presence like the charge of lightning that hung in the air before a storm.

She dare not allow him to look too deep into her eyes. If she did, she would be lost. He would know everything. He would—

With great difficulty, Anne checked her panicky thoughts. She ran her fingers over her neck, telling herself she was being ridiculous. Mandell was not omniscient. Mandell would not be looking into her eyes. He had not even attempted to approach her, content to mock her from a distance with a bow and that quizzing smile. He had likely forgotten her existence and was absorbed in enjoying the play.

She had enough real fears to contend with without inventing new ones. With the back of her glove, she mopped a bead of perspiration from her brow. She was not at all formed for this sort of dangerous intrigue.

She felt as guilty as if she really were plotting to murder someone. Despite her fierce vow to Lucien, Anne had not bought the pistol to harm him, only to threaten him if necessary. Indeed, she hoped she would not have to confront him at all, but would find some way to snatch her daughter from his house when he was away.

Norrie ... Anne had been trying not to dwell on the thought, but in a few short hours, if all went well, she might actually be gazing upon her little girl again, caressing her curls while she slept. Crushed inside the reticule beneath the pistol was a note.

Midnight. The back gate.
L.

The lettering was rough and had obviously been carefully labored over. It was the script of a servant who had been taught only the bare rudiments of printing, Louisa Douglas, apple-cheeked, fresh from Yorkshire, little more than a child herself.

Anne had patiently studied the comings and goings of Lucien's household for nearly two days. She had hoped for a glimpse of Norrie and been disappointed. But she had managed to assess many of the servants, trying to decide who might be useful for her purpose.

In the end, Anne had settled upon Louisa, a homely young woman who, despite her crooked teeth, possessed a warm smile. The little maid was sent out on frequent marketing errands and Anne had found no difficulty approaching her in the street.

Louisa had been wary, sympathetic, and intrigued by turns over Anne's plight. Yes indeed, she saw Miss Eleanor every day. It was Louisa's task to carry the breakfast tray up to the nursery. The poor little mite always looked so pale. Pining for her mama, Louisa expected. Louisa would be only too happy to try to slip Norrie a message or a small present from Anne.

But when Anne had explained what she really wanted, Louisa's eyes had gone round with terror. Smuggling a message was one thing, but sneaking Anne into the house to actually see the child quite another. If they were caught! Sir Lucien had the most formidable temper.

"Then we will pick a time when Sir Lucien is gone," Anne had said smoothly.

"He hardly ever is during the day, ma'am. Mostly just late at night."

"Late at night would be perfect," Anne had said. "The rest of the household would be asleep."

Louisa had allowed that even the governess, Mrs. Anstey, was a heavy sleeper, but she had continued to shake her head. It had taken a great deal of persuasion and coin to convince the girl to help Anne in such a risky undertaking. Even then, Anne was not sure she had succeeded until she had found the note tucked, as prearranged, in the chink of the garden wall.

The simple note that was somehow touching printed in that childlike hand . . . *Midnight. The back gate.*

What troubled Anne most about all her plotting was the deception she practiced upon Louisa. Contrary to what she had told the girl, Anne wanted to do far more than just see her child tonight. She meant to remark the layout of the interior of Lucien's house, the position of windows and doors, the exact location of Norrie's room.

For the next time Anne entered Lucien's house, she had to do it without Louisa's aid. She could not have an innocent serving girl implicated in Norrie's abduction. Abduction? No! Anne's lips thinned at the word. It was not abduction to take back one's own child. Norrie was rightfully hers no matter what Lucien and the law decreed.

Lost in her contemplations, Anne scarce realized how far the performance had progressed. When she managed to focus on the stage, she realized the actress playing Lady Macbeth was drifting through the paces of the sleepwalking scene.

The final act. Soon the curtain would ring down for the intermission between the main bill and the farce. Anne determined to resist Lily's efforts to drag her along to the foyer again. She could not face greeting more acquaintances, trying to keep her worries and apprehensions to herself.

She still had so many arrangements to make in the days to come. She needed to hire a coach to get her and Norrie out of London, and then find some way to gain passage out of the country, far from Lucien. Anne did not as yet have the least idea how to go about such a thing.

She tensed, thinking of the difficulties that lie ahead, her fingers moving back to fidget with her purse. Lily reached out to stop the movement with a tiny smile, an admonishing shake of the head.

That was Lily, forever playing the older sister, trying to curb Anne's inelegant tendency to fiddle with her purses, fans, jewelry, or to nibble her nails. Ofttimes Lily's playful reproofs irritated Anne, but tonight the gesture brought an unexpected lump to her throat. It suddenly occurred to her that if the plan she had formed succeeded, she might never see Lily again. She would have to flee without even bidding her sister farewell.

She wished she could take Lily into her confidence, but no one would be less likely to understand the rash action Anne contemplated, an action that would put her forever beyond the pale of the society Lily so cherished.

Certainly when Anne had first come to London in search of her daughter, Lily had patted Anne's shoulder and commiserated. "It is a deal too bad of Lucien not to allow you to see the child. But I heard he has engaged for her one of the best governesses in England. Mrs. Anstey tutored the Duchess of Biltmore's girls. Do you think that Norrie will be neglected?"

No, Anne could not precisely say that. In his own way,

Lucien was fond of Norrie. All of her sensitive, dreamy-eyed little daughter's physical needs would be met, but Norrie required more affection than any governess could give. Norrie needed her mother.

Anne had tried to explain that to Lily, but her sister had only given her cheek an indulgent pat.

"Dear Anne. You are a lady, not a nursemaid. The child will have a legion of servants to attend to her needs. And I will tell you what I found to be true of my own girls. The older they got, the more interesting they became. When Norrie is quite grown, she may call upon you as you pleases, and you will find that you take much greater delight in her company then."

When Norrie is quite grown. Lily could have no notion what dismay her words had struck to Anne's heart. She had realized then it was useless even trying to explain to Lily about such things as how warm and sweet Norrie felt being rocked at bedtime, the simple joy of coaxing tangles from curls yet baby fine, of enfolding small fingers still sticky with jam. Small stubby fingers that would all too soon grow into long elegant ones slipping out of a mother's reach.

It would be foolish to expect the bright butterfly that was her sister to understand any of that. Not that Lily was callous or unusual. Most of the fashionable ladies in London would have agreed with her. The rearing of children was best left to servants, and though it was sad that Anne could not see her daughter upon occasion, there were far greater tragedies. Great heavens, she might have been refused vouchers to Almacks!

Anne's mouth twisted into a bitter smile. Perhaps having children had come all too easily to those grand ladies. They had never had to endure the heartbreak of so many miscarriages, the even greater grief of laying to rest a tiny still-born son.

When Norrie had been placed into Anne's arms for the first time, warm, alive, she had been like a small miracle. The babe had been at once so frail, so susceptible to every passing fever and sniffle, and yet also so bright-eyed, so quick, so eager to learn. Like a miser with a fragile treasure, Anne had hoarded her child within the secure walls of the nursery, ever fearful the jealous heavens meant to snatch Norrie away from her.

But it had taken Lucien to make that nightmare come to pass.

The clash of swords upon the stage pulled Anne out of her unhappy thoughts. Birnam Wood had come to Dunsinane and Macbeth rushed toward his end. When Kean stepped forward to take his final bow, the applause swelled around Anne, an excitement that did not touch her.

In the midst of the cheering crowd, she felt isolated and alone. Strangely, her gaze was drawn to the one part of the theatre she had sworn to avoid. Her eyes swept the upper tiers, seeking the box opposite.

Mandell's seat was empty. He must have left before the final scene. She experienced a strong relief mixed with a curious sensation of disappointment. The feeling confused her and she sought to ignore it.

The applause had scarce died before Lily gathered up her skirts and rose eagerly to her feet. As much as she adored any sort of performance, Lily also loved to see and be seen, to compare her gown with the other ladies' present.

It was with great difficulty that Anne refused her sister's insistence upon taking another turn about the foyer.

"I find the crowd far too fatiguing," Anne said. "But you go on ahead. I am quite content to remain here."

Lily looked a little vexed with her. Mr. Barnhart, who obviously found Anne's company a bore, merely stifled a yawn and offered his arm to the countess. But the gallant Lord Cecil beamed at Anne, saying, "Then I will stay behind and bear you company, Lady Fairhaven."

"Oh, n-no," Anne cried, dismayed at the prospect of having to make conversation with anyone, even the kindly Lord Cecil. "I will be fine by myself and you must be quite stiff from sitting so long—"

She stilled any further protest by leaning forward and adding in a conspiratorial whisper, "Besides, you cannot have Mr. Barnhart stealing a march upon you."

His lordship glanced anxiously toward Mr. Barnhart, who was already sweeping Lily out of the box. "Well, if you are really sure . . ." he said. He sketched Anne a quick bow and bolted after the others.

Anne sighed with relief, sagging back in her chair. At least for a few moments she could be alone with her hopes and fears. She did not have to keep her expression schooled into a smile, feign interest in Kean's performance, or watch what she did with her hands.

She plucked at her purse, running her fingers over the silk and the heavy bulge of the pistol. The weapon held the most horrible fascination for her. She was beset with a constant urge to keep stealing peeks at the weapon as though if she did not keep checking, the demonic device might explode in her lap.

With an anxious glance about her, Anne bent over the purse. Easing open the clasp, she parted the silk edges just enough to peer inside. She touched the cold ivory of the pistol's handle, then felt for the note from Louisa Douglas to make certain it was also secure.

But at that moment she was startled by the creak of a footfall and realized someone was about to enter the box. Her pulse gave a violent leap, and in fumbling to close the reticule, she dropped it instead.

The slippery silk skidded beyond her chair out of reach. Anne bolted from her seat, scrambling on her knees to retrieve the purse. But before she could do so, she nearly collided with a pair of elegantly shod feet, muscular legs outlined to perfection by tight breeches.

Her heart seemed to stop as she glanced upward at the tall, powerful figure looming over her . . . Mandell, his face a blend of light and shadow. As in that night in the garden, he was garbed in unrelenting darkness from the satin of his frock coat to his sable hair to the black of his eyes.

"What are you doing here?" she said hoarsely. "I hoped that you had already gone."

That expressive brow of his shot upward. "Faith, milady, but you are hard upon a man's vanity. Are you merely overwhelmed by my presence or have you lost something?"

"What? I—I," Anne stammered, becoming conscious of her ridiculous position, kneeling at his feet. "No, I haven't. That—that is, I dropped my—my—"

"I believe you ladies call it a reticule."

To Anne's horror, he bent down beside her, reaching for the purse. His unexpected appearance had caused her to freeze, but now she was galvanized into movement. She dove for the purse herself, but she was too late. Mandell's long fingers had already closed about the reticule.

Anne held her breath, half expecting the damning contents to come tumbling out. But the clasp had miraculously closed in the fall. There was only a slight hesitation on Mandell's part before he handed the purse to her.

Had he noticed anything unusual? If so, he did not betray it by the flicker of an eyelash. He seemed concerned only with placing a steadying hand beneath her elbow and helping her to her feet.

As soon as she was standing, Anne shrank from his touch. She realized her heart was beating again with an almost painful rapidity. Since their last meeting, Mandell had assumed a supernatural presence in her thoughts, something dark, wild, and threatening to her peace of mind.

Resisting the urge to whip the purse behind her back, Anne said with what dignity she could muster, "Thank you, my lord, but—but now—"

"Now that I have performed this trifling service, you wish to send me to the devil. That would be a great pity, with you looking so lovely tonight."

Anne shied as skittishly as a high-strung colt when Mandell reached out to touch the curl at her cheek. "I like what you have done with your hair," he murmured. "The softer style becomes you. And the gown . . ."

His gaze lowered to her décolletage. Lily had selected the design of the dress. Anne had said all along she feared the gown was too revealing. Under Mandell's bold eyes, she was sure of it. He added, "The effect would be even more enchanting in a garden by moonlight."

Anne's cheeks fired. How could he be so shameless as to remind her of their last encounter?

"I have nothing to say to you," she remarked primly. "If you have come to apologize, I would prefer you just sent round a note."

"I would be happy to send you notes, flowers, anything else you desire, Sorrow. But what would you have me apologize for?"

Anne's gaze came uncomfortably to rest upon the outline of that full sensual mouth. "You know full well!"

"Ah, that! You expect me to express my gentlemanly regrets for kissing you. That would be both rude and untruthful." He captured her hand. Holding her eyes with his own, he raised her fingertips to his lips. "I fear I cannot say that I am sorry. Do you really want me to?"

"I—I," Anne faltered. It was so easy for him to fluster and confuse her. The contact of his mouth against her hand was fleeting, but enough to send a shiver of heat coursing through her. "I just want you to go away."

Mandell released her hand, his eyes narrowing. "Why do I get the feeling that I am more than usually unwelcome? Are you worried I will frighten away your other admirers?"

"I don't have any admirers."

"That's where you are quite mistaken, my dear." He cupped her chin, forcing her to look up. Her breath snagged in her throat. She thought he would be bold enough to kiss her again, here in the theatre where anyone below in the pit might see. For a moment, she had difficulty remembering she had vowed never to let this man come near her again.

Somewhat unsteadily, she put his hand away from her. "Please stop teasing me. By now you must be quite aware that I don't know how to flirt. You must have laughed yourself nigh ill at the way I bolted from the garden like a frightened rabbit." She could not prevent the tiny catch in her voice, the hurt and humiliation still so fresh in her mind.

"Nay, Sorrow. I had not the least inclination to laugh. The garden was a cold and lonely place after you had gone." Mandell's words were as warm as a caress. Anne had never known any man so practiced in the art of seduction. He constantly made her feel as though the ground were about to shift beneath her feet.

She frowned. "Then I don't understand. If not for your own amusement, why do you keep seeking me out? What is it that you want?"

"You."

The low spoken syllable sent a jolt through her entire system. All her anxieties over the desperate scheme to get Norrie back were driven clean out of her head. Anne did not remember bending her knees to sit, but she sagged down upon her chair. She barely managed to keep her grip on the purse, burying it in the folds of her gown.

"Are you cold?" Mandell asked.

Anne watched him retrieve her cashmere shawl from where it had tumbled to the floor. He draped the soft folds about her, his hands lingering on her shoulders.

Still in shock, Anne was certain she could not have heard him right.

At last she echoed doubtfully, "You want me? For what?"

His eyes widened in genuine surprise. Then a smokey heat drifted into his gaze. His lashes drifted downward, his stare tracing a slow scorching path from her lips to the exposed flesh above her bodice.

"Oh!" Anne shrank back. She wrapped the shawl tightly across her breasts.

"There is no need for you to bundle up so. It is not my intention to take you here and now."

"Not now! Not ever!"

"That is another matter entirely." He smiled at her, drawing up another chair. He sat so close that his knees brushed against her own.

"You must be quite insane," she said. "You hardly even know me and yet you are telling me that you would . . . you would . . ."

"Indeed I would, and gladly. It does not take me long to decide whether or not I want a woman in my bed."

His bed. Disturbing images sprang to her mind of a place as exotic as a sultan's lair, redolent with seductive incense, satin and sin, Mandell's lean hard frame tangled amongst crimson sheets. Anne swallowed. The fire in her cheeks became an inferno.

"How dare you say such things to me!"

"A lady of your great virtue? Alas, we both know my opinion of that. Virtue—the last refuge of those lacking courage or imagination."

"And in which of those categories do you place me?" Anne demanded indignantly.

"I don't think you are wanting for courage, Sorrow."

He was accusing her of having no imagination then. He was very wrong about that. He could not know how her mind ran riot, focusing on his strong graceful hands, those long lean fingers, imagining the things they could do to her.

Mandell continued, "I am paying you the compliment of being bluntly honest. I could as easily seduce you with soft words, false pledges. But I admit my intentions toward you are quite dishonorable. The only promise I make is that there will be a great deal of pleasure for both of us."

Anne could hardly believe that this fantastic conversation was even taking place. She stifled an outburst of hysterical laughter. For nearly twenty-six years her life had been as placid as a stagnant pond. Now, in the space of one night, she had to plot to abduct her own daughter and fend off an attempt at seduction.

"I have never had an improper proposal before," Anne said. "I am not sure what I am supposed to say. Except, definitely no, thank you. My life is already in enough of a coil at the moment."

"Perhaps I could help you untangle it, Sorrow."

"You cannot help. If anything, you are making things more difficult, and please, stop calling me by that dreadful nickname."

"But it suits you so well. There is a sadness that is never far from your eyes." Mandell leaned forward in his seat. He managed to secure one of her hands. "What is wrong, Anne?"

"Nothing, except for the fact that you are here tormenting me with these outrageous proposals. What makes you think anything else could be wrong?"

"For one thing, most women carry nothing more lethal in their purse than smelling salts."

Anne's startled gaze flew up to meet his. His eyes held hers steadily, knowingly. Of course he knew. She had been foolish to think there was a chance he had not noticed the pistol.

"I am only carrying the pistol for protection," she said. "From footpads like the Hook."

"There could be a dozen Hooks abroad tonight and you would never heed them. What is it that really troubles you, dear heart?"

The softly voiced question inspired her with a strange desire to burst into tears. She shook her head.

"Only you."

"I wish I could believe it was me that caused you to tremble so." He turned over her hand as though examining it, the shaking in her fingers clearly visible. He ran his own fingertips over her palm, lightly stroking, evoking sensations that did nothing to stop the tremors coursing through her. He added with a sigh, "But there has always been something, or someone else. I would have the truth from you, Anne."

A brief moment of madness came over her. She felt overwhelmed with a sudden longing to unburden herself of all the fear and misery she had borne alone these past few months.

It was wicked the things this man could do with his voice, his eyes. He could make it seem as though there were a chance that he might really care.

His grip upon her hand tightened, his voice becoming low and charged with an intensity that almost frightened her. "Trust me, Anne. Whatever, whoever it is who brings that look to your eyes, I will banish it. Whatever your unhappiness, your fears, in my arms, I can make you forget."

Forget . . . Forget Norrie? Mandell's vow snapped Anne back to her senses as nothing else could. She reminded herself of exactly what he was, a callous, cynical seducer of women. Nothing more.

She yanked her hand away. "You are the last person on this earth that I would ever trust. A man like you! A libertine with no honor, no heart, no proper feelings! If you will not leave me alone, I shall go myself."

"That will not be necessary."

Whatever gentleness she had fancied in his face was shuttered away again. He presented the sardonic facade she found far more familiar. Idly, he rose to his feet, straightening his cuffs. "There is no need for you to run away again, Sorrow. I will leave if that is what you wish."

He sauntered toward the door of the box, pausing only to glance back at her, his eyes as bright and hard as onyx.

"But my going changes nothing, Anne," he said. "I want you. I will have you."

He swept her a magnificent bow, then was gone, his soft-spoken threat seeming to linger in the air. Anne found she was trembling so badly, she had to grip the back of her chair.

I want you. I will have you.

Panic lashed through Anne, accompanied by a feeling of strange wild excitement. It was but one more reason to avoid Mandell.

One more reason to gather up her daughter as soon as possible and flee London forever.

Chapter 5

Sara Palmer unfurled the leaves of her ivory-handled fan and waved it before her, trying to enjoy the luxury of what might be her last night attending the theatre. The subscription on the box Mandell had hired for her was due to run out. Such an excellent location it had been, near the stage, rather private from the rest of the house.

If she came to the theatre again, it would have to be at the half-pay rate, coming in after the main bill was over, sitting in the pit. Just another one of the economies she would be forced to practice until she acquired a wealthy and noble lover, hopefully one more marriage-minded this time.

Sara sighed. Her prospects at the moment did not look good. She was a fool to have broken with Mandell before she had been assured of something better. The marquis had been most generous, and under his protection, Sara feared, she had learned to be extravagant. Only three days separated from him and she was already feeling the pinch. Mandell had finished paying for the lease on her apartment and the stabling fees for her horses, but there had been the dressmaker's bill she had forgotten to have him settle, also one from the jeweler.

Sara scarce knew what had gotten into her. She was usually far more efficient and businesslike in her dealings with men. Her only excuse was that she had been distracted of late, and she did not have to look far for the source of it.

Frowning, she glanced at the tall figure of the young soldier who lounged in the chair behind her. With a yawn and a stretch, her brother rose and moved toward the door of the box.

"Where are you going, Gideon?" Sara asked sharply.

"Just thought I would step out a moment to get a breath of air."

"There is plenty of air right here. Sit down. I didn't ask for your company tonight merely to have you abandon me while you slip backstage to flirt with some actress."

"Is that what you are afraid of, my dear sister? Or did you think I was going to nip out to the alley and carve someone else up with my hook? The intermission is almost over and it has been so long since my last murder."

"Lower your voice!" Sara hissed with a nervous glance around her. "There are some here tonight who might not appreciate your dark sense of humor."

"Like that fat magistrate who was sitting in the box next to us?"

"Yes!" Sara was relieved to see that the portly official had stepped from his seat during the intermission, especially since Gideon persisted in talking so recklessly. Her brother had that look in his eye that boded ill. Sara had known it since their childhood, that diamond-hard glitter. Sometimes it almost seemed as though Gideon was begging to have a noose placed around his neck.

She was not soothed, even when he stepped up behind her and began to massage the back of her neck with his large powerful hands.

"Sara, Sara," he chided. "You have to relax about this Hook affair. The beaks in the city are too busy rounding up all the one-handed men to bother with me as a suspect. The only one ready to condemn and send me to the gallows is you. You wound my tender feelings. Positively, you do."

"Your feelings couldn't be wounded with a poleax." Impatiently, Sara thrust her brother's hands away from her. "And if I still suspect you had something to do with that murder, I have good reason. You were always lurking about with Bertie Glossop and that other young idiot Dan Keeler. And I know how vile your temper can be when you have been drinking. And as if that were not enough, you have been flashing around an inordinate amount of money lately."

"It is only my pension, the grand reward our government bestows upon the noble warriors who shed blood for dear old England." His mocking tone was underscored with bitterness as his hand crept to his face in an almost reflexive gesture. He stroked the jagged scar that bisected his chin like a flash of white lightning, the legacy of the French sabre that had nearly cleft his jaw in twain.

"You've never seen a penny of recompense since you have been out of the army," Sara said indignantly.

"I never saw a penny while I was *in* the army. All I have to show for my devoted service is this uniform."

"Stolen off of some officer's back!"

"He no longer had any use for it. He died of dysentery, poor chap."

Sara shuddered. "You should get rid of it. It is dangerous to go around impersonating a leftenant."

"But it impresses the devil out of the ladies." Gideon grinned. "Sometimes I think I should have stayed with the regiment, but things got sadly flat after Waterloo. And I daresay they won't release poor old Boney from Elba merely to suit me. So alas, my dear, I fear your brother must embark upon a new career."

"What worries me is that you have already found one."

"Sara, I assure you one last time. I am not the Hook. I swear upon our mother's grave."

"Our mother is not dead."

"The graves of our fathers then."

"Whoever they might be."

"Not even our own mama knows for sure." Gideon flashed her a dazzling smile. Her brother possessed enough charm to wheedle himself into anyone's good graces, from the local barmaid to the Archbishop of Canterbury. Only Sara had never been taken in by him.

When he reached out to pat her hand, Sara gave his fingers a sharp whack with her fan.

"Ow!" Gideon sucked on his injured knuckle, eyeing her reproachfully. "For all your pretensions, Sara, there is one difference between you and the Quality. I have never seen a real lady use her fan for a truncheon."

"I wish this was a club. Maybe then I could beat some sense into your head," Sara muttered as she checked the handle of her fan to make sure she had not broken it. "I never thought I would say this, but some things were better back in the days when we all lived in the slums of Bethnal Green. If you and Davy didn't mind me, I could thrash you both. Now Davy is almost as tall as you and I can scarce reach to box his ears. He is making a living by stealing dead bodies to sell and you are up to heaven knows what. I daresay I shall end with both of my brothers clapped up in Newgate."

"At least you will know where we are." Gideon's knuckles had apparently recovered enough for him to risk chucking her under the chin. "Old Aunt Peg always said I was a villain child, born to hang. When the day comes, will you shed a tear for me, sweet Sara?"

"Only if you reek of onions." She turned her head away so that he could not see her lip quiver in a rare display of emotion. She had but two fears. One was of ending like her mother, living above a pawnshop, reminiscing about her many lovers and the glories of her youth. The other was of Gideon finishing his life upon the gallows.

Sara was close in age to both her brothers, but somehow it had always been Gideon she had understood and loved too well. How many nights had she lost sleep worrying about him, imagining him taking that final walk up the scaffolding, smiling and defiant even as the thick hemp was slipped round his neck.

If she understood Gideon through and through, then likewise he comprehended her every mood. He settled back into the chair beside her and covered her hand with his own.

"Come on, Sary. Please stop your fretting and scolding." Gideon's charm was never more lethal than when he resorted to using her childhood nickname. "I admit I have done a reckless thing or two which could get me hanged.

But one of my friends has put me onto a scheme for making money that is practically foolproof."

"If this suggestion came from one of those ruffians who carouse with you at the Jolly Tar, I shudder to think what it is."

"No, this has nothing to do with any of my dockside acquaintances. This idea came from the respectable Mr. Keeler. That is, before we had our falling out. That boy is the most reprehensible cheater at cards." Gideon's lips thinned, but the ugly expression vanished as quickly as it had come, as he continued enthusiastically, "But Keeler has his uses, being a banker's son. Before we parted company, he showed me an almost undetectable method of counterfeiting coin."

"Counterfeiting? That is your notion of honest employment?"

"I never said anything about honest employment. I said I had found a good way to *make* money."

Sara pressed her fingers to her temple, feeling the familiar nigglings. She would end by having one of her infamous headaches over this. Counterfeiting coin! What madness would possess Gideon next?

"I think it would be better if you left London. You are doomed to get yourself into some sort of deep water if you remain here," Sara said wearily. "I could lend you enough money to get out of the city."

"Leave London and do what?"

"Rusticate in the country or go abroad or—or—"

Sara was floundering for another suggestion when she was interrupted by someone barging into their box. One of the players burst in, a petite female with a half-exposed bosom and carroty curls.

"Excuse me, madam," the girl squeaked. "I was looking for—oh, Gideon!"

When her brother rose to his feet, the chit all but flung herself into his arms. Wrinkling her nose, Sara attempted to fan away the stench of cloying perfume. Why did Gideon have to have such low taste in females?

Slipping his arm about the creature's waist, Gideon said,

"Cherry, my little love. Allow me to present you to my sister."

Sara gave the girl a look that would have frosted hot tea. She had no desire to be introduced to any threepenny actress. The girl greeted her with a mighty sob, her face pale beneath her layering of garish makeup.

"What's the matter, love?" Gideon asked.

"Too—too dreadful," was all the girl could choke out. She continued to snivel against Gideon's shoulder despite all his coaxing and pressing of kisses to her brow.

Oh, lord, Sara thought. She hoped Gideon had not gotten another stupid wench with child. Unable to endure any more of the nonsense, she shot to her feet.

She spun the girl away from Gideon, saying, "Stop it. Unless you want to be smacked, you'd best save this melodrama for the stage. Either tell us what is wrong or get out."

"Sara!" Gideon protested. But her words had more effect on the girl than all of Gideon's crooning. Cherry looked up at Sara with wide frightened eyes. Sniffing, she wiped her face on her sleeve.

"The—the Hook has been abroad t-tonight," Cherry gasped. "They found another body in the street behind the th-theatre."

A chill shot up Sara's spine. Gideon wrapped his arm around the trembling actress's shoulders and he seemed to be avoiding Sara's eye.

No! She sought to reassure herself. It was all right this time. Gideon had been here with her, watching the play.

But he had not joined her until the second act.

Sara's head gave a mighty throb and she passed one hand over her brow, fearing she was going to be ill. She wanted to press Cherry for more details, but was afraid to.

It did not matter. Having finally found her voice, the girl's words came in a torrent. "It—it was another murder. Some banker's son. The body is still laying there in—in all that blood. And the constables are everywhere. Someone saw something this time an' they might be able to figure out who the Hook is. But I—I am still terrified to go home alone tonight."

The girl clung meltingly to Gideon. Cherry's hysterics were largely feigned. It was quite clear what the girl wanted, and it was a testimony to Gideon's finesse that he was able to steer her back out of the box without promising anything.

Much as Sara wanted the girl gone, she moved to stop them, placing one hand on Cherry's arm. "This banker's son?" Sara asked. "Do . . . do you know who he was?"

"Some young lad named Daniel Keeler."

Sara's hand fell back to her side and she could feel the color draining from her face. She scarce noticed when Gideon hustled Cherry outside.

First Bertie Glossop. Now Daniel Keeler. What was it Gideon had called him? *The most reprehensible cheater at cards.* And she recollected all too well Gideon's hard smile when he had denied knowing anything about the Hook's activities.

Sara blinked. The pain that flared behind her eyes caused them to water. Sometimes it was a great disadvantage to know one's own brother so well.

When Gideon returned to the box, a heavy silence hovered between them. He faced her with a wry smile.

"You may be right after all, Sara," he said. "Perhaps I should leave London."

Sara stared deep into those cold silver-blue eyes.

"Yes, you should," she agreed hoarsely. "Tonight."

Chapter 6

❦

"Twelve of the clock and a cloudy night."

Anne heard the watchman's mournful cry as she huddled in the shadows of the high stone wall which separated Lucien's townhouse from the street. It seemed to her that the old charley no longer sang out as cheerfully as he once had before the Hook had brought his murderous activities to Mayfair.

Before she had left the theatre, she had heard rumors of another killing. But that did not bear thinking of, not when she was creeping alone through the dark. She was nervous enough. More than once she had fancied herself being followed, heard the light tap of a footfall not her own. But when she whipped about, the sound had been swallowed by the clatter of a passing carriage, any mysterious shadows becoming nothing more than the rustling shape of some tree.

Each time she fell prey to such fancies, she chided herself for a fool, but it was a night prime for dark imaginings. Clouds settled like a veil across the face of the moon, the wind whistled around the corners of the houses, and the heavy threat of an April rainstorm hung in the air. Anne shivered and draped her shawl over her head. Tightening her grip upon the pistol, she hastened her footsteps.

She was already late. Slipping away from Lily's house undetected had not been easy, even at such an hour. Her sister had been most persistent, pressing her to attend a late supper at Lord Cecil's. And even after Anne had managed to fob off Lily, there had been any number of servants about, all seeming to regard Anne's furtive movements with curious eyes. Lily's household never settled until the wee hours of the morning.

By the time Anne had succeeded in snatching up her shawl, bolting out one of the side doors, the clock already approached twelve. Anne could only hope that Louisa was not likewise experiencing such difficulties; that even if Anne was a few minutes late, the little maid would bear the patience and courage to wait for her.

Following the high wall surrounding Lucien's garden, Anne rounded the corner, which brought her out onto the narrow street behind the house. Except for the lone hackney that creaked by, the cobblestone lane was dark and silent, making her feel as isolated as though she had crept into the sinister confines of some back alley.

Once more her nerves played tricks upon her, conjuring up sounds behind her, shapes that were not really there. Her heart thudding, she stole one more glance over her shoulder, but she was quite alone. She hastened toward the tall iron gate that led into Lucien's garden. Here at least was a pool of light provided by the two lanterns mounted upon the brick pillars on either side of the gate.

Anne shoved against the latch, but the gate was locked, just as she had expected. She peered through the bars. She had hoped to find Louisa waiting for her, but the house beyond loomed still as a tomb, with scarce any light showing behind the myriad windows.

The garden seemed likewise bleak and deserted, a desolate place overrun with weeds and dying foliage. It must have been badly neglected by the previous tenant and Lucien had done little to set things to rights. Nothing seemed capable of growing there, not shrubs, not flowers, certainly not a child.

"Louisa?" Anne called, praying that at any moment the girl would step out from some place of concealment in the shrubberies. She received no answer other than the mournful whisperings of the night wind.

Could she be more than ten minutes late? Surely Louisa

would not have given up on her after such a short delay—that is, if the girl intended to keep their rendezvous at all.

The prospect that Louisa might fail her was too daunting, and Anne refused to consider it. She continued her vigil, clutching the bar of the gate, staring anxiously at the silent house.

How long she stood there Anne had no idea, the minutes crawling by. The cold damp of the night air seeped through her thin shawl, chilling her to the bone, but Anne scarce noticed it for the numbness stealing into her heart.

She feared that the dawn would find her still clinging to Lucien's gate, wistfully regarding all those windows, wondering which one her little girl slept behind. Louisa was not going to come. Anne knew that with a sick certainty, but she could not bring herself to abandon her hope and start the miserable trudge back home.

If only she had taken more pains with Louisa, been more persuasive, offered her more money to keep their bargain.

"Did I not make you understand?" Anne whispered. "You are my last hope."

She rested her head against the bars of the gate, the pistol she clutched a heavy weight in her hand. The plan she had formed began to seem both ridiculous and pathetic. She was utterly useless at this kind of thing. Getting Norrie safely out of that bleak dark mansion would take someone far bolder, more ruthless than she.

It was disconcerting that an image of the marquis of Mandell should pop into her head. Ruthless Mandell was, and most certainly bold and unscrupulous. But if Anne ever stood alone in the dark with him, she knew that Mandell's thoughts would not be upon rescuing her daughter.

And God help her, perhaps her own would not be, either. Mandell's eyes smoldering with passion had a seductive effect upon her, both hypnotic and strange. He seemed to call to some wild, dark, secret corner of Anne's heart, a part of herself that alarmed her. Even now she could feel that stirring of her blood which was almost a fever.

Anne fought to suppress the unwelcome feeling, to banish Mandell from her mind. She was still struggling to do so when she straightened, suddenly alert.

Was it only her overwrought imagination again or had she actually seen something this time? A shadowy form emerging from the shelter of the house?

Anne strained against the gate. No, this time she had not imagined it. Someone was coming down the garden path. And it was . . . yes, it was a woman carrying a large bundle in her arms.

Anne was momentarily confused. It occurred to her that she ought to step back out of the pool of lanternlight on the chance that this was not Louisa. Her gaze fixed on that mysterious bundle, a bundle that she soon realized was a child swathed in a blanket, the folds falling back enough to reveal a glint of golden curls.

Anne's throat constricted painfully. "Norrie," she rasped. That foolish maid had stolen her little daughter out of her bed and brought her out into the chill damp of the night. But as Louisa stumbled closer, Anne was consumed by an overwhelming longing. She could think of nothing but her need to see her child again, to touch her.

"Lady Anne?" Louisa stopped within yards of the gate, peering cautiously.

"Yes. Yes!" Anne choked out, flinging back the shawl so that she would be more readily recognized. Her daughter stirred awake in Louisa's arms. Norrie raised her head from the maid's shoulder, knuckling her eyes in a familiar gesture that wrenched at Anne's heartstrings.

Louisa crept near the gate whispering, "I'm right sorry, ma'am. But I didn't know what else to do. It seemed much easier to bring the little girl out to you."

Anne nodded, unable to tear her gaze from her daughter's face. The lantern bathed Norrie in a soft glow, illuminating those fragile porcelain features, the rosebud lips, the small upturned nose, eyes such a clear blue they were almost transparent. She was a dream child, an angel child, a golden-haired fairy who had often seemed not quite real to Anne and never less so than at this moment.

She strained her arm to the utmost, stretching through the

gate, able to touch only the blanket, half fearing Norrie would vanish into mist as she had in so many of Anne's nightmares these past months.

Norrie was small for her age, but it was obvious she had already proven a great burden to Louisa's slender arms. With a mighty sigh, the maid set Norrie down. The child was clad in nothing but her nightgown and the blanket, but Anne was relieved to see that Louisa had at least enough wit to have eased slippers onto Norrie's feet.

Anne hunkered down to Norrie's level. Setting the pistol she carried by her knee out of the child's sight, Anne smiled tremulously, reaching both arms through the bars.

Instead of coming any closer, the little girl shrank back against Louisa, the child's sleep-misted eyes regarding Anne with confusion. The memory of Lucien's mocking words echoed inside Anne's head.

I vow the child has forgotten you already.

Anne's chest hurt so that she could scarce breathe, but she managed to croon gently, "Norrie. It's . . . it's Mama."

"Mama?" Norrie took a tentative step forward, blinking at Anne with the solemnness of a baby owl. Then her glad cry rang out, shattering the silence of the brooding darkness.

"Mama! It *is* you. I thought I just dreamed you again."

Norrie flattened herself against the gate, and Anne ran her fingers through the child's silken curls, pressing feverish kisses against Norrie's face, her own tears wetting Norrie's baby-soft cheeks. Her arms ached with the need to gather her child close.

"For the love of God," Anne cried to Louisa. "Unlock this wretched gate."

Her eyes large in her frightened face, Louisa bit down upon her lip. "Oh, I can't, milady. I brung the girl to see you. I daren't do any more."

"Please. Let me into the garden. Just for a moment."

"Nay, ma'am. I am already afeard I done too much. I should never've agreed to any of this. If the master caught me, I'd be turned out for sure and whipped besides. I ought to be gettin' that child straight back to her bed."

"Oh, no! No . . . don't." Anne clutched at Norrie with a sudden desperation. Having seen her, touched her, Anne knew she could not give up her child so easily. She thought of the weapon lying on the pavement by her knee.

Anne had only to raise it, level it at Louisa, and order the girl to unlock the gate. She could grab Norrie in her arms and flee with her into the night.

But flee where? the chilling whisper of common sense demanded. Where could she flee that would take her far enough, fast enough from Lucien's certain and vindictive pursuit? Nowhere. She was not prepared to vanish with her daughter this night. And if she had been, Anne realized that she could not bring herself to threaten poor Louisa with the pistol, likely terrifying both that simple creature and her own little daughter.

Stifling her mad impulse, Anne hugged Norrie as close as she was able, the bars of the gate an impassable barrier between them. Norrie bore this patiently for awhile, then wriggled to be free, protesting, "You are pushing my face against the bar, Mama. I'm getting rusty."

It took all of Anne's self-restraint to release her daughter, to content herself with stroking the child's curls back from her brow. Norrie patted away the last traces of Anne's tears.

"Don't cry, Mama." Norrie had always handed out her commands not with the regal hauteur of a queen, but with the gentle dignity of a princess accustomed to having her slightest wish granted.

"I won't. Not anymore," Anne said. "It is only that I missed you so."

"I missed you, too. Have you come to take me home?"

Anne had to swallow deeply before she could answer. "I—I fear I cannot just yet."

"But Mama, I have been here in London forever."

"It has only been three months, Norrie." Three months . . . eternity.

Norrie opened her mouth wide, pointing to a gap where her front tooth should have been. "I even lost a tooth while I've been with Uncle Lucien. And I had my birthday."

The little girl added in aggrieved tones, "Did you forget all about my birthday, Mama?"

"No! Never. I have presents waiting for you. I even made a new gown for your doll. Is that what Uncle Lucien told you—that I forgot?"

With a troubled look in her eyes, Norrie nodded.

Damn him. Anne gritted her teeth. "What else has he told you about me?"

"I am not allowed to talk about you very much. Uncle Lucien said I don't need a mama anymore. He said that you were tired of taking care of me. But I knew that wasn't true."

"Did you?" Anne's anger at Lucien was dispelled by that sense of wonder Anne had always experienced at her daughter's perception. Those clear blue eyes of Norrie's seemed to see things far beyond her years, far beyond the understanding of many adults.

"Uncle Lucien tells dreadful lies sometimes," Norrie continued with a sad shake of her head. "But I remembered, Mama. You told me you would always be there until I was growed up enough to take care of myself. And you never break your promises."

The child's solemn faith in her almost shattered what remained of Anne's self-possession. The urge to bury her face against the folds of Norrie's nightgown and burst into uncontrollable weeping was hard to resist. But as she had managed to do so often for her daughter's sake, Anne reached inside of herself and found the strength to remain calm.

"I am glad you remembered what Mama said, Norrie. I do always try to keep my promises." Anne lowered her voice so that the hovering Louisa could not possibly hear. "And I promise you will be with me very soon."

"Why can't I come now? Why won't Uncle Lucien let me be with you?"

Because he is a cruel, cold-hearted bastard.

But Anne choked back the words, knowing she could never possibly say such a thing to her small daughter. For the moment, Norrie had to continue to abide under Lucien's roof. It would help nothing to teach the child to fear and despise her uncle.

Groping for a better answer to her daughter's question, Anne at last faltered, "Well, you must think of our time apart as kind of like a game—a game of pretense. Do you remember how we used to playact the stories in your myth book?"

Norrie favored her with that charming gap-toothed smile. "Yes, that was when we named my doll Lady Persifee."

"Only this time, you have the part of Persephone, carried off by the dark lord Hades to his fantastic underground kingdom."

"Uncle Lucien is s'pposed to be Hades? His hair is too yellow."

"We—we are only playing pretend, Norrie." The blanket had started to slip off Norrie's shoulders and Anne tugged it more firmly around her. This damp night air was no good for the child. And behind Norrie, Louisa had begun to pace.

Anne realized she had not much more time and rushed on with her explanation. "I will pretend to be the goddess Demeter, looking for my lost daughter everywhere."

"And making it winter until Hades lets me come home," Norrie said solemnly.

"That's right, my little love. And not until I have you back safe will I ever allow it to be springtime again."

Norrie cocked her head to one side, considering. Then she said with a heavy sigh, "My new governess won't like this game, Mama. Mrs. Anstey says reading about gods and goddesses is heathen. She took away my book of myths. She said I would get mixed up and not remember who the real God is."

Norrie's small chest swelled with indignation. "I told her I wasn't a baby. I knew that myths are just make-believe. But she sent me to bed without supper anyway."

"Oh, Norrie!"

"I didn't mind so very much, Mama. 'Cause I knew I was right." Norrie's chin jutted out at a stubborn angle. For all her air of fragility, Norrie often exhibited a courage and obstinacy that amazed Anne.

"Ma'am!" Louisa suddenly loomed over Anne, breaking in upon her and Norrie's whispered conversation. "I got to be getting the child back before someone notices she's gone."

"I know," Anne said. She looked at Norrie, forcing a smile to her lips. "You have to go back now, love. But remember what we have talked about and don't tell Uncle Lucien. My lord Hades mustn't know we are about to break his spell."

"All right, Mama." Norrie's lip quivered. "But I don't think I like this game very much."

"Neither do I," Anne whispered. She drew Norrie close to the bars to kiss her one last time before Louisa scooped the child back up in her arms, arranging the blanket around her. Stiff from bending, Anne rose slowly to her feet.

Norrie's small sad face peered at Anne from beneath the folds of the blanket. "Don't make it be winter too much longer, Mama."

"I won't. I promise."

Anne was not sure that Norrie even heard her anguished vow as Louisa bundled the child back toward the house. Anne would have liked to thank the maid for the risk she had taken, for allowing Anne even these few precious moments with her daughter. But Louisa fled back along the garden path as though pursued by devils.

Gripping the gate bars, Anne strained against the cold metal, her gaze fixed not upon the maid but upon her daughter, watching until Norrie was swallowed up by the brooding silence of the house.

Only when Norrie had vanished from her sight did Anne allow her shoulders to slump. The pain-filled joy she had experienced at seeing her child again faded to become the more familiar ache of despair.

She had seen Norrie, touched her, but she had accomplished nothing else by this nocturnal visit. She had not gotten to view the inside of the house and she was afraid she would never again be able to persuade the timid Louisa to help her.

She had done little but make Norrie promises that she

did not have the least idea how she was going to keep. It was so easy to form fantastic plans and grim resolves in the warm security of one's own bedchamber. Strange how they all fled before the cold reality of a locked gate, the bitter chill of a damp April night.

Anne stared down at the pistol lying on the pavement at her feet. In her hands it was a useless thing, as useless as she was herself. Utterly dispirited, she bent down and picked it up. As she did so, she thought she detected a sound out of place in the night; not the rustlings of Lucien's ill-kept garden, not the distant rattle of some coach wheel, and not the thudding of her own heart. But she felt drained, too weary to respond even to her own night terrors.

She did not bother looking around until she heard it again, a footstep that definitely was not her own. She glanced up and peered down the street. He stood but yards away, near the corner of the wall, his features obscured by the night, but Anne recognized at once the tall powerful figure enshrouded in the black cloak with the single cape. She should have been astonished to see him, but she wasn't. He was becoming a familiar shadow across her life, my lord Mandell.

As he stalked closer, she flattened herself back against the gate, leveling her pistol at him. "Don't come any nearer or I'll shoot."

"It is only I, Anne. Mandell," he said.

"I know perfectly well who it is."

A soft laugh escaped him. "Do you? Then I am astounded you did not shoot at once."

He stepped into the light, the lantern casting flickering shadows over the angles of that proud aristocratic profile, the black sweep of hair, the fathomless dark eyes. A sense of danger and subtle sensuality emanated from his every move.

"There is no need for such alarm," he said. "I don't intend to assault your virtue in the street any more than at the theatre. I prefer a bed."

"So you have already told me," Anne snapped.

He appeared not in the least perturbed to have a shaking

pistol leveled at his chest. "Is that thing loaded?" he asked in accents of polite interest.

"I am not sure." Anne lowered the weapon, suddenly feeling foolish. "I tried to, but I don't know if I did it right."

"I see. Then perhaps you had better allow me . . ." He eased the pistol out of her grasp. Anne's hands were trembling so badly, she could not have resisted even if she had wanted to. Mandell examined the weapon briefly, glancing at the cocking piece. Whatever he saw caused him to roll his eyes, but he said nothing, slipping the small weapon into the pocket of his cloak.

"You don't seem entirely surprised to see me, Sorrow," he remarked.

"I'm not. I'm beginning to believe you are an evil genius set on earth for the sole purpose of tormenting me for my sins."

"Sins you have yet to commit, milady."

Anne chose to ignore this suggestive remark. "What *are* you doing here? I cannot believe it is merely chance this time that—" She broke off, tensing with a sudden sick certainty, recollecting the number of times this evening she had fancied herself being followed. It must have been Mandell all along. He had witnessed her reunion with Norrie, that private moment of tenderness and heartache, all played out before Mandell's cynical gaze.

"Damn you!" she cried. "You have been spying upon me. Ever since I left Lily's. How dare you!"

"Alas, you must forgive me, my dear. I am a jealous fool. I never dreamed this midnight rendezvous of yours would be with a child."

Mandell . . . *jealous?* Anne eyed him with disbelief. He spoke lightly enough, but with an odd grimace. Yet that was the trouble with Mandell and his sardonic facade. One could never be sure whether he was serious or not.

"How did you even know I would be meeting anyone tonight?" Anne demanded.

Mandell groped beneath the folds of his cloak. He produced a crumpled scrap of paper. "This dropped out of your purse at the theatre. I pocketed it when I retrieved the reticule for you. If you mean to engage in this sort of clandestine adventure, you really ought to get in the habit of destroying your notes at once."

"I would have done so, but I never had the chance. No sooner had I received the message, then Lily—" Anne broke off. Why was she troubling to explain anything to Mandell? She continued angrily, "It makes no difference. You had no right reading my messages or following me."

"Someone must keep watch over you, Sorrow, if you will persist in these midnight wanderings," he drawled. "Who was the pretty child that draws you out at such a perilous hour?"

His question caused Anne to realize something. While he had been able to observe, he must not have been able to hear any of the whisperings between herself and Norrie.

"The child's identity is none of your concern," she informed him loftily.

"I suppose I can always make inquiries of your sister."

"No!" Anne's hauteur dissolved in an instant. "You must not say anything about this to Lily or to anyone. No one must know that I have been here tonight. If Lucien ever found out that I had seen Norrie . . . Please, my lord. If you have any decency at all, you will keep silent."

Mandell regarded her through half-lowered lids. He cupped her chin, tracing his thumb lightly over her lips. "My silence would have a price."

She might have known he would say something like that.

"Very well." Anne raised her head with all the drama of a martyr about to meet her doom. "Take your payment then."

She pursed her lips and closed her eyes, bracing herself to be assaulted as Mandell had done that night in the garden, the blood drumming through her veins.

The moment dragged out and she felt nothing but the wind ruffling her hair. When Mandell did kiss her, his mouth just brushed hers, the contact warm and fleeting.

Anne's eyes fluttered open in surprise to find Mandell's dark gaze glinting with amusement.

"Very sweet," he murmured. "But a kiss was not what I had in mind, Sorrow."

Anne's cheeks flushed hot with embarrassment. "Then why did you take it?"

"How could I refuse what was so prettily offered? But I fear I must demand payment of another sort. I want to know what is going on. Who is ... Norrie, I believe you called her?"

Anne compressed her mouth into a stubborn line.

"We are not going anywhere until you answer me, Sorrow. We will stay here all night if we have to. It will not bother me. I have always been a nocturnal creature by habit."

Mandell leaned back against the gate, inspecting his nails, looking as disinterested as though he graced some boring afternoon tea. Yet Anne knew he meant what he said. He was fully capable of holding her prisoner by Lucien's gate until dawn if need be. And despite the marquis's negligent posture, she doubted she would get very far if she attempted to flee.

"All right," she conceded. "I will tell you whatever you want to know. But can we not continue this conversation elsewhere? I have already risked enough by lingering this long. If Lucien were to catch me, he can be so vindictive." Anne shivered, drawing the ends of her shawl tightly about her. "Can we please leave this place?"

Mandell came slowly away from the gate. He undid his cloak, sweeping it from his shoulders. Before she could guess his intent, he draped it about her, engulfing her in the heavy black folds.

"Oh, n-no," she stammered, finding the contact of the fabric, warm from his body, redolent with his musky scent, disturbingly intimate.

But Mandell ignored her protest, fastening the cloak about her neck. "I want no confessions from a woman with chattering teeth. Let this be another lesson to you. Don't attend a midnight revel so scantily clad."

Anne started to inform him she was not in the least chilled, but until Mandell had gathered her up in the

warmth of his cloak, she had not realized exactly how cold
she was. The garment, which came only to his knees,
swirled to her ankles, nearly dragging the ground, envelop-
ing her from neck to toe.

She should have refused to allow this. She wanted nothing from this man. But she was too tired to argue with him,
too glad of the cloak's sheltering folds.

"Thank you," she said grudgingly.

"The pleasure is mine, milady." Mandell steered her
away from Lucien's house. They crossed the narrow street,
Anne scarce noticing where he led her. At the end of the
block, she could make out the lights of Clarion Way, the
distant strains of a waltz, carriage wheels—the revelry that
never seemed to end in London's Mayfair district.

But Mandell kept her to the side street, for which Anne
was grateful. The night shadows no longer seemed so formidable with Mandell at her side, the darkness almost welcoming.

They walked slowly in silence until they were a good
distance from Lucien's. Then Mandell said, "Who is
Norrie, Anne?"

"Eleanor," Anne corrected. "Eleanor Rose Fairhaven. My
daughter. My only child." She pronounced the last words
with a deal of pride, a deal of sorrow.

At Mandell's prodding, she found herself telling him everything, from the very beginning of Lucien's youthful in-
fatuation for her, a strange passion that had turned to hate.
She described the death of her husband and Gerald's infamous will.

"Gerald always saw me as a helpless little fool. Although
he disliked his brother, he left Lucien in charge of everything. My house, my fortune, even my daughter."

Anne sighed. "It was still all right at first. Lucien was
too preoccupied with assuming Gerald's title to do more
than harass me in small ways—withholding funds, dismissing all my servants, replacing them with his own."

"Small ways!" Mandell echoed. "Sorrow, most of the
ladies I know would be ready to kill if deprived of their favorite abigail."

A sad laugh escaped Anne. "Even that was bearable. It was not until Lucien discovered he could distress me the most by threatening to take Norrie away that—"

Anne came to an abrupt halt on the pavement, shaking her head. "I cannot believe this wretched tale can hold any interest for you, my lord."

"Go on," Mandell insisted.

Anne moistened her lips. "I suppose I never believed Lucien would go that far, but one day last autumn . . ."

Her words trailed away, the glow of the street lamps blurring before her eyes. The memory still had the power to devastate her.

"I was out visiting in the neighborhood. One of Gerald's tenants had taken ill. Since he had become lord of the manor, Lucien always neglected such things. When I finally returned to the house, I knew at once something was wrong."

Anne's voice cracked. "The house was so still, the way a house often seems when someone has died. None of Lucien's servants would meet my eyes. They all avoided speaking to me. But I did not have to ask. Somehow I just knew. I went tearing up to the nursery.

"The place looked like it had been ransacked by a thief. All the drawers hung open. Norrie's clothes were gone, her books, even her doll. I—I remember screaming for Norrie, calling her name, but—but—Oh, God. I thought I would lose my mind."

She could not go on. Hot tears coursed down her cheeks and she was mortified to put on such a display of grief before Mandell. But when she dared glanced up at him, she was surprised to find his expression not unsympathetic.

"My regrets, Sorrow," he said. "But I never seem to have a handkerchief about me."

He caught her face between his hands, brushing away her tears with the tips of his fingers. Anne tried to regain control of herself.

"I was crying that first night you met me. What a perfect fool you must think I am."

"This is neither the time nor the place for me to show you what I think of you."

His husky words and the feel of his hands upon her skin sent a tingle of heat through her veins. Nervously, Anne put his hands away from her, continuing with her tale.

"For a long time, I did not even know where Lucien had taken Norrie. Finally, I traced her to London. That night by your gate I was looking for Lucien's house. This evening was the first time I had seen Norrie in months."

"And so you have found your daughter at last. Now what?"

It astonished Anne that he could even ask such a question.

"I shall take her back from Lucien, of course," Anne said fiercely.

"How?"

"I have a plan. I have already pawned all my jewels at this little shop in Chancery Street."

"What!"

Anne flinched from the sudden flare in those dark eyes.

"Are you quite insane?" he ground out. "That is in Bethnal Green, one of the worst slums in London."

"I had no choice. I told you Lucien controls all my funds and there are no pawnshops in Mayfair. I had to sell off all my jewelry, even the locket with Norrie's picture. I thought it wouldn't matter because I expected to have her back with me soon and—"

Anne swallowed hard, steeling herself. She was not going to start blubbering again. Her plan for recovering Norrie had once seemed so clear, so possible, but as she tried to explain it to Mandell, she realized how ridiculous it sounded, how hopeless.

"So you bribed this maidservant, and were going to find a way to singlehandedly storm the gates and steal away a sleeping child?" he demanded with an incredulous lift of his brow.

"Well, I . . ."

"All the while holding an entire household at bay with a

weapon which, with the way you had loaded it, would be incapable of killing anyone, except perhaps yourself."

"I didn't want to kill anyone. I didn't even want anyone to be hurt. I just want my daughter back."

"Did it never occur to you that you might get hurt making such an attempt?"

"I don't care," Anne cried. "Oh, why should I expect you to comprehend? No one else does. I love my daughter. I would willingly die for her. Is that so hard to understand?"

"No. But you must take my word for this, Sorrow. Your daughter would far rather you live."

This remark was as strange as the expression that passed across Mandell's features, the lines of his face for once achingly vulnerable. But as quickly as the look had come, Mandell shuttered it away again.

"Did it never occur to you, milady," he asked, "that you needed someone to help you in such a desperate undertaking?"

"Who would help me? Lucien has the law on his side. I could scarce imagine any honorable gentleman of my acquaintance deigning to interfere."

Mandell's lips quirked into an odd smile. "You don't need an honorable gentleman. You need me."

"You!"

"Yes. I believe I could devise a better way of recovering your daughter than wandering through the streets at midnight with a half-loaded pistol."

"Then tell me what it is!"

"Your pardon, Lady Fairhaven. But your skills at intrigue leave a little to be desired. You had best leave the details to me."

Anne gaped at him. Either he had run mad or she had.

"You are really planning to help me?"

"Yes." Mandell gave her a slightly bemused smile. "I rather believe that I am."

"You astonish me, sir."

"I astonish myself, madam."

Wild unreasoning hope stirred to life inside of Anne, but she fought to quell it. She still regarded Mandell's offer with suspicion. "And what would you ask in return for your services?"

Her question seemed to give him pause. "In return?" he repeated softly. "Oh, yes, of course, I could hardly be expected to act merely out of the goodness of my heart." Whether he mocked her or himself Anne could not tell.

She wrung her hands together beneath the cloak, saying with a passionate desperation, "I would give anything, do anything to get my daughter back. I would sell my soul to the devil if I had to."

"Careful, Sorrow. The devil just might take you up on that offer."

The look he fired her way made his meaning clear.

"Name your price."

"We both know what I want from you."

For one dizzying moment, it was like standing on the brink of some cliff, dark and fathomless. Anne stared deep into Mandell's eyes and plunged.

"Done!" she said, holding out her hand. "You get Norrie back for me and I pledge that I will come to your bed."

Mandell glanced down at her hand. "This strikes me as an odd sort of bargain to be sealed with nothing but a handshake." His lips curved into a sultry smile which should have warned her.

He seized the ends of the cloak. He dragged her toward him, his mouth closing over hers, hot and hungry.

A faint protest escaped her, but was lost in the fierce sensations his kiss aroused. Her lips parted before the fury of his embrace, his tongue delving into her mouth, sending a rush of heat through her veins that left her weak and shivering by the time he released her.

His eyes held hers in the darkness. "Now 'tis truly done, our pact made. And I give you fair warning, Sorrow. I do not deal kindly with those who break faith with me."

"I will not. Just get Norrie back for me."

By way of acquiescence, he sketched her a brief bow, rife with arrogance, a supreme confidence that filled Anne with more hope than she had known for a long time. She refused to dwell on the nature of the bargain she had just made, only thinking what it would be like to have Norrie back again.

As he resumed escorting her through the darkened street, he said, "Do me one favor, Sorrow, now that you have agreed to allow me to handle this matter for you. Curb your penchant for flitting about the streets alone after sunset. You may encounter far worse than me in the dark. A gentleman known as the Hook for example. There has been another murder tonight."

"Yes, I heard."

"The latest victim, I believe, is not unknown to you. Mr. Daniel Keeler."

Anne frowned in confusion.

"The young gentleman you saved the other night from disgracing himself at the card table."

"Oh, Mandell. How dreadful." For a moment, Anne was deeply shocked and grieved. But nothing could take precedence over her anxiety over her daughter, and what Mandell intended to do.

When they arrived back at Lily's gate, Anne demanded, "My lord, you must give me some idea of what you are planning. How will you go about rescuing Norrie, if not by abduction? I have tried everything else. Lucien won't listen to reason."

"I believe I can persuade him to listen to me." Mandell's smile was not pleasant. He raised her hand to his mouth, his lips warm and lingering upon her bare flesh.

"But Mandell—"

"Keep safe behind locked doors, Sorrow."

With this final command, he stalked off, vanishing into the darkness before Anne could question him further. She suddenly realized she was still wearing his cloak, the garment seeming as rife with secrets and mystery as its owner. She huddled deeper into the heavy folds, torn between hope and fear, a little awed by the dark force she had just unleashed upon the night.

Chapter 7

❧❧❧

The following evening, the porter at Brooks's was astonished when he opened the door to admit the marquis of Mandell. As his lordship swept across the threshold into the marble-tiled hall of one of the most exclusive gentleman's clubs in London, the elderly servant moved to ease the greatcoat from Mandell's shoulders.

"This is a rare privilege, indeed, my lord. We seldom see you in here these days. We have managed to pry you away from White's at last."

The porter nodded disdainfully toward the front window where the lights of the rival establishment could be seen glowing across the width of bustling St. James's Street. Mandell was a member of both clubs. He acknowledged that the interior of Brooks's possessed the elegance and charm of a gentleman's country manor, but he generally preferred the company to be found at White's. However, Sir Lucien Fairhaven did not. And Sir Lucien was Mandell's main reason for venturing abroad tonight. Mandell had made a pact with a lady and he intended to waste no time in fulfilling his side of the bargain.

As he handed off his curly-brimmed beaver to the porter, Mandell inquired casually, "The club is well filled this evening? Most of the members present?"

" 'Twould seem so, my lord. With it being such a foul night, threatening to rain again and all, most of the gentlemen seem content to be here warm and dry rather than seeking other entertainment about the town. It is certainly a deal safer, my lord, if you take my meaning." The old servant gave him a significant look.

Mandell took his meaning quite well, but made no comment. He allowed the porter, whom Mandell had known since the days of his youth, more familiarity than most servants. But he was not about to tolerate any more gossip on the subject of the recent murders, or tiresome speculation about the Hook.

Smoothing out his sleeves, Mandell crossed the imposing front hall, already beckoned by the sounds emanating from the Great Subscription Room. The drone of masculine voices was punctuated by bursts of unrestrained laughter, the kind gentlemen indulged in when no ladies were present. A bewigged servant held open the door and bowed Mandell inside.

He stepped into a chamber vast enough to have been a ballroom. The Great Subscription Room was done up in the classical manner, its towering walls left noticeably bare. There must be nothing to distract one from the club's main and serious purpose—the pursuit of gaming. Brooks's members crowded round myriad felt-covered tables. Standing or seated, they played at hazard, faro, quinze, or whist. Both the stakes and spirits appeared to be high tonight, judging from the number of flushed countenances. Waiters trotted to and fro bearing fresh bottles of port from Brooks's noted cellars while the croupiers intoned wins and losses amidst choruses of groans.

Mandell greeted a few acquaintances while doing a quick scan of the house. As near as he could tell, the gentleman he sought was not yet present. But the night was young. It was barely past one of the clock.

Refusing to be drawn into a game of whist, Mandell chose to stroll about observing the play. He noticed a familiar figure in a scarlet frock coat lounging near a settee by the hearth. He had to give his cousin credit for that much, Mandell thought with a slight smile. In a world of rather drab and sedate evening clothing, Nick always managed to stand out.

Nick appeared to be engaged with two of his Whig

friends, the betting book spread out on the table before him. Both Lord Soames and Mr. Watkin were laughing, Nick looking flustered and annoyed. Chances were good that the other two were roasting Nick upon some of his reformist policies, his humor on that subject often lacking.

Since the pleasure of tormenting his cousin was one Mandell reserved to himself, he went to Nick's rescue. After the way they had parted at the theatre the other evening, Mandell expected a little reserve on Nick's part. But his cousin had never been one to hold a grudge.

His irritation with his companions momentarily forgotten, Nick glanced up with a half smile at Mandell's approach. "Hullo! Mandell. Here's a surprise. What has lured you away from that blasted Tory stronghold across the way?"

"White's seemed a little thin of company tonight," Mandell replied.

"The place has never been the same since poor old Brummell was obliged to flee to the continent," Lord Soames broke in with a sigh.

Mr. Watkin agreed, both young gentlemen sobering for a moment in memory of the elegant dandy Beau Brummell, who had once been London's supreme arbiter of fashion. But Nick growled, "Brummell fled to escape his debts. These two jackanapes will be in the same case if they persist in wagering their blunt so recklessly. Tell them, Mandell."

"I can hardly tell them anything unless I know the nature of the wager."

Lord Soames's eyes had begun to dance again. "Perhaps Lord Mandell will care to lay odds of his own."

Mr. Watkin, the mischevious redhead, spoke up with a chuckle. "We are hazarding as to who the Hook's next victim might be."

"Indeed?" Mandell asked politely. With a bored arch of his brow, he produced his snuffbox, taking a pinch.

"Aye." Lord Soames giggled. He had likely consumed too much port. "I regret to say that it is your cousin Drummond who is the odds-on favorite."

Mandell stole a glance at the scowling Nicholas. "The

Hook would have to be careless indeed to attack a gentleman of such noted temper as my cousin."

"And equally noted for his empty purse." Mr. Watkin grinned while Lord Soames picked up the quill pen. Drawing the betting book closer, he continued to register the wager in a slightly unsteady hand.

"Temper and poverty notwithstanding," Watkin continued, "it has to be Nick. He is positively begging to be attacked, some of the places he has been poking about of late, those lightning houses."

"Flash-houses," Nick said. "I have been investigating flash-houses in Bethnal Green."

At Mandell's inquiring look, he explained. "Taverns that are little better than schools for crime, where street urchins are taught to be thieves, little girls scarce turned twelve taught to be whores."

"How very original." Mandell's lip curled in disgust. "And progressive. One of the most civilized cities in the world now offering formal education for pickpockets and prostitutes."

Lord Soames snorted a laugh, spattering ink over the betting book. "That is just what I was telling Drummond myself."

"Except that Mandell is being sarcastic," Nick said. "While you, you great lubbering idiot, are merely acting the fool."

Taking exception to this form of address, Soames flushed bright red. It was the sort of quarrel between young gentlemen that could easily get out of hand.

Mandell stepped between the two men. "You must excuse my cousin, Soames. We both know Drummond well enough by now to realize he waxes a little earnest over such matters. He offers you his most sincere apologies."

Soames blinked owlishly, then gave a nod of acceptance, even as Nick was crying out in protest. "No, I don't—"

But Mandell seized his arm in an iron grip, hustling Nick away. Nick wrenched himself free, glaring. "Damn it, Mandell," he said. "Why did you interfere? I had no wish to apologize to that ass. It is men like Soames who make me ashamed to be considered a Whig."

"Nicholas, the fellow is half foxed. You cannot attack someone merely for possessing a dull wit."

"Oh, yes I can."

"I cannot risk you engaging yourself to fight a duel at present. That would be most inconvenient."

"Why should you care?"

"Because for once, you may have to act as my second. So do us both a favor. Bespeak a glass of chilled wine and hie yourself off to cool that temper."

With his cousin gaping at him, Mandell started to walk away. But Nick was hard after him. "Second you in a duel! Damnation, Mandell, you cannot simply toss out a remark like that and then not explain yourself."

"There is nothing to explain at the moment." Mandell peered toward the door and frowned. Half past one and no sign of Sir Lucien. He asked Nicholas, "Sir Lucien Fairhaven is still a member of Brooks's, is he not?"

"Yes, he is, but what does that have to—" Nick broke off, his eyes narrowing with suspicion. "This doesn't have anything to do with Lady Fairhaven, does it?"

Before Mandell could answer, Nick paled. "It was Sir Lucien that you meant when you said—My God! You are planning to challenge Fairhaven to a duel over Anne. I know you made that remark about getting rid of your rivals, but I cannot believe it. You have not fought a duel over any woman since that time you were seventeen and you damn near killed Cecily Constable's brother because . . ."

Mandell shot Nick a warning look. His cousin trailed off, possessing enough sense not to pursue that particularly ugly incident any further.

"Calm yourself, Nicholas, and for heaven's sake, keep your voice down." Even in a place as devoted to faro as Brooks's, Nick's agitated manner would soon attract attention. "As usual, your imagination runs away with you. I never said a word about challenging Sir Lucien. I merely want to talk to him."

"You intend to warn him to stay away from Anne," Nick

continued, shaking his head. "I just don't understand it. I have implored you more than once to leave her alone. She is no dasher, no Helen of Troy, not at all the sort to inspire this degree of—well—obsession."

Mandell frowned at Nick's choice of words. It was not obsession to desire a woman, to find it pleasant to conjure her image in those long bleak hours before dawn when he often could not sleep—an image of an angel's face, framed by a fall of honey gold hair, with sorrowing blue eyes that sometimes had the power to banish the familiar nightmare and keep his night demons locked away. But Mandell was not about to try explaining such a fanciful thing to Nick. It might make it sound too much like he actually needed Anne Fairhaven. And, of course, the marquis of Mandell needed no one.

"Let us just say I find the lady's charms unique, well worth fighting for."

"You ought not to be stirring up any trouble here at Brooks's. You will lose your membership. I should know. I have been nearly expulsed myself on several occasions."

"Credit me with a little more subtlety than you possess."

"It scarce matters if you are infernally polite when you are offering to shoot some fellow's brains out in a duel. And if you do challenge Sir Lucien, I daresay that is what it will come to."

"And since when did you become so squeamish about dueling?"

"It is different with me. I never hit anyone when I shoot. Quite the contrary." Nick rubbed the scar on the back of his hand. "I never have regained the full use of my fingers since my last distrastrous engagement. But you—everyone knows you are a dead shot."

"Let us hope Sir Lucien knows it, too."

"If he doesn't, I'll tell him." Nick regarded Mandell unhappily. "You have got the most damnable look in your eye. I feel like I am standing near a powder keg about to ignite."

"You have always been the powder keg, cousin."

"And you are more like a block of ice. But ice still

burns. I wish you would reconsider this. I have no fondness
for Sir Lucien, but if Lady Fairhaven does, she will not
thank you for scaring him off. She will likely never speak
to you again."

"On the contrary," Mandell murmured, thinking of
Anne's passionate vow. "I expect the lady to be excessively
grateful."

"You will create the deuce of a scandal. You might have
to flee the country or—or—"

A laugh of rare and genuine amusement escaped Mandell. Nick flushed, looking deeply offended.

"Forgive me, cousin," Mandell said, when his mirth subsided. "But surely even you must perceive the humor of
you preaching caution to me."

"I'm damned if I will say another word to you then. I
just hope you know what you are doing," Nick flung out,
before pivoting on his heel and stalking away in a state of
high dudgeon.

Mandell chose to linger near one of the green baize tables and hazarded a few passes with the dice to pass the
time. It was an activity that required little of his concentration, which was just as well, for Nick's parting shot kept
echoing through his head.

I just hope you know what you are doing. At any other time, Mandell would have told Nicholas that that was
exactly the case, but for once in his life Mandell was not
entirely sure of himself.

What was he doing? Was he really about to force a quarrel upon a man he scarce knew? Certainly, Sir Lucien had
always filled him with contempt, but the man was not interesting enough to actually detest.

And yet before this evening ended, Mandell might find
himself challenging Sir Lucien. Not over Anne, as Mandell
had led Nicholas to believe, but over a mere child. Mandell
had never been sentimental about children. And yet he kept
remembering that wistful little girl peering at her mother
through the bars of a locked gate, Anne looking as vulnerable as a lost child herself. He kept recalling Anne walking
beside him through the darkened streets, telling him the

story of her loss and grief with quiet dignity. Even her tears had been silent.

He thought he would have promised anything to erase the sorrow from her eyes; pledged to restore her daughter to her, damn the cost to himself.

"The main is seven, my lord." One of the players next to Mandell nudged him, forcing Mandell to realize he had held the dice cupped in his hand too long.

He gave them a careless toss. Perhaps Nick was right. Perhaps he was becoming obsessed. Perhaps he should back away from this affair of the lady Anne. It waxed dangerous when he began to entertain such noble thoughts.

After all these years, it would be disconcerting to discover that he possessed a heart after all. How fortunate it was that he knew better.

In truth, he cared naught whether Anne was reunited with her daughter. It was simply that Anne was proving a difficult conquest. If sending her flowers or showering her with jewels would have done the trick, he would not have bothered himself further. If anyone misconstrued his intervention as some act of chivalry or kindness, the more fool they.

Mandell would know better. And so would Anne.

Strange that that last thought should fill him with such melancholy. Mandell stared down at the table, the tossing of the dice beginning to seem too great an effort. As he walked away, he had to be reminded to collect his winnings.

As the minutes ticked by, Mandell waxed increasingly restless. It annoyed him to think he might be obliged to track Fairhaven down at his house, or worse still, at one of those squalid gaming hells Sir Lucien was known to frequent.

Mandell paced the length of the room, his movements attracting the attention of an acquaintance he had overlooked. Sir Lancelot Briggs was ensconced at the faro table, his hangdog look proclaiming him to be losing. But his face brightened at the sight of Mandell. He leapt up from the table.

"My lord, I did not know you were here. Will it please you to play at faro? You may have my place."

"I should not dream of depriving you, my dear Briggs," Mandell drawled.

He tried to pass on, but Briggs kept pace. "Oh, 'tis all right. I have lost everything anyway." He cast one last wistful glance to where the croupier leaned over the curved slot in the table, raking away the last of Briggs's gaming pieces.

"Have you supped?" Briggs asked. "We could retire to the eating room. I have so many exciting things to tell you."

"I think not."

"Oh, but I do. I had the privilege of encountering your grandfather in the Pall Mall today."

"What a rare pleasure that must have been for both of you," Mandell replied in acid tones. He had been favored with his grandfather's opinion of Sir Lancelot many times.

"Inbreeding," the old duke had sniffed. "One fool mated to another for too many generations. How else could one explain how the man comes to be such a simpleton?"

But Sir Lancelot remained blissfully unaware of the duke's scorn. He confided to Mandell, "I think His Grace may be beginning to like me a little. He actually condescended to speak to me this time. I said, 'Good afternoon, Your Grace. A pleasant day, is it not?' And he said, 'If you like rain, sir.' " Briggs beamed with delight. "He actually said that to me. 'If you like rain, sir.' "

"My grandfather has always been noted for his wit."

"Your relationship to the duke has always intrigued me. Imagine being adopted by one's own grandfather. I mean, do you then call him father or grandpapa?"

"I always called him 'Your Grace,' " Mandell said icily. Sir Lancelot blinked. "Oh. Oh, of course."

Once more Mandell made the effort to move on, but Sir Lancelot trailed after him, saying, "But why am I blathering on about His Grace?"

"I don't know. 'Tis one of the great mysteries of the universe."

"I have far more interesting news to impart. You will

never guess. I, Lancelot Briggs, witnessed the murder at the theatre the other night."

"What!" Mandell was startled enough for once to accord Briggs his full attention.

"Well, I did not exactly see the murder taking place. I arrived on the scene shortly afterward. I saw a suspicious fellow slinking away, wearing a big floppy-brimmed hat with a feather, and I described him to the constable." Briggs drew himself up importantly and Mandell could tell he was about to launch into a long-winded account of what the constable had said to him and just what he had said to the constable. But Mandell's brief flash of attention was already lost.

He had just seen Sir Lucien Fairhaven entering the room.

Never taking his eyes from the doorway, Mandell drew forth his purse and extracted a handful of pound notes. Interrupting Sir Lancelot in midsentence, he stuffed the money into his pudgy hand.

"Here. I will stake you. Go try your luck at faro and see if you can recoup your losses."

To Mandell's surprise, Briggs made no move to pocket the money. His lips quivering, Sir Lancelot regarded Mandell with a wounded expression in his brown eyes. He returned the notes, speaking in a manner that for him was almost dignified.

"If you don't wish for my company, my lord, it is not necessary to pay me to go away."

With a small bow, he turned and shuffled off, losing himself in the throng about the hazard table. A soft curse escaped Mandell, equal parts annoyed with Briggs and with himself for making such a clumsy gesture.

But he had more important things to worry about at the moment than Briggs's injured feelings. If Sir Lucien settled into a card game, it would make Mandell's task that much more difficult.

Thrusting the money into his purse, he made his way across the room. Sir Lucien had paused to berate a page boy for some fancied insolence. Since he had acquired his brother's title, Fairhaven never seemed to feel he was being paid enough deference. But it was often that way with up-start nobility and the noveau riche.

As soon as he finished snarling at the trembling boy, Sir Lucien moved purposefully toward the faro table. But Mandell was in time to intercept him. He stepped into Sir Lucien's path with one graceful fluid movement.

Brummell had always declared that clothes could make the man. But doubtless the Beau had never seen the likes of Fairhaven before. Sir Lucien's attire was faultless, yet there was still an air of boorishness about him. No matter how immaculately he was garbed, Fairhaven always looked like a man recovering from a bad night, heavy sags beneath his eyes, his thick mane of yellow hair slightly unkempt.

Barely disguising his contempt, Mandell said, "Good evening, Sir Lucien."

Fairhaven looked surprised at being addressed by Mandell, but he nodded in return. "My lord."

"I was not aware that you were a member here, Sir Lucien."

"I had the privilege of being elected two months ago."

"Ah, that would explain it. I must have been absent the night the ballots were cast. What a pity."

Fairhaven frowned as though considering whether or not this was meant as an insult. Mandell wondered if he was going to prove as obtuse as Lancelot Briggs.

He beckoned imperiously. "Come join me in a glass of madeira."

"Another time perhaps. I was just sitting down to play."

Mandell offered him a thin smile. "Apparently I did not make myself clear. It is my particular wish you join me. I need to speak to you on a matter of some slight impor-tance."

Sir Lucien looked suspicious and a little ill at ease. But he conceded with an ungracious shrug. "Oh, very well. But I trust this will not take too long."

"That is entirely up to you, sir." Giving the man no fur-ther opportunity to think or change his mind, Mandell led the way toward the farthest corner of the crowded salon.

He was aware that a few heads turned, remarking their

progress. The marquis of Mandell was not known to bestow his attention upon parvenus like Sir Lucien Fairhaven. Nick stared after them with troubled eyes.

Mandell found two chairs in a secluded corner and sent one of the waiters to fetch some madeira and two glasses. As they waited for the wine, Sir Lucien cracked his knuckles, his gaze traveling toward where the bets were being laid, fast and heavy.

Mandell had the opportunity of studying Fairhaven at his leisure. He supposed the man possessed a certain florid handsomeness. But in a few more years, there would likely be no trace of those good looks, the vigor of youth all but vanished.

Mandell had encountered the likes of Sir Lucien before, a hedonist of low tastes and even worse breeding, a man whose decadent soul was rotting him from the inside out. Mandell had heard it said that Sir Lucien frequented the lowest gaming hells and brothels. His sexual appetites were supposed to be so strange that none of the more respectable establishments would have him, no matter what coin he offered.

And it was this creature who had charge of Anne's daughter, that curly haired waif who had been dragged from her bed at midnight, who had to stand shivering in a garden just to be able to feel the touch of her mother's hand.

Something strange stirred inside Mandell the more he stared at Sir Lucien, something cold and hard. He had pledged to help Anne simply as a means to his own ends. But for the first time it occured to Mandell that dealing with Fairhaven might be a pleasure.

When the wine was served, Sir Lucien took a large gulp, then growled, "So? You had something to say to me?"

"Yes." Settling back, Mandell tasted his own wine. "I believe you are in possession of something that does not belong to you."

"You mean something of yours? I think not, my lord."

"Something of Lady Anne Fairhaven's. Stolen away by you many months ago. Her daughter."

"My niece. I am the girl's legal guardian. I have a perfect right to do whatever I choose with her." He paused to scowl. "In any event, my lord, I fail to see that these family matters are any concern of yours."

"I am making them my concern."

"Why?"

Mandell regarded Sir Lucien through half-lowered lids. "Consider me a tenderhearted fellow. It gives me great distress to see a child separated from its mother. So much so, I am afraid I must ask you to return young Eleanor to the lady Anne. By noon tomorrow at the latest."

This cool demand left Sir Lucien dumbfounded at first. Then he flushed, blustering. "And if I don't chose to do so?"

Mandell twirled the stem of his wineglass idly between his fingers. "Then I fear I would be vexed with you, Sir Lucien," he said softly. "Very vexed, indeed. I might even consider your refusal an insult of the gravest kind."

Fairhaven choked on his wine. He set the glass down with a sharp click. "Could you possibly be implying that— that you would challenge me to a duel over the chit? It would do you no good. Do you think I would allow myself to be drawn into such an affair? I know your reputation with a pistol. I have seen Derek Constable still hobbling about on his crutches. And I heard tell about that highwayman on the heath that time. Shot dead through the heart at twenty-five paces."

Sir Lucien snorted. "Challenge to a duel. It would be more like an invitation to die. No, thank you, my lord."

"And yet I could make it impossible for you to refuse. Suppose I were even now to fling the contents of my glass into your face in front of all these interested gentlemen."

Sir Lucien stole a nervous glance about him, waxing pale at the mere suggestion of such a thing.

"Think you that you could then just walk away," Mandell purred, "and ever show yourself in this club or anywhere else again?"

"You are utterly mad, Mandell, or else drunk. Did Anne put you up to this? She scarce seems the sort of woman to have any influence over you. My dour sister-in-law is hardly worth your notice."

A muscle twitched in Mandell's cheek. His fingers tightened so convulsively about the crystal, he nearly shattered it. But keeping the taut smile fixed to his lips, he said, "And you, sir, I find are not worth the waste of this fine madeira after all."

As he drained his glass and rose to his feet, Sir Lucien breathed easier, apparently believing the conversation to have reached its conclusion.

But that was before Mandell began stripping off his glove with a deadly calm.

Fairhaven went ash white. As Mandell stood there, towering over Sir Lucien, the hubbub in the room became quieter. Heads turned, necks craned as the realization spread that something of great interest was transpiring between the marquis of Mandell and Sir Lucien Fairhaven.

Mandell was only vaguely aware of the gathering silence, of Sir Lancelot gaping, of Nick inching closer. Mandell focused on Sir Lucien's bloodshot eyes. The man tried to sneer, but failed, fear creeping unbidden into the hazed blue depths.

How many times had this bastard inflicted a similiar torment upon Anne? Mandell wondered. Sir Lucien mocking her, threatening, making her afraid, not for herself, but for her child.

As beads of perspiration dotted Sir Lucien's brow, Mandell stroked his glove between his fingers, relishing the moment, prolonging it.

"Don't!" Fairhaven rasped hoarsely, his eyes darting about as wildly as a cornered rat's. "I—I will return the girl."

Mandell scarce heeded him. All he seemed able to think of was Anne. Anne's blue eyes drowning in sorrow, Anne describing her agony at finding her child missing, Anne desperate enough to brave the night, clutching that misloaded pistol.

Slowly Mandell began to draw back his arm.

Sir Lucien shrank back, saying louder, "Stop! Damn you,

I said that Anne shall have the child back. By noon tomorrow."

Mandell became aware of Nick's grip upon his sleeve. "He has yielded, Mandell," Nick murmured.

Exercising every last bit of his self-control, Mandell lowered his hand, releasing his breath. Sir Lucien got shakily to his feet. But before he could bolt away, Mandell said, "Noon tomorrow. I trust you will remember. I should not care to have to remind you."

Fairhaven gave a jerky nod. His eyes glittered with all the hatred of a whipped cur, then he brushed past Nick and was gone. Apparently he had lost his taste for gaming, for he made directly for the door.

The room at large seemed to draw a collective breath. The excitement over, interest returned to the cards and dice once more. Only Nick dared to make any sort of remark upon the recent proceedings. "Damme, Mandell. For a moment there, I thought I was going to end up being your second after all."

"I told you there was little chance of that at the outset." Mandell eased his glove back onto his hand. "Sir Lucien was no more than I ever thought him, both a fool and a coward."

"Forgive me," Nick said. "But I overheard a lot of what passed between you. Why did you not tell me earlier what was amiss? That villian actually took away Lady Anne's child. I vow I was ready to smash his teeth down his throat. But you. You were so cool. I never saw anything to equal it. You cowed him without striking a single blow."

"Yes," Mandell said, conscious of a bitter disappointment that this was so. Anne's tormentor had escaped too lightly. How very much he would have enjoyed holding the bastard at pistol point and slowly cocking the hammer.

Mandell checked the savage thought, wondering what was wrong with him. He had achieved what he set out to do. Nothing else should matter. Yet he felt annoyed when Nick caught up his hand, wringing it in a hearty congratulation.

"What you did tonight was wonderful," Nick said. "One

of the most noble unselfish things I have ever seen you do.
I do believe there is hope for you yet, coz."

Mandell wrenched his hand away. His voice held a sharp
edge as he replied, "Noble? Unselfish? And just what do
you suppose my motives were?"

"To help Anne recover her child. What other reason
could there be?"

"It never occured to you, my idealistic young fool, that
there are many ways to seduce a woman. Some want diamonds. Anne wanted her child back. It was that simple."

Nick's smile faded. "You mean you only did this to lure
Anne Fairhaven into your bed?"

"How very astute of you to finally figure it out." Mandell waited for Nick's explosion of outrage, feeling that he
would almost be glad of it. Anything would be better than
having Nick stare at him like he was some sort of blasted
hero when they both knew better.

Nick's expected burst of temper was not forthcoming. He
did look more subdued, the light dying from his eyes. But
he shook his head slowly.

"No, Mandell. I don't think even you fully comprehend
the reasons for what you did tonight."

"You pretend to know me better than I do myself?"

"Perhaps this once I do."

Mandell drew himself up coldly. "I suggest you save
your insights of character for your opponents in Parliament,
Drummond. You may have need of such brilliance come
next election."

Feeling strangely more irritated with his cousin than he
ever had in his life, Mandell turned and stalked away, leaving Nick staring thoughtfully after him.

It was not the fashionable hour for shopping. The shops
on Bond Street stood nearly empty at that hour of the day,
most of the ladies still abed or lingering over their morning
chocolate. But Anne Fairhaven had been scarce able to
sleep or eat since she had parted from Mandell by Lily's
gate.

A day and a night had gone by in which she had heard

nothing from him. She wished he would have given her some hint of how he meant to force Lucien to return Norrie, but Mandell was very much a man who played out his own hand. Anne could do little but steel herself to wait, to try to fill her anxious hours.

That was why she paced down Bond Street at such an early hour, approaching the milliner's shop where she had first seen the child's bonnet. It was still there, displayed in the bowfront window, a confection of satin and lace the color of old ivory, trimmed with pale pink ribbons, with a large poke front that would frame Norrie's piquant features most charmingly.

Anne had glimpsed the bonnet days before when she had been dragged out on a shopping expedition by Lily. Then Anne had been scarce able to look at the delicate garment or anything else that reminded her of the little girl she had lost.

But now she did a most foolish thing. She went into the shop and purchased the bonnet. All during the carriage ride back to Lily's, Anne hugged the bandbox upon her lap, telling herself she was courting heartbreak by daring to dream that she would again have Norrie with her soon.

It was unreasonable to expect Mandell to accomplish anything so swiftly, perhaps to expect that he could accomplish anything at all. But she did expect. She did hope. He was a rake, a cynic, a man who possessed few scruples, but she sensed that he did not give his pledge lightly.

And he had pledged to get Norrie back for her. As to what she had promised in return . . . Anne shivered, choosing not to think about that just now.

When the coach pulled up before Lily's townhouse, Anne handed down her purchase to the footman who flung open the carriage door. She prayed that she had arrived back before Lily rose from her bed. Her sister would be sure to scold Anne for venturing abroad so early and without even the company of a maid. It would also be difficult to explain the purchase of that little bonnet without revealing her hopes and the shocking bargain she had struck with Mandell.

Anne scarce waited for the footman to help her to the pavement. She gathered up her skirts, preparing to slip back into the house as quickly as possible, when she was halted by the sound of someone bellowing her name.

She had little time to turn about before she realized that her brother-in-law was bearing down upon her. Lucien looked quite wild, but Anne took in little of his appearance, her gaze riveted upon the child he dragged by the hand.

Norrie! Anne's heart constricted painfully. The little girl was pale, her eyes wide with fear. Before Anne could move to intervene, Lucien drew abreast of her.

"Here," he snarled. "Take her." He flung the child at Anne. Norrie bounded into Anne's arms with a tiny sob and Anne lifted her, straining her close as though she would never let her go.

As Norrie buried her small face against Anne, Anne stared at Lucien. She was too stunned to do more than stammer. "W-What? Why . . . I don't understand."

Lucien glowered back at her. "Your new friend visited me at my club last night. I don't know what has passed between you and Mandell, but you have won this round. I am returning the girl, but I promise you, Anne. Neither you nor that interfering bastard has heard the last of this."

He hissed this vow with such savage hatred, Anne was glad that Norrie had her face hidden against Anne's cloak. Spinning on his heel, Lucien stormed off down the pavement without another look back.

Still in shock, it took Anne a moment to accept the reality of what had just happened. *You have won . . . I am returning the girl.*

She had Norrie back again. And neither Lucien's fury nor his threats mattered a damn. Tears began trickling down Anne's own cheeks, her joy so intense it was akin to pain. Her knees threatened to buckle beneath her and she was forced to set Norrie down upon the pavement.

She tangled her fingers in the child's silken hair, nearly devouring the little girl with her kisses, soothing away Norrie's tears with hands that trembled.

"I was scared, Mama," Norrie hiccuped on a sob. "Uncle

Lucien was so angry. I thought he liked me. He gived me a pony."

"Well, I am sure that . . . that is, I believe that he— Oh, but what does it matter now?" She caught Norrie in another fierce hug. "You are going home with Mama now, love. And no one shall take you away from me, ever again."

A sigh shuddered through Norrie and she raised her head to give Anne a radiant smile.

"You kept your promise, Mama. You made it spring again. I knew you would."

"Yes," Anne whispered. Now was hardly the time to remember that it was not she who had brought this miracle about, but a formidable man with night-dark eyes and full warm lips that could tempt an angel to sin. Anne's pulse skipped a nervous beat, but she refused to dwell upon the devil's bargain she had concluded with Mandell.

It was enough that no matter how, Anne's promise to Norrie had been fulfilled. There would be time later when she had her little daughter tucked up safe in her own bed tonight, time enough then in the quiet darkness for Anne to lie awake, thinking of the marquis of Mandell.

And the promise she had yet to keep.

Chapter 8

Coal smoke hung in a perpetual pall over the sagging tenements of Bethnal Green. Peering through the grimy window of the hackney coach, Sara Palmer pressed a scented handkerchief to her nose. As the hackney rattled along the cobblestones, she was assailed by far too familiar sights and sounds, ones that she had long tried to forget and put behind her . . . the decaying boarded-up buildings crammed with poverty-stricken families, the shrieks of the ragged urchins chinking stones at the carriage wheels, the bawdy songs of drunks staggering away from the gin shops.

What had once been a pleasant country village on the outskirts of London had now become a teeming part of the great city, a maze of narrow streets and courts, with dark corners where the struggling poor were tempted with the lure of quick money and often an even quicker death.

The brothels, the flash-houses, the back alleys where hardened men plotted desperate deeds . . . it had been well nigh impossible to escape being pulled in and dragged down by such places when growing up in Bethnal Green.

Sara congratulated herself that she was one of the few who had managed it. And she hoped, she prayed, that her brother Gideon might yet prove to be another. She had put him on the stagecoach heading north. Sara hadn't cared where so long as it took Gideon out of reach of the London authorities, far from questions and witnesses that might connect him with those two deaths.

Of course, Gideon had protested his innocence to the last, but Sara had paid him no heed. Her brother could be caught with a bloodied razor in his hand and he would insist he had just nicked himself shaving all the while a corpse lay stone cold at his feet.

Whether Gideon was innocent or not scarce mattered. What was important was that for the moment he was safe, that she had gotten him away from the dark influences and temptations of Bethnal Green. If only she could accomplish the same for her mother.

As the hackney lurched over a rut, Sara braced herself against the side of the coach, frowning. She had tried more than once to persuade her mother to retire to some little cottage in the country. Sara could have easily afforded to purchase such a thing when she had been Mandell's mistress. My lord had been most generous with his money, never questioning how Sara spent it.

But her mother had stubbornly refused. Chastity Palmer had declared she had endured quite enough of provincial village life in her youth. Sara had never been certain of her mother's origins, but Chastity had always claimed she had been a country curate's daughter.

Sara supposed that was possible. Mum did show an amazing tendency to quote the Bible when she'd had a drop too much rum. If such a respectable grandfather did exist, Sara had never met him. Her mother had run off at the age of sixteen and never gone home again. She had come to the great city of London seeking romance.

And, Sara thought wryly, Mum had found it. Again and again and again. And the fact that Chastity Palmer had frequently been paid for her latest amour had never seemed to dim her enthusiasm or her fixed belief in finding her one true love.

Mrs. Palmer still had a strong liking for the men, and during her bimonthly visits, Sara never knew quite what she might find going on in her mother's flat. As the hackney drew to a halt at the curb, Sara hoped for once Chastity might be alone.

Her mother's most recent address was a small flat above the pawnshop on the corner. It was one of the more respectable-looking buildings in the Green, and Mum liked the fact that from her front windows she could see clear up the street and know at once what neighbor was involved in a fight or who was being arrested.

Gathering up the parcel she had brought, Sara alighted from the hackney and paid the driver. Before he even pulled away from the curb, Sara found herself surrounded by street urchins, creeping closer to her skirts like a pack of fierce starving rats.

She had the sense not to wear one of her best ensembles to Bethnal Green, but she was still dressed fine enough to provoke several sneers and comments.

"Look at the leddy, will yer, Sam?"

"La-di-da."

"Hoity-toity."

One sharp-faced lad, a little bigger and bolder than the rest, darted closer, his fingers inching toward Sara's reticule. Despite balancing the bulk of her parcel, she was quicker, spinning around and catching the boy's ear in a merciless pinch.

"Ow-ow-ow," the lad howled, as much astonished as hurt.

Sara released him with a little shove. "Try that again, you little gallow's bait, and I'll rattle your bone box, see?"

She was appalled at how quickly she lost the refined accent she had cultivated over the years, slipping back into the patter of the street. But her fierce growl had the desired effect, the urchins scattering away from her wide-eyed.

Lifting her skirts above the mud and debris, Sara picked her away around to the narrow door at the back of the pawnshop. Mounting a flight of rickety stairs, she made her way to the second floor. She could already hear a burst of raucous laughter from the flat above.

Sara sighed. It was as she had feared. Mum was entertaining again. If she had not already dismissed the hackney, Sara would have been tempted to turn right around and leave.

But then she would have come all this way for nothing. Bracing herself, Sara climbed the last of the steps and rapped halfheartedly on the flat door. The laughter within was so noisy, she was obliged to pound harder.

The laughter stilled at once, and Sara smiled, fully comprehending. In this neighborhood, such a thump on the door could well mean the constable or a tipstaff. After a brief pause, the door was inched open by Chastity Palmer. Her sagging bosom threatened to spill out of her gown, yet Mum's middle-aged face still possessed a certain blowzy prettiness.

At the sight of Sara, Chastity's cautious expression disappeared. She beamed, throwing wide the door.

"Sary! My sweet babe." She dragged Sara across the threshold, embracing her, package and all.

Sara felt relieved. If she was only Chastity's "babe" and not her "heart's darling," at least she knew that Mum wasn't drunk. Sara returned the hug, breathing in the scents that had always meant mother to her, cheap perfume and stale gin.

Peering over Chastity's shoulder, Sara quickly glanced around to see who else was present. It was not as bad as she feared. Mama had not been entertaining her latest "romance."

Seated behind Mum's small wooden table was only a neighbor, old Mr. Haythrope, the beanpole of a man who occupied the flat upstairs. And next to him was a demure woman garbed in black who looked respectable enough to have been a governess.

She was in fact one self-styled Madame Dubonnet, the owner of one of the most exclusive and elegant brothels in the city. Chastity had once worked for her off and on, and even Sara had had her start in Madame's house.

Sara had interrupted them in the midst of their refreshments. The delicate china service she had bought her mother was laid out upon the table, but from the reek of spirits in the air and the flushed countenances of her mother's guests, Sara doubted that anyone had been drinking tea.

When Chastity had had her fill of hugging Sara, she tugged her over to the table, laughing and exclaiming proudly, "Well, would you just look who's come to visit her poor old mama? It's our little Sary. Doesn't she just look grand as a queen?"

Mr. Haythrope managed to get to his feet. "Sharmed to see you again, Mish Palmer. Shimply sharmed."

He would have taken her hand, but Sara shrank away with disgust. The man's dirt-encrusted fingernails reminded her of his profession as a grave robber.

She was distracted by Madame Dubonnet pacing around her, examining the stitching upon her cloak with an expert eye, lifting the garment up to peer at the ruching on Sara's gown.

"Oh, you have done very well for yourself, Sara," she said. "Very well." Madame nodded wisely at Chastity Palmer. "I always knew the girl would never end up a common whore."

"There was never anything common about any of my children," Chastity said loftily.

"You were a credit to my house once, Sara Palmer." The brothel owner gave a sentimental sigh. "The bishop of Barnwell still asks after you."

"Does he indeed?" Sara gave a dismissive shrug as she set her parcel on the table, but she could not help remembering. The bishop had been her first lover. How very strange. Out of all the men she had had, the two who had been best in bed had been his holy eminence and that devil Mandell.

Still, Sara had no wish to indulge in such reminiscences. Unlike her mother, she preferred to put the past behind her. She felt grateful when neither of Chastity's guests elected to linger long. Mr. Haythrope was going to require some help negotiating the stairs.

Both Chastity and Madame Dubonnet followed him through the door of the flat to make sure he did not fall and break his neck. While awaiting her mother's return, Sara removed her cloak and bonnet.

Even though she knew it was useless, she could not help strolling about the flat's single large room, straightening the cushions on the worn settee, wiping dust off the oil lamp, picking Chastity's nightgown off the floor.

Sara started to return it to the curtained alcove where Chastity kept her bed. But as she brushed the drapery aside, she was stayed by the sound of soft snoring, the sight of a large bulk beneath the covers of the bed, a pair of glossy black boots tossed carelessly on the rug.

It seemed she had been too optimistic. Mum had one more guest after all, and Sara had no desire for an introduction. Sara let the curtain fall, draping Chastity's nightgown over the back of one of the chairs.

Chastity bustled back into the room, breathless and laughing. "I declare! That Bill Haythrope. I've never known any man to get so easily foxed. Just wave a cup of stout beneath his nose and he's under the table."

"He's an old drunkard, Mum. I don't know how you can encourage him to hang about or that Madame Dubonnet. I should think you would want to forget that we ever had any connection to her or her house."

"Betty is an old friend, Sara, and Mr. Haythrope is a kind, generous man. It was him as 'pprenticed your brother Davy into a profitable trade."

"As a resurrectionist? Stealing and selling dead bodies!"

"It's nice steady work, miss."

"If Davy were not so lazy, if he had an ounce of ambition in that thick head of his—"

"Now don't you be so hard upon my poor little man. Davy is a good boy, so he is. He looks after his poor old mama."

Sara rolled her eyes, but held her tongue. She had never been fond of her younger brother David, finding him both shiftless and underhanded. But it was useless arguing with her mother on that point. Besides, Chastity's last comment about how well David looked after her had been a broad hint, Mum's gaze fixing upon the parcel Sara had brought.

Sara handed her the package and Chastity pounced upon it as greedily as a small child. Chastity cooed with delight over the tea, the pound of coffee, the chocolates, and sundry other delicacies. But what pleased her most was the box of cigars. Mum had acquired a taste for the nasty things from one of her lovers who had been a sea captain.

As Chastity examined the last of Sara's offerings, several new pairs of knit stockings, Sara reached for her reticule. She fished around inside, drawing forth a small wad of pound notes.

"I am sorry I could not bring you as much as I usually

do," Sara said. "Since my parting from the marquis I have had to be more careful with my funds."

"Ah, don't you fret, babe." As she took the money, Chastity reached out to give Sara a motherly pat on the cheek. "Things will come out all right. So that wretch of a man left you. You'll find a new love soon enough."

Sara started to reply, then closed her lips again. No, it was of no use trying to explain to Chastity that Mandell had never been her love or that it had been Sara who had broken off the relationship. Mum would never understand whistling such a handsome and wealthy lover down the wind any more than she would understand Sara's yearning to be a real lady, to achieve a noble marriage.

"I am sure I will come about in time," Sara said. "But I worry about you, Mum, about being able to bring you enough. I don't want you feeling hard-pressed or thinking that you have to go back to Madame Dubonnet's."

"Lordy, child, as if I would ever have to do that if I didn't want to!" Chastity daintily tucked the money inside the bosom of her gown and gave a proud toss of her head. "Your Mum still possesses a few resources of her own, you know. Besides, you forget I have two strong sons to care for me."

"But that is the other reason I came here today—to tell you something. Gideon had to leave London, perhaps for quite awhile."

"Oh, er—yes. Poor Gideon. Traveling on that horrid stage up north. I have only my little Davy left now."

"How did you know where Gideon went?" Sara asked sharply. "I just sent him off yesterday and I gave him no chance to come back here."

"Well, I—I . . ." Chastity's pink tongue darted out, moistening her lips. "I heard it from Davy. Yes, Davy. He just happened to be at the inn, spying upon you. You know what a rogue he can be sometimes."

Giving a nervous laugh, Chastity's gaze flicked toward the curtained alcove and guiltily away again. Sara stiffened. Her mother had the most transparent features imaginable.

Sara swore. How could she have been so stupid when

she peeked behind the curtain before? The glossy boots that should have been familiar. The snoring, the huddling down beneath bedcovers pretending to be asleep. One of the oldest tricks of their childhood.

Compressing her lips, Sara stalked toward the alcove.

"Oh, no, Sara," Chastity cried. "I have a guest in there I didn't tell you about. You don't want to—"

Ignoring her mother, Sara flung back the curtain. Gideon was already leaping up from the bed. Shoving back the strands of his tousled brown hair, he gave her a sheepish grin. "Hullo, Sara."

Sara's fingers clenched about the end of the curtain. "Damn you, Gideon! I put you on that stage myself. I had you out of here. Why the devil did you come back?"

He spread his hands wide in an apologetic gesture. "Well, my dear, when the stage got past the city, I chanced to look out the window." He gave a mock shudder. "There were pastures, Sara. Cows! Sheep!"

Chastity gave a shrill giggle which died when Sara whipped around to glare at her mother. "This is not amusing, Mum."

"Aw, Sara." Gideon tried to get an arm about her shoulders, but Sara flung him off.

"Come now, Sary," Chastity coaxed. "You have got yourself into a rare state of panic over nothing. Gideon told me everything. Trying to make him run off over a few suspicions. No one is accusing him of being the Hook yet."

"When someone does, it will be far too late," Sara snapped.

"If it's the money you wasted upon the stage," Gideon said, "I will pay you back somehow."

"It is not the money, you fool! I thought you finally understood. I am trying to keep you from being arrested for murder."

"Bah, there is nothing to connect Gideon to those killings. Only rumor." Chastity smiled, preening a little. "Mind you, it has not hurt my reputation in the neighborhood a bit, having people imagining Gideon might be the one. Why, the Hook is getting to be something of a legend like Dick

Turpin or Robin of the Hood. The butcher actually slipped me an extra slab of bacon the other day."

"When you see your oldest son swinging by the neck, I hope you will think the bacon was worth it, Mum."

"Of course I wouldn't." Chastity's smile faded, her chin quivering. "I went to see poor Meg Cuttler's boy turned off just last week for horse stealing. Davy and I attended the hanging. It was dreadful, though Meg did lay out a nice funeral breakfast in her flat afterwards."

"And all the while I suppose Davy plotted to steal the corpse."

"Certainly not!" Chastity said. "I raised your brother up to be a gentleman. He'd never open the grave of anybody he knows."

A smothered choking sound escaped from Gideon, but Sara had no desire to laugh. She did not have much will to be angry anymore, either. Sinking down at the table, she rested her brow upon her hands, determined not to have another headache.

What was the use of arguing? she thought wearily. What was the use of trying to help either one of them? It was hopeless. Life had always been hopeless in Bethnal Green.

Gideon drew their mother aside. After a little whispering between them, Gideon handed Chastity some coin, instructing her to bring back some rum from the shop around the corner.

Snatching up her shawl, Chastity slipped out of the room, promising to be back directly. A silence settled over the flat when the door had closed behind her. Gideon ambled back over to the table, but he did not sit down. Resting his hands on the back of one of the chairs, he stared at Sara and said, "It wasn't any good me running away, Sara. I think we both realize that."

"If you had just possessed the sense to keep on running."

"I have done some checking, Sara. The authorities are as baffled as ever. They have no witnesses, no clear description of the Hook. Bertie Glossop's watch turned up in a pawnshop, but even the broker doesn't remember who brought it in. I am safe."

"For the moment."

"The moment's enough for me. It always has been." He gave a fatalistic shrug. "Bloody hell, Sara. I can't run away from myself. If I don't find trouble here in London, I'll just find it elsewhere."

"You are utterly determined to end up in the dock."

"And when I do, I hope they don't call you in for a character witness."

"I would lie through my teeth for you," Sara said bitterly.

"So you would." Although he leaned forward to chuck her under the chin, an expression of rare seriousness stole into Gideon's grey eyes.

"Don't you understand, little sister?" he asked. "It is you who should run from this place and not come back. Why do you persist in returning for these visits?"

"What a stupid question! Mum needs me. And you."

"Mum can look out for herself and so can I. And even if it were otherwise, don't you see, Sara? You can't help us. You are the only one of us who has ever had dreams, wanting and imagining something much better than all of this."

A hard smile touched Gideon's lips. "Me and Mum and Davy . . . We don't dream. We just exist and we are content with that. But you, Sara, you are different, bright, clever, determined. You'll get what you want someday, but not if you keep coming back here, getting tangled up with us. We will only drag you down."

Sara felt a faint flush of shame stain her cheeks. Gideon was not saying anything that she had not already thought herself more than once.

Gideon finished by giving her cheek a playful flick, forcing the lightness back into his tone. "For what it was worth, that was a piece of free brotherly advice. It is likely the only thing you will ever get from me."

Sara shoved back from the table, a hard set to her jaw. "Thank you, my dear brother. You are quite right, of course. You *are* all fools here. I shall not bother with you again."

"That's the spirit," Gideon said, holding her coat to help her into it.

Sara was just donning her bonnet when Chastity came

rushing back into the flat, bottle in hand. She gave a crow of dismay to see Sara on the verge of leaving.

"You cannot mean to be going so soon, Sary? And without a nip of rum to warm you, put some color back into your cheeks."

"I feel warm enough, Mum," Sara said, though she had never felt so cold in her life. She lied, "I have to get home to change. A gentleman is taking me to supper tonight."

"I daresay it will be some elegant affair." Chastity sighed. "I knew a young baronet once. A little on the simple side, but a good-hearted fellow. He took me to an assembly ball one evening. His mama damn near died."

Smiling at the remembrance, Chastity rustled forward to fuss with the strings of Sara's bonnet, tying it for her. She always could do up the prettiest bows.

"There. Now you look quite the young lady. When will you be coming back to see your mama again?"

Sara hesitated, thinking of her recent discussion with Gideon, what she had just decided. She stared at her mother's face, the age lines feathering eyes that still had the bright sparkle of a young girl's.

If only her mother had had more intelligence and ambition, where might the whole Palmer family have been today? And yet, Chastity had not been such a bad mother, really. Whenever Sara had been sick, Chastity had always been there, and sober, too. It had been Chastity who had taught Sara how to read.

And Gideon . . . the first time her brother had ever killed anyone it had been because of Sara and that drunken dockworker who had tried to rape her. Gideon had been only fourteen.

Swallowing hard, Sara heard herself saying, "I will be back again in two weeks, Mum. Like always."

As Chastity hugged her, Sara met Gideon's eyes over her mother's shoulder. He arched his brows in a look that was both mocking and sad. From across the room, he mouthed a single word.

Fool.

There was only one response to such a thing in keeping

with Sara's dignity. When Chastity was not looking, Sara thrust her tongue out at her brother.

Kissing her mother farewell, Sara left the apartment. Feeling equal parts frustrated and resigned, she was still thinking about all that had taken place in the flat when she reached the street.

It was a grave mistake to walk along woolgathering through the lanes of Bethnal Green and Sara knew better. But before she snapped to her senses, she was roughly shoved from behind, hands snatching for her reticule.

Sara clung to the thin strap, but events proceeded too quickly for any further response. A sly-faced boy with blond hair knocked her off balance, wrenching the purse from her grasp. Sara cursed as she recognized the taunting grin.

"Damn you, Davy. Give me that back before I wring your neck."

"You have to catch me first," her younger brother sang out.

Sara lunged for him, only to topple headlong into the muddy street. By the time she raised up onto her elbow, David had already darted between two buildings and disappeared.

"You little bastard," Sara muttered. Struggling to rise, she felt a hand upon her arm, trying to help her.

Usually they just stepped over you in Bethnal Green. Assistance was rare, the sight of the man who was offering it even rarer.

Sara blinked. She had never seen such a bright-striped waistcoat before, especially not worn with a bottle-green frock coat and skin-tight yellow breeches. A high-crowned beaver was perched upon artlessly combed locks. The man had a face that was pleasant rather than handsome, and vaguely familiar to Sara.

But she was too cross to do other than dismiss him as some dandy who had meandered into the wrong part of town, a complete idiot.

"Are you all right, miss?" he asked as Sara steadied herself on her feet.

"Do I look all right?" she snapped. She attempted to scrub some of the mud from her coat, but her glove was equally dirty.

"I am sorry about your purse," the stranger said. "I could attempt to go after that young villain, but I doubt I would catch him."

"I doubt you would either." Sara was not about to explain to this fool that the rogue who had snatched her purse was her own brother. David would return the reticule in his own sweet time, empty of course. And when he holed up somewhere in the back alleys and corners of Bethnal Green, the canniest Bow Street Runner could not ferret him out, let alone this toff in the fancy waistcoat.

Sara was in no humor to render thanks to any Good Samaritan. She wished the man would have the wit to take himself off, but he hovered by her side, regarding her gravely.

"I am glad to see you have taken no real harm, miss."

No real harm? Her coat was ruined and there was no Mandell to buy her another.

He continued, "After you have had such a fright, I hate to scold. But it is obvious that you are a lady of Quality. It is very reckless of you to be wandering alone in such a part of town, without even a maid to accompany you. This is no place for a respectable woman."

"And what about you? Strutting about Bethnal Green attired like some—some Macaroni!"

The man's stern expression lightened. "Very true," he said with a twitch of his lips. "But I must point out that it was not me who just had my purse stolen."

"Go to—" Sara started to grate out, catching herself just in time. "Go away and leave me alone."

"I will be happy to oblige when I am certain you are no longer in need of my services." He tipped his hat in a brief bow. "Though the circumstances are somewhat unusual, allow me to introduce myself. Nicholas Drummond."

Sara started at the name. Drummond. Mandell's cousin. Of course, Mandell had never introduced her. My lord preferred keeping his mistresses well in the background of his life, Sara thought bitterly. But she had glimpsed the young man in the marquis's company a time or two.

"And you?" Drummond prompted. "Have I seen you somewhere before? At the park or the theatre perhaps?"

"I don't go out in society very much. I am Sara Palmer, Mrs. Sara Palmer lately of Yorkshire."

"Well, Mrs. Sara Palmer lately of Yorkshire, your husband should take better care of you."

"I am a widow," Sara said, slipping easily into the familiar lie. "I have only recently come to London for a change of scene. I have been living here for two months now, taking in some of the sights in a very quiet way."

"Then that would explain why you did not know that Bethnal Green is no place for ladies."

"I would have to be blind not to realize that. I am not stupid, sir."

"No, but you are bleeding." He frowned, stepping closer, drawing out a handkerchief. When she started to shy away, he caught her chin, saying, "Hold still. I am not going to hurt you. You have scraped your cheek."

He dabbed the linen carefully against her skin, his remarkable light grey eyes a study in concentration.

"There. Luckily it is only a scratch. It would have been a shame if there had been . . . had been . . ." He seemed to lose the thread of his thoughts, his face very close to hers. He stared as though seeing her for the first time.

Her bonnet was askew, her face likely dirty, but Sara knew enough of the power of her own beauty, how it could stun a man speechless. Yet Mr. Drummond did not look stunned.

He merely looked as though he liked what he saw. As though he liked it very much indeed.

"What *are* you doing here in Bethnal Green?" he asked.

She should have told him to mind his own damned business, but Sara found herself wanting to offer a reasonable excuse.

"I was bringing a basket of food and clothing to some of the poor families hereabouts. And you, Mr. Drummond?"

"I am a member of the House of Commons, ma'am. We

have formed a committee to investigate some of the shocking conditions of the poor in these slums."

"Does it not occur to you, sir, that the poor could use a little less investigating and a little more bread?" The tart comment startled her as much as him. Had that really come out of her mouth? She had almost sounded as though she cared, when in truth the remark had been born more out of bitter memories of some of the hungry days of her own childhood.

She thought her blunt question would have insulted him, but he nodded in thoughtful agreement and stared at her. She was accustomed to men doing so, but something in Drummond's steady regard unnerved her.

Sara squirmed and said crossly, "What are you gaping at now? Do I still have dirt upon my nose?"

"No, forgive me. I did not mean to be rude. But I have never met anyone quite like you. I have known charitable-minded women before, but they hold teas, collect funds. I have never known any to actually visit the slums, bringing comfort themselves."

"I have always been a woman of action, Mr. Drummond. Now if you will excuse me, it is waxing late and I must find myself a hackney to—"

Sara broke off, re-collecting her stolen purse. She bit her lip in vexation, realizing she would have to return to the flat and borrow back some of the money she had given to Chastity.

Mr. Drummond apparently realized her predicament at the same moment for he said, "Look, Mrs. Palmer. I hope you will not think this too forward or misinterpret my offer, but I have my own carriage near here. I would be only too happy to escort you home."

Too forward? His offer came as a great relief. It would save her bothering her mother and get her safely home. Even if Mr. Drummond's intentions were not what they should be, Sara would know how to handle that.

But she was a pretty shrewd judge of men, and as she stared into those steadfast grey eyes, she was fairly certain that Mr. Drummond was a gentleman. She doubted he had ever harbored a wicked thought toward any woman in his life. Naive, idealistic, a dreamer, a fool. He appeared to be exactly the sort of nobleman that Sara had always told Mandell she meant to find one day and—

Sara caught her breath at the thought. Mandell's own cousin? No, she would never dare. She should not even be considering such a thing, even in passing. Yet she caught herself looking at Nick Drummond, speculating and trying to remember anything Mandell had ever let slip about this cousin—the state of Drummond's fortune, if he stood to inherit a title.

"Now I am beginning to think I am the one with a smudge on my nose," Nick complained good-naturedly. At the same time, he looked endearingly self-conscious.

Sara forced her eyes down, trying to summon a blush. It came naturally for once. She affected a maidenly hesitation before saying, "Thank you so much for your chivalrous offer to take me home, Mr. Drummond. I fear I am obliged to accept."

Drummond seemed quite pleased. When he linked his arm through hers, Sara's heart pounded. She must be quite mad.

Sara knew full well the marquis's opinion of any of his noble family marrying the likes of her. If his lordship ever suspected that she might be courting his cousin ... She shuddered, being quite familiar with Mandell's icy temper. But she was being foolish. She was only accepting a carriage ride from Drummond. He might prove an unlikely prospect for Sara's schemes.

As Nick escorted her down the street, she risked another glance at him. He was definitely not a handsome man. But when he looked back at her, his eyes crinkling at the corners that way, he possessed a charming smile.

And Sara found herself smiling back.

The devil fly away with Mandell, if he had not done so already.

Chapter 9

❦

The black cloak pooled like a shadow in the bottom of Anne's wardrobe. As she bent down, touching the garment, the folds of silk rustled in her fingers, whispering of night breezes, the heat of a kiss, a vow made with passionate desperation.

I would sell my soul to the devil if I had to.

Careful, Sorrow. The devil just might take you up on that offer.

The pact she had made with Mandell seemed fantastic in the daytime, sunlight spilling through the latticed windows, past the lacy curtains and over the elegant satinwood furniture of Anne's room at Lily's. The bedchamber was thoroughly feminine. No place could have been further removed from Mandell's aura of powerful masculinity, from midnight wanderings and reckless promises.

If not for the cloak she clutched in her hands, Anne could scarce have believed that their tryst had been anything more than a haunting dream.

Yet the child napping in the little room just above Anne's own was no dream. For the past week since Norrie's return, Anne had feared she would awaken and find it so. She had kept the little girl with her almost constantly. Even when Norrie slept, Anne stole from her own bed, creeping down to the nursery to tuck the blankets more snugly around Norrie, to stroke a curl back from her cheek, just to touch the child, and reassure herself that Norrie would not disappear with the morning light.

But during that same week, Anne had had the leisure to

wonder how she was ever going to keep her promise to
Mandell. To go to his bed ... her mouth went dry at the
thought. She tried to reassure herself. She was no shrinking
virgin. She had been a married woman, for mercy's sake;
had borne children.

Yet Gerald had always been what he termed "a gentleman" in bed. He had eased up her nightgown, mumbling
apologies for violating her chastity, taking her with merciful
swiftness. Anne knew that what would take place between
Mandell's sheets would be nothing like that mundane
wifely ritual. She had already had a taste of the difference
in Mandell's arms, his lips so hot upon her own.

He would want her naked in his bed and without any
blushes of maidenly modesty. He would never be satisfied
with the tame submission she had shown her late husband.
Mandell would take relentlessly, demand with his mouth,
with his hands, with his lean hard body. He might stir in
her those passions she had learned to keep locked away, desires that often kept her awake nights, a fine sheen of perspiration bathing her flesh.

And when he had done, Mandell would rise from the
bed, offer her her clothes with a mocking bow, and go
coolly on his way. But Anne was very much afraid that she
would never be the same woman again.

She pushed the cloak away from her, stuffing it to the
very back of the wardrobe. She could not go through with
it. She was not the sort of female who could offer herself
up casually to a man. And such a man! A rake who had
known dozens before her, women far more beautiful, more
sophisticated. What could she be to him but one more conquest, another night's amusement, and a disappointing one
at that?

But she had promised, and Anne had never broken a
promise in her life. She bit ruefully down upon her thumb-
nail. She had pledged Mandell one night in his bed. Yet
their bargain had not been a fair one, she argued. He had
taken shameless advantage of her desperation, hadn't he?

Anne's conscience would not allow of that excuse, either.
Who was it who had flung out such a reckless offer that

could not help but tempt a man like Mandell? He had tried to warn her. *Careful, Sorrow. The devil just might ...*

She owed him something. He had kept *his* word. She had her little girl back again. And yet how much had Mandell had to do with that? She did not know for sure. Of a certainty, he must have talked to Lucien, applied some little pressure. But she might have gotten Norrie back some other way even if Mandell had not intervened. Perhaps Lucien had been planning to return Norrie all along.

Anne groaned softly, resting her head against the wardrobe door. Who was she attempting to fool? She would never forget Lucien's hate-filled look as her brother-in-law had thrust Norrie back into her arms. Lucien had never meant to return Norrie, and whatever Mandell had done to him, it had been far more than talk.

But his lordship had made no effort to contact her once this entire week. True, she had kept close to the house, but he had never called or even sent round a note. Perhaps, Anne thought hopefully, moving on to nibble the nail of her forefinger, perhaps Mandell had simply forgotten all about redeeming the pledge she had made.

But this comforting reflection did not last long. She could not block out the memory of his intense gaze, his warning, *I do not deal kindly with those who break faith with me.*

Anne did not know what prevented him thus far from demanding that she keep her side of the bargain, but whatever it was, one thing was certain. Mandell would never forget.

Her second finger bitten nearly raw, Anne shifted to the next nail. She started when the soft rap came at her door.

"Anne, it's Lily," her sister called out. "Are you still abed?"

"N-no. Just a minute." Anne made haste to pile some old shawls on top of Mandell's cloak. Her fingers brushed against something hard; her pistol, which Mandell had shoved into the cloak pocket that night which now seemed so long ago. Anne had all but forgotten her foolish little weapon. She dumped an extra shawl on top of it and shoved the whole pile as far back into the wardrobe as she could. The maid Lily had assigned her, young Bettine, had already once noticed the masculine garment. But Anne had been able to explain that it belonged to her late husband and the girl had sighed, imagining Anne, the brokenhearted widow, clinging to the cloak in remembrance.

But Lily would not be so fooled. Gerald, ever the provincial gentleman from his boots to the severe style of his cravat, had never worn anything so dashing as Mandell's cape.

Closing the wardrobe door, Anne smoothed out her gown and tidied the wisps of her hair. She called out as cheerfully as she could, "Come in."

Lily bustled in, carrying a fistful of sealed letters. "Good," she said. "You are up and stirring. I thought you might be lying down for a nap, poor dear. You have been exhausting yourself, looking after that child."

Although she smiled, there was a hint of reproof in Lily's tone. Lily was delighted for Anne's recent happiness and only too pleased to welcome her small niece into her home. Yet she feared that Anne had become far too absorbed in performing the tasks of a nurserymaid.

But for too many months, Norrie had awakened only to the impersonal ministrations of servants. Anne vowed her child would never do so again.

For her sister's benefit, Anne shook her head, saying, "I am not in the least tired, Lily. I have just been going through my wardrobe, selecting some gowns that are out of fashion to pass on to my maid."

To Lily, that was at least a reasonable occupation for any lady. Her eyes lit up with immediate understanding. "Of course! You have needed some new things for an age. I shall take you round to my modiste this very afternoon. You will need a special gown for the Bramleys' rout come Saturday next, and just look at all these other invitations you received in this morning's post."

Lily laid out the squares of vellum upon Anne's dressing table, gloating over the cards like a miser counting up a treasure.

"How very nice," Anne said.

"Do you not intend to open them?"

"Perhaps later."

"Later?" Lily's elegant brows rose skeptically. "Or will they end up in the fireplace grate again? Anne, this simply will not do. You have been hiding yourself away in this house ever since Eleanor was returned to you."

"That's absurd. I have not been hiding." But Anne's protest sounded halfhearted even to her own ears. That was exactly what she had been doing. Hiding from Mandell, afraid of encountering him again, not knowing how she would react, what she should say, afraid of what he might do.

"You got what you wanted, Anne. Your child returned," Lily said with a tinge of impatience. "Now it is time to cease this moping. You are in London at the height of the season. You need to get out more, enjoy yourself."

"And so I shall. But you know Norrie has not been well. She has been having trouble sleeping and then there is that worrisome cough she has developed."

"You cannot have an apoplexy every time the child sneezes."

"Norrie has always been delicate. Every trifling illness seems to strike her so much harder than other children. There was that time I thought she had but a sniffle. By nightfall, she was in such a raging fever she did not even recognize me. I almost lost her that time, Lily."

"Well, you will not lose her now. I know some of the finest physicians in the city. We shall have Dr. Markheim out to check her cough in a trice. Will that make you feel better?"

Anne nodded reluctantly.

Lily gave her a swift hug although she continued to scold, "But you are still young, Anne. Your life cannot center upon that little girl. And there is another excellent reason you should get out more. I have not liked to mention this, but there have been rumors, Anne. Rumors about you and the marquis of Mandell."

Anne opened her mouth to speak, but found she couldn't. She felt herself grow pale as Lily continued, "The gossip all seems to have started since that ugly scene between Mandell and Sir Lucien at Brooks's."

"What scene?"

"I thought you might have heard something of it, but I keep forgetting. You have been buried in the nursery all week. You will recollect, however, that we both wondered why your brother-in-law experienced such a sudden change of heart regarding Eleanor's future."

Lily had wondered. Anne had kept her speculations on that subject to herself.

"My dear Anne, it would seem you are indebted to the marquis for your daughter's return. I have it on excellent authority—Sir Lancelot Briggs's—that Mandell confronted Sir Lucien in the Great Subscription Room. Mandell had stripped off his glove and was going to fling it into Fairhaven's face."

"Mandell challenged Lucien to a duel?" Anne felt a sudden need to sink into the chair by her dressing table.

"No, it never came to that. Lucien Fairhaven has far too great a regard for his own skin. Mandell is deadly with a pistol, my dear, positively deadly. In any case, Sir Lancelot was close enough to overhear the cause of the quarrel. Would you credit it, my dear? It was over our little Eleanor. Mandell demanded that Lucien give up the child."

Anne pressed her hands to her face. A duel! She remembered being disquieted by the look in Mandell's eye that night he had left her, but she had never dreamed he would have been willing to take things that far.

No matter how good a shot Mandell was, the possibility still existed that he could have been wounded or killed. Barring that, dueling was illegal. Despite his powerful connections, he could have been arrested or forced to flee the country. Did the man consider such a risk worth it merely to have Anne in his bed?

"Mandell has ever been such a discreet devil, so cold-blooded," Lily said. "Whatever could have inspired him to such an extraordinary gesture?"

"I don't know." Anne was unable to meet her sister's eye.

"One does not think of Mandell as ever waxing tender-hearted over a mother and child. Though I suppose this all could have something to do with losing his own mother at so early an age. Poor Lady Celine. Mama knew her well. She always said Celine was a great beauty in her day and as proud as Lucifer, like all the Windermeres. Everyone was stunned when she eloped with some impoverished French nobleman. Such a ghastly mistake that turned out to be. She was trapped in Paris during the revolution and suffered a hideous death. Celine was actually torn apart by an angry mob."

"Dear God!" Anne said hoarsely.

"Did you not know about that part of Mandell's family history?"

"No, I didn't." Anne was fast realizing that she knew very little about the marquis of Mandell. She said softly, "The man has ever been an enigma to me."

"And to the rest of the ton. That is why this chivalrous gesture has so many tongues wagging. Many are saying my lord means to fix his interest with you. His grandfather has been after him for a long time to choose a respectable wife."

"Oh, no!"

"I found that utterly ridiculous, myself. The wicked Mandell and you, my saintly little lamb. Such speculations are almost as bad as the more scurrilous rumors that Mandell is only laying siege to your virtue."

Anne felt ready to sink through the carpet. It was unsettling enough to think she would be obliged to share Mandell's bed, but to hear that half of London was discussing the possibility!

"Then perhaps I ought to go away for awhile," Anne said. "Take Norrie and go home or journey to Scotland and visit Camilla."

"Run away? That would be the worst thing you could do," Lily said sternly. She relented enough to give Anne's shoulder a comforting pat. "My poor pet. I know that you are not at all accustomed to arousing this sort of furor. That is why you must take the advice of your older sister who has walked the fine line of scandal herself a time or two. You must get out more, be seen at parties. When you encounter Mandell, greet him with complete indifference. That will quickly scotch all these rumors."

Greet Mandell with indifference? Anne thought with dismay. It would take a greater actress than the famous Mrs. Siddons to pull off such a thing.

Lily thrust the stack of invitations into Anne's hands. "Here. You can start with these. There must be one amongst them it would please you to accept."

Anne regarded the pile listlessly. All she wanted was for her sister to leave her alone to sort out the bewildering and disturbing array of information Lily had thrust upon her. But Lily would give her no peace until she opened her mail.

Reaching for a letter opener, Anne broke the seal on the first invitation while Lily flitted about, examining some of Anne's gowns. "You know this lilac silk might still do for a casual evening at home if the frock were furbished with some new trimmings."

"Hmmm?" Scarce heeding her sister's sartorial advice, Anne shifted through the stack of invitations. Mrs. Cardiff begged the Lady Fairhaven's appearance at a small supper party. The Duchess of Devonshire was holding a rout. The Renfrew's eldest daughter was about to be presented to society. If the weather improved, my lord and lady Benton proposed an al fresco breakfast.

None of these invitations produced any reaction from Anne other than a weary sigh. She experienced not the flickering of an interest until she reached a note that had been buried amidst the stack of gilt-edged cards.

A small, plain sheet of vellum, folded over and sealed; it had not been franked so it obviously had been delivered by hand. The script bearing her name was elegant, but most definitely the product of a masculine hand.

Somehow before she broke the seal, she knew. Her heart set up an unsteady beat as she unfolded the single sheet.

My lady Sorrow,
Tonight. At ten o'clock. Make your excuses to your sister. I shall have a coach waiting by the front gate.
Mandell.

The signature leapt out at her, dark and bold. Anne tried not to panic. She still had enough time to pack her trunks and Norrie's, to order up the carriage, to convince Lily that she had to leave today, this very afternoon.

Except that she knew she would do none of those things. Mandell had brought Norrie back to her, and at great personal risk to himself. No matter how selfish his reason, how wicked his motives, Anne was vastly in his debt, a debt she had to find the courage to pay.

She sat staring at the note until she was interrupted by the sound of Lily's voice. "Well, Anne? Do none of those invitations appeal to you?"

Anne concealed Mandell's note beneath the rest of the stack.

"Yes," she said quietly. "There is one here that I am obliged to accept."

Hours later as the mantel clock ticked onward to the hour of ten, Anne took one last look at her uninspiring reflection in the mirror. She had woven her hair in the familiar tight crown of braids and selected one of the most demure gowns she owned, a plain muslin whose pale pink shade seemed to wash out what color remained in her fair skin.

Over it she donned a cottage vest of green sarcenet, lacing it so tightly across her bosom that she flattened her breasts, making it difficult to breathe. The ensemble was not likely to please Mandell, but then he knew that he was getting no sultry beauty in Anne Fairhaven. He could hardly expect any miraculous transformation tonight.

Perhaps Mandell would take one look at her and decide to send her right back home again. She touched one hand to her bare neck. Her little gold locket would have gone perfectly with the outfit, but it was still gracing the pawnbroker's dusty shelf. Anne pored over the few pieces of her jewelry that remained, but in the end opted to wear none. It would only be one more thing that she would have to remove when—

She swallowed hard, suppressing the thought. She was

already nervous enough. Her gaze flicked to the mantel clock, the hands moving inexorably toward ten.

She had never known a day to go by so swiftly and she wondered if this was how condemned prisoners felt during their last hours. She had bitten her nails down to the nubs and her hands looked hideous. Was it considered acceptable to engage in intimate relations with a man while wearing gloves?

The thought almost caused her to break into hysterical giggles. She took a deep breath to steady herself. Tugging on her kid gloves, she reached for her brown velvet mantle, the one with the hood.

She had never looked more proper in her life. She appeared as though she was going to do exactly what she had told Lily earlier that day—have a quiet supper with her elderly godmother, Lady Bennington. She had even had the forethought to announce that her ladyship would send her own coach to fetch her.

How adept she was becoming at telling these lies, Anne thought sadly.

Lily had been annoyed with her, of course. Out of all the invitations Anne had had to choose from, she did not see why Anne had to elect to spend her evening with an elderly recluse. But, Lily had remarked sourly, she supposed it was better than Anne wasting another night at home.

Lily had already gone out herself to attend a lively musical soiree to be given at the home of some countess Anne could not remember. Her sister's absence made things easier. As easy as this night was going to get, Anne thought as she prepared to descend to the front parlor. She could pace better there until her hour of doom. The room was much more spacious than the confines of her bedchamber.

But as Anne opened her door, she was startled by the small figure that appeared on the other side—a golden-haired sprite, with bare toes peeking out from beneath a ghost white nightgown, a doll clutched beneath her arm.

"Norrie," Anne gasped.

Her daughter skittered across the threshold. Norrie held up the china doll, whose tangled tresses had seen better days. She announced solemnly, "Lady Persifee couldn't sleep again, Mama."

Anne cast an anxious glance at the clock. Any other time, she would have welcomed the prospect of cuddling Norrie and rocking her back to sleep. But for once Anne did not feel equal to dealing with her small daughter.

She attempted to summon up her sternest expression, but Norrie skipped about Anne, eyeing her gown. "You look bee-yootiful, Mama. Just like a fairy princess."

"More like the wicked stepmama." Anne scooped her daughter up in her arms. "Eleanor Rose Fairhaven, you and Lady Persephone belong back in bed."

Norrie laid her head upon Anne's shoulder, regarding her with wide pleading eyes, giving her most enchanting dimpled smile. But her smile faded as her small frame shook with the cough she tried to repress.

"Oh, child," Anne murmured. "Come, we must get you tucked back up all warm again. This is no good for you, being up so late."

As Anne carried her daughter out into the hall, Norrie protested, "But, Mama, I'm 'ccustomed to being waked up at night. It was awful noisy at Uncle Lucien's."

"That is because your bedroom must have been too near the street. But you have no such excuse here at Aunt Lily's, young lady." Anne took the firmness from her words by giving Norrie's smooth pink cheek a kiss.

"But I like the sound of horses and wheels and people laughing. And it wasn't the street noises that waked me, it was Uncle Lucien. He got angry at night and broked things."

"Oh, Norrie, darling. I am sure Uncle Lucien was seldom at home after you went to bed. You must have been dreaming."

Norrie stubbornly shook her head. "I peeked out my door and saw him. But I was careful. Uncle Lucien didn't like anybody but him to be awake at night. And one time he hurted himself, Mama. He had blood on his sleeve and he kept falling down. And he smelled bad."

Anne scarce knew what to reply. She strained her daughter close lest Norrie see her horrified expression. Anne had always known Lucien to be something of a rake, a heavy drinker, but alas, so were many gentlemen of the ton. Only recently had Anne begun to suspect how far gone in debauchery Lucien might be, how close to the edge of sanity. She could only thank the heavens she had Norrie safely away from him.

No, not the heavens, she reminded herself.

Mandell.

It took her some little while to bundle Norrie back to the nursery and coax the child to sleep again. By the time she saw her daughter resting peacefully, Anne was horrified to hear the clock strike half past the hour of ten.

Snatching up her cloak, Anne tore down the stairs to the first floor. But Lily's stern butler attempted to bar her way. If a coach had been sent for Lady Anne, then it behooved one of Lady Bennington's footmen to come to the door and announce the fact.

With great difficulty Anne persuaded Firken to step aside, the dignified old man scowling with disapproval as Anne dashed out into the night. She half hoped, half feared that Mandell would have given up on her by now.

But through an evening heavy with mist, the phantom outline of a coach and horses appeared drawn up next to the curb. Giving herself no more time to think, Anne flung up her hood, concealing her features. She raced toward the carriage, her heart pounding in tempo with her footsteps.

A servant melted out of the darkness, a stocky young man attired in Mandell's distinctive livery of black and silver.

The footman bowed. "Lady Fairhaven?"

Anne nodded. She wondered if this solemn man knew why he had been sent to fetch her. Of course he did. Servants always knew everything. Anne blushed, shrinking deeper into the shelter of her hood.

"I am John Hastings, my lady," the footman said, opening the coach door for her. "My lord Mandell sent me to insure your safe arrival."

As he handed her into the darkened interior of the carriage, Anne asked, "Where are we going?"

But Mandell had obviously trained his servants to be as enigmatic as himself, for Hastings closed the door without another word. He scrambled to take his place up on the box beside the coachman.

Anne was jolted back against the squabs as the coach lurched into movement. She clenched her hands together in her lap, trying to still her desire to leap back out of the carriage.

She supposed it scarce mattered what their destination might be. She had placed herself in Mandell's power that night she had given him her vow, perhaps longer ago still when she had first permitted him to lead her into a moonlit garden and steal a kiss.

There was no escaping him now.

Chapter 10

The carriage ride was short. Anne did not have enough time to compose herself before the silent Hastings was handing her down into the darkness of a stable yard.

"If it would please you to follow me, my lady," he said.

As if Anne had any choice but to do so. Huddling deeper into her cloak, she stumbled after Hastings through the inky blackness of a starless night, broken only by the bobbing light of the lantern he carried. He took such long strides she had to hasten to keep up with him, having little chance to gain her bearings other than to realize that she passed beneath the branches of some trees, through the shadows of what appeared to be a garden.

It was not until the footman led her across the threshold of a formidable door, and her feet clattered against the cold marble tile of an entranceway, that Anne dared ease back her hood to determine exactly where she was.

She stood in an imposing front hall, cold, elegant and austere, a stairway with a wrought iron balustrade sweeping up to a shadowed landing above her. A shock of realization pierced her and she nearly exclaimed aloud.

Mandell's own London house. She had never been past his front gate before, but she knew with inexplicable certainty that she stood in his reception hall. The coach could have done no more than circle the square a number of times before bringing her back here, to a house only down the street from her own sister's.

Feeling more confused and unsettled than ever, Anne turned to question the footman, but Hastings had vanished, leaving her alone in the chill silence of the hall, the house around her a ring of forbidding closed doors.

There was no sign of Mandell or anyone else for that matter. Now what was she expected to do? Anne wondered miserably. There was not even a fire kindled upon the hall's massive stone hearth. Hastings had taken the lantern away, and if not for the candles flickering in the wall sconces, she would have been left in darkness.

She stood, shifting from foot to foot. The front door loomed but yards away. She could fling it open in a trice. If she ran fast enough, it would be a matter of minutes before she was back safe in her own bedchamber and—

"You are late, Sorrow," a silky voice echoed from the regions behind her. Her heart thudding, Anne whipped around.

The marquis of Mandell stood on the landing above her, his tall shadow cast down the length of the stairs. The candlelight accented the hauteur of his features, giving him an aura of almost satanic male beauty, the glow bringing a sheen to the dark waves of his hair.

He was clad in a wine-colored dressing gown of satin, belted at the waist. The rich folds parted enough to reveal that he wore close-fitting black breeches beneath and a white shirt opened slightly at the neck. He extended one hand toward her, his signet ring glinting in the light.

It was not so much a supplication as a silent command. Anne risked one longing glance toward the front door before drawing in a steadying breath. She raised her skirts, beginning the long climb up toward Mandell.

When she came close enough, he caught her hand, his own fingers strong and steadying as he drew her up to stand beside him.

"It is nearly eleven of the clock," he said. "I have never waited so long for any lady to keep her appointment with me. I had begun to think you intended to fail me."

There was an edge to his voice and when she dared glance up at him, she saw that his eyes were as still and brooding as his great empty house.

"I had difficulty getting away," Anne said. "Norrie woke up and she needed me. I had to soothe her back to sleep."

Mandell's face softened a little. He raised her gloved fingertips lightly to his lips. "I suppose the important thing is that you are here now."

"Yes, but I never expected you would bring me to your home."

His brows rose haughtily. "You thought I would hie you off to some sordid inn where any common knave might look at you? I have a little more regard for your reputation than that, milady. That is why I instructed Hastings to take great care when spiriting you away to me."

"But servants will gossip and—"

"Mine don't. Especially not the one I sent to fetch you. I acquired John Hastings reluctantly at the insistence of my cousin Drummond. He has turned out to possess the two traits I value most in my servants, obedience and silence.

"But I have kept you standing in this drafty hall long enough." Mandell draped his arm about her shoulders. "My house possesses far warmer rooms."

Like his bedchamber, Anne thought with a sinking heart, her mind filling inevitably with that Turkish sultan's den she had once imagined, rife with shameful secrets and satin sheets.

But she allowed Mandell to guide her forward toward a door at the end of the corridor. He pushed it open, urging her across the threshold.

Holding her breath, Anne stepped inside and blinked.

The room was normal, almost sedate, a sitting room of undeniably masculine influence, the glow of oil lamps reflecting off rich paneled walls. A small but comfortable forest green settee was drawn up near the hearth where a cozy fire crackled, a book of Dryden's poetry left carelessly open upon a tripod table nearby. Busts of Mozart and Beethoven peered down from atop the mantel.

Somewhat reassured, Anne crept farther into the room only to draw up short at the sight of the arch which led into the adjoining chamber. She could make out the shape of an enormous four-poster bed, the coverlets already turned down.

Shrinking back, Anne collided against Mandell's hard

frame. She gasped as he reached for her, but he was only seeking to brush back her hood.

"Come out of hiding, Sorrow," he said. "Your presence has been noticeably absent this past week. I wondered if you were seeking to avoid me, if you intended to cheat me out of my promised reward."

Anne felt a telltale flush spread over her cheeks. "Of course not. But it was not the sort of debt I could repay by posting you a bank draft through the mail. You could have sent for me sooner. I would have come."

"Would you have, indeed?"

Anne could not meet his eyes. He placed his fingers beneath her chin, forcing her to look up. "I tried to give you a little time to make up your mind to come to me. You disappointed me, Anne, and my patience finally wore thin."

"And if I had tried to cheat you, what would you have done?" she asked anxiously. "Would you have sought to undo your part of the bargain?"

"There are many things I am interested in undoing, my lady." Mandell reached for the fastenings of her cloak. "But our bargain is not one of them."

His long graceful fingers deftly unbuttoned the braided froggings. Anne exhaled, telling herself she must try to relax. He was only taking off her cloak . . . thus far.

Mandell swept away the garment, draping it over a leather armchair. As he took in the details of her very proper attire, his teeth flashed in a smile of genuine amusement.

"By god, madam, you could be on your way to church. Have you brought your prayer book as well?"

"No, but perhaps I should have," Anne retorted. "No doubt you could use a few prayers said for your soul."

"Alas, milady, 'tis far too late for that."

Anne flushed under his sardonic regard. She smoothed out the sleeve of her gown, saying in a defensive tone, "I told everyone I would be visiting my elderly godmother this evening. I had to dress accordingly."

"Your godmama finds you quite charming, but far too pale as usual. Come, let me offer you some food and drink."

Making her a magnificent leg, he waved her toward the

window, where the heavy velvet draperies had been drawn, shutting out the night. Anne saw that covers for two had been laid out upon a small table, some silver-covered chafing dishes being kept warm on a sideboard.

"You intend for us to dine first?" Anne asked incredulously.

"Would you have me seduce you on an empty stomach?"

Her stomach was tensed into a thousand knots. How could he possibly expect her to eat? When Mandell began to draw back her chair, Anne shook her head.

"I am not hungry."

"Let me at least offer you a little wine then." He picked up a glass of delicate crystal and reached for a dust-covered bottle, a rare vintage that must have graced his cellars for some time.

"If you insist, my lord. But I should warn you it takes very little wine to make me fall asleep."

Mandell paused with the bottle suspended in midair, that expressive brow of his arching upward. "Then perhaps I had better send down to the kitchen for some lemonade."

"I am not thirsty, either," Anne snapped. She did not sound very gracious, but she had never felt more nervous or out of her depth in her entire life. Not even on that dreadful night she had made her debut at Almack's.

"All this politeness is not necessary, my lord. Whatever you want to do with me, I wish you would just do it and get it over with."

"Some pleasures are not to be rushed." Mandell set down the wine bottle. He stepped closer, framing her face with his hands.

His poor Lady Sorrow. It was difficult to remember at this moment that she was a widow, a woman who ought to know a little something of the world and men. She looked young, vulnerable, and scared, as though she expected him to pounce on her, tear off her clothes, take her right there on the floor.

It was not as though the desire burning inside him waxed too cool for such a thing. But he had ever been a man of iron control and possessed more finesse than that. He had taken far too many pains over his conquest of the virtuous Anne, planned too carefully to ruin all by a clumsy burst of passion. He wanted her beneath him, hot and willing, trembling not with fear but with a fire that would match his own.

"I'll have no martyrs in my bed, milady," he said, tracing his thumbs over her cheekbones. "I do not intend to proceed until I feel you are ready, my beautiful one."

"Oh, don't," she cried, clutching at his wrists, seeking to push his hands away. "Don't feel obliged to say things like that, to try to pretend that I am beautiful."

"Pretend? And whatever makes you think that you are not?"

"I have only to look in a mirror."

"Then you have been looking in the wrong one. You should seek your reflection only in my eyes." He kissed her brow, reveling in the sweet fresh scent of her, the warm silky texture of her skin.

"Before this evening is over, Anne Fairhaven," he vowed, "I shall not only have you willing in my arms, but also convinced of how beautiful and desirable you are."

"That could take a very long time, my lord," she said sadly.

"We have all night. So if you truly have no wish to dine, go sit you by my fire and warm yourself. You seem quite chilled."

She obeyed him, marching over to perch upon the edge of the settee with a resigned sigh. Mandell drifted about the room, extinguishing all the oil lamps until the chamber was lit only by the glow of the fire. When he moved to take his place at her side, she sat ramrod straight, her gloved hands clenched together in her lap.

He eased himself down, stretching one arm behind her along the back of the settee, taking as great a care as though she were a skittish dove that would flutter away at his slightest movement.

"You have exquisite posture," he said. "Were you ever in the military?"

His teasing succeeded in coaxing a half smile from her.

"No, but I did have a very strict governess who I am sure could have out-generaled Wellington himself."

Capturing one of her hands, Mandell inched back her glove enough to expose the delicate blue-veined area of her wrist. He pressed his lips to her thundering pulse.

"Mrs. Brindlehurst!" Anne gasped.

"I beg your pardon?"

"That—that was the name of my governess. She always insisted upon proper carriage. She—" Anne eyed him nervously as he began to undo the buttons of her glove. "She always said it was important to remain erect. Otherwise my bos—my frame would start to sag."

"I have never noticed any part of you—um—sagging." Mandell tugged off her glove, delighting in the slender grace of her hands until he saw her fingernails. Anne blushed scarlet and tried to curl up her hand, but he refused to allow it, holding up her fingertips, examining them closer.

"My dear Sorrow, what have you been doing to your poor hands?"

"It is a bad habit of mine," she said in a tight shamefilled voice. "I bite my nails in times of great stress."

Mandell frowned, for the first time understanding the agonies of apprehension Anne must have gone through the past week.

"And I have been the cause of that stress?" he said, kissing her fingertips one by one. He felt a shiver course through her.

"You are not exactly the most restful influence in my life, Lord Mandell."

"Is that what you desire, Anne? To remain calm, no excitement ever to touch your staid and proper world?"

"Staid and proper. That is what I am. I don't know how to be anything else."

"Then it behooves me to teach you."

Mandell had never felt flooded with so much tenderness toward any woman. His need to take her into his arms and soothe away her fears burned equally as strong as his desire for her.

"Come here," he commanded huskily. Urging her to draw

her feet up on the settee, he guided her until she lay back across his lap, cradling her head in the crook of his arm.

Anne's eyes widened as she braced her arms stiffly alongside her.

"Relax, Anne. I am not going to hurt you. Have I been such an ogre thus far?"

"No. But I feel too helpless with you holding me this way and I don't know what you expect me to do."

"I don't expect anything for now. Just talk to me."

"What about?"

"Tell me about Eleanor Rose." He tucked a stray tendril of hair behind Anne's ear. "Has it made you happy at last, my Sorrow, having your little daughter back again?"

"Oh, yes," she breathed. He could feel her begin to melt a little. As he gazed down upon her flushed features, Mandell thought if he were any less a villain, he would put a stop to this now and send her home.

The radiant look shining from her eyes as she talked about her child should have been payment enough for any man. But it also lent her an irresistible beauty, the soft curve of her lips far too tempting.

". . . And it has been all I could do to keep Norrie from making a nuisance of herself," Anne was saying. "My sister Lily does not have a great deal of patience with small children, but Norrie is fascinated with watching Lily attire herself for attending balls. I can remember being the same way when I was still in the schoolroom and Lily was making her come-out. She is so dazzling. You must have been there. You must have seen her that night she first took Almack's by storm."

"I am afraid not. I have ever eschewed Almack's. Too many simpering virgins and predatory mamas. I suppose that is how I also failed to notice you."

"You were not alone in that," Anne said with a grimace. Mandell doubted she realized it, but she had settled more snugly back against his arm. He suppressed a smile.

"I fear I was something of a disappointment after the debut of both my sisters," she continued. "Lily and Camilla, the famous Wendham debutantes."

"Lily and Camilla . . . their names always made me think of a stroll through a botanical garden. Tell me, my dear Anne, how did you ever escape being christened an Amaryllis or a Columbine?"

"I suppose when Mama peeked into my cradle, I did not make her think of flowers."

"You make me think of one," Mandell said, exploring the delicate outline of her lips with his finger. "A blossom whose petals are just about to unfurl."

He bent forward to brush her mouth with a kiss. Anne tensed at the first touch of his lips, but his kiss was so gentle and lingering. It was as though he but tasted her, sampling the texture of her lips, spreading a pleasant warmth through her. Anne's mind reeled. She felt giddy, lightheaded, almost floating in his arms.

She clung to him, her fingers slipping across the open neckline of his shirt, making contact with that exposed patch of warm bare skin. She heard Mandell's intake of breath and drew back immediately, cringing with embarrassment.

"Oh, I—I am sorry," she stammered. "It is only that you made me feel so dizzy."

"It is all right, Sorrow. Feel free to touch me. I promise I won't object."

His smile was like slow heat, curling in the pit of her stomach.

"I can't," she said, blushing hotly. "I am not accustomed to— You must think me so awkward."

"Actually what I was thinking is that it is time to be rid of those braids. May I?"

"Well, I . . ."

But he did not wait for her assent, his fingers moving through her hair, removing pins, untwisting the heavy braids she had fashioned with such care. Her hair tumbled down to her shoulders, spilling over his arm, feeling gloriously free. He combed his fingers back through the tangled golden strands.

"Lovely," he murmured. "You should always wear your hair thus."

"I would look like a half-mad hoyden."

"You can be a hoyden tonight. You can be anything you want with me, Anne."

"What a terrifying offer," she sighed, closing her eyes as he bent to kiss her again, his mouth demanding a little more this time. His tongue teased her lips, coaxing, and she parted for him, allowing him access to the innermost recesses of her mouth, allowing him to fill her with heat, to tease, to mate with her as he would.

His hand moved between them, slowly undoing the laces of her vest. When the fabric parted, Anne found it a great relief, realizing she had done the laces far too tight. She was able to breathe again.

Then Mandell cupped her breast through the thin fabric of her gown and Anne found she could not breathe at all. She no longer felt light, a warm heaviness stealing over her that seemed to center at her woman's core. As he stroked her nipple, teasing it to a state of hardness, a sigh escaped her, and the sheer cotton that separated her from his touch became a torment.

He shifted her to a sitting position upon his lap. Breathing kisses against her neck, he reached around her. No lady's maid could have been more adept at undoing the fastenings of a gown and chemise. But the brief respite gave Anne time to cool down a little.

"No, please," she could not keep from saying as he began to slip the gown down her arms.

He stopped at once, exposing only her shoulders. "But you are lovely." He traced the path of her fragile collarbone with his fingers. "Mrs. Brindlehurst was right about the posture. I am excessively grateful to her."

Starting with her shoulder, Mandell caressed her with his lips, his mouth warm against her tender flesh. Anne drew in a tiny gasp, trying to stem the sparks of sensation he aroused, delicious wild sensations that threatened to overwhelm her.

His own breath coming a little quicker, Mandell eased her gown down farther, exposing the soft upper swell of her breast. As his mouth covered the pulse beating at the base of her throat, Anne stifled a soft cry. The fabric of her gown fell away to her waist, revealing the full round globes of her breasts to Mandell's hungry gaze. She watched the desire flare in his eyes.

No man had ever stared thus at her nakedness, not even her husband. Anne tried to fold her arms protectively across herself, but Mandell stopped her.

"Would you drive me to madness, Anne? Don't seek to hide your beauty from me."

When he kissed her again, Anne thought it was she who would go mad. He caught her lower lip gently between his teeth, sipped at her mouth, his tongue skimming hers, rekindling the fire.

The contact of his warm palm against her bare breast sent spirals of fire through her. He stroked and caressed. She trembled and burned, biting down upon her lip to keep from moaning aloud.

He sought the valley between her breasts and kissed her there. Anne was shocked as much by her own eager response as by what he was doing to her. He whispered against her flesh, "Let your feelings go, Anne. There is no passion you need be ashamed of with me, no desire I would not be pleased to indulge."

Anne caught his head, seeking to stop him as his lips closed over one nipple, his mouth hot and moist as he gently suckled her. She found herself burying her hands in his dark hair instead, arching back her neck and closing her eyes with a long shuddering sigh. The rush of pleasure that coursed through her was wondrous and new, almost unbearable in its intensity.

She squirmed on his lap, striking up against the hard evidence of Mandell's own arousal.

"Oh!" she gasped.

"I think it is time I showed you my bed," he said hoarsely.

Anne gave a dazed nod. He rose to his feet, gathering her up amidst a tangle of gown and chemise, lifting her high against his chest. She wrapped her arms about his neck, clinging to him as he moved away from the glow of the fire, bearing her off to the cool dark mystery that was his bedchamber.

The moon had finally succeeded in piercing the clouds. It shone through the tall latticed windows, spilling its silver-white light across the massive four-poster bed.

When Mandell lowered Anne onto the mattress, she was bathed by a shaft of moonlight, turning her tumbled hair to gold, her soft white skin as translucent as pearl.

Mandell had never brought any woman to his own bed before. This chamber was his inner citadel, a prison of pain-filled memories, tormenting regrets, and empty dreams. But tonight he felt as though he had captured an angel, brought there to drive back the darkness and loneliness that filled too much of his life.

As he gazed down at Anne through eyes hazed with passion, Mandell's throat closed with an unexpected surge of emotion that had little to do with the desire pumping through his veins. Struggling to remove his own dressing gown and shirt, his hands seemed wooden and clumsy.

When he stripped away his shirt, Anne stared up at the bare contours of his chest with a kind of wide-eyed wonder. She half reached out to touch, only to retreat.

As he stretched himself out beside her on the bed, he caught her hand, drawing it against him. Her fingers felt slight and fragile threading through the matting of his dark hair, resting over the thundering region of his heart.

"I've never touched a man's naked chest before," she whispered.

His surprise at this pronouncement must have been evident, for she hastened to explain, "Gerald always wore nightshirts to bed."

Mandell smiled. "Well, milady, I wear nothing at all."

She stole a downward glance. "But you are still wearing your—" Anne broke off, looking enchantingly flustered.

"A condition I intend to remedy." Mandell began undoing the buttons on his breeches when Anne sat up abruptly, her hair spilling forward across her naked shoulders.

"No, wait. Please. Before we go any further, I—I have a confession to make."

"Confessions are best left for the morning after," Mandell said, easing her back down, brushing back the golden tendrils that veiled her small firm breasts from his view. He sought to stir again the sweet desire he had glimpsed in her face before.

But she restrained him. "No, it is something I must tell you now." She averted her face, her voice sounding small and guilty. "I did intend to cheat you of this night, milord. I was going to take Norrie and run away."

Her confession did not surprise him as much as she expected. But he said gravely, "And what made you change your mind?"

"I had promised you and I never break promises."

Mandell pulled her close, settling her softness against his own hard length. Nuzzling his mouth against her neck, he murmured, "And was the prospect of coming to my bed so alarming you considered going back on your word?"

"I thought so, but I realized tonight that it is not you I am really afraid of."

"I am glad to hear that." His lips located the sensitive hollow behind her ear.

A long blissful sigh escaped her. "I discovered it is really myself that I fear. I have been no one but the 'virtuous Anne' for so long. I am not sure who I will be after my night with you."

Mandell stilled for a moment. That was something he had not given much thought to, how Anne would feel about their passionate encounter on the morning after, in the cold light of day. And it was not something he wanted to think about now.

He skimmed his hands over her bare flesh, down to her waist, seeking to remove her clothes the rest of the way. He felt Anne's quiver of response.

"I never imagined it would be like this," she said. "I never thought you could be so gentle and . . . and kind."

Kind? Now there was a word to cool a man's ardor, Mandell thought with a frown. He kissed Anne, long and deep, attempting to put a stop to any more of these confessions.

But when he drew back, she looked up at him, her eyes shining. "I owe you so much, my lord, more than I can ever repay. And I just want you to know that I am ready now to give you whatever it is you want from me."

Mandell stared at her, stunned to silence. Anne took his hand and breathed a kiss along the back of it, then cupped his palm against her cheek. She began running her own fingers over his chest in a feather-light exploration. Mandell had never realized that so gentle a touch could prove such exquisite torture, the promise of all he longed for and now knew he could not take. He held himself as rigid as stone, not responding. Then, with more self-control than he ever dreamed he possessed, he wrenched himself out of her arms. He stalked over to his dressing table, gripping the back of the chair until he thought he would splinter the wood to bits.

"My lord?" He heard Anne's voice behind him, soft and confused.

She could not be any more confounded than he was himself at this moment. He ached with his need of her, his desire to bury himself deep within her welcoming softness. Never could he remember wanting any woman more. So what stopped him from taking her? They had made a pact between them. She had just told him that she was willing and ready to redeem her pledge, to do anything to please him.

Ah, but there was that other blasted word that still seemed to hang in the air. *Kind*. Mandell grated his teeth. From the moment he had met Anne at Lady Sumner's ball, he had schemed and manipulated to get her into his bed, used whatever ploy he could think of, including her love for her child. And she thought him *kind*.

So kind she had overcome her fear of having any regrets. Now the fear was all his. When he had satisfied his selfish desires, taken his fill of Anne, what was he going to do with his virtuous Lady Sorrow after his passion was spent? She would be no Sara Palmer, giving him a cool nod the next time he chanced to pass her out driving in the park. Would Anne hereafter blush with shame every time she met his eye across some crowded ballroom? Would she seek to bury herself back in the country rather than ever encounter him again?

It was the most damnable moment to be asking himself such questions with the lady sprawled out on his bed half naked, her own desires finally awakened. Mandell dragged his hand back through his hair in pure frustration.

"Mandell?" Anne called again. "Is something amiss?"

"Get dressed," he snapped without looking around.

"I don't understand."

"I said get dressed. You can manage that much on your own, I suppose?"

"Yes, but—"

"Good," he growled. "It were as well I did not touch you again."

She fell silent, but he could sense her puzzlement. Then her voice came again, sounding very quiet this time. "Did I do something wrong?"

Mandell swore softly. "No, you didn't. I did. I should know better than to ever permit a woman to talk when I am making love to her."

He heard her shifting off the bed and realized with some alarm she meant to approach him.

"Stay back," he snarled. Unwisely he risked a look at her. Her flow of angel's hair tumbled about her flushed features, her gown dragged up only as high as her smooth white shoulders. It was pure agony watching the rise and fall of her breasts as she breathed, the wistful trembling of her lips.

He turned away, feeling beads of cold sweat break out on his forehead. "Our pact is ended, madam," he ground out. "When you are dressed, I shall summon Hastings to take you home."

"You are releasing me? But why?"

"Because!" Mandell gave a harsh self-mocking laugh. "Who would have ever thought it? After all these years, I have stumbled over my conscience in the dark of my own bedchamber."

He flung over his shoulder before stalking from the room, "And I am finding it most damnably inconvenient."

Chapter 11

ಀಀಀ

A storm was brewing. Mandell stood at the open window of his study, staring at the overcast sky. The wind tore past the draperies, rifling his hair, the raw spring air seeming to cut through the thin linen of his shirt. The room was as cold as his empty hearth. He had had no one in to light the fire and none of his servants had dared to appear unbidden. His humor had not been of the best since he had sent Anne away last night.

He had retired to his empty bed, not to sleep, but to lie awake calling himself every sort of idiot. He might have spent the hours until dawn with Anne's slender warm body clasped in his arms, sampling all those pleasures she had so willingly offered. Instead he had been left to toss and turn, his loins afire, tormented with the ache of unfulfilled desire. He had finally cursed himself to sleep somewhere near daybreak.

He had not awakened until well past noon, bleary-eyed, and in the devil's own temper. A temper that had not improved much as day wore on. His mood was about as dark as the sky overhead, the storm clouds stealing away the daylight earlier than usual.

He ought to close the window. His study was by now cold and damp. But he welcomed the bite of the wind. Perhaps its chill breath might return both his icy composure and his common sense.

What the deuce had come over him last night? He had gone to such lengths to seduce Anne, greater effort than he had ever expended upon any woman. He had pursued her at the theatre, followed her through the streets like some lovesick ass, had come close to fighting a duel all for her sake. In his bedchamber, he had done his best to put her at her ease, murmured such tender words as had ever passed his cynical lips. Then, after such a hard-fought campaign, he had allowed her to escape him because of some wretched attack of scruples.

It was as ridiculous as if Wellington had turned back from Waterloo to avoid distressing Napoleon. Mandell shook his head in disgust. It was just fortunate that he had seen nothing of his cousin Nick of late. If Drummond ever guessed how this affair of the lady Anne had ended, Nick would either roar with laughter or go all sanctimonious and declare that he had known one day Mandell's more noble self would emerge. Either response would be intolerable.

If only he had it all to do over again, Mandell thought fiercely. But that was the pure hell of it. He feared he would end by doing the same thing. What else was there to do when one found oneself drowning in violet eyes, listening to the woman pledging that she was ready to give him everything he wanted?

Did not the little fool understand that no one *gave* to the marquis of Mandell? He took what he wanted. There was nothing to be done with a female that naive but send her packing. Nick had warned him all along that Anne was not suited for the kind of diversion Mandell sought. And he should not have had to be warned. He had always known that virtuous women were the very devil.

He should be glad that his conscience, his better self, or whatever it was, had emerged to intervene. He should be glad to be quit of his Lady Sorrow before things had gone any further, become even more complicated. And he was glad, so long as he did not dwell too long over the way Anne's hair had looked tumbled across his pillow, moonlight outlining the soft whiteness of her breasts.

Slamming the window closed, he stalked over to the corner cabinet and poured himself a large brandy. He raised his glass briefly, his lips curling into a self-mocking sneer.

"Here's to the resurrection of my nobler self," he muttered. "And may it henceforth be buried six fathoms deep where it belongs."

He tossed down the brandy in a single gulp and it burned like fire in his empty stomach. It occured to him that he had never gotten around to eating anything yet today. But at the moment another brandy seemed far more appealing.

Hc was reaching for the decanter to refill his glass when a light rap came at his study door. Composing his features into more implacable lines, he issued a command to enter.

John Hastings stepped into the room. With a solemn bow, the footman presented Mandell with a packet of letters.

"Forgive me, my lord. But I noticed these left lying upon the hall table. They must have arrived by the morning post."

"You certainly took your time about bringing them to my attention."

"Yes, milord." Hastings did not flinch beneath Mandell's icy regard.

Most likely the fault lay with the butler or the timid parlormaid, but Hastings was not a man to offer any excuses. Mandell accepted the letters and tossed them upon his desk.

"Thank you, Hastings. You may go."

The young footman apparently took the "may" in his command quite literally. Instead of quitting the room, Hastings began stacking logs on the hearth, bending down to kindle the fire. The man was obviously too new to Mandell's employ to gauge the danger in the marquis's temper, or else was possessed of the most stolid nerve.

Mandell was inclined to believe the latter. Instead of voicing the acid rebuke that sprang to his lips, he found himself watching Hastings in silence, observing the man's movements with the poker and bellows.

He had not exchanged a word with Hastings since he had summoned the footman to convey Anne home last night. Though he despised himself for doing so, Mandell asked, "The lady you escorted to her house yestereve. You made certain she arrived safely?"

"Yes, milord."

Of course he had. Hastings was as dependable as the sun rising in the east. Otherwise Mandell would never have trusted him with such a delicate commission as looking after Anne. After an awkward pause, Mandell growled, "How did the lady seem when you left her?"

"Seem, my lord?"

"Was she calm? Distressed? Did she say anything?"

Hastings paused in his task, bellows still in hand. He frowned as though in effort of memory. "Well, she bade me good night and offered me a most generous vail." Hastings brightened. "And then her lips sort of trembled and she smiled."

Anne must have been most relieved to be quit of her pact with the wicked Lord Mandell. An unexpected pain twisted somewhere inside him.

"Your lady has a passing sweet smile, my lord," Hastings ventured.

"The fire waxes hot enough. Have done and get out."

Hastings rose to his feet, dusting off his hands on his breeches and started to leave the room. When he had reached the threshold, Mandell brought him up short by adding tersely, "And Hastings . . ."

"Yes milord?"

"She is not my lady."

"No, milord," the footman said quietly, easing the door shut behind him.

When Hastings had left, Mandell let fly an oath. When had he become reduced to holding conversations with his footman, especially about a woman? Irritated beyond measure, Mandell poured himself another brandy. He did not know what the devil had come over him of late, but he knew the cure for it.

Diversion. Fortunately, he was in a city that could provide amusement in abundance for a gentleman of his wealth and tastes. Anything from an evening at the opera to a night at a most discreet and exclusive bordello.

He was in no mood for Mozart. What he needed was a woman, and not one with soft trembling lips and vulnerable blue eyes, but a practical woman skilled in the arts of pleasing a man and grateful for nothing more than the size of his purse. Yet the thought left him strangely cold.

Perhaps what he really required was supper and cards at White's, that all-male bastion that had the good sense to ban any woman from so much as peering across the threshold. He might bid Drummond to come and dine with him. It could be entertaining to discover what Nick had been up to this past week, to torment him over the doings in Parliament. But Nick might be inclined to ask some awkward questions about the lady Anne, questions Mandell felt unequal to parrying.

Frowning into his glass, Mandell drained it. He had fallen into one of those damnable moods when every distraction he could think of seemed stale and meaningless. He supposed he would end by spending the evening at his own fireside.

But to do what? To discard books the first page barely read, to rise from the pianoforte, the melody half finished, to begin a letter only to leave the sheet blank? To pace this great empty house like a caged beast, tormented by his dark memories, questioning everything from the folly of the world to the meaning of his own existence?

Anne was right to have been relieved to have escaped him, Mandell mused. He frequently found his own society quiet intolerable. Mandell started to reach for the brandy again only to check the movement. He was already entertaining enough morbid notions and he wasn't even drunk yet. Instead he forced himself to settle behind his desk, attempting to concentrate on the letters he had received.

The cards of invitation he thrust aside without hesitation to be examined later. The rest were bills, many of them still from when he had had Sara Palmer in his keeping. One from a dressmaker looked surprisingly recent. He wondered if Sara had been desperate enough to attempt to foist one final purchase off on him. Mandell would not have put it past her.

He had never known any female to be bolder or more shrewdly calculating. She would likely one day get her hooks into some noble fool and trick him into wedding her.

In some distant future, Mandell could imagine himself being introduced to her in a crowded ballroom, hearing her styled as my lady something or other, Sara looking as haughty as a grand duchess.

That at least was one thing to look forward to, Mandell thought cynically. It would be amusing to utter some wicked greeting only Sara would understand, to flirt with his former mistress under the nose of her unsuspecting and no doubt oaf of a husband, more amusing still if she were wearing a gown Mandell had paid for.

Smiling a little at the thought, Mandell dipped his quill into the ink, preparing to write out a draft to settle the account. He was interrupted by another knock at the door. Hastings again.

This time Mandell did not even trouble himself to look up.

"Yes? What is it now? More mail that has been left lying about for the past few days?"

"No, my lord. You have a caller."

"Tell whoever it is to go to the devil. I am not receiving."

When Hastings made no move to comply, Mandell glanced up impatiently. "Are you hard of hearing, man? I said I am not at home to any visitors."

"Yes, my lord. But it is your grandfather, the Duke of Windermere."

Mandell's brows arched in mild surprise. His grandfather calling upon him and at such an hour?

Hastings gave a delicate cough. "I am not sure you would really wish me to deliver His Grace such a message."

Mandell flung down his quill with an expressive grimace. "You are quite right, Hastings. One is always at home to His Grace of Windermere. Show him in—"

Mandell broke off, glancing down at his attire. It would hardly do to receive the old gentleman in his shirtsleeves and breeches.

"Place him in the drawing room," Mandell finished. "And express my regrets for the delay. I shall be there directly."

"Yes, my lord."

Hastings rushed off to obey his command while Mandell retired to his bedchamber to make himself more presentable. Some fifteen minutes later he descended the stairs, smoothing out the sleeve of a dark navy frock coat, his cravat arranged to a modest perfection.

He doubted any fault could be found with his appearance, but if there was, His Grace would be quick to point it out. Mandell had long ago abandoned the quest to win his grandfather's approbation. A most useless struggle.

He and the old man rarely spent time in each other's company these days. Mandell had no notion what could have prompted the duke to call upon him this evening. He was certain only of one thing. The visit was unlikely to afford pleasure to either of them.

Shoving open the door, he stepped into the drawing room, a chamber that was at once both somber and elegant with its heavy curtains, mahogany furniture, and thick Aubusson carpet.

The duke stood at the far corner by the pianoforte. Oblivious to Mandell's arrival, he leaned upon his silver-handled cane, staring up at the small painting that had been a gift to Mandell from his cousin Drummond. It was by a Dutch artist after Rembrandt's style of light and shadow, and depicted a cavalier with flowing black locks and pointed beard, an arrogant youth of another time and place.

Mandell reflected that his grandfather likewise could have just stepped out of a portrait of another century, an age of greater elegance. His thick waves of white hair swept back into a queue, His Grace was attired in a powder blue satin coat and knee breeches, the richness of the fabric gleaming in the candlelight. The coat was nudged back slightly to reveal a flowered waistcoat that Nick would have envied, Mandell thought with a wry smile.

His grandfather had never inspired much affection in Mandell, but he did have to admit the duke had a way about him, a regal aura that could put a king to shame. One could not love the old devil, but one did have to admire him.

Mandell pulled the door behind him with a sharp click. His Grace had to have heard him, but he did not trouble himself to turn around.

"Good evening, Your Grace."

The duke finished his inspection of the portrait. "Mandell." He gave a curt nod, regarding Mandell with his heavy lidded gaze, those keen grey eyes that time seemed unable to dim.

"This is an unlooked for . . . honor." Mandell chose his words with deliberate care. "I trust I have not kept you waiting too long."

"Only a quarter of an hour. I have entertained myself by studying your unusual taste in decor. I notice you yet have *that* about." The duke made a sweeping gesture with his cane, bringing it to rest atop the pianoforte. "Do you still play?"

"Occasionally, to amuse myself. And you can hardly have forgotten the pianoforte once belonged to my mother."

"She had little use for it. Like most of the Windermeres, my daughter was not musically inclined." The duke's thin smile was rife with accusation.

Mandell felt his own jaw clench in response. Both he and the duke knew where Mandell had inherited his ability and passion for music, and it had not been from Lady Celine. It was a subject to be avoided. The old man must be in a rare mood to be seeking to provoke a quarrel this soon. Considering Mandell's own edgy temper this evening, his grandfather's visit could not have been more ill timed.

Mandell eased the cane from atop the piano. "I can scarce believe you called upon me to discuss my furnishings. There is a chill at this end of the room. Will it please you to return by the fire?"

The duke held his gaze for a moment, then complied, stalking past Mandell. He settled himself upon a wing chair. Brushing back the lace from his cuffs, he rested both of his hands upon his cane in front of him. His fingers were remarkably smooth and straight for a man of his years.

Mandell knew his grandfather would get to the reason for this visit in his own good time. Curbing his impatience,

Mandell stood by the fire, resting one arm along the mantel. It somehow gave him an advantage, and one needed every advantage when dealing with His Grace of Windermere.

"I hope Hastings looked after you well in my absence," Mandell remarked.

"Hastings?" The duke frowned. "Oh, you mean your footman. An efficient enough fellow, but why will you persist in garbing your servants in black? It seems the most deplorable affectation, as though you were perpetually in mourning."

"So I am," Mandell drawled. "For my lost innocence."

"Spare me your wit, sir."

Mandell acknowledged this rebuke with an ironic bow. "If you do not care for my *wit*, perhaps you would prefer my wine. I have an excellent port in my cellars that—"

"No, thank you. I fear my gout has been flaring up."

"Then it astonishes me that you would choose to venture abroad. Especially on such an evening. The weather promises to turn most foul."

"I should not have had to come here if you would be so obliging as to wait upon me. You did not even put in an appearance last week when I asked you to dine."

"Commanded me," Mandell corrected.

"I suppose I may command my own grandson. That dinner was to have been a special occasion."

"To mark the anniversary of when you adopted me? I marvel that Your Grace still thinks that a cause for celebration."

His grandfather pursed his lips, then said grudgingly, "For the most part, I have been quite satisfied with you, Mandell. You exhibit the traits of a man of intelligence and breeding except for those lapses when the passionate side of your nature gets the better of you."

He scowled. "I have recently heard some gossip about you from Sir Lancelot Briggs which I find disturbing."

"Indeed? I was not aware that Your Grace and Briggs had become such boon companions."

"Do not trifle with me, sir. Briggs is a blithering fool and your association with the man does you no credit. But he did serve one useful purpose. If not for his idiotic chatter, I should never have known how close you came to fighting a duel with Lucien Fairhaven."

Mandell tensed. So that was what had brought the duke descending upon him. Damn Lance Briggs, he thought grimly.

"I await your explanation, sir," the duke said.

Mandell gave him an icy smile. "You raised me to believe the marquis of Mandell is not required to give an accounting of his actions to anyone."

"You are to me! I despise Fairhaven myself. He comes from a family of country upstarts. But I will not have my heir risking scandal and possibly death by challenging such an underbred boor."

"Such considerations did not seem to trouble you when you thrust me into a duel when I was only sixteen," Mandell reminded him coldly. "You did everything but load the pistol for me."

"The dispute with Constable was an affair among gentlemen. You had been insulted. It was a matter of honor."

"Or at least the appearance of honor." Mandell sneered.

"Do not seek to change the subject, sir. You threatened Sir Lucien over a matter that was none of your concern. You forced him into turning the guardianship of his niece back to her mother, Anne Fairhaven."

"Your Grace is remarkably well informed. So why come questioning me?"

"Because while I know what you did, I have no notion why you did it. I can only presume your extraordinary behavior has something to do with Lady Anne Fairhaven."

Mandell gritted his teeth. If it had been anyone but his grandfather daring to question him about Anne, Mandell would have told them to go to the devil. But His Grace of Windermere possessed enough icy hauteur to freeze the depths of hell.

"Is she one of your light-o'-loves?" the duke asked.

"The virtuous Lady Anne?" Mandell arched one brow after his own haughty fashion. "That is hardly likely."

It was illogical. He had done his best to seduce Anne and

yet to hear his grandfather speak of her thus stirred an inexplicable anger in Mandell.

The duke regarded Mandell through narrowed eyes. "Then you must have a more serious motive for currying the lady's favor. It is just as I feared."

"Feared?"

"If you are thinking of marriage, she will not do, Mandell."

No thought of marriage had ever entered Mandell's head, but his grandfather's words brought him up short.

"And just what does Your Grace find so objectionable about the lady?"

"Nothing personally. She is gently bred and from an old, respectable family. But she lowered herself by marrying with a Fairhaven, had a child by him. If you wed the lady Anne, this girl would become your stepdaughter, a child tainted with the Fairhaven blood."

"Then little Eleanor Fairhaven and I would have something in common. My own blood is far from pure according to you."

The duke flinched as though Mandell had struck a raw nerve. But he said levelly enough, "I trust a sound English education has cured any unfortunate traits you might have inherited from— And we decided long ago never to discuss that unfortunate part of your background, to simply forget."

"You decided. I don't recall ever being given a choice." Mandell stared into the fire, carried back to that long ago night when he had watched his grandfather burn up the papers proclaiming his French heritage. "Perhaps the past cannot be so easily ignored, Your Grace. Nick has always thought I should seek to know more about those first years of my life."

"What does Drummond know of anything?" the duke growled. "That young idiot, that wild-eyed radical, that *Whig*. Half the time I am ashamed to acknowledge him as my grandchild."

"Nonetheless, Nick does have an uncanny habit of being right." Some devil in Mandell prompted him to continue goading. "I have been feeling remarkably restless of late.

Perhaps it is time I returned to France and sought some answers."

The duke leaned on his cane, shoving himself to his feet. His face had gone ice white. "I absolutely forbid it!"

Mandell felt the color drain from his own face. It had been many years since the duke had even presumed to say such a thing to him. Compressing his lips, he turned away.

"I believe the storm is likely to break soon. I should summon Your Grace's carriage."

But the duke caught him by the arm. The old man's grasp was surprisingly strong. "You will not go to France, Mandell. What possible reason could you have for doing so?"

"Is it so unnatural that I might wish to learn more of my French heritage, perhaps even my father?"

"The chevalier de Valmiere was a coward. He took my daughter away from her family, carried her off to France. He eventually abandoned her there to die. And you. He made no effort to seek you out for twenty-five years. Is there anything more you need to know about such a man?"

With a great deal of self-control, Mandell forced the duke's grip from his sleeve. "Perhaps not, but I cannot deny that he existed."

"So you would seek him out, return to the land of your mother's murderers. It is unworthy of you, Mandell. An insult to her memory. Can you have forgotten how she died?"

"No, I have not."

"The Parisian police broke down the door of the apartment. They arrested her. They dragged her out, terrified, screaming."

"I remember. I was there."

"They intended to put her on trial. She would have faced the guillotine." The old man's eyes glittered. "But the mob was waiting in the streets. They put their filthy hands upon my proud, beautiful Celine, suffocating her with their vile stench. Clawed and tore at her like savage beasts, smearing themselves with her blood."

"I remember," Mandell repeated tersely.

"And when they had done, they paraded her head on a pike—"

"I remember, damn you!"

Mandell strode away to the window, struggling to regain his composure. The sky beyond the glass was so black, like the suffocating darkness of being shut up in a closet. Mandell had seen nothing that long ago night, only felt the terror. It had always been the visions that the duke conjured that made him feel as though he had actually witnessed his mother's death, the old man's words splashing the night sky with vivid hues of red.

Mandell pressed unsteady fingers to his brow. When he turned back, the duke looked ashen and as shaken as he. But it had been ever thus between them, circling each other like two duelists seeking their mark, only to succeed in re-opening the one old wound that gave pain to them both.

It was his grandfather who recovered enough to speak first. "You were brought to me as a boy, Mandell, frightened, confused, as ragged and shivering as any peasant. I gave everything back to you, your courage, your place as my grandson, the dignity of my own name. I never expected gratitude from you, but I at least thought to have your loyalty."

"And so you have had, Your Grace, beyond question."

"Then you will not go to France?" his grandfather asked. It was as close as the proud duke of Windermere would ever come to a plea. Mandell looked deep into the old man's hooded eyes and was astonished to find fear there. It had never occurred to him that his iron-willed grandfather carried with him his own nightmares and terror of Paris.

"No, I will not go," Mandell said softly. "I never had any intention of doing so."

He half expected his grandfather might require his oath on that, but the duke appeared satisfied with those few brief words. Leaning on his cane, he stumped over to summon the footman and order up his carriage himself.

It was strange, Mandell thought. As a boy, his grandfather had seemed such a looming figure in his life. When he had grown to manhood, it had come as quite a jolt to realize the duke was not that tall. What he lacked in stature, His Grace made up for in his regal bearing.

But as Mandell studied his grandfather more closely, he saw the first signs of stooping shoulders. When the candle-light played full upon the duke's age-lined features, he looked drained.

The old man was clearly no longer up to these little bouts of theirs. Mandell experienced a genuine regret that he had goaded him so. He was moved to apologize, but knew it would do no good. The duke would only perceive that as a sign of weakness.

While they waited for the duke's carriage to be brought round, Mandell sought to introduce more neutral topics and was grateful when his grandfather followed his lead. They discussed the spirited team of horses Mandell had recently acquired and His Grace's plans to dine at Devonshire House that evening.

"The countess has been pressing me to do so and I shall be retiring to the country soon," the duke said.

"In the midst of the season?" Mandell asked with mild surprise.

"London is not what it was. It gets worse every year. So many of my acquaintances have passed on and one scarce knows what manner of person one might meet these days, even in the best houses. This modern world of yours, Mandell, has no proper regard for rank and breeding."

"Not my world, Your Grace, so much as Nick's. He believes it is high time that men should be judged more for their own merit than who their fathers were."

"Your cousin is becoming a most alarming young man. I fear that one of these days Nicholas will carry these mad ideas of his too far." A troubled frown creased the duke's brow.

But Mandell was accustomed to his grandfather's complaints about Nick. Having no desire to set the duke off into another of his tirades, Mandell found it more politic to ignore the remark.

After Hastings had helped His Grace into his cloak and

tricorne hat, Mandell escorted the duke to the waiting carriage himself.

Going down the walk, he attempted to used his tall frame to shield the old man from the bite of the wind. It had not yet begun to rain, but the thunder edged closer, causing the team of bays hitched to the duke's brougham to paw restively.

"Take care, sir," Mandell said. "It is going to be a bad night and Nick seems to be correct about one thing. Given recent events, perhaps this city does stand in need of a little more protection."

"Bah! I suppose you mean that Hook business. I am no fool like young Albert Glossop. I have always known how to take care of myself."

One of the duke's own postilions snapped to open the coach door for him. But Mandell put his hand beneath the duke's elbow to help him up the steps. It was the only touch his grandfather had ever been willing to accept from him.

As the duke settled back against the squabs, Mandell closed the door. His Grace thrust his head forward to peer out the coach window. "One more thing, Mandell. Think about what I have said regarding your dealings with Lady Fairhaven."

Mandell had hoped his grandfather had forgotten or else decided to let the matter die. But that was too much to have expected. His Grace was nothing if not persistent.

"Set your mind at rest," Mandell said. "I have no intention of marrying anyone at present."

"But I want you to think of marriage. It is time you were producing an heir. All I ask is that when you are choosing a bride, remember your station in life—you are my grandson, the marquis of Mandell."

"When would you ever allow me to forget?" Mandell murmured somewhat bitterly. But his remark was lost as the coachman whipped up the team and his grandfather's ancient carriage clattered off down the street.

Mandell felt the first dash of rain against his cheek and did not linger by the gate. He returned to the relative warmth and comfort of his drawing room. But if he had been restless before his grandfather's visit, he now felt tenfold more so.

He applied the poker to the fire, causing the flames to crackle and flare higher about the half-burned logs. It was ironic. His grandfather had striven to burn away his past, commanded him to forget. And yet it was the old man who constantly stirred the ashes of remembrance.

The bitter words he had exchanged with the duke had set ghosts loose upon this chamber. It was a perfect night for such spectres with the rain now lashing the panes, the wind howling like some thrice-damned soul.

One such phantom was waiting for him as he approached the pianoforte, lightly trailing his fingers over the keys. After such a passage of time, Mandell had no clear memory of his father, other than he had been tall and handsome, his eyes brilliantly dark.

But his recollection of the chevalier's hands was crystal clear, those long, sensitive fingers moving as deftly down the keys as a man might caress a mistress he has known long and loved well. And his father's voice . . . It had been as rich and lilting as the music he played.

"Attend-moi, mon petit gentilhomme, if you seek the fire and fury of a man's soul, look to Monsieur Beethoven. But if you want something light and romantic to charm the ladies, it must be Mozart."

And Mandell recollected heeding his words most solemnly, for it had seemed his father was right. When his father had played out the strains of a minuet, his mother leaned across the pianoforte, sighed, and smiled. Mandell's memory of the Lady Celine was that she had hardly ever smiled. She had always been so stern and distant. She only seemed to come alive when his father was present.

Mandell scowled, the softer vision fading as it always did to be replaced by the darker one, that night of black closets, splintering wood, and terrifying screams.

Valmiere had given his mother love and life, only to abandon her to death.

"Where were you that night, my noble father?" Mandell grated. "Why weren't you there to save her?"

He slammed his fist down upon the pianoforte keys with a jarring clang, then stalked away from the instrument. Why had he and his mother been left alone in Paris? Had his father truly been that much of a bastard, and did any of it really matter anymore?

No, it didn't. It was only his grandfather's visit that had stirred up all these memories, these doubts. It was only the storm outside making him so edgy, the lightning cracking and illuminating his windows like a flash of cannonfire.

He could sense the tension building within him until he felt as dark and dangerous as the night itself. It was going to be a wild night, a night in which he dared not sleep, for he knew he would dream. And dreaming was always bad.

Anne was fortunate she was not with him now, for he could never have been merciful enough to let her go. Not tonight.

"My Lady Sorrow, if you were in my arms at this moment, I would crush you against me, plunder your sweetness until I found forgetfulness. I could almost admit that I need—"

But Mandell was quick to check that wayward thought. Of course he had no need but the most primitive male urge. He had survived many such nights of torment without Anne Fairhaven. And he would get through this one as well.

Summoning Hastings, he commanded the footman to fetch his greatcoat and beaver hat. "I shall be dining away from home this evening," Mandell informed him.

Hastings ventured a doubtful glance toward the windows, where the storm raged outside, but all he said was, "Yes, my lord."

"And you may tell my valet not to wait up for me. I do not expect to return until . . ." Mandell hesitated. Until dawn streaked the sky, dispelling the night shadows, until he was exhausted enough to sink into oblivion.

He concluded aloud, "I shall not return until very late."

"Very good, my lord. Does that mean the rest of the staff

might retire early as well?" There was a hint of eagerness in Hastings's usual respectful monotone.

Mandell shot his footman a curious glance. He suddenly recalled the reason for Hastings's introduction into his household. "You were planning to be married soon, were you not, Hastings? My parlor maid—er—Agnes."

"Emily, my lord. You must have forgotten. We were wed last Tuesday morn. You granted us a half-day holiday."

"Did I? How unusually gracious of me." Mandell drew on his gloves. "So you are a newly wedded man. Yes, perhaps you should retire to your bed early."

Mandell was amused to see the stolid Hastings flush a deep scarlet. The marquis's lips curved into a genuine smile, which was rare for him. Accepting his hat from the footman, he said, "Be off with you, John. Hie yourself away to the heaven of your lady's arms." Mandell's smile faded to an expression more grim. "I intend to seek my comfort tonight in far different regions."

Chapter 12

⎯⎯⎯⎯⎯⎯

The storm abated long before the one that raged within Mandell's soul. The night was still young when he swept down the steps of White's where he had taken his supper alone, his forbidding scowl for once keeping even Lancelot Briggs at a distance.

Mandell had eaten too little and drunk far too much, but he was sober enough to keep a steady pace as he stalked along the rain-wet pavement. The amount of brandy he had consumed had done nothing to dull the pain of old memories. It only gave a sharper edge to the tension coiling inside him.

The storm had kept many a more prudent person from venturing abroad tonight. The usually bustling St. James was thin of traffic. The wind tugged at the flaps of his greatcoat and disheveled his hair. Mandell shoved back the straying locks and stepped off the pavement. He was looking to summon a hackney cab when he heard someone hailing him by name.

He turned to see Lancelot Briggs hastening down the steps of White's. Mandell's lip curled with disgust. Briggs's plump frame appeared ridiculous swathed in a cloak with several capes. It was an exact imitation of the one Mandell had swirled about Anne's shoulders that night that now seemed strangely long ago.

Thoughts of the lady only drove the ache inside Mandell deeper. He awaited Briggs's approach, fixing an expression on his face black enough to keep Briggs from bounding up in his usual exuberant manner.

"Excuse me, my lord," Briggs said timidly as he held out a high-crowned beaver hat. "But you forgot this. It's your hat. You left it back there. At White's, remember? Where you had supper."

Mandell yanked the hat from his grasp.

"My lord is making an early evening of it. You are going home?"

"No!" Turning on his heel, Mandell walked away. To his irritation Briggs followed. It was difficult for Briggs to keep pace with Mandell's long legs, but he managed.

"You have another engagement? You are going somewhere else, my lord? I would be pleased to accompany you."

Mandell came to an abrupt halt. "I am going to the devil."

"Oh." Briggs looked a little daunted. But he forced a smile. "What a coincidence," he jested weakly. "I was just going there myself."

"It is not a journey that requires company, especially not that of a spy."

"A spy, my lord?"

"That is what you are, is it not? Forever hovering near me, watching what I do, only to go bruiting my affairs about half the city."

"No, my lord. I assure you. I never speak of anything that you do—"

"The incident between myself and Sir Lucien," Mandell reminded him. Even in the darkened street, he could detect Briggs's guilty flush.

"Oh, *that*. Perhaps I did tell just a few . . . It is only that it was such a noble thing you did, forcing Sir Lucien to return Lady Anne's daughter. You are too modest to ever speak of it yourself, so I could not help—" Briggs squirmed beneath Mandell's glare. "I am sorry, my lord. I am a rattle-pated fool."

"So you are. And a dead bore besides. Good night, sir." Mandell set off again. He was annoyed past bearing to discover Briggs still dogging his steps. He drew in a sharp breath, but was forestalled by Briggs saying, "It will do you no good, my lord. You may insult me as you please. But I shan't leave you."

"Indeed?" Mandell said with a dangerous softness.

Briggs looked a little frightened, but he held his ground. "I—I have been observing you. You do not seem yourself this evening. I would not be any kind of a friend if I let you go off alone in this state."

"You are not my friend, you encroaching idiot. I don't want your damned friendship."

"I know that, my lord," Briggs said quietly. "But the choice is not yours. I would not presume to ask what is troubling you—"

"How very wise of you."

"But I do not think you should be wandering the streets this way when you are so distracted. It is not safe. The Hook was seen abroad again last night. He robbed two men near the Temple Bar."

"And you mean to protect me from him and other such brigands. How touching."

"I would do my best, my lord."

"Go back to your club, Briggs, or go home or anywhere else you damn well choose. Just get the devil away from me."

Mandell was thunderstruck when Briggs shook his head. "You may curse me or mill me down, but there is nothing you can do to prevent me following you."

Briggs's plump chin set into an attitude of amazing stubbornness, his brown eyes filled with unwavering devotion. Mandell took a menacing step forward, but Briggs did not flinch from the expected blow.

Mandell heaved an exasperated sigh, but found himself unable to proceed further. He turned away with an angry shrug.

"Very well," he snarled. "Follow me to hell if you choose. But I give you fair warning. You'd best be able to look out for yourself when we get there."

And Mandell strode away without another backward glance.

* * *

The Running Cat tavern near Covent Garden was not precisely hell, but close enough. A haze of smoke blanketed the dingy taproom, half obscuring the group of coarse men dicing at one of the tables. A buxom serving wench slapped away the hand of a bold customer while an old sailor slumped in a corner over his bottle of gin. The pipe falling from his slack lips seemed in danger of setting the entire place afire.

But the den of noise, stifling heat, and stale beer made little impression upon Mandell, no more than did the scantily clad woman who had settled herself upon his knee. She possessed a hardened kind of prettiness, her long black hair spilling about her half-bare shoulders, her expression as weary and jaded as Mandell himself. She pressed kisses against his neck with a practiced skill and nibbled at his ear, but Mandell struggled to focus on the murky darkness beyond one of the tavern's narrow windows. How many more hours would it be until dawn, he wondered. How long until he was exhausted or drunk enough to find the oblivion of dreamless sleep?

He sought to reach past the wench nuzzling him, groping toward the table to find his glass of whiskey again, but she stopped him, murmuring, "I've got a little room upstairs, m'lord, an' it would please you to bear me company there."

She began to undo the buttons of his shirt with a kind of rough impatience. It was then that Mandell realized his frock coat and cravat were missing, but he had no notion what he had done with them over the course of the evening. The girl slipped her hand inside his shirt and began to knead the hair-roughened flesh of his chest. Mandell attempted to conjure some stirring of response, but all he could think of was the gentle way Anne had touched him last night in his bed, her slender fingers skimming over him with a kind of wonder. Would he never be able to get images of that lady out of his head? He gritted his teeth, but the vision of Anne's blue eyes persisted. The cloying odor of the black-haired woman's perfume repulsed him. With an oath, he thrust the doxy off his knee.

She staggered a little, but regained her balance. Her full

lips curved into a sullen pout. "Did I do something wrong, m'lord?"

It was a painful echo of the same thing Anne had said to him.

"No!" Mandell snapped. He groped about for his purse. In this place, he was astonished he had not already been relieved of it.

"You aren't the first man who ever got hisself too drunk to perform," the girl said. "But there are other things I could do to—"

Mandell cut off her suggestion by shoving a handful of guineas at her. "Go upstairs and try sleeping for a change."

The girl regarded him with surprise, then shrugged and took the money. As she sashayed away from him, Mandell leaned his head back against the rim of his chair and closed his eyes.

He had no idea how he had got himself to this place or even what else he had been doing this evening. He had foggy memories of White's, lurching along in a hackney cab, frequenting some other gaming hells that all blurred into one. He had stumbled along some refuse-strewn back street and rousted a shopkeeper from his bed to . . . Mandell believed he had bought something, but that was absurd. What would he have wanted to purchase at this hour of night?

Massaging the bridge of his nose with his fingertips, he frowned, beginning to feel the throbbing effects of the amount of spirits he had consumed. He was drunk, but not drunk enough to blot out the things he most wanted to forget—Anne, his grandfather, the nigglings of the ages-old nightmare that still threatened to claim him if he dared to sleep.

Mandell forced his eyes open and realized someone was hovering over him. Lancelot Briggs, wearing that whipped puppy look that Mandell so despised.

"Damme," Mandell growled. "You still here? I thought I'd finally lost you back . . . back in—well, somewhere."

"No, my lord." Briggs perched himself on the edge of

the wooden chair opposite Mandell. He had Mandell's frock coat and cravat draped over his arm.

Struggling to an upright position, Mandell demanded, "So what're you about now? Applying for a post as my valet?"

"No, I am simply trying to make sure you leave here without misplacing anything." Briggs regarded him hopefully. "My lord is ready to go home now, perhaps?"

"And perhaps not," Mandell said, locating his whiskey glass. "What's the matter, Briggs? Are you not enjoying yourself?"

"No, I—I don't like it here."

"Surely you are not afraid? The bold Sir Lancelot who once encountered the Hook himself, who has pledged to aid in that villain's capture and eventual hanging?"

"Don't taunt me, Mandell. I am frightened and I am not ashamed to admit it. There are all manner of evil wretches hanging about this part of town. Especially that soldier over there by the rum keg. He has a wicked-looking scar on his chin and he has been staring at us in a most suspicious manner."

Mandell bestirred himself enough to glance in that direction. He saw no one but a scullery boy in a greasy apron.

"You're imagining things, Briggs," he scoffed. "Have another whiskey. If you're going to hallucinate, you might as well be as drunk as I am."

Briggs declined. He drew forth his pocket watch. Snapping open the gold case, he consulted it with a weary sigh. "It is not so very late. Maybe we could leave and go call upon your cousin Nick. Yes, that would be the very thing. He would know what to do."

"What the devil would I want with Drummond? I am in no mood for any speeches."

"It only seemed to me that you are not finding much amusement here, either. This hardly is the place for a man of such fastidious tastes as your lordship."

"Ah, that is because you are unfamiliar with the darker side of my nature, Briggs." Mandell took a gulp of the whiskey. It was vile stuff, but his palate had gone dead so it scarce mattered. "I have bad blood, y'know."

"Then maybe you need to see a doctor. I have heard being bled a little helps when a man falls into these black humors."

Mandell gave a snort of mirthless laughter. "I'd have to slit my damned throat."

Briggs paled with alarm. "Oh, no, pray, my lord. Don't even jest about such a thing."

As Mandell reached to refill his glass, Briggs pleaded, "I think your lordship has had too much to drink. You have consumed enough to have felled an ordinary man."

"But then I am not an ordinary man, Briggs. I am the marquis of Mandell."

Mandell splashed some whiskey into the glass and started to raise it in a mocking salute when he was distracted by a sudden commotion. The buxom blond serving wench stumbled into Briggs's chair, emitting a shrill protest as she fled to escape the customer who had been harassing her.

"No, I won't be after going upstairs with you. You are a deal too rough, sir."

"I'll get a lot rougher, you little bitch, if you don't do as I say."

The familiar snarling accent grated upon Mandell's ear. He looked up slowly, focusing on the girl's tormentor. Staggering across the room in pursuit was Lucien Fairhaven, flushed, sweating, and stinking of gin. Mandell had not seen Fairhaven since he had permitted the man to stalk out of Brooks's unscathed. He remember regretting that Sir Lucien escaped so lightly for all the misery he had caused Anne. A regret that Mandell was surprised to realize still gnawed at him.

Fairhaven closed in upon the blond girl, seizing her wrist and causing her to cry out, "Ow, let me go." Her predicament evoked not the slightest ripple of interest in the crowded taproom. Sir Lucien dealt the wench an openhanded slap and started dragging her toward the stairs.

"I believe the woman asked you to release her, Fairhaven," Mandell called out. It was a slurred imitation of his usual icy tone, but it had the desired effect.

Lucien twisted around, peering in Mandell's direction. He was startled enough to let go of the girl. Clutching her reddened cheek, she whirled and fled up the stairs. Fairhaven made no effort to follow, his attention now fixed upon Mandell. He took a wavering step toward the table, his bloodshot eyes dilated with unmistakable hatred.

"Oh, no!" Mandell heard Briggs moan softly, but he ignored him, never taking his eyes off Fairhaven's approach.

"Well, well, the high and mighty Lord Mandell and his favorite toady." Lank strands of dirty blond hair tumbled across Lucien's brow as he leaned across the table. "What brings you to this part of town, m'lord? Still playing the knight errant. Championing whores now?"

"Please, Sir Lucien," Briggs piped up. "We don't want any trouble."

"There isn't going to be any trouble," Mandell said. He was only vaguely aware of how hard his hands were gripping the edge of the table. "Sir Lucien is just leaving. He knows I find his company most . . . distasteful."

"Leave? The devil I will!" Sir Lucien thumped his fist against the table, rattling the glasses. "What're you going to do, Mandell? Threaten me with your glove? Do you think I am afraid of you?"

"No, you appear to have finally located your courage. Where was it? At the bottom of a gin bottle?"

Fairhaven's face darkened to an alarming hue, but to Mandell's surprise, it was his own wrist that Briggs seized in a restraining grasp.

"Oh, don't, Mandell. Can you not see the fellow is drunk? He is not worth your trouble."

Mandell shook himself free of Briggs with an irritated gesture. What was Briggs talking about? He was behaving as though Mandell were the one likely to lose control. He was no Nick Drummond, possessed of a volatile temper. Everyone knew that the marquis of Mandell had ice in his veins.

Sir Lucien straightened, swaggering a little. "That's right,

Mandell. Mustn't create a scandal to disturb the fair and virtuous Anne. Why aren't you with her tonight? Could it be that after all your heroic efforts, you couldn't get beneath her skirts after all?"

The ice in Mandell's veins pierced and burned. He shoved back from the table. "Don't you even dare to speak her name, you whoreson dog!"

Sir Lucien's face twisted with an ugly satisfaction. "Whoreson dog?" he taunted. "A rather common insult coming from you, my lord. What's happened to the famous cool wits? Could it be my dear sister-in-law has addled them?"

Mandell's breath quickened. He felt his heart commence an erratic and savage rhythm. Ignoring Briggs's feeble attempts to restrain him, he struggled to his feet.

"Mandell!" Briggs's protest was lost in Sir Lucien's bark of harsh laughter.

"You fool!" Fairhaven smirked at Mandell. "You could have had her in your power, but you didn't know how to use it, did you? When I had the child in my possession, I actually brought the proud Anne to her knees."

"You what?" Mandell hissed.

"Didn't she ever tell you? She knelt down to me in the gutter, begging, crying for the return of her brat. And I spurned her, left her groveling in the murk where she—"

The rest of Sir Lucien's boast went unfinished as Mandell's fist smashed against his jaw. Briggs shrieked as Fairhaven stumbled back, his mouth smeared with blood. A low growl of rage escaped Sir Lucien and he lunged for Mandell.

But the ice inside Mandell shattered, splintering into myriad white-hot shards. Before Sir Lucien could strike, Mandell leapt upon him, dragging him to the floor of the tavern to the accompaniment of crashing tables and shattering glass.

Lucien got off a blow that glanced off Mandell's cheek. Mandell felt nothing but the force of his own blind fury. He drew back his fist again and again. Fairhaven's head snapped back, his features slick with blood.

"Stop! Mandell!" Briggs cried out. "You'll kill him." But his frantic plea was all but drowned out by harsher voices, cheers of encouragement coming from cruel mouths. Greedy eyes gleamed like the demons of hell.

Lucien went limp, his eyes fluttering closed, but Mandell could not seem to check the beast that raged within him. His breath coming in ragged gasps, he drew back his arm to strike again. But something struck him hard from behind, his world exploding in a flash of bright light and pain.

Mandell wavered and fell, darkness misting before his eyes, a darkness that ebbed and flowed, in waves of agony. He no longer knew where he was or what was happening to him. Dimly, he realized that he was lying on some hard surface and cold water was being dashed against his face. He tried to turn away from it and open his eyes, but the effort proved too great. From a great distance, he heard a man's voice sobbing.

"Mandell? I'm sorry. I didn't mean to hit you so hard. Please open your eyes. Say something. Oh, dear God, I've killed you."

Killed him? Mandell's pain-fogged mind latched upon the word. Was he dying then? Surely there was peace to be found in dying, not these sharp spirals of pain, this terrifying feeling of being suffocated in the dark.

"You'll be all right," the voice promised. "I'll get you out of here. I'll get you to a doctor."

No. Mandell tried to form the word, but it would not come. He wanted no doctor. There was only one person he wanted, needed. The thought pierced his haze of pain with astonishing clarity.

"Anne," he whispered. "Take me . . . to Anne."

Then, with a great sigh, he allowed the darkness to claim him.

Chapter 13

Anne had no idea what time it was, only that it was well past midnight. Bathed in the glow of the lamp in the nursery, she cuddled her daughter in her lap, attempting to lull Norrie back asleep by reading to her from her favorite book of myths.

Disturbed by another of her coughing spells, Norrie had had a restless night. So had Anne, for vastly different reasons. Exhausted as she was, she felt grateful for this opportunity to snuggle Norrie's warm little frame close, to breathe in the sweet scent of her silky curls. Seated in the old wing chair, watching the fire in the grate burn low, restored some sense of normalcy to her world. Heaven knew Anne needed that after what had happened last night.

She was tormented by the memory of struggling to get dressed in the darkness of Mandell's bedchamber, bewildered by his abrupt change of heart, even more bewildered by her own. Of a sudden, it had been Mandell remembering the proprieties, commanding her to leave him when she had been more than willing to stay. The recollection left her feeling confused and shamed, angry with him and with herself.

"Mama." Norrie tugged at the sleeve of Anne's dressing gown, reclaiming her straying thoughts. "You stopped reading again."

"What? I'm sorry, my love." Anne deposited a kiss upon her daughter's smooth brow, then glanced down the page with a frustrated sigh, trying to relocate her place in the text.

". . . and because Lady Persephone had eaten the seeds of the pomegranate," Anne read, "she was ever after obliged to spend six months of the year in Hades's underground kingdom."

"Autumn and winter," Norrie murmured against Anne's shoulder. "Do you think it made Lady Persifee sad to stay with Hades?"

"I really don't know, Norrie," Anne said wearily, attempting to go on with the tale, but Norrie persisted.

"I don't think so," said Norrie. "I think p'rhaps she did not really want to leave the underground kingdom forever. P'rhaps she started to like the dark lord a little and that's why she ate the seeds."

"Nonsense, Eleanor." Anne was disconcerted to find herself thinking not of Hades, but of Mandell. "I am sure the lady was merely desperate with . . . with hunger. She could not have truly wished to stay with someone that wicked."

"Why do you think the dark lord behaved so naughty, Mama, forcing Lady Persifee to go away with him?

Anne grimaced. "I've often wondered the same thing myself."

Norrie's small brow furrowed in frowning concentration, then she brightened. "He must have just been very lonely there in his dark kingdom with no one to love him."

"That is still no excuse for—" Anne brought herself up short as she remembered what she and Norrie were really discussing, a man of myth, not one of flesh and blood. If Mandell so mastered Anne's thoughts that she was reduced to arguing with a seven-year-old child, then she was indeed in a wretched state.

She shifted uncomfortably upon the chair, and when Norrie started to pipe up again, Anne silenced her with a swift hug. "If you don't stop interrupting me, Eleanor Rose Fairhaven, we will be awake reading when the sun comes up and Aunt Lily will scold us both."

"Aunt Lily never sees the sun. She's always still sleeping," Norrie giggled. But she subsided, nestling back against Anne's shoulder.

Anne managed to get through the rest of the tale, intoning the words without making much sense of them. When she had finished she was relieved to see Norrie's eyelids looking heavier. Casting the book aside, Anne lifted her daughter in her arms and carried her over to lay her in her small bed.

"But I'm still not sleepy, Mama," Norrie mumbled as she burrowed deeper against the pillow. She groped about as though feeling for something, a movement that Anne had already anticipated. She bent down, retrieved Lady Persifee from where the doll had slipped to the carpet, and placed the bedraggled object within Norrie's reach.

The child gathered the doll to her with a contented sigh. By the time Anne had tucked the coverlet about her and kissed her cheek, Norrie's eyes were already closed. The child appeared likely to rest quietly now, untroubled by that persistent cough. Anne was glad that Lily's doctor was scheduled to visit in the morning.

Straightening, she rubbed the small of her back. It was more than time that she retired to her own bedchamber and got some sleep herself. As she moved to make sure the fire on the hearth was properly banked, Anne noticed that it had begun to rain again. The storm had ended hours ago, but the droplets continued to beat out a monotonous tattoo upon the nursery window. The sound was dreary and depressing without the majestic clash of thunder and lightning.

As quiet and dreary as the entire day had been. Anne gave herself a brisk shake, annoyed with her own dissatisfied thoughts. What was the matter with her? She should be content. Her little daughter was safely back in her care. She had nothing more to worry about, no dangerous midnight quests to undertake, no more reckless pledges to redeem, no more marquis stalking her with wicked intent in his dark eyes.

She ought to be grateful instead of feeling as restless as a sleeping princess only half awakened by a kiss because the prince drew back before he had properly finished the job.

What an absurd thought that was. Mandell was certainly no fairy-tale prince simply because he had experienced one fleeting noble impulse. He was an unscrupulous rake who had been doing his best to seduce her and had nearly succeeded. Why did she have trouble remembering that fact?

That was as unanswerable as some of Norrie's wonderings about the myth of Persephone and Hades. Anne caught herself musing over the child's innocent remark.

Perhaps she started to like the dark lord a little.

Like him? Anne frowned. How did one begin to like a dark menacing stranger when all one knew of him was the power of his kiss to turn one's veins to molten fire, his merest touch enough to make one forget all one had ever learned about the virtues of being a perfect lady?

She could not speak for Persephone, but as for her own dark lord, Anne could not begin to comprehend him. How could one man be at once so kind and so cruel, so mockingly aloof and so passionately tender?

Mandell could have taken her at once last night. Anne had expected him to do so. What she had never expected was such patience, such gentle effort to stir her own desires. He had even tried to make her feel beautiful in his arms. And he had come so close.

And then, when he had her more than willing to do anything he asked, he had wrenched himself away, snapped at her to get out. What was it he had said—something about stumbling over his conscience and finding it damnably inconvenient.

"It would have been much more convenient if you had happened upon your conscience a little sooner, my lord," Anne murmured indignantly. Before he had put her through such agonies of apprehension waiting for him to claim his due from her, before he had summoned her to him in that humiliating fashion like some mighty sultan beckoning to his harem girl, before he had taught her what it was like to experience passion in a man's arms.

Why had he drawn back at the last possible moment? Did the wicked marquis truly possess some scruples, a finer side to his nature? Or when it came down to it, had he simply not found her desirable enough? That thought gave her small comfort, but at least it was one explanation for his behavior that she could comprehend.

She sighed. The clock upon the nursery bookcase told her that it was now past three in the morning. She was beginning to fear she would be up until dawn fretting over Mandell's puzzling behavior when she was interrupted by a rap on the nursery door. Alarmed lest Norrie be disturbed, Anne hastened across the room, but the door was already opening. Bettine thrust her head across the threshold, calling, "Milady?"

Anne frowned, nodding toward the sleeping child and raising a finger to her lips. She whispered. "Bettine, what are you doing up? I told you I had no more need of you."

"Oh, madam, I thought I would find you in here," the maid said. She appeared far too agitated to keep her voice down. "You'd best come belowstairs at once. There's such a commotion."

"What's the matter?"

"Some drunken lunatic has forced his way into the front hall. And he won't leave. He kept calling for you and he nearly knocked poor Mr. Firken down. Now the fellow seems to be in danger of passing out and Mr. Firken doesn't know what is to be done with him."

Lucien was the first dread thought that popped into Anne's head. Who else did she know capable of such barbaric behavior? If he was in one of his drunken rages, Anne feared that neither her sister's elderly butler nor the footmen would be capable of subduing him. Lucien was adept at bullying servants even when sober.

What could have possibly induced him to come here? Anne remembered the last time she had seen Lucien, and his threats of vengeance. She stole a look at her sleeping child and shivered, then drew herself up sharply.

"Bettine, I want you to stay here with Norrie," she said, "and lock the door."

"Oh, milady!" Bettine's eyes went wide. "What do you think is going to happen?"

"I don't know, but I am taking no chances. Just do as I say. Lock that door and open it for no one but me."

Bettine nodded, her face going pale with fear. She needed no further urging and when Anne stepped out of the room, she heard the lock being fastened with a resounding click.

Her heart thudding with trepidation, Anne steeled herself to remain calm. She did not know exactly what she was going to do, but thoughts of the pistol buried in the bottom of her wardrobe chased through her head.

But as she tiptoed along the landing above the stairs, she heard none of the uproar that she anticipated. The hall was strangely silent. Perhaps by some miracle Lucien had already been persuaded to leave.

Peering over the imposing mahogany balustrade into the shadows below, she saw Lily's butler, clad in his nightclothes, bending over one of the high-backed chairs near the fireplace. A pair of masculine legs clad in dark breeches and Hessian boots stretched toward the hearth. The face of the man slumped in the chair was obscured from view, but one thing was certain. Those legs were too long to belong to Lucien.

Anne did not know whether to be relieved or more alarmed. Whoever the intruder was, he appeared to have been calmed for the moment.

"Firken?" Anne called as she crept toward the top stair.

The butler straightened. Stepping into the pool of candle-light, his dignity appeared rumpled, his nightcap askew. "Oh, milady, I am sorry to have disturbed you in this matter, but the countess has not yet returned from the rout she attended tonight and I did not know what else to do."

"What is amiss?" Anne asked as she started down the stairs. The butler hastened forward. Anne had never seen the old man so disconcerted.

"You must forgive me, Lady Fairhaven. If it had been anybody but his lordship, I would not have let him in. I would have summoned the footmen to throw him into the street, but one cannot treat the marquis in such a fashion."

His lordship? The marquis? Anne felt her heart give an erratic leap. She brushed past the butler as she raced the rest of the way down the steps. The candle left burning in the wall sconce illuminated the face of the man sprawled back in the chair, those blade-sharp features, the aristocratic profile that possessed a certain hauteur even in the marquis's disheveled state.

"Mandell!" she gasped. Anne had to blink several times to be certain she was not dreaming.

His eyes were closed but he stirred a little at the sound of his name, groaning and rolling his head against the back of the chair. He was clad only in his breeches, shirt and waistcoat soaked to the skin, his dark hair plastered to his brow.

"He is very drunk, I am afraid," Firken said, clucking his tongue.

"I can see that," Anne replied, recovering from her initial shock. After last night, she had not expected to see the cool, arrogant marquis again, and certainly not collapsing in Lily's hall. "What is he doing here?"

"I don't know. He asked for you, my lady. Gentlemen will do odd things when they are in their cups. But I am sure you will agree, the important thing is to avoid any unpleasantness. One would not wish to offend a man as important as my lord Mandell."

"Offend *him*!" Anne exclaimed. Once more Mandell had turned up when she least expected him, giving her a dreadful fright. As if that scene in his bedchamber had not been enough, now he must arrive on her doorstep at three in the morning, wreaking havoc with her emotions all over again.

Anger coursed through her. Ignoring the butler's pleas for caution, she strode over and shook Mandell.

"My lord?" she demanded. "Wake up. At once! Do you hear me?"

He gave another moan. His eyes flickered open, his brow furrowing as though the effort cost him a great deal. He gazed up at her, confusion in those dark depths. Then his lips twitched in a lopsided smile.

"An angel? 'stonishing," he mumbled. "Funny . . . always thought . . . end in other place."

"I always thought so, too. But you are not dead yet, my lord. Don't you even know where you are? Who I am?"

"Sorrow . . . my Lady Sorrow."

"Lady Fairhaven," Anne snapped. "You must try to come to your senses, my lord, and go home. You are quite drunk. You have come to my sister's house by mistake."

Mandell shook his head, the movement causing him to wince. After a struggle, he managed to sit upright, rubbing one hand over his face.

Anne gave a horrified gasp. There was dried blood on his sleeve and his hand . . . that strong, beautiful, elegant hand was hideously bruised and swollen.

"Dear God, Mandell!" Anne took his hand carefully in her own. "What have you done to yourself? You are hurt."

"Of no 'portance, Sorrow." He sighed, and there was a weariness in his eyes that went far beyond the amount of drink he must have consumed and whatever paths of hell he had been stalking this evening. "Had to see you one last time. Had to give you this." He raised his other hand and pressed something cool and smooth between her fingers.

Anne stared at the object he had given her. A cry of astonishment escaped her. It was the gold locket, the one bearing Norrie's likeness that Anne had been obliged to abandon in that dreary pawnshop. She cupped the precious treasure in the palm of her hand. Wonderingly, she raised her eyes to Mandell.

"My locket. You got it back for me. I—I don't understand. How did you . . . I mean, why would you bother?"

But Mandell was beyond answering any more questions. His eyes drifted closed and he swayed dangerously forward. Anne did her best to steady him, but he sagged against her, his weight threatening to drag her to the floor.

"Firken!" she cried.

Even with the old man's help, there was no way to prevent Mandell collapsing onto the cold marble. He sprawled on his back, his face ice white.

"Out cold for sure this time," the butler lamented. "Perhaps I should go rouse Thomas and one of the other footmen. We could send his lordship home in the countess's carriage."

"No!" Anne said, surprised by the vehemence in her own

voice. "It is raining outside and the marquis is already soaked through. Would you have him catch his death?"

"No, milady. But what is to be done with him then?"

Anne glanced at Mandell's still features, the lines of pain that unconsciousness failed to smooth from his brow. She clutched the locket tighter in her hand. She did not know how or why, but she found herself in the wicked marquis's debt again. The least she could do was offer him a haven until he was more himself.

Her shoulders squared with sudden decision. "Have the footmen convey my lord upstairs to the front bedchamber."

"I don't know whether that would be fitting, my lady." Firken said. "If only the countess would come home! She is so adept at handling these extraordinary situations."

"More so than I, I daresay. But Lily is not here." Anne brushed the damp locks of hair back from Mandell's brow and added more softly, "It would seem I am obliged to look after the dark lord myself."

Anne found herself alone in the bedchamber with Mandell. She could not help reflecting upon the irony of that as she arranged a pitcher of cold water, ointment, and strips of linen upon the dressing table. During the course of her very proper marriage to Gerald, she had rarely been closeted thus with her husband, perhaps twice a month. But she had seen Mandell abed twice in as many days.

Anne supposed that for propriety's sake she should have had one of the servants remain with her while she attended Mandell. But she experienced a surprising protective urge toward the unconscious marquis. It had been bad enough allowing the footmen and Firken to strip Mandell out of his wet garments and thrust him into the butler's spare nightshirt. She did not wish to expose the proud Mandell to any more of the young men's snickering comments or the older butler's disapproval than was necessary.

And as for her maid, Bettine had been terrified when she had been informed the lunatic stranger was being tucked up in the best front bedchamber. Bettine had dove for her own bed, pulling the covers up over her head, behaving as if

Anne had brought something wild and dangerous in out of the night.

Which perhaps she had, Anne thought as she picked up the candle and drew closer to the oak bedstead with its heavy brocade hangings. Mandell made a formidable presence, even sprawled out flat on his back.

He was no longer resting with that deathlike stillness that had so alarmed Anne in the hall below. He had begun to toss and turn upon the pillow, twitching the sheets into a tangle below his midriff, the nightshirt pulled taut against the muscular contours of his chest.

The sight brought back a flood of memories from last night and Anne felt her cheeks heat. Gingerly she tugged on the sheet, managing to get it up to his shoulders. But when she tried to bathe his injured hand, he pulled away from her, mumbling a protest.

She was able to do little more than clean the dried blood from his knuckles as Mandell began to thrash about in earnest. A darkness settled over his features. That was the only way Anne could describe the tension that corded his jaw and caused deep slashes to appear alongside his mouth.

Anne knew little about what it was like to drink oneself into such a state, but had heard it laughingly described as a condition when one felt no pain. Yet Mandell seemed to be experiencing a great deal of it, a guttural cry breaching his lips.

Perching herself on the edge of the bed, Anne sought to soothe him, bathing his brow with cool water, murmuring some of the same absurd comforting sounds she often used with Norrie. Mandell looked younger somehow, more vulnerable when unguarded by his customary mask of cynicism.

She was relieved when he quieted at her touch and she continued to stroke his cheek. She was finally able to apply the ointment to his hand, bandaging the swollen knuckles with the strips of linen.

Brushing her fingers one last time across his brow, she checked for fever. His brow felt almost too cool, damp and clammy with perspiration.

Even though she knew he could not hear her, she murmured. "Try to rest now, my lord. Sleep is what you need. I fear you will not be feeling quite well when you awaken, but I will need to talk to you."

She touched the locket which she had fastened about her neck. "I know you do not usually condescend to answer questions, but this is one time you must oblige me."

She eased herself away from the bed and reached for the candle. But a startled cry escaped her when Mandell suddenly lashed out. His eyes flew open wide and he seized hold of her wrist.

"Don't," he said hoarsely. "Don't . . . go."

Anne took a tremulous breath, trying to recover from the fright he had given her. "But I must, my lord. It will be dawn in a few hours and you must try to—"

"Don't go out there!" His fingers tightened on her wrist to a painful extent. He stared up at her, his expression so wild it caused Anne's heart to pound.

"They'll kill you," he said. He stared straight at her, but his eyes were glazed and Anne realized he was in the grip of some delirium. She sought to pry his fingers away.

"You are dreaming, my lord. There is no one here to harm me or you. You are at my sister's house. Do you not remember?"

He wrenched her forward as he pushed up onto one elbow. "No!" His voice was low, savage.

"Please, Mandell. Let go. You are hurting me."

"They will destroy you as . . . as did her."

"Destroyed who?" Anne cried. Struggling to make sense of his madness, she wrenched herself free.

"Mother."

Anne had never before heard a single word breathed with such anguish. Her own fear dissolved before the torment that twisted his lips and haunted his eyes.

"Mandell, you are having a nightmare," Anne said. "What happened to your mother was a long time ago. It is over."

"Never over. Ev-every time close my eyes. C-can't get out. Can't save her."

Anne managed to ease him back down onto the pillow, but a ragged sob tore through him, a despairing cry that Anne seemed to feel echo in her own heart.

He clutched at the sleeve of her dressing gown. "Dark . . . too dark," he rasped. "Help me. Don't . . . leave me."

"I won't. I promise." Anne ran her fingers back through his hair. "I am right here."

Her assurances soothed him enough that he closed his eyes, but he continued to cry out, tossing and turning, murmuring of a secret pain Anne was certain that no one had ever been meant to hear.

She knew that when he was once more himself, the haughty Mandell might never forgive her for this, witnessing the tear that leaked out of the corner of his eye, the childlike sob that wracked his frame.

But what could she do? Once more she had given him her promise. Perhaps she could bring him no comfort, but she could not leave him like this, either. Leaning forward, she pressed a soft kiss across his brow. Clinging to his hand, Anne watched helplessly as Mandell descended into his own dark world.

Chapter 14

❦

Mandell awoke to bright sunlight stabbing at his eyes. With a low groan, he flung one arm across his face, shielding himself from the intensity. Despite the warmth of the rays, he felt chilled. His eyes mere slits, he studied his surroundings, the costly brocade bedhangings, the heavy oak pillars of the bed, the dressing table with its jar of ointment and bandagings. All quite unfamiliar.

He shivered and groped for the coverlet, at the same time groping for his memory.

Where the devil am I?

He scowled, then nearly cried aloud, the simple act of contracting his brow making him conscious of the pain exploding inside his head. Damn! He felt as though someone had been using his skull for a blacksmith's anvil.

Gingerly, he attempted to explore his forehead for any sign of injury and was further mystified by the linen cocoon wrapped about his hand. Had he been in some sort of an accident?

Moistening his dry lips, he grimaced at the feel of his own tongue, thick as a wad of cotton. His splitting head and the stale taste in his mouth were sensations he recognized.

He had not been in any accident. This disaster was one of his own making, his and too many tumblers full of brandy. He emitted a soft sigh, part disgust, part agony. It had been many years since he had drunk himself into such a state, not since the uncultivated days of his youth. And never had he gone so far that he had awakened in a strange bed, wearing someone else's nightshirt, not even knowing where he was, much less what he had been doing.

As he flexed his sore hand, he wondered what manner of folly he had been guilty of last night. It made his head swim even to try to think about it. Confusing scenes flashed before his eyes; the quarrel with his grandfather, telling Hastings not to wait up, setting off for White's determined to drown his black thoughts.

Apparently he had done a good job. He could recall nothing after his arrival at White's. His memory was like a dark mirror that had shattered into a dozen shards. Mandell had a strong foreboding that gathering those shards would prove an agonizing task, one that might leave him cut and bleeding.

Managing to prop himself up on one elbow, his bleary gaze tracked round the massive four-poster bed. He supposed he could have ended up in worse places; a brothel, some stinking tavern, the gutter. This bedchamber belonged to a fashionable household, one of wealth and elegance.

But whose? And how did he arrive here? He could not remember. So what did he do now? Attempt to summon a servant? He flattered himself that he could handle any situation with aplomb. But he was not certain that even the haughty marquis of Mandell was equal to demanding a hot bath, his clothes, and by the bye, could you kindly tell me where I am.

Mandell was not aware that he had muttered these last words aloud until a small voice piped up, "You are at my aunt Lily's."

The sound, soft as it was, startled him into jerking upright. A grave mistake. His head spun and a wave of nausea swept over him. It took all of his iron control to suppress the desire to be sick, to bring the whirling room back into focus.

A focus that settled upon a diminutive figure at the foot of his bed. Mandell wondered if he were having a hallucination. The little girl stared back at him through solemn blue eyes. She could have been an apparition, all pink and gold, garbed in delicate white muslin, a blue sash knotted at her slender waist. Except that Mandell had seen this fairy child before, locked behind the cruel iron gates of an unkempt garden.

"Eleanor Rose Fairhaven," Mandell said in dumbfounded accents, as though he needed to convince himself of that fact. "Anne's daughter."

The child must have perceived this as a form of introduction, for she dropped into a graceful curtsy. "Good afternoon, sir," she said, and then inquired politely, "S'cuse me, but have you lost your wits?"

"That is a strong possibility," Mandell murmured, feeling quite dazed. Norrie Fairhaven . . . If she was in truth standing at the foot of his bed and he had not run quite insane, then at least he knew where his drunken progress must have ended.

At the Countess Sumner's, Lily Rosemoor's doorstep.

No, not Lily's. Anne's. Mandell stifled a groan. He would have preferred the gutter.

"I heard Bettine telling cook about you," Norrie continued. "That you burst into our front hall like a luny-tic." The little girl frowned as she struggled to pronounce the next words. "Bettine says you are a fitting candi-ake for Bedlam."

"A woman of vast perception." He winced. "Just who is this Bettine?"

"Mama's maid. She helps take care of me. She is very kind most of the time, but she did think we should have throwed you back into the streets."

And what did Mama think? Mandell longed to ask, but why should he care what Anne would have thought? It only irritated him to realize that he did.

The little girl's shoulders shook as she struggled to suppress a cough. Norrie crept around the side of the bed as though she approached some dangerous but fascinating beast. Mandell could easily have outstared the most haughty of duchesses. But something about the child's steady regard unnerved him. It was almost as though those clear blue eyes could peer straight through to his soul, not a pretty sight for anyone, let alone a little girl.

Drawing the coverlet up to his chin, he sagged back against the headboard. In his current state of misery, he would have told anyone else to get the devil away from him. Instead he surprised himself by murmuring gently, "Begging your pardon, Miss Fairhaven. I am not precisely up to receiving visitors at the moment."

"You look very sick," Norrie agreed. "You have tiny little black hairs growing out of your face."

Mandell rubbed his hand along his unshaven jaw. "That is one of the consequences of calling upon a gentleman before he has had recourse to his razor. Surely you must have seen your own papa—" Mandell broke off as Norrie's face fell. He silently cursed himself for reminding the child of the father she had lost.

"I never saw my own papa very much," Norrie said in woebegone accents. "I was sick too many times and my papa had a 'version to sickness."

"Did he, indeed," Mandell said, thinking God rot the saintly Gerald.

"I get the sniffles and cough too much." As though to demonstrate, another hacking sound erupted from her throat which she fought by stuffing her hand against her mouth. "You see? It makes my face turn too red. Most un-un-'tractive, Papa used to say."

"He was quite mistaken. Your face is not red at all, but a most becoming shade of pink. You are a very pretty young lady, Miss Eleanor."

Norrie beamed. "Thank you. You are very pretty, too."

Mandell started to chuckle, but it hurt too much. "In my present state? I hardly think so."

"Not pretty, but handsome," Norrie corrected. "Those dark bristly hairs make you look fierce and your eyes are red. I used to pretend my uncle was the king of the underworld, but you would make a better dark lord than him."

"I always had a strong presentiment that I looked like the devil. But thank you for confirming it, young lady."

"Not the devil. The god of the underworld. Don't you know who he is?"

"Yes, Hades." Mandell pressed his fingertips to his

throbbing brow. "But I am not quite up for a mythological discussion at the moment and I think you had better return to your—"

"You read myths, too?" Norrie wriggled in delight. "Which ones?"

"All of them, I expect, but—"

"Uncle Lucien never did."

Lucien. Out of all the child's prattle, the single word struck Mandell like a blow. He stared down at his injured hand and closed his eyes as one of the shards of memory slipped into place. The smoke-filled tavern, Lucien Fairhaven crumpled beneath him, the sickening sound of fist connecting to bone, the blood . . .

Lost in the memory of that grim scene, he realized that a small hand was patting his where it lay extended along the coverlet. Opening his eyes, he found Norrie peering at him, her small brow furrowed with concern.

"Are you feeling very poorly?" she asked. "There is a doctor coming."

What ailed him was past the power of any physician to cure. To the child, Mandell merely said, "I don't need a doctor."

"Neither do I, but Mama thinks I do because of my coughing." Norrie fretted her lower lip. "What would you do if a doctor came to see you and you didn't want him to?"

In a painful effort, Mandell arched one of his brows. "I would simply say to him, 'Sir, you can retire at once.' "

After absorbing this with intense concentration, Norrie pranced over to peer at herself in the mirror suspended above the dressing table.

"Sir," she said, "you can be tired at once." She could mimic Mandell's haughty tone to perfection, but his expression gave her more difficulty. After much scrunching and grimacing, she was obliged to take her fingers to press her eyebrow into the upraised position.

For the first time since he had wakened, Mandell felt the inclination to smile. But he tensed as he heard the door opening. From his angle on the bed, he could not see who it was that tiptoed into the room.

He heard a soft gasp, then a feminine voice whispered, "Norrie! What are you doing in here? Come away before you awaken Lord Mandell."

Norrie spun about. "He already woked up by himself, Mama."

Anne. Mandell had not yet steeled himself for encountering her again, especially under such humiliating circumstances. But he had no time to brace himself, for she appeared at the foot of the bed, standing where he had first seen Norrie.

Anne's primrose morning gown rustled softly as she stepped closer. Her honey blond hair was tucked beneath a lace cap, silken wisps of gold caressing her pale cheeks. Deep shadows rimmed her eyes and she looked as though she had not passed a much better night than he.

Their eyes met across the length of the bed and both made haste to look away. Heat washed over Mandell's face. It had been so many years since he had experienced such a thing, it took a moment for him to realize what was happening to him.

Damme! He was blushing.

Anne's hand fluttered to the lace at her throat and she seemed to find it easier to address her daughter. "Norrie, you should not have come in here."

"I only wanted to peek at the strange gentleman, Mama. He is not mad as Bettine says, but very nice. He reads myths, too."

"This is not a proper way to be making Lord Mandell's acquaintance. I want you to go back to the nursery right now."

Norrie's lip quivered at Anne's stern tone, and Mandell spoke up. "I fear the fault was mine. Miss Eleanor kindly came in to inquire after my health, and I kept her engaged in conversation."

Anne looked astonished, but Norrie flashed him a brilliant smile. "It was nice being 'quainted with you, Lord

Man. I will remember how you told me to get rid of the doctor."

"Get rid of . . ." Anne faltered. She shot Mandell such an accusatory look, he made haste to say, "It was good advice only if one is quite well, Miss Eleanor. However, if I had a cough, I would demand that the doctor make me better at once."

"You would?" Norrie asked.

"Indeed, I would."

Looking thoughtful, Norrie left the room, still practicing the trick with her eyebrow. As she passed through the door, she could be heard to say imperiously, "Make me better at once."

After the child had gone, an awkward silence ensued. Mandell found himself thinking of the last time he and Anne had been alone together in a bedchamber, but he struggled to suppress the thought. He had enough aches to torment him without adding the agony of frustrated desire.

Anne gave a faint sigh, shaking her head. "I am sorry if Norrie disturbed you, my lord. I have not yet engaged a governess for her and I fear she has been permitted to run a little wild. I will have to have a discussion with Eleanor about the impropriety of—of—" Her gaze skittered over Mandell's frame stretched beneath the coverlet. "Of invading a gentleman's bedchamber."

Despite his splitting head and sense of embarrassment, Mandell possessed enough of the devil in him to murmur, "That should be a most enlightening discussion. I would love to hear it."

Anne turned a bright pink and took a step nearer to the door. "I am glad to see you looking a bit more fit. I took the liberty of sending word to your household. Your valet has arrived with fresh clothes for you. I will send him in immediately."

As she started to retreat, Mandell called out, "Anne. Wait!"

She hesitated, glancing back at him.

"My head is still not quite clear about exactly what happened last night," he said. "I have a fair idea that I made a nuisance of myself. I understand your maid thinks I should have been thrown back into the street and no doubt she was right. Please convey my thanks to your sister for her forbearance."

"My sister?"

"Yes, I assume that she must have directed her servants to put me to bed and—"

"Lily was not even here when you arrived."

Mandell glanced up sharply at that. Even though his wits felt far from keen at the moment, he perceived a difference in Anne, something so subtle he had not noted it before. He could find none of the condemnation primming her mouth that he had expected. There was a gentleness in her tone, a light in her eyes that was softer than the sunbeams streaming through the window, turning her hair to gold.

"I don't understand," he said.

"Lily did not arrive home until sunrise and—" A tiny smile curved Anne's lips. "Her head was not quite clear, either. She always sings tunes from the Beggar's Opera when she has had a drop too much champagne. Did you not hear her in the hall?"

"Er—no. That was one performance that thankfully I missed. But then who admitted me to the house?"

Anne said nothing. She merely smiled at him again and then slipped out of the room. As Mandell heard the door close behind her, he sank back down into the pillows, feeling more dazed than when he had first regained consciousness.

The drawing room that hosted so many of the countess's balls and other brilliant gatherings stood still and silent in the afternoon. Most of the draperies had been drawn to protect Lily's delicate silk-striped chairs from exposure to the sun. The gilt mirrors, the towering ceiling, and the magnificent chandeliers were all cast into shadow, like part of the scenery on a vast unlit stage.

As Anne wandered aimlessly down the length of the room, she felt much like an actress waiting for the curtain to go up, an actress no longer sure of her part. But this was foolish. Nothing had changed.

Despite all that had happened, Mandell was still ... Mandell, and she was the virtuous Anne. But as Anne fingered the gold chain about her neck and felt the cool weight of the locket hidden beneath the bodice of her gown, she knew that was not true.

Something *had* changed, and she could not say how or when it had begun. Perhaps the moment when he had pressed the locket into her hand. Or had the change come sometime during those hours before dawn, watching Mandell struggle with his own private demons, realizing that the arrogant marquis could ache and bleed like any other man? Or was it when she had seen him being so kind to her little girl?

Anne was not sure. She only knew she would never be able to view the wicked marquis in quite the same way again. As she waited for him, something compelled her to remove her lace cap, allowing her hair to tumble freely about her shoulders. She was considering retiring to change her gown for something a little less matronly when the drawing room's massive double doors were eased open.

Anne expected it to be one of the servants come to inform her that the marquis had emerged from his room and was asking for her. But it was Mandell himself who paused, silhouetted on the threshold. He turned his head, searching the room. Anne felt her heart miss a beat the moment his eyes found hers.

He stepped quietly into the room, drawing the doors closed behind him. A remarkable transformation had taken place during the hour since she had left him. In assuming the clothes his servant had brought—the cravat, the buff-colored breeches, the frock coat of midnight blue—Mandell appeared to have reassumed some of the arrogance of his stance as well. Clean-shaven, his ebony waves of hair swept back, the only sign of his recent misadventure was a certain paleness, his cheekbones standing out in gaunt relief.

Yet as he stalked the length of the room, coming toward

her, his Hessians echoing off the tiled floor, Anne sensed a hesitancy in his manner that had not been there before.

He stopped within an arm's length of where she stood before the French doors leading down into the garden. They stared at each other like two strangers waiting to be introduced, which was absurd. She had nearly been this man's lover.

Nearly . . . Anne had never before realized what a world of regret could be found in a single word.

Mandell said, "I was told I might find you in here, milady. May I speak to you for a few moments?"

"Certainly. I have been hoping—that is, I was expecting you would wish to do so."

"And well you might. Though I scarce know how to begin. Anne, I . . ." He trailed off, grimacing. "It is deuced strange. I can tender the most handsome apologies when I don't mean a word of it. When I want to be sincere, which isn't often, I can't seem to think of a thing to say."

He turned away from her, his arms locked behind his back. The sunlight that filtered in through the French doors played over the bladelike tension of his profile. "I remember enough of what happened last night to realize that I behaved like a complete idiot."

She should have agreed with him. Instead she found herself trying to soothe. "It was no great matter, my lord."

"No great matter? I burst into your sister's house, roaring drunk, assaulted the butler, roused you from your sleep, and passed out on the floor. I expected a box to the ears this morning or at least a lecture on the evils of intemperence."

"I was exasperated with you at first. You have a habit of disconcerting me. I suppose I am getting accustomed to it."

"I am sorry, Anne," he said stiffly. "When I was in such a state, I do not know why I chose to inflict myself upon you, of all people."

"Don't you remember? You came to bring me this." Anne tugged at her gold chain, drawing forth the locket from inside the neckline of her gown.

Mandell stepped closer to examine it. The jewelry seemed more delicate when contrasted to the strength of those long tapering fingers. He opened the locket, exposing the minature of Norrie as a babe, her eyes wide and blue, her halo of tumbled curls and dimpled cheeks making her look like a mischevious cherub. His grim expression lightened a little.

"I do have a vague recollection of rousting some pawnbroker from his bed, forcing him to open his shop."

"I am astonished that you even remembered my telling you about the locket, let alone where to find it."

"My memory is a peculiar thing. It is amazing what I choose to forget, what I am forced to remember." A sadness clouded his eyes, and Anne knew the source of it.

She had pieced together the nightmare of his childhood from his ravings, and the knowledge weighed heavy upon her heart. She longed to offer him some comfort, but she had a fair notion of what that would do to Mandell's pride.

Instead she asked him the question that most troubled her. "You went to a great deal of bother to retrieve this locket for me. Why did you do so?"

"A drunken whim, I suppose." He snapped the locket closed. "If you are worried that it is another attempt to get you in my debt, don't be. I don't expect any repayment."

"I did not think that you did."

She thought she saw a flash of gratitude in his eyes. He tucked the locket back inside the lace collar of her gown, allowing it to slip beneath her bodice. As he did so, his fingers brushed against the column of her throat, lingering. She waited breathlessly for what he might do next, but he allowed his hand to drop away, his thick lashes drifting down, hooding his expression.

"You look exhausted," he said. "I recall enough to know that you took the time to bandage my hand. I hope you did not feel obliged to hover over me while I raved my way through some drunken delirium?"

The question sounded casual, but she was aware how intently he studied her from beneath his lowered lids. She understood what he was seeking to discover. Mandell had suffered enough humiliation from this episode. She had best take care with her answer or she knew with certainty she would never see him again.

And she knew with even more astonishing certainty she did not want that to happen.

"I did stay long enough to bandage your hand," she hedged. "But when I left you, you were sleeping like the dead." She had never been good at lying, and she was not certain Mandell would be put off by this half-truth.

He appeared satisfied, if not relieved. "And when I first arrived here," he said. "Was I alone?"

"Yes, of course. Why do you ask?"

"No particular reason." Mandell frowned. "Only that somehow I managed to misplace Sir Lancelot Briggs. No easy feat, I assure you. I daresay he will turn up again. He always does."

Reaching for her hand, he bowed over it and made one final attempt to apologize for his conduct. Anne realized he was preparing to take his leave. Why should that dismay her so?

Surely everything that needed saying had been said. What more was she waiting, hoping for? She didn't know, but she found herself attempting to delay him.

"Your bandage looks a little soiled," she remarked. "Perhaps you should allow me to redo it with clean linen."

"No, thank you. My hand feels much better. I can probably dispense with the bandage altogether." As he undid the wrapping, his knuckles still looked raw, but the swelling had gone down. Mandell flexed the fingers, but his gaze seemed fixed on some distant point. He compressed his lips as though he debated something with himself.

"There is one more thing that happened last night," he said reluctantly. "I suppose I should tell you about it before you hear about it from someone else. That fool Briggs has difficulty keeping his mouth shut."

Mandell held up his hand for her inspection. "You must have wondered how my knuckles came to be in such a disreputable state."

"You planted someone a facer?"

Mandell's eyes widened in such surprise, Anne smiled.

"I had a young male cousin who was very much into blood sports. Am I correct? Did you mill someone down?"

"Yes, I did, as you so aptly put it, 'plant someone a facer.' The face in this incidence might be of some concern to you. It belonged to your brother-in-law."

"Lucien?" Anne's smile vanished as she felt the beginnings of dread coil inside her. "You were fighting with Lucien? Why?"

"My dear Anne, two drunken fools at a tavern do not need a reason."

But Anne was not about to be put off with this glib explanation. "It was because of me," she said. "Lucien vowed he would have his vengeance because he had been forced to return Norrie. I hoped he would come to his senses and simply forget all that had passed. I should have known better."

She squared her shoulders. "I will not tolerate his making any more trouble for you. I will have to speak to him and—"

"You won't go anywhere near that bastard." Something dangerous flashed in Mandell's eyes, but Anne refused to be intimidated.

"Lucien's quarrel is with me, not you. I know how foolish men can be when their tempers are roused. The next thing I shall hear is that the two of you are meeting to fight a duel."

"You confuse me with my cousin Drummond. I don't fight duels."

When Anne shot him an incredulous look, he grimaced. "So even you have heard about the Constable affair. Is that to haunt me for the rest of my life? I was nothing but a green youth."

Anne did not think he would deign to tell her any more. She was surprised when he continued, "Cecily Constable, despite her spinsterhood, was a lady of vast experience, and she took great pleasure in sharing that experience with me, initiating me into the rites of—ah, er—" Mandell broke off with a irritated gesture. "I was silly enough to fancy myself quite smitten with her, that is until the afternoon I discovered her also playing tutor to the stable boy. I was angry, my pride wounded enough to make some imprudent remarks about the lady's virtue in her brother's hearing. Derek knew what a trollop she was, but for the sake of the family honor, he challenged me to a duel. For the same reason, my grandfather insisted that I accept.

"So there we were, two young idiots squaring off with pistols at the break of dawn, quaking in our boots. I was certain my hour had come, but when the smoke cleared, by some miracle I was left standing and Constable was on the ground, clutching his leg. I had shattered his kneecap."

Mandell looked as though the memory still sickened him and he rushed to finish his tale. "Eventually the leg had to be amputated below the knee, but the strange thing was, Constable did not seem unduly upset. He had defended his sister's nonexistent virtue. He was satisfied. Cecily was satisfied. My grandfather was satisfied. The only one who didn't find the conclusion satisfactory was me."

His face was raw with the bitterness and disillusion of youth. But he was quick to take refuge behind his mask of cynicism.

"I suppose it was a valuable lesson. I learned that it is not honor so much that matters as the appearance of it. Ever since then I have had the good sense to eschew dueling."

"But you nearly challenged Lucien at Brooks's," Anne could not help reminding him.

"That was different."

"How so?"

"Damn it, I don't know. It just was. Perhaps Nick was right. Perhaps . . . perhaps for once in my life I had found something worth fighting for."

"To have me, a prize you did not even fully claim? Tell me, Mandell. Why did you choose to let me leave your bed that night?"

He could not seem to meet the directness of her gaze. He turned away, saying impatiently, "I already told you. My conscience finally caught up with me."

"Was that really the reason? Or did you simply realize

that you made a mistake—that I was not quite so attractive after all?"

"No!" He spun around, his eyes blazing. "I have only ever made one noble gesture and I'll be damned if I'll have it misinterpreted. I wanted you, Anne, so much that I ached with the longing. God help me, I still do."

Stepping closer, he ran his fingers through the tangle of her hair, holding up the golden strands to catch the sunlight. The hunger was in his gaze, stronger than ever, causing her to tremble, but no longer with fear.

"You are a beautiful, desirable woman," he murmured. "Obviously your esteemed late husband never made you aware of that fact. Do you want to hear something truly absurd, Sorrow? The rest of your jewels are still in that pawnshop. I remember the owner pointing them out to me. But I chose to leave them because I didn't want you to have anything back that Fairhaven had given you."

"Those other jewels meant nothing to me. You have returned to me everything that I ever held precious."

"Did you love Sir Gerald?" Mandell demanded. "Whatever induced you to marry a self-righteous prig like that?"

With Mandell standing so close, his fingers rippling through her hair in that slow, seductive fashion, Anne had difficulty remembering. "Well, I suppose Gerald was handsome and he could be charming when he wished. That first night at Almack's when I looked up and saw him bending over me, he seemed like some prince out of a fairy story. I thought I fell madly in love with him, but sometimes I have wondered. I have wondered if I was merely afraid there would never be anyone else interested in me."

It was the first time Anne had ever confessed such a thing to herself, let alone anyone else. She flushed, waiting for Mandell's reaction.

"I wish . . ." he said hoarsely. "I wish I could turn back time to that night. I wish I had been there."

Anne smiled sadly. "You would have never noticed a poor little mouse like me. There were many more dashing belles present."

"We would have to turn the clock back for me as well,

to a time before I had too many Cecily Constables in my life." His dark eyes were wistful. "Back to when I was a more tender fellow. Is such a thing possible, Anne? Are you any good at pretending?"

"It would not be too difficult. I can remember exactly what I did that first evening." Pulling away from Mandell, she sat down in one of Lily's chairs, primly folded her hands, and stared at the tiles. "I spent the entire time studying a crack in the floor that resembled the outline of Ireland."

"Would you have looked up if I had approached you?" Mandell stepped in front of her.

Anne regarded the tips of his Hessians. "I would have contented myself to admire your shoes."

"What if I summoned one of the hostesses, Lady Jersey perhaps, to introduce me? 'Miss Wendham, may I present to you the marquis of Mandell as a very desirable dancing partner.' "

Anne laughed. It was all nonsense, but her pulse fluttered and she felt suddenly, absurdly shy. "Then I suppose I would have been obliged to look up." Anne raised her head slowly.

She had no difficulty imagining how Mandell would have appeared in a candlelit ballroom, the soft light bringing out the sheen in his waves of ebony hair, the white folds of his cravat only serving to accent the lean masculine line of his jaw.

The look on his face was so solemn, his smile one of rare sweetness. His eyes glinted like the facets of some mysterious dark jewel and held no trace of his usual mockery. Her breath caught in her throat.

"And after I finally induced you to look at me?" he prompted. "And then?"

"Then," she whispered, "there is a chance I might have seen no one but you."

He took her hand and drew her to her feet.

"I believe Lady Jersey has given permission for us to perform the waltz."

"Did she? I am hearing a minuet."

"I hate to correct you, Miss Wendham," Mandell said gravely. "But it is most definitely a waltz."

He rested one hand at her waist, gathering her other hand in his own. Maintaining a decorous distance, he led her into the first steps of the dance.

She followed his lead, marveling that she did not feel foolish. It was as though she could hear the strain of violins and the chatter and laughter of other couples but from a great distance, a world obscured by mist.

As Mandell whirled her in a slow circle, the room became a blur and she felt as though she were losing herself in his eyes.

"Are we not moving too slow, my lord?" she asked. "We are out of tempo with the music."

"Maybe. And maybe it is the rest of the world that is out of step."

He drew her closer until the front of her bodice brushed against his chest. His movements became slower, waltzing her about the floor in a sensual sway which caused her pulse to race.

"You should be warned, young Miss Wendham," he murmured close to her ear. She could feel the warmth of his breath tickling her hair. "I am already acquiring a reputation for being a little wild."

"Young Miss Wendham is not so quick to judge as the prim and proper Lady Fairhaven. She has a notion you are not so wicked as you would like everyone to believe."

"Does she? And where would she get a notion like that?"

"Perhaps it was from watching you be so kind and patient with a certain little girl. A little girl who was quite enchanted by you today. Even while the doctor examined her, she could talk of nothing else but Lord Man who liked to read myths and told her how pretty she was."

"I suspect that was only because the little girl fancied me to be like one of the characters in her stories."

"Hades. I've noticed the resemblance myself," Anne said. "The dark lord who was so lonely he felt forced to steal a bride."

"There is something I have never understood about that

myth. What did Hades want with a foolish little chit like Persephone when there was Demeter, a woman of strength and determination? If it had been me, I would have carried off the mother."

They were barely moving, their bodies slowing to a sultry rhythm that caused Anne's blood to warm, her voice to become unsteady.

"If—if you had taken away Demeter, you would have plunged the world into eternal winter."

"I am a selfish man. The rest of the world could shift for itself and be damned."

Mandell gathered Anne close in his arms until she was pressed up against the hard wall of his chest. The waltz music in her head faded to become the pounding of her own heart. His eyes darkened as he bent toward her. Anne raised her head to meet his kiss.

His lips were gentle, his kiss poignant, rife with an innocence of days gone by. Anne slid her hands up his chest, wrapping her arms about his neck in unashamed response. Her lips parted for him, allowing his tongue to invade the recesses of her mouth in sweet exploration.

Innocence gradually faded to become knowledge, knowledge of what they both wanted, desperately needed. Her body's response to his hard masculinity reminded Anne she was no longer a green girl of seventeen, but a woman. And Mandell was making her heartily glad of it. As he deepened his kiss, he ran his hands over her. A low cry caught in her throat when his fingers skimmed over her breast. She clung to him, returning his embrace with unchecked passion, offering herself to him, offering him anything that he desired to take.

It was Mandell who first came to his senses, thrusting her away. His breathing was unsteady, but he managed a lopsided smile.

"And thus would I have succeeded in getting us both denied vouchers to Almack's forevermore."

He attempted to jest, but his eyes were hazed with a combination of desire and a melancholy that struck deep to Anne's heart.

"So much for our little game of pretense, Sorrow. I fear it is too late for any new beginnings. It was ever thus with me."

Anne started to protest but she was stayed by a knock at the drawing room door. Never had any interruption been so ill timed, she thought, biting her lip in vexation. She and Mandell had barely enough time to draw apart before Bettine burst into the room.

The girl had got herself worked up into another of her agitated states. Wringing her hands, she cried, "Oh, my lady Fairhaven, the most dreadful thing has happened. Oh, mercy!" She finished with a shriek when she spotted Mandell.

"It is all right, Bettine. Lord Mandell is quite himself this morning," Anne said. However, she was not as sure about herself. She pressed her hands to her flushed cheeks in an effort to cool them. "Whatever is the matter now?"

Bettine eyed the marquis warily, but since Mandell had stalked away to the window to regain his composure, she dared to speak. "It is terrible news, milady. I heard it from the stable boy who heard it from Lady Eliot's cook—"

"Bettine, will you just tell me what it is?"

"We've all got to stay inside today and lock the doors. The Hook has been at it again. This time he attacked Sir Lancelot Briggs and—"

"What!" Mandell whipped about to stare at Bettine.

His harsh exclamation reduced the girl to a state of terrified speechlessness. Her own heart sinking with dread, Anne prompted the maid gently, "Tell us what happened clearly, Bettine."

"Well, I-I . . ."

Mandell strode across the room, glowering at her. "What nonsense are you talking, girl? Briggs dead? That's impossible."

Anne sensed that Mandell's voice was sharpened by fear, but Bettine cowered away from him. He seized Bettine by the wrist. Anne's protest went unheeded as Mandell gave Bettine a brisk shake.

"I was just with Briggs myself last night. You must have made a mistake."

Bettine's eyes were wide with terror, but she managed to sniff, "N-no mistake, sir. They found Sir Lancelot early this morning. He is mortal bad wounded. They—they don't expect him to live out the day—Ow!"

Mandell's grip must have tightened cruelly, for Bettine let out a howl. His face had turned ashen.

"Mandell, please," Anne said. "You are hurting the girl."

It took a moment before he appeared to hear her. He blinked, releasing Bettine. The maid fled sobbing from the room. Mandell stood as though turned to stone, the look in his eyes unreadable.

"What a dreadful thing," she faltered. "I was not that much acquainted with Sir Lancelot, but he always seemed such a sweet harmless sort of little man. Did you know him well, my lord?"

"Of course not!" Mandell's mouth set into an angry, bitter line. "He was a fool, a chattering idiot, a nuisance. But I believe—" He swallowed hard.

"I believe he was my friend."

Chapter 15

❦

The marquis of Mandell never had difficulty making an entrance. He had swept through doors of anywhere from a king's drawing room to the most dangerous of gaming hells without a blink, treating the stares of both royalty and rogues with a cool disdain. His arrogant confidence had never failed him until he prepared to enter the humble parlor of Sir Lancelot Briggs's London residence.

The place was already thronged with sorrowing relatives speaking in hushed voices, a few of the women sniffing into their handkerchiefs. Mandell stood just outside the room, feeling awkward, wondering why he had come.

After hearing the tidings about Lancelot, he had bolted from the Countess Sumner's, scarce taking the time to bid Anne farewell. He had not even realized where he was going until he had found himself upon Briggs's doorstep.

Why had he come? To fill in the blanks left in his drink-fogged memory about all that had happened last night? To assure himself that whatever had befallen Lancelot was not his fault?

Either motive was hardly a noble one. And Mandell had never felt less noble in his life than when he steeled himself to face Sir Lancelot's mother. Usually a bustling woman, as plump and cheerful as her son, the Dowager Lady Briggs sat at the far end of the parlor, staring into the empty hearth with red-rimmed eyes. Her large brown eyes were filled with a mournful bewilderment as though she could not quite take in what had happened to her son.

Mandell recalled meeting the woman only once. Sir Lan-

celot had proudly insisted upon presenting his mama to his
good friend the marquis. Mandell had given her such a frozen stare, the poor woman had been too awed even to
speak.

Like so many of his memories, Mandell did not find it a
comfortable one. His discomfort increased when the servant
intoned his name and Lady Briggs leapt up to greet him
like an old and valued friend. She rushed to the threshold
with her hands extended, tears glistening in her eyes.

"Oh, my lord Mandell. I knew the moment you heard
about my poor Lancelot you would come rushing to his
side."

Mandell flinched, but he managed a stiff bow. He resisted Lady Briggs's urgings that he join the others in the
parlor, drawing her out into the hall instead. "I do not wish
to intrude upon your family at such a time. But I had to
know. Has the doctor been to attend Briggs yet? How does
he fare?"

"As well as can be expected, poor lamb." Lady Briggs
groped for her handkerchief. "That fiend who did this
wounded him twice. By the time he was found down by the
river, my son had lost a powerful deal of blood. The sur-
geon says there is no more to be done than let Lancelot rest
and—and hope for the best.

"But I know he is going to be all right," she added
fiercely, mopping at her eyes. "Lancelot has always been
such a sturdy boy. I wanted to sit with him, but I am not
brave enough to contain myself and I upset him so. It has
always distressed him to see his mama cry."

"He is conscious then?" Mandell asked, feeling a flicker
of hope. Perhaps the reports of Lancelot's injury had all
been greatly exaggerated. "Would it be possible to visit
him? Would he want to see me?"

"Lancelot would always want to see you, my lord. I shall
summon his valet to conduct you to him. The dear man has
not left my poor boy since he was carried home this
m-morning." The thought of the servant's devotion over-
came her ladyship for a moment. She wept into her handkerchief while Mandell stood by uncomfortably.

He was wondering if he should step into the parlor and summon one of the other women to her aid when Lady Briggs struggled for command of herself. She blew her nose gustily, then glanced up at him with a pathetic attempt to smile.

"Forgive me for being such a fool, my lord," she said. "But this is so hard to bear. I cannot understand why this should have happened to my son. He is such a dear kind boy, never harming anyone and so—so good to his mama. And—and he hardly ever carries more than two farthings in his pocket. Why should this Hook person have wished to attack him?"

"I don't know," Mandell said. But another shard of memory fell into place, this one more piercing than any of the others. Through the smoke-filled haze of the tavern, he seemed to hear his own jeering voice, unguarded, speaking far too loud.

The bold Sir Lancelot who once encountered the Hook himself, who has pledged to aid in that villain's capture . . .

And equally clear came Briggs's pleading reply, *Don't taunt me, Mandell. I am frightened . . .*

Who else might have heard his drunken jest besides Briggs, Mandell wondered. Briggs had kept insisting that someone was staring at him, some sailor with a beard or a scar or something like that. And what had Mandell replied? Some rejoinder full of mockery and wit, no doubt. He was ever good at that, Mandell thought bitterly.

Mandell found it difficult to continue his conversation with Lady Briggs. He was relieved when the valet, a scrawny fellow with sorrowful eyes, appeared to conduct him upstairs.

The curtains had been tightly drawn in Lancelot's bedchamber, only one candle left burning. It took Mandell's eyes a moment to adjust to the darkness. The servant did not leave the room, but he stood back respectfully, allowing Mandell to approach his master's bedside.

A deathlike silence had already fallen over the chamber. It was broken only by the ticking of Briggs's watch, which had been left lying open upon the dressing table. The sight of the timepiece disturbed Mandell in an odd way, stirred some fragment of memory that hovered just out of reach. He closed the watchcase before stepping nearer to the bed.

Sir Lancelot lay unmoving upon the mattress, his upper chest and neck swathed in bandages. The linen was no whiter than the pasty shade of his complexion. His eyes were shut, his face drawn in lines of silent suffering.

Mandell's chest constricted with a mixture of sorrow, remorse, and anger. "You bloody fool! Why couldn't you have heeded me last night when I told you to go home?"

His voice, low as it was, caused Briggs to stir. He shifted upon the pillow and his eyes fluttered open. The brown depths clouded with confusion and fear as though he thought a stranger hovered over him.

"It is I, Briggs," Mandell said. "Don't you know me? It is Mandell."

Briggs blinked, the confusion replaced with that pathetically pleased expression Mandell had always found so annoying. Now it brought a lump to his throat.

He drew up a chair and seated himself beside the bed. Briggs moved his lips in an effort to speak. His face puckered and he pointed to the bandages at his throat.

"It is all right. I understand," Mandell said. "Don't try to talk."

Briggs held out his hand. After an awkward hesitation, Mandell grasped it. Briggs's flesh felt cold. Mandell squeezed the soft plump hand as though trying to infuse some of his own warmth and strength into the man.

"You are being quite a nuisance, you know that, don't you, Briggs? Giving everyone such a scare, making all the clubs fear they will have to close their doors if you do not return soon to lose your money."

Mandell's voice did not even sound like his own. It rang with a false heartiness he despised, and Briggs was not fooled. His eyes drifted down with a hopelessness, a lack of faith in his own recovery.

"You are not going to die. I forbid it." Mandell said. He was astonished by the fierceness of his emotion. Taking a deep breath, he strove for a lighter tone. "Who else would there be to endure my company when I am in one of my uncivilized humors?"

Briggs's lips quivered. Mandell pressed his hand one last time and released him. "We had quite a night of it last night, didn't we?"

Briggs nodded sadly.

"The last I recall you prevented me from murdering Lucien Fairhaven. I suppose I should thank you for that, but then I believe you carted me up to some flea-ridden bed and half drowned me with water. And then . . ." The effort to recall caused Mandell's head to ache again. "Then I have this notion you left me. You were going to fetch something, is that correct?"

Briggs nodded again, but his gaze skittered uneasily away from Mandell's.

"How did you come to end up down by the river? Do you remember who attacked you? Was it the Hook?"

Briggs shuddered and nodded.

"Was he someone from the tavern? Would you recognize him again?"

Briggs cast him a piteous glance. Mandell continued to prod gently, "Was he the same fellow you glimpsed before, the one with the plumed hat? Could you manage to write out any sort of description? I may abuse my own friends, Briggs, but I am damned if I will allow anyone else to do so. I will track this bastard down and tighten the noose about his neck myself if—"

Mandell broke off as Briggs became quite agitated. He clutched at Mandell's sleeve, shaking his head in vehement denial.

"Steady on, old fellow," Mandell said, attempting to soothe him. "You don't remember who attacked you? Or you are afraid for me to go after him? I don't understand what you are trying to tell me."

Briggs allowed his hand to drop back to his side, his eyes filling with tears. But Mandell had no opportunity to question him further. The valet who had stood quietly in the shadows all this time now crept forward.

"Please, my lord. The doctor said as how the master should be kept quiet. He needs to rest."

"Of course." Mandell stood up, reluctantly saying, "I am sorry. I shall come back when you are feeling more fit, Lance."

It was the first time he had ever used Briggs's Christian name, let alone abbreviated it in such friendly fashion. Briggs appeared quite overcome. He managed to roll onto his side and buried his face in the pillow to conceal his silent sobs.

Mandell was elbowed aside by the valet, who stared at him reproachfully and sought to calm his master. Mandell saw there was nothing more he could do. He had unwittingly caused enough damage.

Stepping out into the hall, he cursed himself. He had been a fool to come here, more foolish still for spouting such nonsense and upsetting poor Briggs. What was he trying to prove by vowing to capture the Hook, blustering threats of vengeance that only added to Lancelot's misery? The bitter truth was that Mandell had not been considering Briggs's feelings at all, but merely seeking to appease his own guilty conscience. He had never been Briggs's friend. It was too late to start pretending as if he were one now.

Just as it had been too late with Anne. He had been doing the same thing with her earlier that afternoon, playing games of pretend. Making believe that he could go back to a time when he was not yet so well schooled in arrogance and cynicism, indifferent to anyone else's needs but his own. He had tried to be not a gentleman, but a more *gentle man*.

It had not worked. The soft touch of her skin, the sweet scent of her perfume, the warm womanly feel of her in his arms and his own selfish desires had raged out of control. That she had responded in kind only made matters worse. It was just a sign of how far he had succeeded in seducing her. And he had been so tempted to take full advantage of her willingness.

It is too late for any new beginnings. It was ever thus with me.

As he dwelled upon this grim truth, he became aware that one of the maidservants was approaching him. She would wish to conduct him back to the parlor, but Mandell could not bring himself to face Briggs's grieving mother again.

He called for his hat and walking stick instead, and quit the house. Drawing on his gloves, he bolted down the stone steps of the brick residence and collided with his cousin.

Nick staggered back, his curly-brimmed beaver nearly flying to the pavement. He grasped at it, looking a little taken aback at the sight of the marquis.

"Mandell!" he exclaimed. Appearing to recover himself, he straightened his hat back upon his head.

It had been over a week since Mandell had seen his cousin, and he should have evinced more pleasure at encountering Nick. But he felt too raw from his visit with Briggs to do more than mutter, "The long lost Drummond. Where have you been keeping yourself, Nicholas?"

Nick smiled, but the expression was strained, lacking his usual warmth. "I have been preoccupied with . . . Parliamentary sessions, government details too tedious to bore you with. But I rushed over as soon as I heard about the attack on poor Briggs. I was told that he is not expected to live."

"He looks very bad, but he is conscious."

"Oh?" Nick asked anxiously. "You—you have spoken to him?"

"I visited with him for awhile, but he cannot speak."

"Then he cannot describe who attacked him?"

"Cannot or will not." Mandell frowned, remembering Briggs's strong reaction to being questioned. "It seems to distress him to remember anything about the attack. The shock of the whole incident appears to have been too much for him. I fear it may have disordered his mind."

Nick vented a frustrated sigh. "Well, I did try to warn everyone, but no one would listen. The activities of the Hook won't be stopped until we have a better police force. The government always refuses to do anything until it is too late."

"For Briggs, it already is," Mandell reminded him sharply.

"Perhaps what happened to Briggs will finally be the leverage I need to get my bill through Parliament. He is the Hook's third victim. Surely now—"

"Don't, Nick," Mandell snapped. "I am in no mood to listen to one of your homilies about the social benefits to be derived from murder."

"Damn you, I have never said anything like that," Nick protested hotly. "Of course, what happened to Briggs was dreadful. But if some good could come of it, if the House could at last be brought to realize . . ."

When Mandell shot him a dark look, Nick bore enough sense to subside, but he added bitterly, "Besides, what makes you so self-righteous all of a sudden? You have probably wounded Briggs with that cutting tongue of yours far worse than anything the Hook did to him."

Nick's biting words struck too close to the mark. Mandell flinched, but he drew himself up icily. "Yes, I daresay you are right. But I think Briggs's family has enough to endure without the pair of us quarreling on their doorstep. I bid you farewell, cousin."

Mandell brushed past Nick. He started to stalk away along the pavement when he was halted by the sound of Nick's voice.

"Mandell!"

Mandell glanced back. Nick stood poised by Briggs's steps. He still looked flushed with annoyance, but there was an unaccountable sorrow in his eyes as well.

"I am sorry," Nick said. "I did not mean to sound so callous. I guess I never realized how much you cared about Briggs."

Mandell started to voice his usual denial, but he ended by saying softly, "I guess I never realized it, either."

"If I had only known—" Nick broke off. He looked as though he wanted to say something more but ended by shaking his head sadly. "You are right. This is not a good time or place to talk about . . . about anything."

He turned to walk away himself in the opposite direction.

Apparently he had forgotten his own intention to visit Briggs or had decided against it.

Mandell stared after Nick, frowning. It occurred to him that Drummond was behaving rather oddly. It was not like the impetuous Nick to hold back with anything he desired to say, no matter what the circumstances. Mandell was left with a strange sensation of a distance widening between them, a distance that stretched much further than the yards of pavement that separated them.

It only added to Mandell's feeling of being isolated and alone, but he attempted to shrug the emotion aside. He was being foolish, he chided himself. Likely Nick was, as he had said, preoccupied with some blasted political matter. Even as he turned the corner, Drummond consulted his pocket watch and hastened his steps as though he had forgotten some important meeting.

It was the sight of that pocket watch that drove thoughts of Nick and everything else out of Mandell's head. His breath quickened as he was assaulted by a memory, the memory that had eluded him earlier in Briggs's bedchamber.

But now he could recall it so clearly—Briggs performing the same action at the tavern last night, checking the time on his watch, urging Mandell to leave.

The same watch that now sat ticking upon Briggs's dressing table hours after he had been assaulted, supposedly by one of the most notorious brigands in London. As the full implication of this struck Mandell, his brow knit in a heavy frown.

What manner of villain was he dealing with here? What kind of a common footpad would carve up a man to rob him, only to leave his victim still in possession of a solid gold watch?

The last minutes of daylight faded. Clarion Way was enveloped in a purple mantle of twilight, the first stars winking in the sky.

"Seven o'clock and all's well," Obadiah called out. But the old watchman no longer intoned the time with the confidence and serenity he had felt before Bertie Glossop's murder. Now, if a stray cat so much as brushed against his legs, he startled half out of his skin.

When he saw the gentleman in the long black cloak come striding up the street, Obadiah's heart gave a flutter of fear, although there was nothing furtive about the man's movements. It was only the marquis of Mandell approaching his own front gate.

But the haughty marquis had ever made Obadiah nervous and he was quick to step out of his lordship's path. He expected Mandell to sweep on past, taking no more notice of Obadiah than he ever did.

To his astonishment, the marquis came to an abrupt halt and nodded in his direction. "Good evening."

Even then, Obadiah glanced about to see whom his lordship might be addressing.

"I am talking to you, sir," Lord Mandell said with a tinge of impatience in his voice. "You are the night watchman, are you not?"

"Well, I-I—," Obadiah babbled. He had always been in terror of Mandell's fierce dark gaze. But seen close up, he realized that the marquis's face possessed none of its usual hauteur. And his eyes were dulled with a bone-deep weariness, a feeling Obadiah recognized all too well. It gave him the courage to reply.

"Why, why, yes, m'lord." Obadiah managed a nervous but respectful bow. "I am Obadiah Jones, your lordship. At your service."

"You, I believe, are the one that I heard found Albert Glossop's body. Do you remember the night he was killed?"

The question astonished Obadiah into blurting out, "How could I ever forget it, sir? 'Twas the most terrifying night of my life, finding young Mr. Glossop that way, all bloodied over and seeing that villian run away, laughing like some pure devil from hell."

The marquis's eyes narrowed. "You actually saw the Hook then?"

" 'Deed I did. All garbed in black he was, like some phantom, that strange hat aflopping over his eyes."

"And his face?"

"Well, I couldn't see that, m'lord. It was a terrible foggy night."

"Then what made you so sure it was the Hook?"

"Why—why because the rogue has been on the prowl for months, terrifying honest folks. Who else could it have been?"

"Who else indeed?" the marquis murmured. He frowned, but Obadiah had the impression Lord Mandell was not scowling at him so much as at some disturbing thought of his own. The marquis's curiosity on this subject surprised Obadiah a little, but then he had never fully understood the ways of the Quality.

So he waited respectfully while the marquis continued, "After you found Glossop, did he still have his valuables on him? His watch perhaps, his purse?"

"I—I don't know, m'lord. After I first touched Mr. Glossop and saw that he was—was dead—" Obadiah shuddered, remembering the sensation of his fingers coming away, warm and sticky with blood—"I didn't examine the young gentleman too close after that."

The marquis seemed so disappointed with his answer, Obadiah hastened to add, "But the Hook must've taken away Mr. Glossop's valuables. Stands to reason, don't it? Him being such a notorious cutpurse and all."

The marquis did not answer. He merely regarded Obadiah and said gravely, "Thank you, Mr. Jones. You have been most helpful."

"Have I?" Obadiah quavered. "I wish I could think I have been. I still remember how Mr. Glossop screamed that night. I never had much liking for Master Bertie, but it was a terrible way for any young fellow to die. I lay awake sometime awondering if I could've done things any differently that night. If I might've moved a little faster, done something to save him."

"Regret ... it is the poison of life, Mr. Jones." Lord Mandell rested his hand upon Obadiah's shoulder. "But I fear it is a curse that many of us are doomed to experience."

He smiled sadly and passed on his way, leaving Obadiah staring after him. This surely had to be one of the strangest encounters Obadiah had ever had on Clarion Way.

And yet, for a moment he had felt an odd kinship with Lord Mandell. The man's touch upon Obadiah's shoulder had been fleeting but there had been a deal of comfort in it. It was almost as if the marquis really understood Obadiah's feelings of guilt and remorse over what had happened to Mr. Glossop.

And to think he had once fancied the marquis such a hard, cold man. He had much more of a liking for Lord Mandell's cousin. But lately it was Mr. Drummond who seemed less than kind, distant and curt. The last time he had called upon his sister, Mr. Nick had actually snapped at Obadiah to get out of his way.

Obadiah meandered on his way up the street, slowly shaking his head. It only went to show. One never knew any man as well as one thought one did.

Chapter 16

❧❀❧

Twilight had long faded into darkness by the time Anne approached the marquis of Mandell's gate. Clutching the heavy bundle of cloth to her chest, she eased back her hood, peering up at his house. A faint glow of light shone through one of the lower story windows, but the rest of the stone structure appeared dark and forbidding.

She wondered what madness had compelled her to come. There had been a sad finality in his voice when he had bidden her farewell earlier that day. He might not want to see her. He might not even be at home. It was absurd, her conviction that he paced the shadows of this vast and lonely house, just as she had been pacing her empty bedchamber these past hours.

Yet the conviction was strong enough to carry her past his gate, up the steps to his front door. He needed her tonight. She was as certain of that as of her own aching need, a longing that she finally dared acknowledge.

Before her courage could desert her, she shifted her bundle under one arm, lifted her hand to the brass knocker and sounded it. Only then did it occur to her to wonder what she would say when her summons was answered, especially if by a shocked and disapproving butler like Firken. Yet she could not imagine any of Mandell's servants being easily scandalized.

All the same, she felt relieved when the door swung open, revealing the familiar and reliable figure of John Hastings.

"My lady Fairhaven!" The young man's eyes widened in surprise, but he struggled to conceal it.

"Is his lordship at home?" she asked.

"Yes, milady."

"I need to see him."

Hastings cast a doubtful glance toward the darkened regions of the house behind him. "It is very late, milady. I don't know if the master would be—"

"Please," Anne said, raising her eyes to his.

Hastings hesitated a moment more, then stepped aside to allow her to enter. "My lord is in the drawing room," he said with a solemn bow. "Will it please you to wait here while I announce you?"

"No! I—I think it would be better if I just went in."

She dreaded Mandell having opportunity to fix his mask of hauteur in place, or worse still, simply refuse to see her.

Hastings nodded in silent understanding. "The drawing room is through that door at the end of the hall."

Drawing a steadying breath, Anne stepped forward. Mandell's entrance hall was as austere and unwelcoming as she remembered it. But as she crept farther into the house, the silence was broken by the distant sound of music. Someone was playing upon the pianoforte and with a great deal of mastery.

She glanced back to Hastings who stood behind her in the shadows. "Is Lord Mandell alone?"

"Always, milady," the footman said with a sad smile.

Anne continued on her way, her heart hammering with every step. When she opened the door, the music seemed to assault her in a great wave, echoing off the rafters with all the power and majesty of thunder. The velvet draperies were drawn, the room dark except for the fire blazing on the hearth and the branch of candlesticks atop the pianoforte, their glow reflecting upon the glossy rosewood surface. Absorbed by his playing, Mandell did not even look up when she entered.

His hands rippled over the keys, the notes ringing out with a hard, angry brilliance. It was as though all the passion, the torment, the longing he kept guarded in his soul flowed out through his fingertips, finding expression in a storm of music that took Anne's breath away.

Closing the door quietly behind her, she crept forward. The candles illuminated his profile and the sheen of his midnight satin dressing gown. He wore nothing else but his breeches, the robe parted to reveal a glimpse of his hair-darkened chest, the strong cords of his neck.

His face was a study in intensity, his lashes lowered to veil his eyes, a flush staining his high cheekbones, his lips half parted.

She walked toward him, captured by the fury of his music as much as if he had seized her in a fierce embrace. She stood beside him and still he did not look up until he reached a place where his fingers faltered.

His brow furrowed in concentration as his hands moved back, trying to repeat the phrase. It was at that point that he sensed her presence. The music died away on a final jarring note that reverberated about the room, finally echoing to silence. He stared up at her as though gazing at an apparition as she brushed back her hood.

"Anne!" He shot to his feet, the darkness in his eyes replaced by an eager light. He reached for her, his own hands a trifle unsteady, and all Anne's doubts were swept aside. She knew she had done right to come.

She awaited his touch with breathless anticipation. But as he recovered from his initial surprise, he seemed to recollect himself. He drew back, frowning.

"How did you get in?" he asked. "And what the devil are you doing here?"

"Hastings admitted me," she replied with more calm than she felt. "I came to return this to you."

She thrust toward him the bundle she had carried tucked under her arm. He appeared puzzled until he shook out the heavy folds and recognized his own caped greatcoat, the one he had draped about her shoulders the night they had first made the pact between them, the pact that had nearly made them lovers. She wondered if the garment stirred for him the same memories as it did her. It was difficult to read his expression.

"I have had it hidden in the bottom of my wardrobe all this time," she said. "I kept forgetting to give it back to you."

He tossed the coat over the back of one of the chairs. "You came here alone?"

"Yes, it is only a short walk from Lily's to here and—"

"You little fool!" The sudden flare of anger in his eyes put an end to her explanation. "There is a murderer on the loose and you decide to go for a late night stroll?"

"The street lamps are all lit and the watchman was making his rounds."

Mandell clenched his hands into fists, looking as though he wanted to shake her. She hastened to add, "Perhaps I did behave a little unwisely. But it scarce matters. I am in no danger now."

"That is a highly debatable point," he ground out. "How long have you been standing there?"

"Only a few moments. I was listening to you play. A symphony by Beethoven, wasn't it? You did it so magnificently. I wish you hadn't stopped."

"I could not recollect any more. I play by memory only."

Her gaze flew back to the pianoforte, noticing there were no sheets of composition propped in the music stand. "You don't read music? You play that way by ear?"

He shrugged. "I never took any instruction. Some musical accomplishment is tolerable, but a gentleman should hardly perform as though he were obliged to earn a living at it like—like some opera-house player."

The acid words seemed to be an echo of someone else's sentiments, not his own. He stepped away from the pianoforte and disconcerted her by asking, "Why did you really come here tonight, Anne? And don't tell me any more nonsense about returning that cloak. You could have despatched a servant to bring it back days ago."

Her cheeks heated. If he did not understand why she was here, she hardly knew how to begin to tell him, especially when he was fixing her with such a hard stare.

"You left so abruptly today," she said. "And you seemed

so distraught about your friend. I was worried. I wondered if you had heard how Sir Lancelot is faring."

"He may live, but I doubt he'll ever recover."

"Do they know yet who is responsible for the attack?"

"I am," Mandell said harshly.

When she looked at him, startled, he added, "I don't mean that I was the one who pierced him through, but I might as well have done. I allowed him to accompany me last night, then got so drunk that I forgot all about him. I abandoned him at that wretched tavern, leaving him to the mercy of some damned brigand, some murderous phantom ... whatever or whoever this accursed Hook might be."

Mandell's lips twisted in a bitter smile. "Briggs hated jaunting about such low places. He only came to try to protect me from myself. Because I once did him a misplaced kindness, he conceived this notion that I am somehow worth saving. A mistaken concept that you seem to share. Is that why you came, Anne? To be my ministering angel? You cannot minister to the devil, my dear."

His words were hard, jeering, inviting her to share in his self-condemnation. But one look into his eyes was enough to see how Mandell damned himself.

His face was taut with the strain of the past hours. A few dark strands of hair drooped over his brow. Anne had longed to smooth them back ever since she had entered the room. Closing the distance between them, she gave way to the impulse now, caressing his forehead.

"I came to you because I thought you might want ... you might need a friend tonight," she said.

He tensed at her touch and caught her hand, holding it in an iron grip. "My friends pay a high price for the privilege of my company. If you don't believe me, ask Briggs. He could tell you—that is if he were still able to speak."

"I am prepared to take the risk, my lord. I am not afraid."

"You should be." He kissed her hand brusquely and returned it to her. "Go home, Anne. You need not worry about me. I am not likely to go off into a decline over

Briggs. I am after all a cold-hearted bastard. I will have forgotten all about the poor fool by tomorrow."

Would he? Anne wondered. Or would what had happened to Briggs become one more painful memory for Mandell, buried only to resurface, haunting him in his dreams? His mouth, she suddenly realized, had never been suited for such hard mockery, but had always been formed for a more sensitive cast. She brushed her fingers lightly over his lips. He flinched as though she had burned him.

He retreated a step, saying, "I will summon Hastings to escort you home."

"No." With trembling fingers, Anne began to undo the fastenings of her cloak.

Mandell stared at her. What the deuce had come over Anne? Even she could not be so innocent that she failed to realize the temptation she was putting in his path, coming alone to his house at such an hour, rising up before him like a golden-haired vision, the better part of his dreams. Ever since he had glanced up from the pianoforte, to find her so close, he had burned with the longing to pull her into his arms, seek comfort from her sweet lips, find solace for the emptiness in his soul.

He was doing his best to resist the selfish urge, but she was not making it easy for him. She brushed back the folds of her cloak and Mandell's mouth went dry. She had on the clinging gown she had worn that night to the theatre, the one that revealed all her womanly curves, the low décolletage exposing the soft white swell of her breasts.

Desire shot through Mandell, so intense it was painful.

"Anne," he said hoarsely. "What folly is this? Do you have any idea what you are about?"

Her eyes met his, those blue depths startlingly clear. Mandell's breath caught in his throat as he realized she knew full well what she was doing. The longing in her gaze reflected his own, and a deeper emotion that he was too afraid to explore.

She allowed her cloak to drop to the floor. "I want to stay with you tonight, my lord." Her voice was low, but filled with a quiet determination.

Mandell summoned up all the self-control he possessed. Clenching his jaw, he retrieved her cloak from the floor. He managed to drape it around her shoulders, touching her as little as possible.

"You are confused, Anne," he said. "I suppose it was that foolish game we played in your sister's drawing room that has brought this on, making you see me in a different light. But I assure you I am still what you once deemed me . . . a libertine with no honor and no heart. I cannot change. I thought I made that clear to you this afternoon."

"I am not looking to change you, Mandell." She cupped his face between her hands. Standing on tiptoe, she brushed her lips against his in a questing that stirred him more deeply than the most passionate embrace. Every muscle in his body tensed with the need to respond. But he held himself rigid, making no movement to enfold her in his arms.

She glanced up, her lips quivering in a tremulous smile. "Does my boldness shock you, my lord? You once told me I could be whoever I wished with you. Do you now deny me that permission?"

"I never gave you leave to be a fool," he rasped. When she slipped her arms about his neck, he swore. He sought to thrust her way, but his arms seemed curiously lacking in strength.

"Anne." He gave a hard laugh that was more of a plea. "Self-denial is not one of my virtues. It took me years to locate my conscience the first time. I don't think I can do it again."

"Let me be the keeper of your conscience then," she whispered. She melted against him and breathed kisses along the line of his jaw.

Her lips were too warm, too close, her slender frame fit too perfectly against his own body. He crushed her in his arms, his mouth claiming hers. Her lips parted, her tongue mating with his in a kiss that stole away his reason and resolve. The fiery embrace burned away everything but his hunger for her.

"Anne! Anne," he groaned, burying his face in the shining gold strands of her hair, making one last effort to bring her to her senses. "I can offer you nothing but heartbreak. Leave me while you still can."

Looking up at him, she shook her head, her eyes glittering with unshed tears. "You have made me realize some truths about myself, Mandell. I feel like I have lived my whole life in a dream, and someday I am going to wake up an old woman with nothing to look back on but days spent stitching samplers by my fireside. I—I want something better to remember, Mandell."

"I can give you memories if that is what you truly want," he said sadly. He only prayed that they would not be remembrances as full of bitter regret as his own.

Mandell's hands shook as he lit the candles, dispelling the darkness in his room. He could not help reflecting how different this was from the last time he had brought Anne to his bedchamber. Now it was Anne who appeared sure and confident while he felt more awkward than he ever had, even in the raw days of his youth.

The irony of this was not lost upon him. She was seducing him tonight, his prim and proper Anne. Yet he had always flattered himself he was a man of iron control. He could resist the charms of any woman if it pleased him to do so.

He glanced to where Anne stood waiting by his bedside. Her face was pale except for the soft rose that stained her cheeks. Her hair tumbled down her back like a veil of gold.

Yes, he could resist any woman ... any woman but this one.

She glided toward him, her eyes as soft and luminous as the candle flame. He held out his arms and gathered her to him, for the moment content to do no more than strain her close to his heart.

It was she who drew back. Solemnly, she gathered the fullness of her hair, brushing it over one shoulder to expose the fastenings of her gown in a gesture that was poignantly childlike. Turning her back to him, she waited for him to undress her, her breath coming quickly.

Mandell's throat thickened with some emotion that had

nothing to do with his desire. His fingers moved over the ribbon ties of her gown with a reverence that made him clumsy.

It seemed to take him an eternity to work through the layers of her garments, during which he was aware of nothing but her soft breathing and the thundering of his own heart. He pushed aside the fabric of her gown and chemise, baring the smooth ivory skin of her back.

Bending, he trailed kisses along the ridge of her spine up to her shoulder blade. Anne leaned back against him with a long rapturous sigh. Then she turned and began easing her gown down over her arms.

His pulse racing, he watched her garments, one by one, fall to the floor. The full white globes of her breasts were outlined in the candlelight, the slender line of her waist, the swell of her hips.

She stood before him, her only adornment her golden sheen of hair. Mandell worshiped her nakedness with his eyes, her supple body a white silhouette, the mysteries of her female form intensifying his desire, leaving him weak and trembling with his need of her.

She seemed a woman more born of mists and dreams. He half feared if he touched her, she would vanish, leaving him alone in the darkness. He stroked his fingers tentatively along the curve of her cheek.

"God, Anne, you are beautiful. If it were only within my power to make you see how beautiful you are."

"It is enough that you make me feel that way," she whispered.

He drew her close to him, capturing her lips in a kiss that was lingering. Somewhere within him a fire raged, a fire that demanded he possess her immediately. But the desire was overruled by a greater need to take things slowly, to make this night last forever.

He kissed her temple, her eyelids, her cheeks, his hands running down the length of her back, delighting in the feel of her skin, as warm and smooth as silk. Her face flushed, Anne tugged at the belt that held his dressing robe closed.

She undid the knot and parted the satin folds of the garment.

Her fingers skimmed his chest as she worked the robe off his shoulders. Mandell drew in a sharp breath. He had never liked to have a woman undress him, finding the notion too strangely intimate, leaving him less in control of the lovemaking.

Yet he found himself reveling in the gentle way Anne removed his robe. He closed his eyes as her fingers roved over his chest and shoulders in tentative exploration. Her caress was almost enough to bring him to his knees.

He gathered her in his arms, kissing her again, molding her breasts to his naked flesh, the warmth of her body flowing into him, sending heat rushing through his veins. Nothing stood between them and the culmination of desire except the coarse fabric of his breeches.

Anne managed to undo the buttons, but he had to help her edge the tight cloth down his hips, his hands covering hers, gently guiding her. She bent before him, tugging the breeches to his ankles so that he could step out of them.

Then she looked up, her gaze filled with a kind of wonder as she studied his legs, the hardened evidence of his arousal, the breadth of his chest, her glance finally coming to rest upon his face. The piercing clarity of her blue eyes shook him to the core of his soul.

To have her kneeling before him in an attitude of adoration was so unbearable it was painful. Mandell made haste to draw her to her feet. Swooping her into his arms, he carried her to his bed and laid her upon the mattress.

As he settled down beside her, her mouth sought his with a sweet eagerness. Her hands moved over his back and shoulders, exploring his body with increasing boldness. Anne had spoken earlier of her own desires, but he sensed she was striving mostly to bring him pleasure.

He sought to match her generosity. He had little enough to offer her but the consummate skill as a lover he had acquired over the years, his intimate knowledge of a woman's body, her most secret needs.

As he stroked and caressed her, he wanted to be able to

do more for her, to murmur soft words in her ear. But the practiced endearments he usually employed seemed too hollow for such a moment, and as for whisperings of tenderness, he had none. So he had to content himself to make love to her in silence, communicating his need for her with his hands, his kiss.

His fingers skimmed over her curves. Gently capturing her breast, Mandell placed his lips over the rosy-tipped crest, caressing it with the rough heat of his tongue. Anne arched back with a whimper of pleasure.

She had seen the promise of passion in Mandell's dark eyes from their first encounter in a moonlit garden. It was a promise he now fulfilled, his kisses hot and sweet, his long graceful fingers working magic, making her feel things she had never imagined possible. No, not for the dull virtuous Anne.

But she was a different woman in his arms, wanton, free and . . . yes, beautiful. She could see the effect she had on Mandell and she could not suppress a tiny thrill that she possessed the power to stir him so.

As he pressed her onto her back, holding himself poised above her, his face was flushed with passion, desire melting away the hauteur and the lines of mocking distance he usually maintained between them.

A fine sheen of perspiration bathed his flesh, sweat glistening on the muscular contours of his shoulders and chest. His eyes burned into her, the sensual cast of his mouth both warm and tender as he kissed her.

She was struck with a sense of awe at the sheer masculine power he possessed and knew a brief flickering of fear as he parted her legs.

But he eased himself inside her so gently, tears sprang to her eyes. A sad thought came unbidden to her mind, that this was as close as she would ever come to Mandell, this union of their flesh. She would never touch his heart or soul.

She embraced him with near desperation, seeking to take all of him into herself, striving to meld her body with his. He began to move inside her and she forgot all else but the bittersweetness of this moment when no barriers seemed to exist between them.

Anne kissed him, arched against him, her body moving as one with his. The pleasure he brought her spiraled into something so intense, she cried out, digging her nails into his back.

He groaned her name, escalating the rhythm, taking her with him into his own land of fire and shadow, seeking a mutual fulfillment that left Anne feeling shattered, spent.

For long moments, Anne was conscious of nothing but clinging to Mandell, feeling the pounding of her heart slow to a more steady pace. As his own ragged breathing became quieter, he continued to hold himself inside of her. Anne savored the warmth, the intimacy of that joining, never wanting it to end.

But he eased himself from on top of her. Although he gathered her in his arms, nestling her head against his shoulder, Anne had a chilling sensation that something was wrong.

She had heard that once the passion was spent, a man would be done with the woman. It had certainly been thus with Gerald. When he had finished with her, he had buttoned his breeches, gave her a peck on the cheek and left the room.

It was some comfort to Anne that Mandell yet clasped her tight in his arms, his face resting against her hair, but she could already feel him slipping away from her.

She shifted enough so that she could see his face. His features were still, his eyes dark with some emotion she failed to comprehend. Disappointment in her perhaps? The confidence that had been born in her this night slowly began to die.

He was so quiet she felt impelled to speak. "What—what happened between us was—was incredible," she said shyly. "It was like nothing I have ever felt. I will never forget it."

Anne silently cursed herself for the inadequacy of her own words. She wished she could find some way to explain to him that what she had experienced in his arms had been wondrous, something bright and beautiful. She only wished it had been the same for him. When he still failed to speak, she knew it hadn't been.

"Did—did you enjoy it, too?" she asked.

"Yes, of course I did." The kiss he pressed to her brow was as abrupt as his words. Anne sensed he wanted her to be silent, but she could not seem to do so.

"I keep forgetting none of this is new to you." She sighed. "You must have experienced such pleasure dozens of times before."

Her voice was anxious and Mandell realized she was seeking reassurance. He should have been able to give it to her, but he was too thoroughly shaken. He was used to making conquests. But he had never surrendered so much to any woman as he had done with Anne tonight. It was as though in holding her so close to his body, he had also allowed her to draw too close to his heart. He could scarce admit such a thing to himself, let alone to her.

Before she could stir any more such disturbing reflections, he sought to silence her. Turning her in his arms, he kissed her, her mouth soft and pliant after their lovemaking. When he broke off the embrace, he saw that he had appeased her anxieties if not his own.

Nibbling at her ear, he strove for a lighter tone. "I fear you are far too easily pleased, my lady. Your late husband's performance in the bedchamber must have been quite unremarkable if you were so impressed by my poor skill tonight. The next time, when I am better rested, I will show you far greater pleasures."

"Will there be a next time?" Her eyes were far too wistful, too eager.

He should have said no for both their sakes. Yet he found himself replying, "If you wish it."

"Then I shall become your mistress?"

Anne watched Mandell's brows draw together in a frown. Her question seemed to disturb him.

"Could you be comfortable in that role?" he asked.

Anne hesitated only a moment over her reply. "Yes. Neither of us are bound by vows to anyone else. It would be different if I were not a widow and if . . . if you were married."

"There is no fear of that difficulty arising."

"Do you never intend to marry, my lord?"

"I suppose I will be obliged to one day, find some haughty dame with enough ice and ambition in her veins to make a proper marchioness. Trade off my title and wealth to put an heir in the cradle of the august house of Windermere."

He meant to sound flippant, but Anne detected an underlying bitterness beneath his words.

"It sounds like a very cold arrangement," Anne ventured, reflecting that she certainly ought to know. Except that instead of ice and ambition, Gerald had wanted propriety and virtue.

Mandell smiled at her, stroking his fingers through the length of her hair. "One generally saves all one's warmth for one's mistress."

"You will have to forgive me, my lord, and remember that I am quite new to the rules that govern a relationship such as ours."

He dropped a kiss on her brow. "To begin with, you will have to learn to be more demanding. Tell me what carriages, what jewels, what expensive presents you expect from me in return for your—er—affections."

Anne swallowed to conceal the hurt his words gave her. "My affections don't come so dear. All I want is more moments like we shared tonight, perhaps occasionally for you to play your music for me."

"You expect too little, my dear. Once again you make me doubt whether you are the sort of woman suited for this kind of liaison."

"What sort of woman do you think I am?"

"The kind who will always need the prince on a white charger, whisking you off to the security of his castle, keeping you safe from all ogres and dragons."

"I already tried the prince," Anne said, running her hand lightly up his arm. "It was very dull. I prefer to take my chances with the dragon."

"Even if he devours you?"

"That would be a preferable fate to being buried alive in some silk-lined palace."

"I hope you still think so when you have been reduced to ashes," Mandell said, his eyes intent and somber. "But now that I have known what it is like to have you in my bed, I am too selfish to forego that pleasure. I suppose I am exactly like that greedy fellow in Norrie's story, the one who robbed the world of spring."

"My lord Hades," Anne murmured, tenderly stroking back the strands of hair that stubbornly persisted in falling over his brow.

"And now I have succeeded in dragging you down into my darkness."

Unless she were able to lead him up into the light. It was a foolish hope, but a persistent one. Yet Anne was wise enough to keep it to herself as Mandell gathered her close in his arms.

Chapter 17

࿖࿖࿖

Over a fortnight had passed since the attack on Sir Lancelot Briggs, and the surly proprietor of the Running Cat hoped that all questions regarding the doings in his tavern had finally ceased. Since that fateful evening, Mr. George Nagle had been beleaguered by a succession of constables, Bow Street detectives, and even a magistrate. Many of the activities at the Running Cat would not bear close scrutiny by the minions of the law, and Mr. Nagle heartily wished that the Hook would be considerate enough to look elsewhere for his next victim.

As he swept out the taproom, he reflected it was the first peaceful afternoon he had known since that wretched night. The tavern was empty except for the sailor, old Tom, passed out beneath one of the benches as usual, and one other customer who stood sipping a pint of porter near the back door.

The quiet suited Nagle, who was in a bad humor, the lazy barmaid Jenny having neglected to clean up again. The girl was only good for such occupation as involved her being flat on her back on one of the beds upstairs. Nagle plied the broom with vigor, stirring up dustmotes in the bright spring sunlight. He did not feel up to greeting any customers, not even with his usual irritable growl.

But he straightened instinctively at the sight of the dark-haired gentleman who entered the tavern. He was tall, the cut of his frock coat severe, his whipcord riding breeches immaculate. Though the color was of a most somber hue, there was no mistaking the quality of the garments or the value of the signet ring the gentleman flashed on his lean aristocratic hand.

Nagle stared in momentary astonishment. His tavern was occasionally frequented by members of the nobility, but none like this gent, who looked mighty high in instep, his lip curling with distaste as he crossed the threshold.

Nagle had the odd feeling he had seen the man before. But he was discouraged from any further ogling by a pair of imperious dark eyes that stared him down, making Nagle feel it might be prudent to take shelter behind the bar.

"Afternoon, sir." Nagle nodded, infusing his voice with more respect than he showed most of his customers. "How can I serve you? A pint of ale perhaps? Or I do have a tolerable brandy."

"No." A slight shudder appeared to course through the gentleman. "I am merely seeking information about something that happened two weeks ago."

Dropping his respectful mien, Nagle bristled like a cat stroked the wrong way. "I hope this is not about that bloody night that little fat fellow wandered out of here to get hisself skewered, because I answered all the questions I'm going to on that score. I am not going to be plagued with every constable this side of the river."

"Do I look like a constable?" the gentleman inquired icily with a lift of his brow. He drew an elegant calling card from his pocket and slid it across the counter.

Nagle squinted at this, his reading abilities none of the best. He was able to make out that he was dealing with a marquis of some sort, but that did little to ease Nagle's belligerent stance.

"All I want to know," his lordship continued, "is if you or any of your staff noticed when Sir Lancelot left the tavern and if he was alone."

Nagle scowled, but gave a grudging reply. "I can only tell you, m'lord, the same as I told the magistrate. We cannot keep track of everybody's comings and goings around here. I can hardly remember what happened last night, let alone two weeks ago."

"But that night must have stood out in your memory. There was a fight, was there not?"

"That's not such an unusual occurrence round here. Why must everyone keep bothering me about this business? Why not go ask your questions of the fellow best able to answer, that little Sir Whatsit that was attacked?"

"Because Sir Lancelot Briggs has never recovered full use of his faculties. He remains unable to speak of what happened to him." The marquis's hard stare did not waver, his haughty features, if anything, assuming a more rigid cast.

"Out of his wits, eh? Too bad," Nagle grunted uneasily. "But I cannot help you, m'lord. The most I recollect is that sometime after that brawl, the one gentleman as was fighting and that there Sir Briggs up and vanished. And as for the blond-haired fellow that took the worst of the drubbing, when he managed to get to his feet, he left howling for blood and vengeance against the whole world. Perhaps somebody ought to be asking that fine gentleman a question or two."

"I already tried. Sir Lucien has given up the lease on his house and left London. Gone to Bath for the sake of his health, or so his butler says."

"How convenient for him." Nagle sneered. "I wish I was there m'self."

The marquis lowered his eyes and Nagle found it a great relief to be spared any more of that piercing gaze. But his tension returned as the marquis asked, "And what of this notorious footpad, the Hook? You must have heard something about him, some speculation as to his identity perhaps, some whisperings from your patrons?"

Nagle began to polish the mugs behind the counter with a scrupulous attention they had never received before. "I've only ever heard enough to know the Hook is one person I want to stay clear of, and if your lordship is wise, you'll do the same."

Nagle did not look up from his task, but he could feel the power of those dark eyes boring into him. He heard the marquis's purse jangle as he laid it upon the counter. Nagle could not keep his eyes from straying to where his lordship fingered the soft leather in suggestive fashion.

"Are you certain you remember nothing else about the night Briggs was attacked?" the marquis purred.

Nagle licked his lips, but he had not entirely forgotten the presence of his other customer, the one who lingered in the shadows by the rear door.

Nagle said, "If I remembered anything, I would have said so."

He could almost feel the weight of the marquis's displeasure. But all his lordship did was to lay several pound notes by his calling card. "If your memory should improve, sir, I trust you will wait upon me. I could make it worth your trouble. My name and direction are written upon the card."

Nagle nodded in jerky fashion. He did not feel able to breathe freely until the marquis had turned and strode back out of the tavern. Then Nagle pounced upon the card and the money, shoving them deep in the pocket of his dirty apron.

The customer who had been lounging at the back of the tavern now stepped up to the bar. Nagle tried not to give a nervous start.

"What was that all about, George?" the young man asked.

But Nagle knew enough about Gideon Palmer not to be fooled by the deceptive pleasantry in Palmer's voice.

The tavern host forced a shrug. "Only some high and mighty lordship with nothing better to do than bother an honest working man with a deal of questions he can't answer."

"Mandell," Gideon muttered.

"What?"

"Nothing." Palmer stroked the scar that disfigured his chin. "So what did his lordship wish to know?"

"Just a deal of nonsense about the night that Briggs fellow was attacked and—and about the Hook."

"And what did you tell him, my dear friend George?"

The question was soft, but Nagle felt the hairs prickle along the back of his neck.

"I had nothing to tell his lordship, did I?" Nagle blustered. "And I wouldn't if I did. I have too much regard for my own skin and—and besides that, I have no patience for fellows as would squeak for a handful of coins."

"At least that is one thing we have in common, George," Gideon said with a silky smile. "Neither do I."

Mandell urged his black gelding through the gates into St. James's Park, the fresh smell of the grass and warm spring breeze dispelling the stench that clung to him from the Running Cat tavern, a noisome combination of sour spirits and stale smoke. There was nothing so enlightening, Mandell thought wryly, as returning to the scene of one's drunken revels when one was stone cold sober.

He had only returned to the tavern out of sheer frustration at Briggs's continued silence. Although Lancelot had recovered enough to sit up in bed, he seemed to retreat deeper into himself each day, shrinking from receiving any visitors, especially Mandell. If Briggs's assailant was to be apprehended, Mandell realized he would have to seek information from some other quarter.

Wheeling his horse into the leafy path that led toward the lake, Mandell grimaced at the image of himself visiting the tavern, playing at Bow Street Runner, a piece of pure foolishness that had gained him nothing. He did not know why he had bothered. Briggs was obviously beyond caring whether the Hook was captured or not. It would do little to aide his recovery or even assuage Mandell's guilt to charge about acting like some heroic avenger.

What he needed to do was to forget the whole sad and frustrating affair and regain his aura of cool detachment, something that he strove to do as he drew back on the reins, checking both his own impatience and the gelding's urge to break into a gallop.

Mandell focused his thoughts upon the rendezvous he had come to keep, in its own way a folly as great as his efforts to unmask the Hook. These visits to the park were a far sweeter pursuit, but equally as mad.

Since the weather had turned fine, Anne brought her daughter to St. James's before the park became too crowded with young bucks showing off their flashy phaetons and ladies unfurling their parasols, determined to be seen abroad at the fashionable hour. Mandell had taken to joining Anne and Norrie on their daily walk by the lake.

It was a strange habit for the cynical marquis of Mandell to have formed, he reflected. Certainly not his usual mode of courting a woman, strolling with her through the sedate walkways of St. James, helping her little girl feed bread to the ducks. No doubt it was the spring air filling his lungs, the breeze upon his cheek as warm and heady as a kiss that made him so eager for these afternoon jaunts.

As he drew closer to the pond, he caught himself leaning forward in the saddle, straining for his first glimpse of Anne.

His mistress.

The word still seemed wrong to him when applied to Anne, almost unholy. Despite the fact that he had managed to steal her away to his bed twice more since the first night they had made love, he preferred to think of her as his friend. It was a question of semantics, a way perhaps of avoiding the harsh realities of their relationship. But it was the only way he seemed able to continue to meet the innocence of her gaze and that of her daughter.

As he rounded a bend, the lake stretched out before him, and in the far distance, the stately buildings of the Horse Guard and Downing Street. The water shimmered in the sunlight, smooth as a looking glass, the surface broken only by the wakes of the majestic swans swimming near the embankment. A willow bowed over the embankment, its slender green branches trailing like a maiden's hair to the water's edge.

It was a scene of enchantment, a fitting setting for the little girl with the fairy-gold curls astride the snow-white pony. The leading reins were grasped firmly in the hands of a sturdy young groom, but Mandell found the picture incomplete.

He drew up with a frown of surprise when he saw no sign of Anne. She was usually never far from Norrie's side. Mandell had teased Anne about her tendency to hover, assuring her that for all of Norrie's air of fragility, she was a sturdy imp who would doubtless give her mama many uneasy moments when she grew a little older.

But he was given no time to reflect upon the mystery of Anne's whereabouts, for at that instant, Norrie spied his approach. She whipped her chip straw hat off her head, hailing him with its flowing pink ribbons as he approached. Her small face lit up with a joy and adoring trust that touched a corner of Mandell's heart he was not even aware existed.

He halted the gelding within yards of her pony, the young groom acknowledging Mandell's arrival with a respectful pull at the pony's forelock.

"Good afternoon, Miss Eleanor," Mandell said with mock gravity as he dismounted. "I see you are out exercising Pegasus this afternoon. But where is your mama?"

"She walked ahead down that path." Norrie's bright smile faded as she complained with all the dignity of an injured princess. "We did not think you were coming today. You are dreadfully late, Lord Man. Where have you been?"

"A thousand pardons, milady," Mandell said, sweeping the little girl his best leg. His hands encircling Norrie's waist, he lifted her out of the saddle, holding her high in his arms. "I was detained by a fool's errand."

"Who was the fool?"

"No one of any consequence," Mandell replied drily.

"Never mind then." Norrie patted his cheek in consoling fashion. "I am just very glad you are here now."

She took Mandell by surprise, flinging her small arms about his neck in an impulsive hug. He returned the embrace with an awkward pat on her back. Someone ought to inform Miss Eleanor about the impropriety of young ladies making such affectionate displays in public, but Mandell knew that he was not going to be the one to do so.

As he set her on her feet, she turned toward the gelding who was cropping at the tender green shoots of grass.

"You brought your horse today instead of the carriage," she said. "May I pet him?"

Mandell could see no reason why not. The gelding was a town-bred animal, selected for its docility in dealing with the chaos of London traffic. All the same, Mandell took a tight grip on the reins as Norrie patted the animal's velvety soft muzzle.

"What's his name?"

"Er—well . . ." Mandell had never troubled himself to think of sobriquets for his horseflesh. "I don't believe he has one."

"Did you forget it?" Norrie asked sadly. "The same as you forget what your mama used to call you?"

Mandell winced, recollecting their conversation of a few days ago, a discussion of nicknames. Norrie had wanted to know what he had been called when he was a small boy. Like Anne, the child had a habit of asking discomfiting questions.

To forestall any further mention of the subject, Mandell hastened to say, "I think I do recall the horse's name. It is . . . Nightmare."

He was left to reflect on the irony of the first choice that had popped into his head, but Norrie appeared satisfied with it.

"Nightmare," she crooned, giggling a little when the gelding nuzzled her hand. "I can hardly wait until my Pegasus grows into a horse as big as you."

Mandell laughed. "I am afraid he has a better chance of sprouting wings."

"Does he?" Norrie exclaimed.

Behind the child, Mandell saw the young groom rolling his eyes. Mandell hated to be the one to disillusion her, but he saw no remedy for it. He cleared his throat.

"What I meant, Miss Eleanor, is that ponies do not grow to be horses. Pegasus is already as big as he will ever be."

"Oh." She looked so crestfallen Mandell was goaded into making a rash promise.

"When you are old enough, I will get you a horse, a pretty little filly every bit as milky white as your Pegasus."

Norrie's eyes sparkled like the glitter of raindrops in the sun. "Thank you," she said. "Uncle Lucien gave me my pony, but I know he would never buy me a horse because he does not like me and my mama anymore. When we went past his house, he made mean looks at me this morning."

"This morning? But, Norrie, there is no one living at your uncle's house anymore. He has gone away."

"That's what Mama says. But I know I saw Uncle Lucien looking out the window, making faces like a hobedy-goblin." Norrie heaved a deep sigh. "Mama says I have too much 'magination."

"I fear Mama may be right." Mandell tweaked one of the child's curls. "And speaking of that wise lady, perhaps it is time we went and looked for her."

"She went down the path that way." Norrie said, pointing one stubby finger. "With your grandpapa."

"My grandfather?" Mandell echoed. He froze, certain he could not have heard the child properly. "You don't mean His Grace of Windermere?"

"Norrie nodded solemnly. "He's a duke, you know."

"Yes, I know that, babe, but my grandfather rarely ever visits the park."

"He came today, taking the air in his carriage and lo and behold!" Norrie spread her hands in an expressive gesture. "There we were. He just chanced upon us."

"Did he indeed?" Mandell muttered, knowing full well the duke of Windermere never did anything by chance. What reason could His Grace have for seeking out Anne? Mandell could not suppose it was a good one, considering the last conversation he had had with his grandfather regarding the lady. A strong sense of foreboding stole over him and he made haste to lift Norrie back onto the pony's saddle.

Turning the reins of his own mount over to the groom, Mandell said, "I will act as Miss Eleanor's chevalier."

"I wish Mama would let me ride the pony by myself sometimes," Norrie said.

But Mandell scarce heard the little girl's soft grumbling as he lead the pony back along the path. When they turned down the part that forked away from the lake, he could see his grandfather's shiny landau pulled off to one side, the old man's liveried servants standing to attention as they awaited his return.

His Grace stood with Anne beneath a copse of elm trees. For a moment, Mandell had eyes for nothing but her willowy form. She looked cool and elegant, as ever his proper Anne.

But he had no difficulty remembering how different she could be in the welcoming dark, turning into a woman of passion and fire in his arms, her slim white body melting against his, their hearts pounding in unison.

Mandell had always found that gratification of desire soon lessened his hunger. He was shaken to find that his yearning for Anne grew greater every time he saw her.

He suddenly realized that the moments he spent here in the park with her and Norrie had become precious to him, something to be jealously guarded. And the stiff old man standing by Anne's side was an intruder; winter come to put a blight on the first spring Mandell could remember delighting in for a very long time. He did not know what His Grace was saying to Anne to drive the color from her face, but he had a fair idea.

They were both too absorbed in their conversation to take much notice of Mandell and Norrie's approach. Mandell heard his grandfather's voice carry to him with disastrous clarity.

"It distresses me to speak so plainly, madam. But I trust I have made my feelings clear regarding your relationship with my grandson."

Anne nodded.

"Perhaps you had best make them clear to me," Mandell called out.

Anne looked up, her face coloring with dismay. The

duke came about more slowly, leaning heavily upon his walking cane as Mandell closed the distance between them.

"Ah, Mandell. There you are at last." The duke's heavy-lidded gaze traveled over Mandell, flicking from where his hand grasped the leading rein to the little girl mounted upon the pony. The sight appeared to afford His Grace no pleasure, for he said in ironic accents, "Something amiss with the child's groom, Mandell?"

"James is taking care of Nightmare," Norrie piped. "Lord Man is acting as my ... my shoveler."

The duke gave her a thin smile. Ignoring his grandfather, Mandell held out his hand to Anne. After a brief hesitation, she slipped her fingers into his grasp.

Mandell fought a strong urge to pull her to his side, drawing both her and Norrie into a protective circle that excluded the hard-visaged old man. But he contented himself with carrying Anne's fingers to his lips, smiling into her eyes. He noticed the duke's hand tighten upon the handle of his cane.

"I am sorry that I am late, my lady," Mandell said. "I was unavoidably detained."

"That is quite all right." Anne withdrew her hand, looking flustered under the duke's stern frown. "Your grandfather happened by and—and ..."

"And has endeavored to keep you suitably entertained?" Mandell's voice had an edge to it. He met the duke's gaze with challenge in his own. "You perceive me all agog to hear what His Grace has been saying to you."

"I don't think ..." Anne trailed off, casting a significant glance at Norrie. As though sensing the tension amongst the adults, the little girl had fallen silent, burying her hands in the lengths of her pony's mane.

"It is time that I was on my way," the duke said. "Perhaps you would care to escort me back to my carriage, Mandell."

"It would be my greatest pleasure, sir," Mandell grated.

He watched as his grandfather took his leave of Anne, sweeping her a courtly bow. But then the duke was the soul of chivalry. Mandell had no doubt His Grace had exercised the greatest of politeness while shredding Anne's heart and pride to ribbons.

Mandell pressed the pony's reins into Anne's hand. Her eyes were full of trouble and a deep sorrow that made him long to curse his grandfather. He wished he could offer her some reassurance, but he was not enough in command of himself to do so.

He strode after his grandfather, the two of them walking in tense silence back to His Grace's carriage. Mandell barely contained his mounting rage until they were out of earshot. Then he rounded upon the old man, saying tersely, "How did you know to come here today? How the devil did you know I would be meeting here with Anne? Have you set spies upon me now?"

"That would hardly be necessary, Mandell. You and your lady have not exactly been discreet, choosing to hold your lovers' trysts in such a public locale."

"Lovers' tryst!" Mandell choked. "With Anne's daughter present?"

The duke's lip curled. "That makes your conduct all the more distasteful."

Mandell clenched his hand. For a moment he almost forgot the duke's advancing years and relation to himself. Taking a cleansing breath to steady himself, he said, "And is this the sort of muck you have been spouting to Anne?"

"No. I merely took the opportunity to offer her the sort of advice her own father would have done were he still alive."

"And which is?"

"To put an end to whatever sort of liaison she has formed with you. Lady Fairhaven has always been noted for her virtue. She is far too good to be your mistress."

"But not good enough to be my wife!"

"I believe we had already settled that point in our last conversation, Mandell. Lady Fairhaven understands the inequities in your situations even if you do not."

"Anne is a damn sight too understanding," Mandell snapped. "What would you say if I told you that I agree we are unequal. I realize more all the time that the lady is quite far above me."

"I would say that your passion in this matter alarms me, Mandell. I raised you to have a better awareness of what you owe to the name I have given you."

"You raised me to be a cold-hearted, unfeeling bastard, just like yourself."

Something flickered in the old man's eyes, something that might have been pain in a countenance less icy. He clutched his walking stick, the lines about his mouth deepening as he stalked the rest of the way to his carriage. One of the bewigged footmen sprang forward at once to let down the steps and open the door.

The duke paused long enough to command, "You will end the connection, Mandell. I endured seeing your mother cast her life away on a mésalliance. I will not tolerate you making the same mistake. I brook no interference with my wishes."

"That is but one more way in which we are alike, Your Grace. I tolerate no interference, either."

Their eyes locked in one final clash of wills. Then Mandell turned and strode away, without glancing back. He heard the coachman give the signal and the clatter of wheels as the carriage lurched into motion and vanished down the lane, leaving that part of the park silent except for the twittering of some sparrows. But the peace of the afternoon seemed irrevocably shattered.

Mandell started back to where Anne waited for him beneath the trees. His gelding was tied off to a low-lying branch, but Norrie and her groom were nowhere in sight.

Anne had watched the entire scene, observing with dismay Mandell's white-hot rage, the old man's rigid disdain. It was strange. Anne had always known *of* His Grace of Windermere. One could not help having an awareness of a personage of such rank and such regal dignity, but the duke had always seemed far removed from the sphere of Anne's quiet existence.

Even as she had grown closer to Mandell, she had not thought about the duke's role as his grandfather. But then, she reflected ruefully, she had not allowed herself to think about much of anything these past weeks. She had learned to measure her life in moments instead of days, moments of strolling through the park with Mandell, of hearing him delight Norrie with legends of water nymphs and tree dryads, of glances exchanged above the child's head, of smiles both secret and tender. Of moments more private when Mandell played his music just for Anne, notes that conjured a majestic passion trapped within Anne's soul that only Mandell's caress could release. Moments when his eyes appeared darkened with a power beyond desire, when her heart fluttered with foolish, unspoken hopes . . . moments of a warm, romantic spring that seemed likely to spin on forever.

But it had taken only a few well-chosen words from His Grace of Windermere to bring the magic slamming to a halt. Anne rubbed her arms as though she had taken a sudden chill as she watched the duke's carriage vanish through the trees.

Mandell strode back to her across the grass, his face still gaunt with anger.

"Where's Eleanor?" he demanded.

"I asked James to take her back to the lake until—I thought it best if they gave the pony some exercise."

"Very wise of you." Mandell's eyes were full of such ironic understanding, Anne felt the color rise in her cheeks.

"Mandell, I never thought—that is, I never realized that I might be the cause of such discord between you and your grandfather. I am so very sorry."

"Damn it. Don't you dare, Anne Fairhaven!"

Anne retreated an involuntary step before Mandell's blaze of fury. "Don't you even think of apologizing for what is none of your fault simply because that old devil—"

Mandell spun away from her, pressing one hand to his brow, struggling for command of himself. Anne had never seen the ice-cool Mandell lose such control of his temper. He presented a stark figure set against the soft green of the park, the sunlight dappling between the trees.

Anne had often perceived him thus, standing so solitary,

possessing no close ties to anyone or anything. She realized that was in part what drew her to him, the sense that she might indeed have something to offer a man who always seemed too much alone. She had forgotten that he was also a marquis, an heir to a dukedom.

No matter what Mandell might say, she felt responsible for his quarrel with his grandfather. Going to him, she laid her hand gently upon Mandell's arm, seeking to mend some of the damage she had inadvertently caused. "My lord, I am sure the duke meant no harm. Your grandfather has been hearing rumors about—" Anne swallowed. "About the illicit nature of our relationship, and it worried him."

"His Grace has never fretted overmuch about my lack of morals before."

"He seems to perceive some difference in our affair."

"And so it is different." Mandell gave a harsh bark of laughter, pulling away from her. "I scarce know what I am about myself these days. Meandering through the park, stopping by to take tea with you, bringing dolls to your daughter instead of diamonds to adorn your neck. This is not exactly my customary procedure with a mistress, Anne."

Anne regarded him sadly. "Would it have been better if you could have set me up in an establishment, bought me carriages and expensive presents? Would you have preferred our relationship to be more . . . more common?"

He stared at her for a long hard moment. "No," he said at last, his eyes softening a little. "It has all been perfect just as it was."

Was. Anne tried not to allow that single word to sink too deep into her heart.

"Exactly what did my grandfather say to you?" Mandell demanded. "How badly did he insult you? I suppose he took great pains pointing out how unsuitable he finds you as a candidate for a marchioness."

"No, there was no need for him to do so. There has never been any question of marriage between us, Mandell, and so I told him." Anne attempted to suppress the wistfulness in her voice. "His Grace spoke only of the improprieties of a liaison such as ours. He expressed a great concern for you."

"For me or for the marquis of Mandell, the precious family honor?"

"At first, I did believe His Grace only worried about the possibility of scandal, but after you walked back with him to the carriage, Norrie said something most strange." Anne cast Mandell a half-embarrassed glance. "Lily always laughs at me for paying such heed to the notions of a child. But Norrie's perceptions often astonish me, my lord. When you and His Grace had gone, I attempted to soothe her, thinking the duke's gruff manner might have frightened her. But she just shook her head in that quaint serious little way she has and said, 'The duke is such a sad old gentleman, Mama. He looks at Lord Man like you look at me sometimes when you are afraid you might lose me again.' "

Mandell gave an impatient frown, half raised his hand as though he wanted to brush Norrie's words aside as nonsense, but could not manage to do so. He shrugged. "The child may be part right. Even in the midst of our quarrels, I sometimes feel a stab of pity for the old man. You must have heard about what happened to my mother. She was his favorite child, likely the only person he ever loved. He never recovered from her death. It poisoned his life."

"And yours?"

Mandell chose to ignore the question, retreating behind his familiar wall of reserve. "We stray from the subject, Anne," he said. "You are trying to paint for me this picture of the duke of Windermere as the doting grandparent, warning you most kindly about engaging me in improper behavior. Pardon me if I do not quite believe it, my dear."

"I never said your grandfather was kind to me. But he was civil."

"Civil as a duelist, observing all the niceties of the code, while circling with his foil, striking unerringly at your most vulnerable spot."

When Anne could not suppress a betraying flinch, Mandell gave a hard smile. "You see how well I know him, Sorrow. Did he find your vulnerability? It took far more than a scolding about being a naughty girl to drive the color from your cheeks. What else did he say to you? Tell me."

Anne moistened her lips and admitted reluctantly, "He—he did mention something that I had foolishly and selfishly not considered, a possible repercussion of an indiscretion such as ours."

"Repercussion?"

"He said that I was not only risking my own reputation, but that if any scandal attached to me, it would eventually attach itself to Norrie and ruin her future as well."

"Damn him! Damn him for using such a weapon against you." Mandell compressed his lips, then added, "And damn him for being right."

"Then you agree with him that the gossip about us might grow bad enough to do her harm. Oh, Mandell, I could not bear that."

"Neither could I. I could not endure bringing harm to either of you."

"It all seems so unfair," Anne said with a hollow laugh. "Lily has had scores of lovers, as have half the married women of the ton, I daresay. I stray once from the path of virtue and I am threatened with the direst of consequences."

"That is because you do not understand the rules of the game, my dear. Virtue is not so important as the appearance of it."

"Then we must learn to be more discreet, to greet each other in public as if we were strangers."

"It is far too late for such measures now. I see only one solution to the difficulties His Grace of Windermere has so graciously presented to us."

"You mean we must stop seeing each other altogether," Anne said in a voice of quiet misery.

"No." Mandell drew himself up to his full height, his dark brows crashing together. Anne thought he had never looked so formidable. "You will have to marry me."

"Wh-what?"

"Marry me," he repeated fiercely.

His words stunned Anne to silence. She could feel her

heart go still with a hope she dared not acknowledge. She raised her head, earnestly searching his face, delving into the black depths of his eyes. She found anger, pain, confusion, but not the emotion she sought. The hope died inside her, stillborn.

She eased her hands from his grasp and somehow found the courage to utter the most difficult word she had ever spoken in her life.

"No."

Mandell glared at her. "Did you not understand me? I just asked you to marry me."

"Demanded that I do so."

"Did you want me to go down on one knee, flatter you with some flowery speech of devotion?"

"It would make no difference. Not while your motive for doing so remained the same."

"And what would you know of my motives?"

"I can read them in your face." Anne brushed one finger upon his temple near the darkness roiling in his eyes. "Here, I see defiance of your grandfather." She trailed down to touch upon the implacable line of his jaw. "And here, I see the stubborn determination to offer me and Norrie the protection of your name."

"Rubbish. We both know I am not afflicted with such noble impulses. I already told you I consider myself obliged to marry one day, and contrary to His Grace's opinions, I have decided you would make me a suitable bride."

"You also told me your conception of marriage. The bartering of lands and title to beget an heir. A very cold bargain, Mandell."

"But not very different from the contract you willingly entered with your first husband," he sharply reminded her.

"I was younger then and a great deal more foolish. And at least with Gerald, I started out with the illusion of love."

"Is that what you are looking for, illusions?" He sneered. "So much for all your bold talk about being content with a few moments of passion. What was it you were really hoping for, Anne? That I would eventually fall in love with you, that your dragon would turn into a prince and carry you off to his castle to live happily ever after?"

Anne flinched at his acid tone.

"I don't believe in such romantic folly," he continued. "You knew that at the outset. The search for eternal love is nothing but some idiot's dream that can only lead to pain and sometimes . . ." He swallowed hard. "Sometimes even death."

"It would be better to risk both than to go about with your heart encased in ice, afraid to ever feel anything," Anne cried. "To spend your life as though you were still trapped in some dark closet—"

She broke off, horrified at what she had been betrayed into saying. But it was already too late. Mandell fixed her with an accusing stare, his face gone white.

"What the devil do you know of dark closets?" he asked.

"Nothing. I—I . . ."

"You merely chanced to overhear me sobbing in my sleep like some frightened child? When, Anne?"

When she did not answer him, he gripped her wrist. *"When?"*

Seeing that it was pointless to attempt to deny it, she confessed in a whisper, "The night that you collapsed at Lily's, when I had you put to bed in the guest room. You were delirious, caught in the throes of some hideous nightmare."

"You told me you heard nothing that night. You lied to me. Why?"

"Because I feared you would not have wanted me to have seen you when you were so devastated."

"You are quite right about that." He released her, stalking a few steps away. His reaction to her knowing of his most secret pain was all she had ever feared it would be. His eyes darkened with the haunted expression of a proud man suddenly stripped of all his defenses, left brutally exposed.

She wanted to touch him, draw him into the comfort of her arms, but she knew she did not dare.

"Mandell," she said softly. "It is nothing to be ashamed of that you should still feel grief and pain over what happened to your mother. You cannot simply forget such a terrible thing. Being vulnerable is no disgrace."

"That is where you are mistaken. Being vulnerable is the worst sin a man can commit." His jaw hardened. "It only leaves one open to the ridicule of the world and the misplaced compassion of tenderhearted fools such as yourself. Don't waste your pity upon me, Sorrow, simply because you saw me plagued by a nightmare.

"I may not be able to control my dreams, but I assure you I have always been in command of my waking hours, never allowing them to be cluttered by the sort of useless sentimentality that torments lesser men."

"Then it was quite wrong for you to propose marriage to me," Anne said. "A tenderhearted fool would never make you a good marchioness."

He stepped back, sketching her a stiff bow. "There seems nothing more to be said. I suppose at this juncture I am expected to utter some noble rot about wishing you every future happiness, but I am not that generous."

His bitter words stung her like a lash. She had thought his reaction to her refusal would be his usual shrug of indifference or even relief. What she had not expected was the depth of his anger, a flash of hurt in his eyes.

Pivoting on his heel, he strode to where his gelding was tied, undid the reins, and vaulted into the saddle. Anne pressed her fist to her mouth, swallowing the urge to call him back. She had to remind herself that if she had wounded anything, it had been his pride and not his heart.

As to the condition of her own heart, it was something she did not care to examine just now. She watched him wheel the black gelding about and thunder off through the park.

He had just vanished from view when Norrie cantered toward Anne on her pony. The child had coaxed James into allowing her to ride without his guiding hand upon the leading reins, but Anne felt too drained to remonstrate.

Norrie reined the pony to a halt, crying out in dismay, "Mama, where is Lord Man going? He did not even say good-bye to me and I wanted to show him how I can ride Pegasus all by myself."

Anne felt unequal to dealing with her daughter's disappointment, but she managed to reply, "Lord Mandell recollected something important he had forgotten to do. We cannot take up all of his lordship's afternoon, babe."

"Do you think he'll 'member about Aunt Lily's sore-ay tonight? Can I wait up to tell him about Pegasus then?"

Anne winced. She had forgotten about the cursed soiree herself, and she had promised to help Lily hostess.

"No, Norrie," Anne said dully. "I don't believe we shall be seeing Lord Mandell at Aunt Lily's tonight."

Or ever again.

But that thought was too bleak for Anne to acknowledge to herself let alone to her sad-eyed little girl.

Chapter 18

The party was what Lily termed a quiet evening, a little supper and cards for a select gathering of forty or fifty of the countess's most intimate acquaintances. She wished to introduce to her friends a passionate young poet she had met who promised to be as scandalous and infamous as Lord Byron.

Anne found Mr. Percy Shelley a little alarming, with his views that encompassed everything from atheism to the banishment of the monarchy. After dinner, when the gentleman was coaxed to recite some of his poetry, Anne was content to retreat behind the rosewood table in the drawing room, helping to serve the tea and coffee. She felt out of place amongst such brilliant company, but it seemed preferable to the solitude of her room this evening. She knew she would have done nothing but stare out the window into the gathering gloom, listen to the mournful sough of the wind through the trees, and think too much about Mandell, wondering what she would say to Norrie when he did not come to join them in the park tomorrow, wondering what consolation she could whisper to herself when he never came again.

Any distraction was better than such torment, though she wished Lily's party was livelier. The drawing room had become oppressively solemn, with the only sounds the crackling of the fire and the earnest cadence of Mr. Shelley's voice reciting a sonnet he had been working on of late.

Lift not the painted veil which those who live
Call Life: though unreal shapes be pictured there,
And it but mimic all we would believe
With colours idly spread . . .

From the fidgeting of many of the guests, Anne wondered if they comprehended Mr. Shelley any better than she. Only one listened with rapt attention, a latecomer who stood apart from the others, barely inside the threshold of the room.

Anne's heart gave a jarring thud. Mandell. She had so convinced herself that he would not come tonight, she had ceased to look for him. She had no idea at what juncture he had slipped inside the drawing room, joining the other guests.

The sight of him occasioned her as much pain as joy. The unrelenting set of his shoulders reminded her of his behavior when they had first met, proud, sardonic, aloof. She saw no trace of the man who could be so laughing and tender with her little daughter, nor the lover who had wooed Anne with such gentle passion, nor even the man who had been vulnerable enough to tear out of the park in a rage of hurt and anger. He was the marquis tonight, garbed in that style of severe elegance, the contrast of black and white that became him so well. His dark fall of hair was swept back from his forehead, candlelight flickering over the plane of his high cheekbones.

When Mr. Shelley finished his recitation, the company broke into a polite smattering of applause. Mandell strolled away from the doorway and glanced about the room. It was then that his eyes met Anne's. She saw at once that it was more than the length of the chamber that separated them. The distance was in his eyes tonight.

Her heart sank. So he had not forgiven her for slighting his proposal of marriage. Then why had he come? She could not believe it was to hear Mr. Shelley declaim his poetry.

As Mandell approached her refuge behind the tea table, Anne busied herself with rearranging the spoons and helping the dowager Lady Mortlane to coffee. With the duke of Windermere's words of warning about scandal still ringing in her ears, Anne fancied a dozen pair of critical eyes upon her and the marquis.

When the dowager moved away to chatter and whisper with some of her acquaintances, Mandell took Lady Mortlane's place in front of the table. As he towered over her, Anne was too much aware of the silk-sheathed contours of his hard masculine figure. She strove to maintain a calm outward facade.

"Good evening, Lord Mandell." It was difficult greeting him as a mere acquaintance, but if she did not look up at him, she found she could succeed. "Such a surprise to see you here this evening."

"Where did you think I would be?" he murmured low enough so that only she could hear. "Languishing at home with a broken heart?"

The cold sneer in his words cut her deeply. It had been so long since he had used that tone with her.

"No, you are looking very . . . fit," she said with forced cheerfulness. "May I pour you some coffee?"

Her fingers trembled so badly when she offered him the cup, Mandell was obliged to steady her hand with his own. The contact was warm and all too fleeting.

"You appear to be a little overcome this evening, my lady," he drawled. "Perhaps it is owing to the force of Mr. Shelley's poetry."

"I scarce understand it and what I do comprehend saddens me, all this talk of raising painted veils and discovering only fear and disillusionment beneath."

"I found his little sonnet most amusing and quite apt. How did that one part go? Ah, yes. 'He sought, For his lost heart was tender, things to love, But found them not, alas!' "

He quoted the words with a harsh mockery that tore at Anne's already raw nerves.

"Please don't, Mandell," she begged, casting a nervous glance around, relieved that Lily's other guests were out of earshot.

"Don't what, my dear? Sigh over Mr. Shelley's words? I thought such behavior would be expected of me. I am not certain how one plays the role of rejected suitor."

"I wish you would be honest enough not to do so at all." Anne met his gaze with a look of quiet reproach.

He scowled at her. She thought he meant to pivot on his heel and stalk away. But after a brief hesitation, the hard line of his mouth relaxed. His dark lashes drifted down, veiling the intensity of his eyes.

"You are right, Anne," he said at last. "I am sorry. I don't know what madness came over me today. I fear you unmanned me when you confessed to knowing about the nightmares. It was generous of you to have spared my pride for so long, pretending to have witnessed nothing, and I behaved like a perfect ass about the whole thing."

"It was natural that you were distressed. I was too blunt when I blurted out the truth, and I should have refused your offer of marriage with more tact."

"You mean by thanking me in the conventional manner for the great honor I had done you, saying you felt compelled to refuse me with deepest regrets?" he asked. "No, Sorrow, I am glad one of us retained their integrity and common sense this afternoon."

Anne winced, wishing she deserved the praise. But she did not feel very sensible with Mandell so near. He set down the coffee cup. Bending over her, he half started to reach for her hand, but like herself, he was forced to remember they were not alone. He drew back as several ladies bustled up, clamoring for tea.

After Anne had served them and they had drifted away again, Mandell complained, "Is it necessary for you to attend to this? The countess has enough servants milling about doing nothing. I would like you to walk out with me onto the terrace."

Anne stole a glance toward the French doors and thought of losing herself with Mandell in the whispering darkness of Lily's garden. She steeled herself to resist the temptation.

"It would be too chilly."

"It is a deal warmer than the first night you allowed me to lure you into the gardens."

"I fear a night as warm as that one will never come again, my lord."

Mandell vented an impatient sigh. "Then at least take a turn about the room with me. I need to speak to you, Anne."

Before she could protest further, he summoned one of the footmen to take Anne's place behind the tea urn. Most of the other guests were gathering about the pianoforte where Lady Mortlane swept back her train with a flourish and sat down to delight the company with a few selections.

The dowager played competently enough, but without Mandell's soul and fire. As he escorted Anne away from the tea table, she saw him grimace. He led her to the far end of the drawing room, to the shadowed recess of one of the tall curtained windows. Anne affected to admire the view of Lily's gardens, but all she saw was Mandell hovering behind her, his reflection shimmering phantomlike in the night-darkened panes.

He sought again to apologize for his conduct. "I am astonished you can forgive me for my surly behavior, abandoning you like that at the park."

"You will have more to do to appease Norrie," Anne said. "She was disappointed when you left so soon. She has grown to be very fond of you."

"You must convey to her my deepest regrets."

"You do not intend to come and see her again yourself?" Anne asked, although she already knew the answer.

"No, I think it best that I do not." Although he smiled, the lines about his mouth were deep, carved with weariness and resignation. "We appear to have reached an impasse in our relationship, my dear. You do not make me a very conformable mistress and it is obvious I will never make you a worthy husband."

"I think you could make a worthy husband someday," Anne said wistfully. "If only you would learn to set more value upon your heart than your estate and title."

"And to think I once said you demanded too little, Sorrow. You ask far too much."

Anne's hand fluttered to the lace at her throat, attempting to massage away the constriction she felt gathering there.

"No, Mandell. I never expected that you would—that our time together would last forever."

"You told me you were seeking only a few memories. Have I given you that much, milady?"

"Oh, yes! I spent so much of my life being afraid of the dark. I will always remember you as the man who taught me to love the power and beauty of night."

If only she had not also learned to love the man himself, difficult, forever distant, locked away behind that wall of reserve she doubted he would ever permit anyone to breach. Those brief moments she had spent in the park with his grandfather had served to clarify for her the enigma that was Mandell. She could see it all now, how it must have been for the frightened child who had endured the horror of his mother's death and the pain of his father's defection, only to be thrust into a strange land, placed in the care of a stern and embittered old man. The duke of Windermere had obviously taken great pains with his grandson's education, fashioning a sensitive boy into the haughty marquis, the cynical nobleman who believed in nothing, not even himself.

It was ironic, Anne thought. Never had she been able to understand Mandell so well as she did at this moment and never had they been further apart. Fearful lest her face betray her thoughts, she moved closer to the window. She sensed a movement of his hands as though he meant to rest them upon her shoulders. But his touch never came.

"You will take care of yourself and young Eleanor?" he said.

Anne nodded, not trusting herself to speak.

"If you should ever need me for anything, you know you have only to send for me. If Lucien should return to torment you—"

"I don't believe that he will."

"But if he should— Norrie made an odd remark to me

in the park today. She said she thought she saw her uncle peering at her from the window of his house."

"She told me that, too, and I sent one of the footmen to check. The house is all closed up. There is no one there." Anne felt composed enough to face him again. "You must not worry about any more danger from Lucien, my lord."

"I would not if you gave me your promise never to receive him again, never to be alone with him. I have felt uneasy ever since I learned of his abrupt departure from London. I found it rather odd coming so soon after the attack on Briggs."

"But Lucien had nothing to do with that. Your friend Sir Lancelot was set upon by the Hook, was he not?"

"Yes, the dread Hook, the brigand so desperate for riches he kills and leaves his victims' gold watches behind. I find something deuced odd about that, Anne, so much so that I wonder if the authorities have been wrong to search for the Hook amongst the alleys and slums of the east side; if they should not be looking in more respectable quarters."

"What do you mean?" Anne asked uneasily.

"I'm damned if I know myself. It is only a parcel of vague suspicions that persist in tormenting me. Just promise me that you will be careful, Anne, and I shall be satisfied. I do not wish to waste our last moments together talking about the Hook."

Our last moments.

Anne bit down upon her lip to prevent its trembling.

"I promise," she said. She held out her hand, adding bravely, "Then this truly is farewell."

"I fear that it is." He raised her fingers to his lips. The kiss he placed there was achingly tender, warm, and lingering. "This time I can honestly wish you every happiness, my dear. I do not believe in love or forever afters, but—"

He hesitated then added hoarsely, "But, by God, Anne, you make me wish that I did."

Mandell had never meant to say anything like that. Having decided that it was right this relationship should end, he had meant to say his good-byes with merciful swiftness. It should not have been this difficult, this painful, bidding her farewell. But nothing with Anne was ever as it should have been.

Mandell found himself still clinging to her hand until they were interrupted by the approach of her sister, and he was obliged to release her.

"Ah, there the two of you are." The countess raised an arched eyebrow. "My dear Anne, you must not keep Mandell sitting in your pocket all evening. The loose tongues have enough to wag about already."

Not giving Anne a chance to reply, Lily turned to Mandell. Rapping him playfully with her fan, she affected a pout of displeasure. "I have a complaint to lodge against you, my lord."

"Indeed?" Mandell's voice yet sounded husky and he struggled to regain his composure.

"I thought we were old friends. How could you keep such a secret from me?"

Mandell saw a telltale flush mount in Anne's cheeks and he moved instinctively to shield her.

"I don't know what you mean," he said.

"There is no use pretending anymore. How is your grandfather taking the tidings of the connection? Not well, I daresay."

Mandell had hoped that no one save himself and Anne knew of that grim scene in the park.

"Well, I—" he began hesitantly.

"His Grace could not have been more stunned than I was," Lily rattled on. "I am certain we all thought your cousin would end a crusty old bachelor. Drummond never seemed the sort to do anything so wildly romantic as elope."

"Drummond?" Mandell echoed. Lily's conversation had often made him feel as though he were trying to swim upstream. He had his first inkling that the countess was not speaking of the thing that he had feared, the affair between himself and Anne. But what she did seem to be talking about was equally confounding.

"Nick. Elope?" he said scornfully. "My dear countess, wherever did you hear such nonsensical gossip?"

"The proof, my lord, stands yonder. When I invited Drummond tonight, I never expected him to come with a new bride in tow. I gather he wed her just yesterday morning, this mysterious beauty no one knows. You must tell me all about her, Mandell, who her family is, where she is from. Then perhaps I shall forgive you."

With a sweeping gesture, Lily nodded toward the cluster of people near the door. Mandell had been so absorbed with Anne these past minutes, the drawing room had faded to insignificance. They might well have been alone. But now he became aware of the excited hubbub of voices, of Drummond's brightly garbed figure surrounded by Lily's guests, his hand being pumped in earnest congratulations. The other newcomer was less visible except for the elegant train of her gown. All view of her face was blocked by the waving fans and headdresses of the other females.

Mandell's brows drew together in a heavy frown.

"My dear Mandell, you look positively thunderstruck. Could it be you actually did not know of your cousin's intent to wed, either?" Lily purred in delight. "I fear this will quite put an end to your reputation for uncanny perception. Never mind, sir. It shall be my privilege to be the first to entertain the newlyweds and to introduce you to your own cousin's bride."

Lily linked her arm through Mandell's. He glanced back for Anne only to discover she had quietly slipped away. Mandell would have been grateful for the chance to do so himself but he was too stunned to do other than permit Lily to lead him across the room, chattering as she did so.

"Actually Drummond's startling news has proved a godsend. This party was getting excessively flat. Mr. Shelley turned out to be such a disappointment. His poetry is depressing enough to make one want to hang oneself. If only he could be more like Lord Byron, so deliciously rude, dark, and brooding. Mr. Shelley is a pleasant young man, but I fear he will never take in society."

Mandell scarce heeded one word in ten, his mind still reeling. Drummond elope? Mandell could not credit it. He had never known Nick to spare any female a second glance except for that dour Quakeress he had once admired for starting schools for the poor. But even the flighty countess would hardly describe Miss Abdingham as a mysterious beauty.

Mandell eased out of Lily's grasp and elbowed some of her guests aside, as both his curiosity and impatience mounted. Drummond glanced up at his approach, his face flushed with a strange mixture of happiness and defiance.

"Mandell, I hoped you would be here tonight. There is someone I have to present to you."

"So I gather," Mandell said. "What the deuce sort of mischief have you been about, Nick?"

"None I fear that you will approve." Nick flashed him a smile. It struck Mandell that Nick's gaiety was forced, so bright as to be almost feverish.

"My dear, come here." Nick disengaged his bride from the cluster of excited females, dragging her forward.

For Mandell, all sound, all movement in the room faded to a blur. He could focus on nothing but the face of the dark-haired woman immediately before him, a face of sultry beauty with bright eyes that had ever reflected his own cynicism.

Sara.

He inhaled sharply, feeling as though a heavy blow had forced the breath from his lungs. Too shocked to say anything for several seconds, he finally managed to growl, "Is this some sort of a jest?"

"I would hardly jest about anything that means so much to me." Nick's hand tightened possessively on Sara's arm as he said, "My love, allow me to introduce you to my cousin, the marquis of Mandell. Mandell, this is my bride, Sara."

"I believe the *lady* and I have already met," Mandell said through clenched teeth.

Sara waxed pale, but she was still brazen enough to offer him her hand. "Ah, yes, we were introduced once at . . . at Drury Lane Theatre, was it not? How have you been, my lord?"

She tipped up her chin in a challenging manner as

though daring him to contradict her, to say anything more. She knew full well that he could not, damn her. Not in front of a roomful of curious eyes, not without shattering Nick completely.

Mandell had suspected this day might come, when he would meet his former mistress again, Sara triumphant, at last breaching the doors of the society she had always craved, leaning on the arm of some poor fool she had snared to realize her ambition. Mandell had expected to derive great amusement from the moment. But he did not feel in the least like laughing.

Sara and Nick. How was it possible? How could they even have met? With Nick always so buried in his Parliamentary doings, Sara would have had to have arranged it, have deliberately sought Nick out, knowing him to be Mandell's cousin.

The silence stretched out. Mandell was aware of Nick's burning gaze upon him. He was forced to take Sara's hand. Bending over it, he murmured for her ears alone.

"You bitch."

"Thank you, my lord," she muttered back, her teeth gritted in a smile. "That was exactly the sort of felicitation I expected from you."

Sara slipped her hand from his grasp, only to be swept off by Lily to be introduced to the rest of the pack of cooing females. Mandell seized Nick by the arm and pulled him roughly to one side.

"You young idiot," he hissed. "What the devil have you done?"

"Fallen in love and gotten married, Mandell. Some men do, you know."

"Not with some—some—"

"Take care," Nick warned, his eyes blazing.

"Some female." Mandell amended the epithet he had been about to apply to Sara. "Some woman that you cannot have known for very long. Can you possibly have any idea of who she is, what her background might be?"

"I know Sara far better than you could ever imagine."

Did you know she had once been my mistress? Mandell

had to bite his tongue. It would be unthinkable to blurt such a thing aloud, unthinkable and cruel. For all his hard defiance, a hint of vulnerability lurked about the corners of Nick's mouth, the trust of an idealistic dreamer. Small wonder that Sara had found him such easy prey.

Mandell expelled a deep sigh. "Why, Nick?" he asked wearily. "Why could you not have come and talked to me first before you did anything so rash as to elope?"

"Oh, yes, cousin, you are just the sort of tenderhearted fellow I would have sought to confide in about Sara. You would have told me to go take a cold bath or—or something worse." Nick's throat worked. "There has been so much I have wanted to discuss with you, but you have never taken me seriously. No one ever has."

He gave a shaky laugh. "Now it is too late. Everything seems to have spun out of my control. We just came from calling upon grandfather. He has cut me off completely and I don't give a damn. As if I would ever want anything from *him*."

Nick pronounced these last words with a savage vehemence that astonished Mandell. "I love Sara, Mandell. She is the only thing I have to cling to in a world gone mad. So if you have any insulting remarks to make about her, you had best be prepared to meet me with pistols at dawn. You always did say if we ever fought, it would have to be over a woman."

"But not this one," Mandell said bitterly. As he looked deep into Nick's stormy grey eyes, he could see how well and truly Drummond was caught in Sara's toils. He raised his hand in a gesture rife with frustration and hopelessness, then started to stalk away. He was stayed by Nick's hand on his sleeve.

"Damn it, Mandell," Nick pleaded. "Even if you do not approve, can you not at least wish me well? That is all I am asking."

Mandell shook him off.

"Congratulations," he muttered. Unable to meet Nick's eyes any longer, Mandell forced his way past the throng of Lily's guests and strode out of the room.

* * *

Huddled on the stone bench in Lily's garden, Anne stared at the lights that blazed in her sister's drawing room. But the silhouettes that passed before the windows seemed to grow fewer and fewer. Most of Lily's guests must have gone home.

How long had she been sitting out here? Hours perhaps. Anne was not sure. After Mandell had bade her good-bye, she had felt the need to escape before she was overcome by her emotions and disgraced them both. Lily's interruption had been fortuitous. While her sister had distracted Mandell, Anne had been able to slip out through the French doors unnoticed.

Seeking the veil of darkness, the trees whispering about her like sheltering arms, Anne had sunk down upon a stone bench. A moonlit garden was such a perfect place for a stolen kiss or to sit in solitude and allow one's heart to quietly break.

But strangely, the urge to weep had left her. She remained dry-eyed, her heart numb. She supposed the unbearable ache of loss would strike later, but for now she sat perfectly still, feeling nothing but the cool night air upon her cheeks, listening to the rustling of the newly minted spring leaves, the distant clatter of carriages passing in the street beyond the garden wall.

Lily's flowers had begun to bloom in earnest, but they would not reach their full exotic glory until early June. Lily would have closed up the house by then, preparing to join the fashionable crowd flocking to Brighton. She had invited Anne and Norrie to join her and Anne supposed that they would. Norrie would so love the sea. It would give the child something to look forward to when Anne told her that Mandell would no longer be—

No. She could not think about that just now. Anne shifted upon the bench, wrapping her arms more tightly about herself, trying to concentrate on the more distant future. After Brighton, she would retire with Norrie to the country, find some way to resume the placid life Anne had once known. Given enough time, she could surely find a measure of contentment, could she not? After all, she still had her daughter, and Lily, for all her flightiness, was a most affectionate sister.

But who would Mandell have? Anne found that it was him she grieved for more than herself. No doubt he would resume his rakehell lifestyle, likely find another mistress who would be . . . what was the word he had used? More conformable. Maybe he would even acquire that wife he had spoken of, the elegant, ambitious lady who would want nothing more from him than his name.

But he would be alone as he always had been. His nightmares would still come, with no one to soothe him as he slept, no one to understand.

Anne thought she would never forget the anguish in his eyes when he had said, *I do not believe in love or forever afters, but by God, Anne, you make me wish that I did.*

Until that moment, Anne had never realized how close she had come to touching his heart. It had made the parting from him that much more painful, more poignant, as she saw so clearly what they might have had together. She had longed to kiss him, to hold him, to desperately find some way to give him back the part of himself that had been torn from him long ago by a terrible black night in Paris, by the enduring bitterness of an old man. But she realized the impossibility of such a thing.

"I wanted to lead you from the darkness, my love," she whispered. "But I could not do so. I fear you must find your own way back."

Her eyes burned, and she was able to weep at last, but only a single tear that cascaded silently down her cheek. She dashed it away with the back of her hand.

Glancing back toward the house, Anne saw that the lights from the drawing room no longer shone so bright. Someone had begun to extinguish the candles. It must be even later than she had realized. She was a little surprised that her absence had not been noted. The furor over Mr. Drummond's elopement must have absorbed everyone's attention, even Mandell's.

Lily probably supposed that Anne had retired to her room, and Anne was glad that no one had come in search of her. She did not feel equal to facing her sister. Lily had been too preoccupied with her own affairs these past days to notice much of what had passed between Anne and Mandell. But Anne feared that Lily had observed enough tonight to ask Anne some awkward questions, questions Anne had no desire to answer.

But she was not eager to find herself locked out of the house, either. Shivering, she noticed the air seemed cooler than when she had first ventured outside. Clouds sifted across the face of the moon, making the garden darker, no longer so soothing, somehow more unfriendly.

Anne rose from the bench, shaking out her skirts. She prepared to follow the path leading back to the terrace steps when she heard the sharp snap of a twig. Peering through the gloom, she thought she saw a shadow pass behind one of the trees. Perhaps Lily had sent one of the footmen in search of her after all.

Surely she would have noticed someone coming down from the house. Anne fretted with the lace at the neckline of her gown, a sense of uneasiness stealing over her. She started when she detected the crack of another branch. This time the sound seemed to be coming from behind her.

She spun about, her heart thudding uncomfortably. "Is—is anyone there?" she called. "John? Matthew? Firken?"

No one responded. The path threading through the plants and flowering shrubs remained empty. Feeling a little foolish, Anne ventured a few steps along the gravel walkway. As she neared the stone wall, she was disturbed to see the garden gate standing ajar.

Left unlatched, it had been blown open by the wind, she tried to tell herself. Except that the breeze was hardly strong enough to disturb the delicate branches of the rose bushes, let alone move a heavy iron gate.

The night itself seemed to stir around Anne, taking on a presence. She could feel the hair prickle at the back of her neck and experienced a strong urge to flee for the shelter of the house.

"Stop being ridiculous, Anne Fairhaven," she scolded

herself. It would be a bold intruder indeed to invade the
sanctuary of someone's private garden. The open gate was
a sign of nothing but one of the servant's carelessness.
Anne forced herself to go forward, intending to slam the
gate closed and lock it.

But her fingers had no sooner touched the cold metal of
the bars when a figure loomed out of the shadows cast by
the wall. Anne started to scream, but she was roughly
seized, one arm pinned behind her back. Her cry was
choked off by the gloved hand clamped over her mouth.

"Don't scream, Anne," a familiar voice rasped. "It is
only me. Lucien."

His words conveyed to Anne no sense of reassurance.
Rather, her heart gave a terrified leap and she put up a frantic struggle to free herself. Lucien's grip only tightened
more cruelly, the leather of his glove bruising her lips.

"Anne, please. I am not going to hurt you. I must talk to
you."

Anne sensed a level of desperation beneath Lucien's
harsh whisper. His body reeked of stale sweat and strong
spirits. Dear God! He had been drinking. The realization
only deepened her fear.

"If you will promise to be quiet and not to run away," he
breathed close to her ear, "I will let you go."

Although her heart pounded madly, Anne attempted to
subdue her panic, sensing that cooperation might gain her
more than her futile efforts to break loose of Lucien's
grasp. She made herself go still, and after a few agonizing
moments she felt Lucien's hold on her slacken, his hand
easing away from her mouth.

She twisted free of him and backed away a few steps,
gasping, "Lucien! What—what are you doing here?"

"I had to find you . . . needed to see you."

"Then c-come up to the house and—"

"No!" He swayed slightly forward and Anne gained a
fleeting impression of his appearance, his hair unkempt, his
clothing dirty and rumpled as though it had been slept in
for many days. He sounded too sober to be drunk and yet

there was a wildness about him she found even more unnerving.

She glanced toward the house, attempting to gauge the distance and the chances of reaching the security of those walls before Lucien intercepted her.

As though guessing her intent, Lucien shifted, planting the solid outline of his stocky frame directly in her path.

"I—I don't know what you want with me," she said. "We have nothing more to say to one another. You are not even supposed to be here in London. Norrie said she saw you peering out the window at her, but I did not believe her. What sort of game are you playing with us now?"

"No game. I have been hiding, trapped in my own house."

"Hiding? From whom?"

"That devil. Your high and mighty Lord Mandell." Lucien spat out the name with loathing and dread.

"N-nonsense," Anne faltered. "Mandell has no more desire to seek your company than you do his."

"Is this nonsense?" Lucien stumbled closer, gesturing toward his face. The moon had drifted from behind the clouds enough to illuminate the ravaged contours of Lucien's features.

Anne choked back a soft cry. His nose was bent to an angle, a large bump forming where the bone was not healing properly. His face was yet streaked with sickly yellow bruises, the pockets of flesh beneath his eyes puffy from lack of sleep. But it was the eyes themselves that truly horrified her, glazed over, bloodshot. He looked exhausted. He look haunted. He looked . . . mad.

When Lucien thrust his face even closer, Anne could not refrain from shuddering and looking away.

"What is wrong, Anne?" he asked. "Can you not bear the sight of what your lover did to me? He wanted to kill me. He still does."

Lucien's voice rose on a note of hysteria. "He's been stalking me. Every time I look over my shoulder, he's there. I catch just a glimpse of his cloak. Even in the daytime, even hidden away in my own house, he watches me. I should have destroyed him when I had the chance. I should have had my revenge on all of you. Even the child."

Lucien's eyes gleamed wildly and Anne did not wait to hear more. She made a panicked effort to dart past him. He clutched at her arm, but she managed to wrench free. Her heart thundering, she raced up the path, expecting to hear him come crashing after her.

But instead his voice shattered on a mighty sob. "Anne! Please. I am sorry. I didn't mean that. Don't leave me. You have to help me. You have to make Mandell stop. You have to m-make him . . ."

Anne hesitated long enough to glance back. She saw Lucien sag to his knees. Burying his face in his hands, he rocked back and forth. His ragged sobs seemed to go right through Anne. He sounded so much like the pathetic boy she had once known, she was moved to pity in spite of herself.

Although she knew it was less than wise, she found herself returning. Maintaining a cautious distance between them, she said soothingly, "Hush, Lucien. I don't know what has put such strange notions in your head, but I assure you Lord Mandell has not been following you. He does not even realize you are still in London."

Lucien raised his tear-streaked face to stare up at her. "Is—is that what he says? He lies. He has been after me day and night, just—just waiting for his chance. And I'm all alone. My servants have deserted me. The c-cowards fled the night I saw Mandell's reflection and I had to shoot the mirror."

Lucien crushed his fingers against his brow so hard he seemed to be trying to shatter his own skull. "I cannot bear it anymore," he wept. "I can't sleep. This accursed pain in my head grows w-worse every moment. Even the tincture of opium does not help anymore."

Opium. Dear God, Anne thought. At least that accounted for his strange delusions. "You should go back home," she said, making one last effort to reason with him. "And try to rest. I will summon a doctor for you."

"Doctor? What doctor? The sort that would have me

clapped up in Bedlam?" Lucien shrilled at her, glaring through his tears. "You'd like that, wouldn't you, Anne? Shutting me away would be as good as having me killed. Maybe you are even helping Mandell to do this to me."

His sudden shift to anger alarmed Anne into retreating again. Attempting to humor him, she said, "I—I don't want to hurt you, Lucien. I will make sure you are safe. I will fetch some of Lily's footmen to escort you home. They will protect you."

But Lucien was clearly no longer listening to her. He had tensed, jerking upright, like some wary beast sensing the approach of the hunter. He whipped about, staring, and pointed a shaking finger. "There! What did I tell you? He's there again."

"W-where?" Anne asked. She peered into the darkness at the end of the garden, seeing only the breeze stirring the tendrils of ivy along the side wall.

"There! Over by the gate!"

"Lucien. There is no one here," Anne whispered.

"Can you not see him?"

Anne watched stunned as Lucien lurched forward, shrieking.

"Curse you, Mandell. Show yourself. If you want to kill me, do it. But I can bear no more of this hellish torment."

He staggered forward, thrashing about amongst Lily's rosebushes. Anne stood momentarily paralyzed with a mixture of horror and pity. She had never seen anyone driven by madness before. The sight was dreadful. She knew she had to force herself to move, summon aide from the house, find some way to stop Lucien before he brought harm to himself.

But as she turned to go, Lucien vanished from her line of sight. She could still hear his hideous sobbing and cursing. She took a cautious step along the path and looked for him. He was by the gate.

Her blood froze. She wondered if she had been afflicted with Lucien's madness. She saw him grappling with a phantom, a creature that should have had no existence outside of Lucien's insane imagination. The spectre's ink black cloak blended with the night, his features shadowed by a large plumed hat as he attempted to level a pistol at Lucien.

Anne's throat closed with terror as she watched Lucien make a desperate grab for the weapon. The force of the struggle carried the two men beyond the gate, out onto the pavement.

Anne attempted to scream for help. She rushed forward to Lucien's aid, scarce knowing what she meant to do, what she could do. A loud retort rang out and Anne saw Lucien stagger back, clutching his chest.

Anne forced her trembling limbs to move faster, but by the time she reached the gate opening, the cloaked man had vanished, melting into the darkness like the vision from a nightmare.

There was only Lucien, sprawled out on his back, the light from the street lamp glinting on his golden hair, the crimsom tide of his blood staining the pavement. Shaking, Anne crept to his side.

His face was contorted with pain, a rasping noise emanating from his throat as he struggled to breathe. He stared up at her through half-closed lids.

"Anne . . ."

She glanced frantically along the darkened street, praying that someone had heard the shot besides herself. To her relief she heard the echo of distant footsteps, and behind her she saw more lights begin to glow behind Lily's windows. The household had been aroused.

Anne knelt down beside Lucien, her knee striking up against something. The pistol. Lucien must have wrenched it from the man's hand even as he was shot. Scarce thinking what she did, Anne picked up the weapon.

"Anne," he groaned. "What have you done to me? Would never have happened . . . but for you."

"Hush, Lucien," she said, touching trembling fingers to his brow. He already felt so clammy and cold. "Try to be still. Help is coming.

"Too late. Curse you, Anne. You've . . . you've killed me."

His chest heaved in a violent convulsion as he made a

desperate effort to draw air into his lungs. A horrible rasping noise came from his throat. His head lolled to one side and he went suddenly still, his eyes vacant and staring.

"L-Lucien?" Anne whispered. She blinked as light fell over his distorted features. Only then did she realize she was no longer alone. Someone stood over her, holding up a lantern.

Dazed, Anne glanced up to see a pool of stunned faces, some she recognized as Lily's servants. But the swaying light was held aloft by the old charley who patrolled Clarion Way, and he was staring down at the pistol still clutched in Anne's hand with a deep reproach in his ancient eyes.

Chapter 19

Morning sunlight streamed through the windows of the marquis's study, but the warmth did not touch Mandell where he sat slumped in the wing chair by the hearth, lost in troubled slumber. He had known if he dared sleep, the dream would come, but he could no longer bring himself to care. Since his parting with Anne, he had struggled with feelings of desolation, of utter hopelessness. Sometime near dawn he had surrendered, falling into an exhausted sleep, eventually allowing the nightmare to claim him.

But it was different this time. Mandell frowned, sensing it even in the depth of his slumber. He heard the knocking at the door, the thunder of the dream command. *Open! Open in the name of the tribunal!* But this time it was not his mother's soft hands seeking to thrust him into the closet, but bony fingers, gnarled with age.

A mocking voice cackled in his ear. *Forget, boy. Forget everything except that you are the marquis of Mandell.*

"No." Mandell muttered, tossing his head against the chair's hard cushion. He could not forget. "You don't understand. Have to save her."

Struggling to free himself from those clutching hands, he peered down the length of a mist-shrouded street. He could see the distant forms of the mob, mad, howling like a blood-crazed beast with a hundred mouths. And she was there, in their midst, being hauled away by a black-cloaked phantom in a plumed hat.

Anne! Anne!

The phantom glanced back when Mandell called. He

could sense the burning mockery of its gaze, but its features were obscured by a death white veil, clinging to its face like a gossamer layer of skin. The phantom dragged Anne toward a towering scaffold and Mandell could see the guillotine, its sharp blade already rich with blood.

He had to get to Anne, had to tear away the veil that hid the phantom's hideous features. It was the only way to save her. Mandell fought against the restraining hands, but it was hopeless. The aged fingers seemed only to grow stronger, entwining him like vines, pulling him back into the suffocating darkness of the closet.

When he was thrust inside, the door slammed closed. He could hear insane laughter and then the hammering. The door was being nailed shut so that he could never escape . . .

"No!"

Mandell's head snapped forward. He wrenched awake with a start. His breath coming quickly, his gaze roved round the study as he tried to recollect where he was and shake off the last vestiges of the dream. It bewildered him because he was now certain he was fully awake. And yet the hammering had not ceased.

He blinked, then realized that someone was knocking insistently upon the study door. Before he could recover his wits enough to issue any command, the door inched open. Hastings thrust his head through the opening and inquired anxiously, "My lord?"

Mandell pressed his fingertips to his eyes and indicated with a curt gesture that the footman could enter. Hastings stepped inside.

"I am sorry, my lord. I did not mean to disturb you."

"You didn't. I had merely dozed off for a few minutes."

Hastings frowned. "Did my lord sleep all night in that chair?"

"No." Mandell ran a weary hand over his unshaven jaw. "I came down to read just before daybreak." He looked for the slender volume of Shakespearean sonnets and discovered it tumbled to the floor. Upon the small tripod table stood a pool of wax that had once been a candle. "What time is it?" he demanded.

"Near nine of the clock, my lord."

Mandell grimaced. Obviously he had dozed off for more than just a few minutes. He noticed Hastings regarding him with a troubled expression and snapped, "Well, what is it, man? What did you want?"

"Begging your pardon, my lord, but there is a lady that insists upon seeing you."

"A lady?" Mandell straightened, unable to help the eager note that came into his voice.

"It is not your lady, sir."

"Oh." Mandell sagged back in the chair, then murmured, "I did not suppose that it would be. I no longer have a lady, Hastings."

"I am very sorry to hear that, my lord."

Mandell averted his gaze, discomfited by the level of sympathy and silent understanding he read in the younger man's eyes. He asked with no real interest, "What wench is it that would plague me at such an ungodly hour?"

"It is me, Mandell," a soft feminine voice spoke up.

Hastings had left the door open and Mandell glanced up to find Sara Palmer silhouetted on the threshold. She wore a pelisse of pink china crepe, complemented by a Caledonian cap of plush silk trimmed with rich bands and fox-tail feathers. Mandell remembered the hat well. He had paid for it.

His jaw tightened. He could hardly believe that Sara would possess the boldness to come here, but nothing about her should surprise him.

"May I come in?" she asked.

"You already appear to have done so."

"I did not quite trust your footman to announce me properly."

"You refused to give me your name, madam," Hastings said.

"This is the Honorable Mrs. Nicholas Drummond, John," Mandell sneered. "You may make her acquaintance as you escort her out again."

Hastings looked startled by this information, yet more than ready to carry out the command. Every line of his stolid form radiated disapproval of Sara.

But Sara moved into the room, deposited her parasol upon Mandell's desk, stripped off her gloves. "I only require a few minutes of your time, Mandell."

"I thought you would be gone on your bride trip. Does your husband approve of his wife calling upon single gentlemen?"

"You and I are cousins now," she reminded him. "Besides, Nick doesn't know I am here."

"Nick doesn't know a good many things."

At least she had the grace to color a little at that. Mandell was sore tempted to evict her from the house himself, but whatever her reason for coming, he sensed that Sara was determined to stay put until she had her say. Loath as he was to admit it, Mandell felt a stirring of curiosity.

After a reluctant pause, he dismissed Hastings. The footman retired with a stiff bow. When the door closed behind him, Mandell rose to his feet, suddenly conscious of his disheveled appearance. He was clad in nothing but his breeches and satin dressing robe. Sweeping back the strands of hair from his eyes, he adjusted the folds of the robe, which gapped open about his bared chest, and he belted the sash more snugly about his waist.

Sara demurely turned her gaze away during the procedure. Her affected modesty only served to sharpen Mandell's anger with her. He did not invite her to sit down, but she did so anyway. Perching upon the edge of his desk, she glanced about his dark-paneled study with bright curious eyes.

"This is the first time I have ever been privileged to enter your house," she said. "It is exactly what I would have expected of you, elegant but cold. Very severe."

"Is that why you came here? To discuss my decor?"

"No." Some of her bravado slipped away, her features becoming more subdued. "You might be interested to know, Mandell, that we left the countess's party not long after you did last night. Nick got very quiet. He hardly spoke a word during the carriage ride back to our flat."

"That would be a first for Drummond."

"He was not at all himself. When we arrived home, he gave me a quick kiss goodnight. Then he went out alone and did not come back until well after midnight."

"And the pair of you wed only two days? Can it be your charms are wearing thin so soon, my dear?"

Her cheeks flooded with color at his mocking tone. "I believe Nick's distracted state had more to do with you," she accused. "You told him something that upset him. Or—or at least I think you did." Sara fretted her lower lip. "It is not always easy to tell with Nick. He seems such a straightforward sort of man, but I've come to realize he can be very good at dissembling."

"He doesn't hold a candle to you, my dear," Mandell said. "So you are worried about what I might have said to him? Whether I asked if you still have that charming habit of dragging all the covers to your side of the bed? Whether I warned him not to waste too much money on stays and chemises because you don't often wear them?"

Sara paled. "Mandell, you didn't."

"No, I didn't, curse you. As you well know I would not after the shock of hearing that you were already married, of seeing Nick trail after you like some lovesick calf."

Sara gave a tiny sigh of relief. She eased off the desk and came to Mandell with contrition in her eyes or at least the appearance of it. "I am sorry, Mandell. Truly I am. I wanted to tell you about Nick and me sooner, but everything happened so fast. And—and I knew you would not be pleased, so I turned craven. I thought it would be better to wait until . . until—"

"Until you had him well and truly hooked?"

She tried to place her hand on his arm, but Mandell shook her off. He said bitterly, "Tell me just one thing, Sara. Out of all the trusting noble fools in London, how did you happen to settle upon Nick? Was it some sort of twisted vengeance against me because I would not gratify your ambitions?"

"No! It was nothing like that!"

"Then what was it? You could not have fancied Nick any great matrimonial prize! From a worldly point of view, you could have scarce done worse than Drummond. He is not a wealthy man."

"I did not realize his grandfather would cut him off."

Mandell gave a hard laugh. "There was not much for His Grace to cut. Nick was never a favorite with the old man. The most the duke ever offered Drummond was that wretched palace down by the river, a crumbling Tudor wreck. He would never have allowed Drummond even that if he had realized that Nick meant to convert the place to a charity hospital someday.

"No, my dear, Nick has but a modest income from the estate his father left and whatever stipend he might earn from his political offices. And what little Nick does have, he tends to give to any beggar that crosses his path."

"I know that," Sara said with a wry smile.

"So you wed him for his title? Because he is the grandson of a duke."

"The Honorable Mrs. Drummond?" Sara pulled a face. "No, I don't even like the sound of it, and as for being related to His Grace of Windermere, I don't see how anyone could benefit from kinship with that old curmudgeon."

Mandell regarded her with a puzzled frown. "Then you must have believed that Nick will rise to a position of some political importance. Perhaps you fancied yourself the wife of a prime minister one day?"

Sara laughed outright. "With Nick's radical views? He will be lucky to keep his seat in the House of Commons."

"Then what the devil did you marry him for?"

"He asked me and I accepted. I'm not getting any younger, you know."

For the first time, the bold Sara could not seem to meet Mandell's gaze. Scowling, he studied her face, noticing a difference in her that he had been too angry to perceive before. There was a change in Sara, something subtle, the slightest softening about her mouth, an added lustre in her eyes.

A suspicion dawned upon Mandell, so incredible he hesitated to voice it aloud. "You could not possibly be—that is, you could not actually have learned to care for Nick?"

"Care for Drummond? Don't be ridiculous. Do you think I would fall in love with a man simply because he has a winsome smile?" Sara stalked away from Mandell, waving her hands in an agitated gesture. "He's not even handsome. He's—he's impossible. A starry-eyed fool, an eternal optimist, forever babbling on about this cause and that one. He is not even the sort of man ever to permit a woman to come first in his life."

Sara continued to bluster on in this fashion until Mandell wondered just whom she was trying to convince. He circled round her, slipped his fingers beneath her chin and forced her to look up.

Her eyes blazed with bright defiant tears. Her lips trembled.

"Good God," he said softly. "You fell in love with him."

"So what if I did?" She dashed his hand away. "There is no law against it and . . . and don't you dare to laugh at me, you cynical bastard. I daresay you think you are far too clever to fall in love yourself."

"No," Mandell said, his mind clouding with a vision of Anne that was both poignant and painful. "Not too clever. Too much the fool to do so."

His response caused a momentary surprise to flicker over Sara's features. Reaching into her reticule, she produced a handkerchief and scrubbed at the moisture in her eyes. "Well, I always thought that I was a damn sight too clever for such nonsense. Then I elope with someone I have barely known for a fortnight.

"Do you realize that Nick was such a gentleman he did not even touch me until we were wed?" Sara's voice echoed the depths of her own disbelief. "I married a man without even knowing what he would be like in bed. As it happens, Nick is rather wonderful when he is not in a rush to get to Parliament."

Mandell's lips twitched, tempted for the first time that morning to smile. "Forgive my continued amazement," he said. "I still cannot imagine a more unlikely pairing than you and Drummond. Where the deuce did you meet him?"

"I was—er—lost in the wrong part of town. I just looked up and there he was, strutting through the slums of Bethnal Green in all his sartorial splendor."

She sniffed and gave a shaky laugh. "Nick actually believes he can make a difference, you know, with his investigating and reporting on the conditions of the poor. That if he writes well enough and speaks loud enough he will induce everyone to be reasonable and see the need for reforms as clearly as he does. When that shows no sign of happening, he gets frustrated. So much so that ... I am afraid for him."

Mandell discovered that he believed her, detecting a genuine caring and concern behind her words. He even found himself attempting to reassure her. "You need not worry about Drummond, my dear. I have watched him for years, like the fabled Don Quixote, forever tilting at windmills. And he never seems daunted when the giants don't fall."

"He is more daunted than you could ever imagine, Mandell. He waxes so angry and desperate when no one heeds his proposals. Sometimes I fear that he—" Sara's eyes clouded, but whatever thought troubled her, she shook it off, saying ruefully instead, "He has such dreams, not shallow ambitions like mine, but real dreams for a better world where everyone would be warm and safe and well fed. Dreams that are absurd, impossible and—and absolutely wonderful."

"My cousin appears to have disordered your reason, Sara. You sound ready to embrace his causes yourself."

"No, I am only interested in embracing him. That is the difficulty. Nick imagines me to be this respectable widow, an angel of mercy to the poor and destitute, ready to march at his side to right the wrongs of the world. And I will march if he wants me to, but I live in dread of him finding out who and what I really am."

"And that is why you came to see me."

Sara nodded. She reached out to clutch at Mandell's arm. "I beg you, my lord. Maintain your silence. Don't tell him anything you know of my past. Give me the chance to make him happy."

She spoke quietly, the strength of her plea in the luminous depths of her eyes. Mandell hesitated but a moment, then covered her hand with his own. "It is an odd thing, but I believe you do love Drummond, that you will make him a good wife, far better than any proper lady with only birth and breeding to recommend her."

Sara gaped at him. "Did such a remark actually come from you, my lord?"

"Astonishingly, it did." Mandell gave her a wry smile. He pressed Sara's hand and returned it to her. "Set aside your fears. Drummond will never hear anything ill of you from me. On the contrary, I wish you both great joy."

"Are you sure you are feeling quite well, Mandell? The most I had hoped for was an uneasy truce between us for Nick's sake. I never imagined you would give me your blessing."

"My blessing would not be worth much, but I will give you some advice. We were discreet, Sara, but this is London, after all. Someone had to know of our previous connection, some avid gossip who will take delight in whispering the tidings in Nick's ear. You would be better off telling him yourself, along with any other dark secrets you might harbor."

Sara said nothing. Mandell could tell she found his advice most unpalatable, but before he could further urge the wisdom of such a course, they were interrupted.

Sara started as the study door burst open and Hastings rushed into the room. Mandell prepared to deliver a rebuke until he noted how flushed the footman looked, panting as though he had run a great way.

"My—my lord," he gasped. "Your—your pardon. Something d-dreadful." He paused, clutching his side, struggling to get the breath to continue.

"Calm yourself, Hastings. Unless the house is afire, I can see no reason for you to—"

But Mandell's words were stayed by the footman's vigorous headshake of denial.

"A—another murder, my lord. Last night. Here on Clarion Way."

"Oh, no!" Sara gave a soft cry of dismay. She pressed her hand to her mouth as though to quell any further reaction.

But Mandell's attention was riveted on the footman. "Take a deep breath, Hastings," he said, "and regain command of yourself."

Hastings nodded, struggling to obey.

"So the cursed Hook has struck again," Mandell murmured. Behind him, he heard Sara sink down upon one of the chairs. "Who has been killed this time?"

"S-sir Lucien . . . Lucien Fairhaven," the footman managed to get out.

"Fairhaven?" Mandell frowned. His mind reeled with this strange development. First the death of Bertie Glossop on this same street. Next that Keeler boy behind the theatre. then the attack on Briggs, with Fairhaven disappearing only to surface again to be murdered. None of this affair made any more sense than it ever did.

But he shrugged, saying, "Well, it seems the Hook may actually have performed a service this time—that is if his victim was indeed Sir Lucien. Are you sure of your facts, Hastings?"

Hastings nodded. "I—I heard about the murder from the postboy. I—I thought your lordship would wish to know more, so I took the liberty of running down to the Countess Sumner's to see what I could discover."

"The Countess Sumner's? What did you go there for?"

"That's where Sir Lucien was killed, my lord. In the garden. Near midnight."

Mandell inhaled sharply. Sir Lucien murdered by the Hook in Lily's garden, such a grisly thing taking place within yards of the house that sheltered Anne . . . Norrie. Mandell could well imagine the horror, the distress Anne must be feeling this morning. Even in death Fairhaven had found a way to cut at her peace. Mandell silently damned the man to hell.

"Sir Lucien was supposed to be gone from London," he said. "What was that devil doing in the countess's garden?"

"Getting himself killed, my lord," Hastings said glumly.

The first icy fingers of an inexplicable dread stroked along Mandell's spine. He had the disquietening feeling that there was something more that Hastings had not told him yet. The young footman possessed a steady, unexcitable disposition. He seemed unduly distressed for mere tidings of Sir Lucien's murder.

"What else is amiss, John?" Mandell asked. He could scarce bring himself to voice the question. "Is—is Lady Fairhaven all right?"

Mandell's dread only increased when Hastings avoided giving a direct answer. Instead he said, "They—they have arrested someone for Sir Lucien's murder."

"The Hook? They have captured the Hook?"

An odd, strangled sound escaped Sara, but Mandell did not turn round. He fixed Hastings with his gaze, a gaze that the footman no longer possessed the courage to meet.

"No, my lord," he said. "There was no Hook. Not this time. Sir Lucien was shot by . . . by your lady." Hastings spoke the last words so low, Mandell scarce heard him.

"What!" He gripped Hastings shoulder so hard the younger man winced. "Where did you hear such a damnable tale?"

"From the countess's own butler, my lord. He was that broken up about it, was Mr. Firken. But the servants at Sumner House and the old watchman . . . they know. They heard the shot, they saw Lady Fairhaven in the garden, standing over Sir Lucien with the pistol."

"Those prating fools," Mandell rasped. "Anne didn't— She couldn't—She can't even load a pistol properly."

"Mr. Firken did say that her ladyship swears there was someone else in the garden, a cloaked figure."

"Then damn you, there was. The Hook. It must have been."

"But no one else saw him, my lord. And with his dying breath, Sir Lucien accused Lady Fairhaven."

"Lying bastard! If he was not already dead, I'd cut out

his tongue." Mandell released Hastings, then stepped back, his lips setting into a taut line. "I must go to Sumner House and see Anne at once. I'll fast put a stop to all this madness."

"You don't understand, my lord," Hastings said miserably. "Your lady isn't there. They have already arrested her, taken her to Newgate."

Hastings's words slammed into Mandell's consciousness with the force of an explosion. He felt the blood drain from his face. Pressing his hand to his brow as though to ward off a blow, an uncomfortable thrumming commenced in his head.

The room seemed to rock, shift beneath his feet, the present slipping away to melt with the past. The sunlight was pouring through his window, his eyes were wide open, and yet he could hear it. The pounding. The infernal pounding at the door.

Open. Open in the name of the . . .

"No!" He breathed harshly. The nightmare had come again and this time there was no waking to escape it. He could envision it so clearly, the rough hands seizing her, dragging her off into the blackness of night, her face pale with terror. But it was not his mother's face he saw. It was Anne's.

The past shifted to the present and Mandell shivered, sickened with a dread and fear that he had not known since that long ago night. The pounding continued and he realized it was his own heart.

"Mandell?" Sara's image drifted into his view. He had all but forgotten her presence. "Mandell, you are looking very queer. Are . . . are you all right?"

He managed to bring the room back into focus, becoming aware of her troubled frown, of Hastings's anxious concern. The footman was attempting to press a glass of brandy into his hand.

"Here, my lord. Perhaps you had best drink this."

Mandell gulped down the contents of the glass, scarce thinking what he did. The fiery liquid burned his throat and sent a rush of warmth through his veins. The chilling terrors of the boy slowly dissolved to become the anger and fire of the man.

Mandell thrust the empty glass back at Hastings and said in an impassioned rush, "I have got to get Anne out of that accursed place."

"My lord?" Hasting's eyes widened in alarm, but Mandell was already striding for the door.

It was Sara who caught him, blocking his way. "Where are you going, Mandell?"

"To Newgate," he snapped. "Don't you understand what has happened?"

"Yes, this—this lady friend of yours has been arrested, but it will do you no good charging off in this agitated state."

Hastings spoke up. "Indeed, my lord, I fear Mrs. Drummond is right. Firken said that the countess had done all that she could to secure her sister's release."

"They do not let one leave Newgate for the asking," Sara said.

"I didn't say I was going to ask." Mandell started forward again, but Sara splayed her hands against his chest to stop him. He tried to thrust her aside, but she clung to him with a stubborn desperation.

"There will be nothing that you can do, Mandell. It is not as if they will take this Anne out and hang her at once. There will be inquiries, a trial."

Mandell gave a harsh laugh. "And what sort of trial will it be with a dozen servants being forced to say they saw Anne standing over Lucien with a pistol? Or perhaps you think the Hook will step gallantly forward and confess, place his own neck in a noose to save her?"

His sardonic suggestion seemed to strike Sara forcibly. The blood was driven from her cheeks. "N-no. That would be most foolish of the Hook. And yet it is the sort of gesture a certain gallant sort of rogue might make, a man bent on throwing his life away."

"The Hook is more interesting in taking lives. But he'll not sacrifice Anne's." Mandell shook her off savagely. He did not bolt out the study door as he had intended, realizing himself that he must strive for some measure of calm. He would do Anne no good if he rushed out behaving like a madman.

He paced to the window, drawing in cleansing breaths, struggling to find his customary cool logic. But he sought in vain. Pressing his palm against the glass, he peered out into the sun-dappled street and thought of the house at the end of the square, of Norrie waking sobbing and frightened to find her mama gone, of Anne cut off from the sunlight, thrust into some dank, dark cell, prey to vermin, prison fever, and God knew what other horrors. He thought of Anne wrenched out of that same cell, only to be displayed in the dock, his Lady Sorrow exposed to the rabble's pitiless gaze. And the most dread thought of all, he imagined a rough hemp rope being fitted about her slender neck, over that warm delicate pulse he had so often placed his lips against when making love—

No! He clenched his hand in his hair. He could not even imagine such a thing, or he would go mad. If Anne were to die, he would die as well. Even if he continued to draw breath, his heart and soul would be lost.

Because his heart was lost already. He had left it in Anne's gentle hands last night when he had bid good-bye to her. That thought stunned him with a truth he had been afraid to acknowledge for so long, even to himself. He stepped back from the window, shrinking from the sunlight as he suddenly realized just how much of a fool he had been.

Yet he felt strangely calmer as he turned to face Sara and Hastings. With an iron edge in his voice he said, "I will have Anne out of Newgate by sunset today, no matter what it takes. Bullying, bribery, even if I have to break down the gates."

"Perhaps you had better get dressed first," Sara said drily.

Mandell flushed, but before he could do anything, Sara sprang into action and began issuing commands to the footman.

"Tell the marquis's valet to lay out his most expensive

and ostentatious suit of clothes. His lordship will also need a small pistol, and then, Hastings, you must go to Newgate and make some subtle inquiries. Find out exactly where Lady Fairhaven is being kept. Given her rank, she will likely be held in the prison portion of the warder's own residence. If she has not been shackled, getting her out could prove easier than you would suppose."

Hastings nodded in eager agreement. But recollecting himself, he turned toward Mandell, as if questioning whether Sara's commands were to be obeyed. Mandell frowned at Sara.

"What do you think you are doing?" he demanded.

"Helping you," Sara said calmly. "I have decided you are right. It is best that you fetch Lady Fairhaven out of prison as soon as possible. Newgate is not impregnable. Escapes are arranged all the time. The trick is to know the way to go about escaping and to keep from being recaptured once you have done so."

"If I find the way to get Anne out of that accursed hellhole," Mandell said fiercely, "I shall permit no one to drag her back again."

"I believe I can show you the way, if you have the boldness to carry out my plan, which no doubt you do."

"You possess some passing strange knowledge for a respectable widow from Yorkshire, Mrs. Drummond."

"I am acquainted with some passing strange people," Sara murmured.

Mandell folded his arms across his chest, not certain he trusted her, this sudden eagerness to come to his aide.

"Why would you offer to help?" he asked.

"It holds no risk for me. I don't intend to assist you in the actual escape attempt, only give you my expert advice on the best means of rescuing this lady."

"But Anne is nothing to you. You don't even know her."

"Perhaps I have a curiosity to meet the woman who could inspire the haughty marquis of Mandell into almost storming Newgate clad in little more than his dressing gown."

But Mandell was not to be put off with this flippant answer. "Why, Sara?" he persisted. "What is your real reason for involving yourself in this matter?"

She cast her eyes downward and Mandell detected a shading of some emotion he could not read. But then she glanced up and met his gaze with her customary boldness.

"I will help you because I feel I owe you a debt, my lord. A payment due from one very clever person to another."

She flashed him a brilliant smile. Mandell was not sure he was entirely satisfied, but there was enough honesty in her answer that he was able to quell his suspicions. He turned to Hastings to give him leave to follow Sara's instructions. But he discovered the footman had already gone.

The prison room was small and cramped, with little furnishings beyond the narrow cot. The Countess Sumner had paid dearly for a few extra luxuries for Anne; a thin comforter, a washstand with pitcher and basin, a generous supply of fuel for the coal burner. Anne knew that there were far worse places she could have been lodged at Newgate than this chamber in the warder's own house.

But the fact remained that when she turned the knob on the door, it did not yield. It was irrevocably locked, dispelling any illusions. She was as much a prisoner as any of the miserable beings who crowded the common cells, her future as precarious as any desperate pickpocket, thief, or murderer.

Shivering, she rubbed her arms. Despite the heat that emanated from the coal burner, she did not seem able to get warm. Perhaps because the chill had its origin in the despair to be found in her own heart.

Glancing out the room's single window, she saw late afternoon shadows slanting across the yard below. The distant figures of prisoners less fortunate than herself shuffled along, weighted down by the irons shackling their arms and legs. They struggled to drink in what air and sunlight they could before being herded back to the dark confines of their cells.

Those were the condemned, the turnkey who guarded

Anne's quarters in the state side of the prison had confided. Already tried and convicted, they would soon be taken to the transport ships to be conveyed off to some distant penal colony. Some would face a much shorter journey, traveling only as far as Newgate's front gate where the hangman awaited.

Anne stepped back, shrinking from the sight of those wretched souls who only served as a reminder of the grim possibilities of her own fate.

"But I am innocent," she sought to remind herself over and over again. "I have done nothing wrong." The protestation had become like a monotonous litany that she chanted in her mind, one that began to have little meaning.

What did it matter if she was innocent if no one would believe her, not the servants, or the constable who had taken her into custody, or the magistrate who had remanded her to be held for trial. Not even her own sister.

"Why did you do it, Anne?" Lily had wailed. "And if you had to shoot that scoundrel, not that I blame you, why couldn't you have told me first? I could have arranged the matter more discreetly, buried his remains beneath the begonias."

And the servants, from Firken to the youngest footman, in their efforts to be loyal, had declared Sir Lucien a proper villain who more than deserved whatever Lady Anne had done to him. What they failed to realize was that their indignant protestations only served to damn Anne further.

Despite the nightmare into which she had descended, Anne might have been tempted to laugh at the absurdity of it all, especially Lily's remarks. Except that her sister's distress had been far too real. When Anne had been hustled away by the constables, Lily had collapsed.

Yet she had turned up at the prison first thing that morning, paying out an exorbitant fee to make sure that Anne was given the best of accommodations and treatment that Newgate offered. Her sister had looked drawn and pale, for the first time making Anne aware of the span of years that separated them. Lily declared it was simply because she had misplaced her rouge, and although Anne had begged her to go home and rest, Lily had insisted upon setting out to engage for Anne the best solicitor in London.

Anne feared it would take a clever lawyer indeed to help her explain away such suspicious circumstances as her being alone in the garden with Lucien at midnight, being found with the pistol in her hand, and Lucien's dying accusation. But Anne had kept her terrors and her growing sense of hopelessness to herself. Lily was distraught enough already without Anne giving voice to the doubts that gnawed at them both.

It had been less than twenty-four hours since Anne had been incarcerated at Newgate. But she found herself already marking the time, pacing the small confines of her cell. She occupied her mind by fretting over the most foolish things—wondering if Lily had found her rougepot, if Bettine had remembered to mend the tear in Norrie's pink muslin, if Norrie would take the time to finish her lessons before she settled down to have a tea party with her dolls.

It had been so remiss of her not to have engaged a new governess for Norrie, Anne thought ruefully. A good, caring governess would have been of great use just now. She would have kept Norrie busy and distracted. She would have found a gentle way to explain to the little girl Anne's absence. Anne dreaded what gossip Norrie might pick up from the servants. A good governess would have prevented that. She might even have been able to soothe Norrie's grief if . . . if the worst should happen and no trace of that sinister phantom was ever found, if Anne stood trial for the murder of Lucien and was found guilty. If—

Anne sank down upon her bed and buried her face in her hands. No, those were the *ifs* she must not think about if she were to survive this madness. Far better to worry whether Bettine would remember to drape a shawl about Norrie's shoulders when she took the little girl for her afternoon walk. Anne pressed the heels of her hands against her brow as though by so doing she could blot out more terrifying concerns.

She remained in this posture until she heard the chink of

the key in the lock. The door eased open and the scrawny figure of the turnkey slipped into the room.

Mr. Griffiths was a cheerful little man with hair like damp straw and a bright red nose that suggested his fondness for rum. But he was obsequiously respectful to Anne and dipped into a deep bow that would have done credit to an equerry at a monarch's court.

"Pardon to disturb, m'lady." He beamed. "But you have a visitor."

A faint protest rose to Anne's lips. She feared it must be Lily again and she was feeling strangely protective of her older sister. She did not want Lily to keep coming to see her in this place. But before Anne could say anything, the individual hovering in the hall outside impatiently thrust his way into the room.

Anne stifled a glad cry. The vision that appeared before her was one that she had not dared to conjure up, even to comfort herself during these past frightening lonely hours. She stared at the tall dark man.

Was it just that she yearned after the sight of him, or did Mandell indeed look more magnificent than she had ever seen him? His dark cloak with the many capes draped lightly over his shoulders, he wore a blue frock coat and tight-fitting cream breeches, his feet encased in gleaming black Hessians. He swept in with all the hauteur of a king.

Anne trembled, rising to her feet. She had never expected he would come to her. They had severed their relationship, said their final farewells last night. But of a sudden, she also remembered something else Mandell had said to her.

If you should ever need me for anything, you know you have only to send for me.

Her heart swelled with a joy and renewed sense of hope that was almost painful in intensity. If there was one man in London who would believe in her innocence, she knew it was Mandell.

It was all she could do not to cast herself into his arms. She was restrained by the presence of the turnkey and by Mandell's own manner. He bowed over her hand with as much studied elegance as though he greeted her at teatime in Lily's parlor.

"Good afternoon, my lady," he said. "Your sister commissioned me to bring you the shawl that you requested."

Shawl? Anne could not recollect requesting any such thing, but she was too dazed by Mandell's unexpected appearance to do any more than murmur her thanks. Mandell dropped a paper-wrapped parcel on her bed. Anne started to open it, but Mandell prevented her doing so.

His casual aspect was belied by the way he gripped her hand. He crushed her fingers within his own as though he meant never to let her go, his eyes filled with dark hauntings, shadings of a nightmare only she could understand.

"They have not harmed you?" he asked tersely.

"No," Anne was quick to reassure him. She sensed a tension in him that she had not at first perceived, a subtle hinting of danger that she began to find alarming.

Mr. Griffiths piped up indignantly, "Of course, 'er ladyship 'as not been 'armed. She 'as been treated well, as befitting a female of 'er station with a sister as what possesses such a gen'rous purse. You can see, m'lord, the lady 'as not even been shackled."

"So she has not been," Mandell murmured, glancing down at Anne's wrists. The smile that touched his lips struck Anne as being etched with a strange sort of satisfaction. Her inexplicable feeling of apprehension deepened.

"This is the room where the marquis of Sligo was kept before 'is trial," the turnkey continued eagerly.

"You don't say," Mandell drawled.

"Aye, just look at all the 'menities."

"Indeed, most excellent accommodations. Such a pity the lady will not be staying."

"Eh? Beg yer pardon, m'lord?"

By way of reply, Mandell eased a pistol from beneath the folds of his cloak. Anne gasped, but Mandell's lips were still curved in that hard smile. His eyes glinted with a reckless light as he leveled his weapon at Griffiths's scrawny chest.

"Dear God, Mandell! What are you doing?" Anne cried.

"Rescuing you from this vile place." He arched one brow as though surprised that she could even ask such a thing.

"Oh, n-no. You must not. Please put that pistol away."

"Aye, do, m'lord and I'll just forget I ever saw you had it," Griffiths quavered. "It is mightily against the law to help a prisoner escape."

"Is it indeed?" Mandell mocked. "How remiss of me to forget that fact."

"Mandell, please listen to him," Anne begged. "You could be imprisoned yourself for attempting such a thing."

"Neither of us shall be imprisoned if you make haste and do what I say, Anne." Mandell jerked his head toward the parcel upon the bed. "In that package is a suit of masculine garb, my footman's livery. I will request Mr. Griffiths to kindly avert his gaze while you put it on."

"No, Mandell. I cannot allow you to put yourself in such peril for me."

"Damn it, Anne. Will you stop arguing and do as I say?"

She stubbornly shook her head, her heart already pounding with fear for him. He shifted to glare at her and in the split second Mandell's attention wavered, Griffiths bolted toward the door.

He started to shout for aid, but Mandell moved with lightning swiftness. Raising the butt end of the pistol, he clipped the turnkey alongside the head, cutting him off in midshout.

Griffiths collapsed in a heap.

"The bloody fool," Mandell swore.

A fleeting regret clouded his features as Mandell bent over the turnkey's inert form. Then he glanced up at Anne, who stood frozen with horror. The determined light came back into his eyes as he said, "I trust this puts an end to any further argument, milady."

Chapter 20

‿∾◌∾‿

The house stood in decaying splendor near the banks of the Thames, a private palace abandoned by time and the changing whims of fashion. It was an impressive collection of gables and projecting bays, although the magnificent stonework had been rendered a dingy grey by layerings of coal smoke, and many of the windows on the west wing had been boarded over. What glass remained at the front of the house caught the rays of the dying sun, the latticed panes glinting red like fire-toned jewels.

The mansion's gates opened onto the Strand, a cobblestone thoroughfare now cluttered with coffeehouses, shops, and more modest dwellings whose occupants took little notice of this last relic of ancient grandeur left in their midst. The front of the manor was so overgrown with weeds, shrubbery, and untrimmed trees that no one from the street could even see the two strange figures that crept toward the house's gatelike stone porch—a nobleman in a flowing cloak closely followed by a slender servant clad in ill-fitting black and silver livery.

It was fortunate that no one observed their movements, for anyone watching would have been scandalized to see the tall man draw his footman into the shadows of the porch, and seize the lad into his arms for a long hard kiss.

The low-crowned hat which had covered Anne's head tumbled to the ground, her hair spilling about her shoulders as Mandell strained her close. For a moment the nightmare of the past hours, the nerve-racking moments of her escape from Newgate all faded to insignificance. Nothing was real

317

except for Mandell, the heat of his lips against hers, the fiery shelter of his embrace.

His kiss braced her, warmed her, comforted her more than the most potent of brandies could have done. He drew back, and even in the fading light she could see the tender shadow of his smile.

"Faith, my dear," he said huskily. "And to think I have always believed Hastings to be a most superior sort of footman. You perform services that make his devoted polishing of the silver pale by comparison."

Anne realized he sought to relieve her apprehensions with his jest and she wished she could have obliged him by smiling. But the chill of those forbidding prison walls still seemed to cling to her and she shivered.

Observing this, he released her and produced a ring of keys which he proceeded to try upon the mansion's imposing front door. Anne leaned wearily against one of the pillars, the recent escape already fading to become a blurring montage of scenes in her mind—helping Mandell to truss up Griffiths's unconscious form, scrambling into the footman's livery, locking the cell door, creeping down to the courtyard.

Only one moment stood out with terrifying clarity. All had gone smoothly until they were to pass beneath the shadows of the prison lodge itself. The guards were too busy harassing and checking the more humble visitors. None of the turnkeys presumed to question the lordly figure that was Mandell any more than they had dared to search him on his arrival. But one of the younger guards had frowned at the sight of Anne, perhaps realizing that my lord the marquis had somehow acquired an odd-looking footman within the prison walls.

As the guard had approached them, Anne's heart had threatened to stop, not with fear for herself, but for Mandell. Despite his cool exterior, she saw a wildness in his fierce dark eyes, sensed the danger in him. In that instant she had realized he was prepared to fight to the death before he would have allowed anyone to touch her.

But the guard had only winked and offered to clear a path for the marquis and his servant through the common herd. Mandell had nodded tersely, slipping a small purse into the man's calloused palm. Anne had felt so weak with relief, she marveled that she had been able to continue playing her part, following a few steps behind Mandell until they had cleared the final gate.

After that she had a dazed remembrance of being bundled into a hackney cab, alighting to trail Mandell on foot through a maze of streets and alleys designed to confuse any pursuer until they had at last slipped into the grounds of this strange abandoned house.

Going through key after key, Mandell muttered an impatient oath until he slotted in the one that fit the lock. The door creaked loudly as Mandell shoved it open. Anne bent to retrieve her hat and followed him inside.

She felt awkward and self-conscious in the masculine clothing Mandell had provided to disguise her for the escape. Hat in hand, she gazed nervously about a great hall, the gallery above where musicians must have once piped tunes for ladies in farthingales and ruffs, the gentlemen in doublets. But the vast chamber stood empty now, cobwebs clinging to the lionhead brackets upon the chimneypiece.

"Mandell, what—what is this place?" Anne whispered.

"Windermere Palace, one of the family icons." Mandell grimaced at the layering of dust he dislodged as he brushed up against the wall. "A relic of late Tudor times. Anyone with any sense sold off their riverfront property at a great profit, but my ancestors persisted in clinging to this lumbering pile and my grandfather upheld the tradition. He wanted to give it to me, but I made haste to decline the honor. The property was then to have reverted to Nick, but since his recent marriage . . ." Mandell gave an expressive shrug.

"Is is safe for us to be here?"

"Safe enough for the present. No one ever comes here anymore except perhaps Nick. Most of the locals tend to avoid this place like the plague because of the legends about the house being haunted." Mandell slipped his arm about her shoulders. "You don't believe in ghosts, do you, Sorrow?"

"After what I saw happen to Lucien, I am no longer so sure," she murmured.

"We will discuss that presently." He caressed back a stray tendril from her cheek. "But first permit me to escort you to less daunting quarters."

Linking his arm through hers, Mandell cautioned her to beware of rotting floorboards and guided her toward the end of the hall. An L-shaped staircase stretched upward, the intricately carved newels adorned with snarling lions the same as on the fireplace.

When she and Mandell reached the top, Anne saw there was a landing that led to a long gallery, pale splotches on the wall bearing testimony to the portraits that must have once hung there.

Mandell went along the gallery, trying door after door. "I know there was one of these chambers that Nick had partially restored. Ah, here it is," he said as he opened the last door but one. He beckoned to Anne to join him.

She stepped across the threshold of what had once been a large bedchamber. When Mandell located a tinderbox and managed to light a candle, Anne saw that unlike the rest of the house, this room was furnished. A worn Turkish carpet covered the floor, a faded tapestry of a hunt scene graced one wall. A massive bedstead minus its hangings dominated the room, a small chest tucked at the foot. To one side stood a small battered desk and chair.

The chamber was damp and musty, reminding one of the house's close proximity to the river. Anne rubbed her arms to dispel the chill. Seeing her do so, Mandell frowned.

"I wish I could light a fire, but I cannot risk anyone seeing the smoke and becoming curious enough to pay us a call. Nor can I vouch for the condition of this chimney. I daresay it has not been cleaned for years."

He whipped off his cloak and draped it about her shoulders. "And this time I trust you will remember to return it sooner, milady," he teased gently, trailing his fingers against the curve of her jaw.

She caught his hand. "Please don't, my lord. It is not necessary for you to try so hard to delude me with this show of good cheer. I fully realize what a desperate case we are both in. They will soon be searching all over London for me, and you, too. I should never have allowed you to take such a risk for me."

"So you have protested several times, and at the most inconvenient moments. Damsels are not supposed to raise such a fuss when being rescued."

Although he was still smiling, Anne sensed the underlying edge of his own tension starting to pierce through. But she could not refrain from saying, "I should not have let you do it. I should have guessed what you were about as soon as you entered my cell. I should have found a way to have stopped you."

"You had grown so fond of Newgate, then, that you wished for a longer residence there?"

"No, God help me, wretched coward that I am. The prospect of the trial, of being found guilty terrified me so, I would have given anything to have been free."

"Well, then?" Mandell said impatiently.

"Anything but sacrificing you to do so. Now you are as much a fugitive as I. They will want to arrest you for helping me."

"So they will. What of it?"

"So perhaps if I surrendered myself now, your conduct would be excused."

Mandell swore, a fire leaping into his eyes that was as much fear as anger. He gripped her shoulders so hard it hurt. "Don't you dare even to think of such a thing. Or I swear to God I will bind you up and hold you prisoner myself if I have to, to keep you from such folly."

When she flinched he eased his grip, but she felt the tremor in his hands. "I fully understood the dangers when I set out to free you, but I did not give a damn. Do you think I could have endured leaving you in that place, waiting upon the whim of some oafish judge to decide your fate? I would have gone mad, do you not understand that, Anne?"

She comprehended far too well. She could see the shadows of the ages old nightmare, the anguish roiling in his remarkable dark eyes.

She reached up, gently brushing her fingers over his brow, trying to ease the lines of pain she found there. "Yes,

I do understand, Mandell. This whole thing stirred memories for you . . . of what happened to your mother."

"It was worse than that," he said. "I thought I knew what hell was, but I didn't, not until I stood outside those damned prison gates, fearing that you might already be exposed to that cursed gaol fever, to the brutalities of some coarse guard."

A shudder of strong emotion wracked through him. "No, Sorrow, I could not have endured you being in that foul place another moment. I could not take such risks with the woman I . . ."

He broke off. The word he could not bring himself to say seemed to hang suspended in the air between them. Anne's heart hammered so wildly she could scarce breathe, for she found the thought completed in the depths of his eyes.

The woman I love.

The moment was too intense and solemn for Anne to feel a flooding of joy. Mandell turned away from her, grinding his fingertips against his eyes. He said shakily, "You see, Anne, it is not you who is the coward. I have never known any woman possessed of such quiet courage and strength, capable of feeling such compassion, even for a wretch like me who—who cannot tell you what you deserve to hear even now."

"Mandell," she breathed. He refused to face her. The most she could do was rest her hands upon his shoulders, press her face against the iron line of his back.

His voice cracked as he continued, "You deserved a prince, my dear. Not one like Gerald Fairhaven, but a real nobleman who would— Instead you got the dragon." He raised his hand in a gesture of hopelessness. "I wonder if all dragons are like me, on the surface fire and bluster, but beneath it all, nothing but smoke and fear.

"You were right that day in the park when you accused me of living my life as though I were still trapped in a dark closet, afraid to allow myself to feel anything but the most shallow emotions. But sometimes you are forced to confront the things you fear, whether you will or not."

He turned slowly to face her, his eyes glistening. "I love

you, Anne. And it hurts as much as I always feared that it would."

She cupped his face tenderly between her hands. "It is not supposed to be all pain, my love."

"I know that." He caught one of her hands, pressing a heated kiss within the center of her palm. "But now I am vulnerable. Now I have something to lose."

"You will not lose me," she promised fiercely. "I am here with you now and everything is going to be all right."

She flung her arms tightly about his neck. He responded with a low groan, crushing her in his embrace. His mouth sought her lips, her cheeks, her brow, raining feverish kisses over every inch of her face.

"I love you, Anne," he repeated again and again, as though each word was a prayer, a blessing, a miracle. Anne returned his kisses, for one moment allowing herself to sweep all pain aside, to be deliriously happy.

His arms tightened about her, straining her close as though he would gather her into the recesses of his heart and hold her safe there forever.

"There was a great love between my mother and father," he murmured. "Even as a child, I was aware of that. But in the end, she died alone, horribly. Her death left me so confused, so bitter. My grandfather taught me it was better not to love, that it was an emotion reserved for fools, and I believed him."

Mandell buried his face against Anne's hair. "He wanted me to forget . . . and to remember. And so the nightmares started, tormenting me until I would cry out in my sleep, a child wanting his mother."

Anne stirred in his arms, realizing there was something about those dreams that Mandell did not even comprehend himself. She drew back a little, saying hesitantly, "But Mandell, the night that I watched you, that I overheard what you said . . . you were not crying for your mother. It was your father whose name you called."

He frowned down at her, his eyes clouding with uncertainty and disbelief. "But I hated him. I always have. He failed my mother when she needed him most. I swear that will not happen with you.

"I won't fail you, Anne," he vowed passionately. "I will find a way to keep you safe. But you must tell me everything about that night in the garden with Lucien."

Lost in Mandell's arms, dazed by the admission of his love for her, nothing else seemed to matter to Anne. It was as though the events surrounding Lucien's murder were a bad dream, an illusion already half forgotten. Only this moment was real.

But Mandell persisted. "Obviously you did not slip away to your bedchamber as I had supposed. And after you had faithfully promised me to stay away from that bastard, that there would be no more midnight wanderings! Then I hear that you have been arrested for shooting Fairhaven."

"I did not kill Lucien, Mandell, I swear it."

"It would not matter to me if you had, love. Now go slowly and tell me everything that happened."

Anne forced her mind back to those last hideous moments of Lucien's life. Haltingly, she related to Mandell every detail of the terrifying encounter that she could remember.

"Thus the accursed Hook claimed yet another victim," Mandell murmured when she had done. "And for no reason apparent to any sane man. But why the deuce did he use a pistol this time?"

"I don't know." Anne managed a shaky laugh. "He did not tarry long enough for me to ask him."

Mandell cradled her close, depositing a kiss upon her brow. "One thing is now certain. We are dealing with no common footpad. This brigand marches to some tune of his own devising, and it has nothing to do with mere robbery. Yet I fear your innocence cannot be proved until this villian is unmasked."

"But how, Mandell? He is indeed like a phantom. No wonder poor Lucien was so terrified, being stalked by such a creature. He rose up in the garden like—like some spectre from hell, and vanished just as quickly. No one can guess at his identity."

"There is one man who might be able to do so. Briggs."

"Sir Lancelot? But—but you told me that you feared he had lost his reason."

"Then I must endeavor to help him find it again."

Anne heard the grim note in Mandell's voice. She tipped her head back to peer anxiously at him. A determined light had come into his eyes.

"I have felt all along that Briggs knows something about the Hook, something that he feared to tell. He was so shattered after the attack that I felt loath to press him, but now the matter is more urgent. I will find a way to slip into his house to see him this very night, induce him to—"

"No!" Anne caught at the folds of Mandell's frock coat. "You must not go, Mandell. If you are seen upon the streets, you could be arrested."

He covered her hands with his own. "I must take the risk, Sorrow. Briggs is our only immediate hope. Besides, I never intended that we should spend our lives as the resident ghosts of Windermere Palace. Even now, Hastings will be working to ready provisions, arranging a passage for us away from London. It was all I could do to keep the young fool from storming Newgate with me."

Mandell's lips crooked into a deprecating smile. "I seem to have inspired this misplaced devotion and concern for my welfare in Hastings . . . and you."

He bent to whisper a kiss upon her trembling lips. "Don't be afraid, Anne. I will be careful, I promise you. If I have no success with Briggs, we shall be gone from the city this very night. I shall tuck you away someplace safe until your innocence can be proven."

"And if that day never comes?"

"Then I shall find a way to fetch Norrie, and the three of us will make a life elsewhere. I have heard tell that America is not quite so barbaric these days. We—we could be a family. I would do my best to make Eleanor a good father, and you a tolerable husband. That is, if you would have me."

Anne had never thought to hear such a humble request from Mandell. Still, she was obliged to shake her head in sorrow.

"What! The lady rejects me again?" He cupped her chin,

his eyes shining with tenderness. "But I thought my wretched heart was all that you desired, Anne. And that is what I am offering you."

"It is all that I desired, all I ever dreamed of. But Mandell, I could not permit you to make such a sacrifice for me, abandoning your estates, your title, everything that you are."

"Everything that I am, everything that I want to be, I find reflected in your eyes, milady."

His words touched an answering chord within her own heart. He pulled her close, his mouth covering hers to still any further objection. His kiss was fierce and demanding, claiming all of her, body, mind, and soul, as though he would bind her to him forever.

Reason was no match for a force so powerful as Mandell's embrace, and Anne surrendered, molding her body to his hard muscular frame, remembering all that he had taught her of passion, returning it to him with love, the two powerful emotions blending to become one.

They kissed, clung, and caressed until they both stood in danger of forgetting the time, the place, and the peril that threatened them. It was Mandell who first came to his senses and wrenched himself away.

He drew an unsteady breath and laughed. "You make it deuced hard for a man to leave you, Sorrow, but I must. I want many more nights in your arms, and without any shadows cast over our lovemaking."

He caught her hand and held it to his lips for a long moment. "I shall return very soon. You must wait for me. You will not be afraid to be alone here?"

Anne shook her head, summoning up her bravest smile. "I shall always have the palace ghost to bear me company."

"As long as he quite understands that you belong to me." But Mandell quickly abandoned the jesting tone, his eyes turning dark, intent. He drew her into his arms one last time, saying, "Everything will be all right, Anne. You must believe that."

She believed anything when he looked at her that way, holding her within the circle of his arms. He kissed her, this time more tenderly, and Anne basked in the glow of his love, a rush of warmth thrumming through her veins.

Only when he had gone did she begin to feel the cold.

As time crawled by, the bedchamber at Windermere House began to seem worse than a prison. Anne felt isolated and alone, trapped in a place where time had frozen like the hands of a clock that ceased to move. She paced the worn Turkish carpets, watching the candlelight flicker over the dark heavy furnishings. The faded tapestries breathed of a grandeur long past, an age of splendor that had vanished.

The security and warmth Anne had known in Mandell's arms diminished as she watched the candle burn lower in the socket. How long had he been gone? One hour? Two? Three? An eternity. She shivered, trying not to think of all the things that might have gone wrong. The heavy silence of the house thickened about her until she felt as if she would suffocate.

She knew it would be prudent to stay away from the windows, but she could no longer resist the urge to peer out. She forced open the shutters and rubbed away some of the grime that smeared the pane, pressing her face to the cool glass, assuring herself that a real world beyond her present madness did indeed still exist.

She could not guess the hour, but the moon had risen, bright and full, casting a glow that even the dark of night could not dim. The moonlight illuminated the tangled wilderness which had once served as vast gardens to this palatial mansion. And beyond that she could make out the black moving shadow that was the Thames, the spires and masts of the ships at dock, towering like the barren tree trunks of some mighty forest.

Ships that carried people away to far off places like America . . . Anne could not help picturing herself huddling on the deck of one of those with Mandell and Norrie, fugitives fleeing to some strange new land. No, how could she ever allow herself to be the cause of such a thing, dragging the man she loved and her delicate little daughter off into the perils of an uncertain future, uprooting them from all that they knew—their home, their heritage, their birthright. But that was surely the worst scenario, one that would not come to pass. There would be some way to prove her innocence. Mandell would persuade Briggs to talk. He would provide some vital clue or—or the Hook would eventually have to grow careless, be caught some other way. He would be made to confess that he had murdered Lucien.

But if that never happened? She attempted not to torture herself with such grim possibilities, to think only of Mandell's love for her, a love stronger and more powerful than any she had ever hoped for.

If only he would return . . .

And if he did not? Anne rubbed her throat, wondering what she would do, where she would find the courage to face such a thing, when the candlelight wavered wildly as though struck by a draft. She turned to see that the flame had burnt near to the end of the wick and stood in danger of being extinguished by the liquid pool of wax.

The prospect of being left in darkness in this chill mausoleum of a house daunted Anne. She hoped that Mr. Drummond's endeavors to restore this house had extended to laying in a supply of candles.

She first searched the small desk, but the drawers contained nothing but writing supplies—vellum, ink, quills, sealing wax. The only place anything could be stored was in the battered trunk that stood at the foot of the bed.

Anne bent over the chest, which smelled of leather and must, whose scarred wood spoke of hundreds of long ago voyagings. Tugging at the lid, she half feared to find it locked, but the ancient clasp had rusted and already given way.

She raised the heavy lid and propped it open against the bed. Her heart sank with disappointment to discover the trunk crammed with nothing but old clothing. But she rummaged past the thick folds of a heavy black cloak and was fortunate enough to find some candles tucked beneath.

As she unearthed one of the wax tapers, her fingers brushed up against the remaining item in the trunk. She slowly lifted the object out into the light and frowned. It was a man's hat with a jaunty white feather, the soft floppy brim of the style once affected by the dashing cavaliers. Anne's heart skipped a beat. She tried to reassure herself there could be a dozen old hats identical to this one tucked away in trunks and attics.

But there were not. She knew that with an inexplicable dread certainty, the same certainty that told her she had seen this particular hat before, shading the features of a dark-cloaked phantom who melted out of the night to leave death in his wake.

Her mind scarce had time to absorb the implications of finding such a thing hidden away in Nick Drummond's house when she heard the creak of floorboards out in the hall. Her heart skittered, torn between hope and a sudden nervous fear.

It was Mandell returning. It had to be. Who else could it be?

She was seized with an unreasoning urge to bury the hat and cloak back inside the chest, shove aside this terrible knowledge that she had not sought and did not want.

But it was too late. The door was already being eased open.

Anne shot to her feet, trembling. "Mandell," she whispered. "Is that you? I—"

Her greeting died in her throat, her heart going still. It was not Mandell silhouetted on the threshold, but Nick Drummond. Anne stared at the familiar countenance, a young man's face that she had always thought so pleasant, so cheerful. He looked haggard in the dim light, but he managed to smile at the sight of her, appearing as concerned as ever, anxious to be kind.

"Lady Fairhaven," he began. Then his gaze drifted down to the hat she gripped in her hands.

Anne could not seem to move, to breathe. The moments ticked on forever as she watched Drummond's smile fade to an expression more grim.

When he raised his gaze to hers, she saw a deal of sorrow in those steady grey eyes, a regret that left her feeling strangely cold.

"My dear Anne," he said with a chilling softness. "I am sorry you had to find that. Very sorry indeed."

Chapter 21

Anne clutched the hat to her like a shield, fear and doubt warring within her. Nick Drummond, the Hook? The murderous brigand who had attacked Briggs and killed Lucien? It was impossible. It had to be. And yet, as Nick stepped farther into the room, Anne shrank instinctively back against the bedstead.

She moistened her lips, forcing a casualness into her voice that was belied by the unsteady thrumming of her pulse.

"Mr Drummond. Wh-what are you doing here? I was expecting Mandell."

"I know," he said. "Mandell should not have brought you here. He could not have picked any place in London that would have been less safe."

"Indeed, this house is in a sad state of disrepair and . . ." Anne's voice trailed away as Drummond shook his head at her.

"It's no use pretending, Anne. I should know. I have been doing too much of that myself for far too long." He stalked nearer and plucked the hat from her nerveless fingers. "I know you are intelligent enough to understand the significance of what you have found."

"It—it's just a hat and some old clothes."

"Anne," he admonished. His eyes were filled with that unnerving regret. He stroked the back of his knuckles along her cheek, sending a chill up her spine, his face hovering above her own. It was like gazing at a familiar sunlit landscape only to find the scene shifted to something bleak and ominous.

"It might have been a relief to have someone else discover the truth if it had been anyone but you," he said. "But you are far too gentle a soul to be dragged into the midst of all this. I am very sorry."

"But I don't have the slightest idea what all *this* is," Anne cried.

"Unfortunately there is no time for explanations." He cast the hat aside, allowing it to tumble to the carpet with a soft thud. At the same moment, the candle gave one final flicker, guttered, and went out.

As the room plunged into darkness, Anne felt Nick's swift movement. A choked scream escaped her as his hands groped over her shoulders. She struggled wildly lest he gain a grip upon her throat.

"Anne," he growled.

Flailing with her fists, she landed several blows upon his face, driving her knuckles in the soft pocket of his eye. He grunted with pain and surprise, whipping his head back and cracking it against the bedpost. With a sharp oath, he released her. Anne stumbled past him.

Through the haze of blackness and her rising panic, she could make out the silhouette of the open door. Hurling herself across the threshold, she dared to slam the door closed behind her. Leaving Nick trapped in total darkness purchased her a few precious seconds.

Her breathing coming in ragged gulps, Anne ran blindly forward down the gallery. Mandell's heavy cloak tangled about her legs. She tripped on the hem and crashed to her knees. Struggling to regain her footing, she realized the cloak had caught on something, a loose floorboard or a nail.

Tearing frantically at the fabric, she heard the sound of Nick hurling open the bedchamber door and his muttered curses. Terror threatened to overwhelm her. She wrenched at the fastening of the cloak and flung it off her shoulders.

Scrambling to her feet, Anne made it as far as the upper landing. A ghostly mist of moonlight poured through the front windows, illuminating the gallery below.

Behind her, Nick roared out her name. Anne glanced about wildly, desperate for any avenue of escape. The twisting flight of stairs leading down to the hall seemed her best, her only hope.

But before she could take another step, Nick lunged. Out of the shadows behind her, she felt his arms close about her. She clawed at his hands even as she struggled to maintain her balance, feeling herself sway precariously on the topmost step.

A cry for help breached her lips as hoarse as it was unavailing, echoing along the palace's indifferent corridors.

Swearing, Nick sought to clamp his hand over her mouth.

"Damn you, Anne," he panted. "Stop it! What are you—"

"Let her go, Drummond."

The icy command issuing from the foot of the stairs caused them both to freeze. Twisting in Drummond's hard grasp, Anne stared downward, her breath snagging in her throat. It was as though her frantic plea had summoned some dread spectre to her aid, a stern gallant of another time and place in his stiff silvery-grey brocade, lace spilling over his ancient hands.

He held aloft a lantern, the light illuminating those aged aristocratic features, the flow of white hair bound back into a queue.

"Release the lady, Nicholas," His Grace commanded again.

Nick was startled enough to do so. With a choked sob of relief, Anne started down the stairs. But Nick recovered himself enough to come after her, seizing her upper arm.

"No, Your Grace," he said. Anne had never heard any words choked out with such hatred and anguish.

The duke set the lantern down, the light reflecting upward, bathing his face in an eerie glow, making his flesh seem translucent, his skin stretched too taut over his prominent cheekbones. Gripping his walking cane, he started up the stairs, coming as far as the first landing.

The sight disturbed Anne in an odd way she could not

name. Perhaps it was because she could feel the tension coil in Nick. She should have warned the old man to take care. But she could not bring herself to believe that Nick would harm his own grandfather.

"Don't come any closer," Nick snarled. "Get back to hell where you belong. I am taking Lady Fairhaven with me."

"No, boy. I have endured enough of your defiance. You have already dishonored me past all bearing."

"I dishonor *you*?" Nick gave a wild laugh.

As the duke came closer, something in his movements again gave Anne a ripple of unease. Then she realized what it was. It was the cane, the silver-handled walking cane. He was carrying it. He had no need of its aid, his step steady and sure.

"Lady Fairhaven's well-being concerns you not," the duke said softly. "Leave while you still may."

He tugged at the cane's handle and a swordstick unsheathed in a lethal hiss of steel. Anne's blood turned to ice as she suddenly realized the mistake she had made, a foolish fatal mistake. She realized it even as Nick thrust her behind him and shouted, "For the love of God, Anne. Run!"

He charged at the old man, but the duke was too swift for him. Like an arc of lightning, the sword flashed. Anne cried out as he drove the sword through Nick's shoulder.

She heard Nick give a guttural cry, watched his face go white with shock. The sword yet buried in his flesh, he leaned upon the duke's shoulder for support. For one brief moment, horror at what he had done flickered over the old man's features. Then he wrenched his sword free. Nick screamed. As he sagged onto the steps, Anne pressed her fist to her mouth so hard she tasted her own blood, but she felt too numb to notice the pain, or to be aware of anything save the crimson stain spreading over Nick's waistcoat.

Whatever remorse the duke might have known, Anne saw that he had already shuttered it away beneath his heavy eyelids. He watched his grandson's lifeblood flow out with a curious kind of detachment.

The sight pushed Anne beyond the realm of horror, beyond any fear for her own safety. Galvanized into movement, she rushed down the steps to Nick's side. Ignoring the old man who hovered over her, the bloodstained sword still gripped in his hand, she stripped off the frock coat she wore.

Bundling it up, she pressed it to Nick's shoulder in an effort to stop the bleeding. Nick groaned, his mouth clenching with pain.

"I tried to warn you, boy," the duke said. "But you have always had a habit of rushing into things headlong, never taking heed of sage advice."

Anne glanced up at him, unable to believe he could stand there and observe Nick's agony so calmly.

"Can you not see how badly you have injured him?" she cried. "You must go and fetch someone to help."

For all the response she received, the old man might have been made of stone.

"He is your grandson," she said fiercely. "I don't care what else you may have done. You cannot allow *him* to die."

The duke produced a laced-edge handkerchief and proceeded to wipe Nick's blood from his sword. It was most strange, Anne thought. It had been hard for her to imagine Nick Drummond as a murderer, but she had no difficulty casting His Grace of Windermere in that role.

"There is an old saying, my dear," he said in his low cultured accents. "It goes something like, 'If thine eye offends thee, pluck it out.' I have just done so. Drummond is no longer any kin of mine."

"He is mad, Anne," Nick panted. "Get out of here. Save yourself."

Anne only shook her head, desperately trying to apply more pressure to Nick's wound.

"Is it madness then?" the duke asked. "To attempt to defend what is yours, to try to preserve the world you have always known?"

"That's your justification . . . for murder?" Nick rolled his head to one side, whether in an effort to escape the pain or simply because he could no longer abide the sight of his grandfather Anne could not tell.

She was a little heartened to realize that she had managed to stop the flow of blood. Glancing toward the front door, she prayed for Mandell's imminent return and calculated her chances of being able to escape and rouse some help from one of the houses on the Strand. Could she possibly make it down the stairs before the duke attempted to cut her down? And even if she were able to do so, how could she abandon Nick to the mercy of a man who was clearly dead to any human compassion?

As though guessing at her thoughts, the duke shifted his position behind her so that he now completely blocked the stairs, toying with his sword.

"At least let Anne go," Nick murmured. "She is no threat to you."

"On the contrary, Lady Fairhaven poses the greatest threat of all." The old man's icy facade cracked a little, some of his bitterness beginning to seep through. "I bred Mandell to be as hard and polished as a diamond, to accept the rights and privileges that are his due. But she has changed him, softened him, inflicted him with some sickly notion of love."

"And I am glad that I have," Anne cried.

"It is the same curse that destroyed his mother, lured my Celine away from me to die."

"Lured! She probably fled from you. If you raised her with as much heart as you've shown Mandell, how I would have pitied that poor lady."

The duke's eyes flashed dangerously. "My proud Celine would have had no need of your pity. Any more than does Mandell."

He seized Anne's wrist, his grip amazingly strong. He dragged her away from Nick, hauling her to her feet. Despite the realization that she could be dead soon, Anne met his ferocious gaze with a look of defiance.

"You cannot hope to get away with any more killing," Nick gasped. "You will be caught this time."

"Perhaps I shall. But at least I will have saved Mandell from committing the same folly his mother did."

Nick made a feeble effort to grip the staircase banister,

trying to pull himself upward. "Damn you. Leave—her—alone."

The duke ignored him, demanding of Anne, "Where is Mandell? I heard about his foolish heroics, rescuing you from Newgate. I thought I should have to send out runners to overtake the pair of you on your flight. Then my dolt of a butler finally saw fit to confide in me that Mandell had sent round earlier to obtain the keys to this place."

He gave Anne a rough shake. "Where is Mandell now? Where has he gone?"

"He has gone seeking the truth," Anne said. "And I would give my life to shield him from it."

"I will have to take you up on that offer, my dear."

Nick kicked out wildly, sobbing with his efforts to rise only to sink back again. He cursed, saying, "You will have to deal with me first."

"I presumed I already had." Releasing Anne, the duke shifted, staring down at Nick. Anne saw the sudden flex of tension in the old man. As he drew back the sword, she flung herself at him, deflecting his sword arm upward. He lashed out, shoving her hard. With a small cry, Anne lost her balance. She banged up against the banister, then tumbled down the stairs, catching herself at the first landing.

Bruised and shaken, she could only watch in horror as the duke whipped around, preparing to run Nick through. She would never reach him in time.

"Anne!"

Someone roared her name, but the cry did not come from Nick or the duke. Mandell's voice echoed from behind her. The duke froze at the sound of his voice, the old man's face draining as white as the moonlight that bathed his features. Anne choked on a sob of relief and struggled to her knees.

She had not heard the door flung open or witnessed his return. She was only too glad to see him now, taking the stairs two at a time. He pulled Anne to her feet, dragging her into his arms. "Anne, thank God. I—"

He broke off as his gaze slid past her to Nick's inert form. He appeared to have lapsed into unconsciousness, his eyes closed.

"What the devil!" Mandell exclaimed. He attempted to go to him, only to find the way barred by his grandfather's sword.

"I fear Drummond is beyond your help, Mandell," the duke said.

"My God, old man, what have you done?"

"Attempted to keep you from flinging your life away upon this woman."

Mandell's jaw hardened. "It is all finished, Your Grace. Briggs has remembered. I know everything."

"You know nothing and you understand even less. And I . . . I have no more time to teach you." The first hint of regret crept into the old man's tone, but he was quick to quell it.

He started down the steps toward Mandell and Anne. Mandell wrapped one arm protectively about Anne's waist. With his other hand, he drew forth a pistol and leveled it at the duke's chest.

The duke paused, regarding the weapon with a brief flash of pained surprise. Then his lips curved in a smile laced with irony.

"So it comes down to this, does it?" he asked. "We were ever adversaries of a kind, Mandell. But now that we reach the sticking point, I wonder— Do you possess the ruthlessness to fire that weapon?"

"I beg that Your Grace will not put me to the test."

Anne held her breath, glancing from one taut male face to the other, alike in hauteur and unyielding pride. But where the duke's eyes were empty and cold, Mandell's roiled with pain and despair.

The duke took another step down. "Are you in truth my grandson?" he purred. "Or only still that puling brat that sprang from de Valmiere's loins? Do you possess the steel to do whatever you deem necessary without remorse or regret?"

"I have no desire to hurt you, Grandfather." A fine beading of perspiration had broken out upon Mandell's brow, but the hand holding the pistol remained steady.

"Grandfather?" the duke mocked, descending another

step. "You have not called me that since the day you were first thrust weeping into my arms. I soon cured you of it, your French tendencies toward an unmanly display of emotion. But did you learn your lesson well enough to be utterly without mercy, without sentimentality? Can you kill me, Mandell, even to save your lady?"

With a malevolent smile, the duke pointed the tip of his sword toward Anne. Mandell inhaled sharply, his eyes dilated. He cocked the pistol.

"Mandell, don't," Anne cried. "Don't you see what he is doing? He is goading you a purpose. He wants you to be his executioner."

Mandell blinked and hesitated while Anne wheeled upon the duke. "Leave him alone," she said. "Haven't you done enough to him? Would you torment him with yet one more nightmare? Are you such a coward that you would seek this way of escaping all the pain you have caused?"

The duke flinched at her words. He stared at her, but Anne refused to be intimidated by his icy gaze. He was the first to avert his eyes. He lowered the sword as though all the strength had suddenly gone out of him.

"No," he said. "You are right, milady. The fate of a duke should rest in no other man's hands."

Mandell exhaled a deep breath, easing back the hammer on his weapon. The duke turned away. Sparing not a glance for Nick, he stepped past his fallen grandson and began a slow ascent up the stairs, only to disappear into the darkness beyond.

Anne and Mandell raced up to Nick. Mandell bent down to feel for a pulse. "Thank God!" he said. "He is still alive."

As gently as Mandell could, he managed to heft Nick into his arms and carry him to the hall below. He laid Nick out upon the floor. But it was Anne who worked over Drummond, fashioning a makeshift bandage out of Mandell's neckcloth.

Mandell could feel the numbness of shock begin to creep over him, born of these last dread-filled hours, forcing himself to accept Briggs's terrible revelation about the old duke, racing back to Anne only to walk into that hellish scene upon the landing. If Mandell had been but a few minutes later, when he thought what might have happened to Anne, to Nick . . .

Mandell gave himself a mental shake. This was hardly the time for such grim contemplations. He eased himself out of his frock coat. Bundling it up, he used it to pillow Nick's head.

Anne touched one hand to Nick's cheek. "He has lost so much blood, Mandell," she murmured. "We must get him someplace where he can be attended properly."

"Hastings should be here at any moment. He was coming right behind me with the carriage."

Even under Anne's gentle ministrations, Nick groaned and stirred. His eyes fluttered open, at first hazed and bewildered. Then he focused upon the marquis.

"Mandell," he said, weakly raising one hand.

Mandell clasped it between the strength of his own.

"Grandfather . . ." Nick muttered. His eyes roved fearfully.

"It is all right," Mandell soothed him. "His Grace is gone."

Nick fixed him with a look of pure misery. "S-sorry, Mandell. When Sara told me about—where going to take Anne. I knew. Knew it was not the Hook doing the killings. But when began to suspect . . . It was too horrible. Couldn't tell you."

"Don't try to talk," Mandell commanded. "We'll soon have you out of here. Back safe with your Sara."

Nick's lips quivered into a fleeting smile, but the expression fast faded. He pressed Mandell's hand with a renewed intensity. "You are going to have to go after the old man, Mandell. We cannot allow him to continue . . ."

Mandell nodded.

Anne regarded Mandell with troubled eyes. "But he is, after all, your grandfather, my lord. What will you do with him?"

Mandell fingered his pistol and stared upward toward the gallery, the darkness where the old man had vanished.

"God help me," he said hoarsely. "I wish I knew."

* * *

His Grace of Windermere sat behind the small desk amidst the faded splendor of the restored bedchamber. Scratching the quill pen across a sheet of vellum, he paused to move the candle closer so that the light fell across the page. When Mandell appeared upon the threshold, the duke continued to write, not even bothering to look up.

Mandell entered, the loaded pistol still gripped in his hand. He had not quite known what to expect, but certainly not this degree of sangfroid even from the duke of Windermere.

It might have been just like dozens of times from Mandell's childhood when His Grace had summoned Mandell to his study to account for some transgression, the duke forcing Mandell to cool his heels until His Grace was ready to deal with the matter.

Mandell found himself staring at the old man, looking, almost hoping to perceive some change in him. Surely murder must leave some mark upon a man.

His eyes did appear a little more sunk deep with weariness, but the brow was as ever untroubled, as smooth as marble. It was like looking upon the face of a stranger. But then His Grace had always been a stranger to Mandell.

The quill continued to scratch across the paper, the duke pausing only long enough to remark, "There was no need for you to have brought the pistol, Mandell. As you can see, I am making no effort to escape. Put that thing away."

Mandell paced over and dropped the weapon upon the bed. He turned back, saying, "We managed to get Drummond off in the carriage. In case you are interested, I believe he will live."

"Indeed?" The duke dipped his quill into the ink and resumed writing. "And your lady? I presume you have also whisked her out of harm's way."

Mandell nodded. The duke paused briefly. He frowned and said, "I do not know if it will much matter to you at this juncture, Mandell, but I did not begin with the intention of harming Lady Fairhaven. It was pure chance that she happened to be there when I finally chose to despatch Sir Lucien."

"I did not see you come rushing forward to clear her name. And if I had not arrived in time tonight, what would have happened to Anne?"

"I suppose she would be dead. That might have been a pity. She possessed more courage than I supposed. If not for her tendency to wear her heart on her sleeve, she might have made a tolerable marchioness after all."

Mandell bit off a savage oath. The duke looked up at him with a cold smile. "What did you expect of me, Mandell? Some sign of remorse?"

"No, but an explanation would be appreciated. You have murdered three men. It would have been four if Briggs had died."

"In another time, another era, no one would have dared to question me. The power of life and death would have been merely another of my rights as the duke of Windermere."

"This is not another era. This is now, damn it! There are no more feudal lords, Your Grace. Even a duke is expected to account for the taking of a life."

The lace at the duke's cuffs brushed the desk as he indicated the paper with a graceful gesture. "I am writing the confession of my actions even as we speak. All the details of time and place, how I managed the business of my disguise. Everything, in short, except for my motives. Those are no one else's concern."

"Not even mine?"

The duke hesitated. "I could explain to you, but I doubt you will understand."

"I beg you will attempt to do so," Mandell ground out.

The duke compressed his lips and began to write again.

"You did not do it for robbery, that I know," Mandell said. "The phantom in the cavalier hat is not, as everyone supposed, the Hook."

"The duke of Windermere, a common footpad!" The duke gave a snort of laughter. "Hardly, but it was useful, my doings being confused with the Hook's petty theft. While the constabulary searched thieves' kitchens for a one-handed rogue, it kept them from interfering with me."

"And so you are not a common thief. Only a common murderer."

"Far from common, Mandell. A dispenser of justice, a killer of fools, a social arbiter perhaps. But never a common murderer."

"What sort of justice was it that made you attack poor Briggs? He had never done any harm to you."

The duke's lip curled with contempt. "He was stupid enough to come and inform me of how he had injured my grandson and heir in the process of halting a drunken brawl."

"Briggs was frightened that night. He came to you for help."

"And he received it. The only possible help for such a simpleton, a yard of naked steel. He looked surprised when I ran him through." The duke sneered. "I rather believed I wounded his feelings as much as anything else."

Mandell probed his grandfather's eyes for some sign of madness. It would have been a comfort to think the old man mad. But his eyes remained remarkably clear with that same cold reason, that lack of compassion that had ever characterized the duke.

"Briggs was . . . is my friend," Mandell said hoarsely. "His devotion to me—"

"The relationship was never a credit to you," the duke interrupted.

"His devotion to me," Mandell continued through clenched teeth, "was such that even after you had nearly killed him, he preferred to keep silent rather than expose you, for fear of giving me pain. When I forced him to tell me tonight, he wept like a babe."

"How touching," the duke said, arching his brows. "I could have spared you both the discomfort of such a maudlin scene had my hand been a little steadier that night."

His Grace flexed his fingers. "My rheumatism, you know. It interferes with my capabilities. I am not the swordsman I once was as a younger man. That is why when I despatched Sir Lucien, I decided that I had better be certain and employ a pistol at close range."

He shot an ironic glance at Mandell. "You will not pretend to mourn his death, I trust?"

"No, but I would not have shot him down in cold blood, either."

"He was a dog, not a man. A sniveling cur who presumed to attack one of my blood in a vulgar tavern. I derived a great deal of amusement from tormenting Sir Lucien first, stalking the coward until I believe I drove him quite mad.

"But in the end, there could only be one fitting payment for Fairhaven's offenses, and that was death."

The duke gave a slight shrug as though already dismissing all thought of Sir Lucien from his mind.

"So you have been committing these murders—" Mandell began.

"Executions," the duke corrected softly.

"You performed these *executions* merely because certain people chanced to offend you?" Mandell asked in disbelieving accents. "What about that young man Kiefer? He was little more than a boy."

"A boy who presumed to sit down to play cards with a duke and attempted to cheat his betters. An upstart banker's son."

"And Albert Glossop?"

"Ah, Mr. Glossop. He was the one who showed me the possibilities of what a blade of steel could do when wielded by a man not afraid to use it to rid the world of inferior beings. It was so easy to cut Glossop down and vanish into the night. The braying ass! The conceited popinjay."

"And that was how it all began? You had no other reason for killing Glossop than you thought him a fool?"

The duke frowned and did not answer him. His hand tightened about the quill and he resumed his writing with a vengeance. Mandell was left with the uneasy sensation that there was something more that his grandfather was not telling him. After so many other horrors, what else could there possibly be?

Mandell felt impervious to any further shock. He was determined to have the truth from the old man, all of it.

Splaying his hands upon the desk, he bent over the duke and repeated his question. "Why did you begin your night stalking with Albert Glossop, Your Grace?"

The duke flinched, but said, "Stand erect, Mandell. Do not lean upon my desk. You know I have always found that an annoying habit."

When Mandell did not move, the old man flung down his quill. He stirred restlessly in his chair, his brow furrowing as he seemed to wrestle with some inner dilemma. He stared past Mandell toward the window, as though he expected to find the answer somewhere out there in the dark of the night.

At last he sighed and murmured, "I suppose I may as well tell you the whole. It can make no difference now."

He waited until Mandell removed his hands from the desk and straightened. Then the duke began slowly, "Glossop was indeed a fool, but that was not my main reason for despatching him. The young idiot had recently acquired a friend ... a friend from France who was acquainted with the de Valmieres."

A tension shot through Mandell. He thought he was prepared to hear anything. But matters suddenly promised to take a direction he had never anticipated.

"My—my father?" he asked numbly.

"No, your father's family. It seems the French king finally decided to overlook the de Valmieres' questionable loyalty during the revolution and restored them to their estate. This finally left them at leisure to send an envoy to make awkward inquiries.

"An envoy that I sent back with false answers. Mr. Glossop, unfortunately becoming aware of this fact, threatened to tell you unless I paid him a considerable sum. Scarcely the action of a gentleman."

"And what was the nature of these inquiries, Your Grace?"

The duke stared down at his paper and fidgeted with his quill.

"The envoy was sent to ask about me, was he not?"

Mandell prompted. "My father's family was seeking to discover my whereabouts."

"Yes ... but mostly they were trying to find out what became of your father."

"My father? Why would they come to you for—" Mandell broke off, stunned by sudden comprehension. "You *know*. You know where my father is."

The duke rested his head against the back of the chair, his heavy-lidded eyes seeming weighted down by a great weariness. "Yes, I have known. All of this time.

"He came to me, journeying to my estate in the north, not long after you had been placed in my care, Mandell. De Valmiere expected to find both you and your mother awaiting him with open arms."

"How could he have expected that? You told me my father abandoned my mother and me in Paris," Mandell accused.

"He may as well have done. He ordered Celine to take you and come to England. If the young fool could have got his head out of the clouds and away from his infernal music, he might have known my Celine better. She was not a woman to tamely accept such commands. She took you and went back to Paris to look for her husband, but he was gone."

"Gone where?"

"To make certain his own family, his brother and sisters, got out of the country, when his first duty should have been to his wife and child."

"But he assumed my mother and I were already safe."

"He should have made sure." The old man slammed his fist against the desk in a rare display of passion. "Instead he comes jaunting to see me months after it was too late to save my beautiful Celine."

The duke's lips twisted with a bitter cruelty. "I took great satisfaction in informing the fool how his feeble efforts had gone awry. I described to him Celine's death in vivid detail, and for added measure, I told him that you had perished, too."

"You bastard!" Mandell said. "And all these years, you

permitted me to believe that my father had deserted me, that he was a coward."

"And so he was. After I told him about your mother's death, he still could not act the part of a man. He wept like a babe, with that vulgar Gallic emotion I find so repulsive. He sobbed until I could endure the sound no longer. I got down my sword."

"No!" Mandell rasped. But his denial was to no avail.

The duke continued relentlessly, remorsely. "He was a coward to the last. When I approached him, sword drawn, he only looked at me. He made not one move to defend himself, profaning Celine's name by whispering it with his last breath. It was but simple justice, his life in retribution for hers."

"Oh, God!" Mandell groaned. After so many years of denying kinship with his father, he suddenly felt at one with the man, could feel the complete despair and agony of the young chevalier's final moments, the way he must have welcomed the sword thrust that ended his life.

Mandell stared at his grandfather, the regal old man dwindling to become something twisted, evil, hideous in Mandell's eyes. His breath shallow and rapid, he stalked toward the duke, his hands clenching and unclenching, scarce realizing what he did.

The duke did not stir. Only his eyes shifted to regard Mandell with a chilling understanding.

"And so now you would like to kill me? And you could do it swiftly and without mercy. You are not so very unlike me, Mandell. Except that you are driven to act from passion, whereas I have always been ruled by cold logic."

His words brought Mandell up short. He was horrified to realize the old man was right. Gazing into the duke's face was like staring into some demonic mirror, a reflection of the dark recesses of his heart. Mandell glanced down at his own trembling hands, inches from reaching for the old man's throat. With great effort of will, he steadied them. Lowering them to his sides, he stepped back, feeling drained.

"No, Grandfather," he said dully. "You are not ruled by

logic, but the bitter poison in your soul that drove you to destroy my father, that will destroy you as well."

The duke said nothing. Hooding his eyes, he reached for his quill and signed his name to the confession with a final flourish. Mandell paced a few steps away, striving to regain the rest of his composure before he could ask, "And what did you do with my father after—after you had—"

"I concealed his body in a winding sheet, and turned him over to the parish as a wandering vagrant who had died upon my lands. He was buried in a pauper's grave in the cemetery of the little church near my estate. I daresay the old vicar can point it out to you if you are sentimental enough to wish it."

After sanding the ink dry, the duke folded the vellum. Using the candle, he melted some red wax upon the closure, then affixed his seal to it.

"Here," he said, holding out the signed confession to Mandell. "This is yours. You may do as you like with it."

Slowly, Mandell turned and came back to the desk. As he reached for the paper, the duke's hand closed about Mandell's wrist. It was the first time Mandell could remember his grandfather volunteering such contact. The old man's fingers were remarkably cold.

"After you mother died, Mandell," the duke said, "I felt that you were all that was left to me. I both . . . cared for you and hated you. Your physical resemblance to your father was pure torment to me, so much so that—that I would often gaze at you as you slept and think of taking up the pillow, and suffocating the life from you."

"After what I have learned tonight, I almost regret that you permitted me to live," Mandell said in low, savage tones. He stared pointedly at the duke's fingers until the old man released him. Wrenching the confession out of His Grace's hand, Mandell turned and stalked from the room.

Only when he was certain that Mandell was gone did the duke allow himself to murmur, "But I have never had any such regrets, my Mandell."

The duke began to put away his ink, quill, and wax, clearing the desk as he had always done. He could not tol-

erate disorder nor had he ever liked servants handling his
private possessions. He rose to his feet and went to peer at
the surface of the bed with a tiny smile of satisfaction.
Good. The boy had forgotten to take the pistol away with
him. That simplified matters a great deal.

Going to the window, the duke forced open the casement,
taking in a reviving breath of sharp cold air. Then, smoothing back the lace from his cuffs, he took up the pistol.

Moments later a shot rang out in the night as the duke of
Windermere claimed his final victim.

Chapter 22

⋘⊙⋙

Braced by a score of pillows, Nick managed to sit up to take his breakfast. Bending over his tray, he attacked a large juicy beefsteak with a hearty enthusiasm that was unhampered by the thick wadding of bandages wrapped about his shoulder. Watching him, Sara could only marvel at his recuperative powers. It was difficult to remember that he was the same man who had been fetched to the doorstep of their modest townhouse only five days ago. Pale, drawn, he had hovered on the verge of death, and Sara had prayed to a God and all manner of saints she had not even believed in until that moment.

Her prayers had been heard and answered by someone, for Nick made a rapid recovery. Sara had discovered her husband possessed a remarkable resiliency of spirit as well as body. Whatever shock and disillusionment he had suffered from uncovering the truth about his grandfather seemed to have healed as swiftly as his wound. There would always be the scar creasing his shoulder, perhaps the lines about his mouth a little deeper for sorrow. But the sparkle in his eyes told Sara that his ultimate faith in the reason and goodness of mankind had not dimmed. Nick still believed.

But would that shining belief remain untarnished when faced with a far greater disillusionment? No longer having to fear for her husband's life, Sara had been freed to torment herself with other worries, Mandell's warning echoing through her mind again and again.

You would be better off telling him . . . any dark secrets you might harbor.

The terrible events that had occurred that night at Windermere Palace had but postponed the inevitable. Sara knew that Mandell was right, yet she could not seem to summon the courage to act upon his advice.

While Nick devoured his breakfast, she sat by the hearthside in silence, mangling the stitches that she attempted to set in a linen handkerchief. Nick's bedchamber was small and close, seeming scarce large enough to contain the mounting tension. But Sara knew the tension was all locked within her. Nick remained blissfully unaware that anything was wrong, or at least so she thought.

She was startled when he shoved his tray to one side and cheerfully demanded, "Out with it, Sara. What is troubling you, my love?"

"T-troubling me?" Sara tried to look astonished. "I have no notion what you might mean, Nicholas."

Nick grinned. "Our marriage has been brief, I will admit. But I can always tell that when you start wreaking havoc on some piece of unoffending fabric with a needle, it is a sure sign that something is wrong."

She winced at his perception. This could be the opening she sought, but it would still be easier to laugh and deny his words. She had been such a good liar all her life. She did not know how to stop dissembling, had never wished to do so until falling in love with Nick. How did one begin to tell the truth, especially when one knew with a sense of inevitability where it must lead? Perhaps the best course was to spare them both a great deal of pain and begin with the end.

Plucking at the snarled threads of her embroidery work, she said dully, "I was only wondering . . . how long one could be married and still obtain an annulment. Or barring that, how difficult it would be to obtain a divorce."

Nick said nothing for several moments. Sara could almost feel the weight of his silence pressing upon her heart. She heard him shift, settling back against the pillows. Then he said with a quiet sigh, "Your question is not entirely unexpected and certainly not one that I blame you for asking. My prospects when you married me were bad enough, but after this scandal with my grandfather—"

"No!" Sara looked up, Nick's misconception a painful reproach to her. "It has nothing to do with that or your prospects, but everything to do with me. There is something that I have to tell you, and then it will be you who wishes for a divorce."

Nick did not receive this dramatic pronouncement in the grave manner that Sara anticipated. His taut features relaxed with relief. He was almost smiling, and Sara did not know how she was going to continue, how she could do this to him. Damn him! Did he have to look quite so adoring, so infernally trusting?

Flinging her embroidery down, she shoved to her feet. It seemed easier to continue when she paced restlessly about the room, when she did not have to look Nick directly in the eye.

"There are many things about me you don't know, Nicholas. Things . . . things like—"

"Like the fact you are not a widow from Yorkshire?" Nick supplied amiably when she floundered again. "That your mother lives above a pawnshop in Bethnal Green? Or are you more worried about telling me of your—um—recent history with my cousin Mandell?"

Sara whipped about to gape at Nick, stunned. His lips quirked in a lopsided smile, his expression so fond and foolish, Sara had to fight a strange desire to burst into tears.

"Then—then you already know everything?" she whispered. "How—how long . . ."

"Oh, since a day or two before our wedding."

"And yet you married me anyway." Fully comprehending the extent of Nick's love for her, Sara felt dazed, curiously humbled by it. "Who—who could have told you such things about me, my family? You know more about me than Mandell ever did."

"My cousin never had any occasion to visit Bethnal Green. You forget I am a frequent caller there. I was doing some of my investigations when I was accosted by a young boy named Palmer who tried to relieve me of my watch."

"Davy," Sara said darkly. "Why can't that fool stick to robbing dead bodies? He possesses no talent for being a pickpocket."

"Er—yes, I do agree he should choose another career. In any event, your brother must have observed our encounter in the street that day. He assumed I had replaced Lord Mandell in your affections and sought to use that knowledge to dissuade me from handing him over to the magistrate. Instead David took me around to—uh—tea at your mother's flat."

"You met Mama, too?" Sara asked with a sinking heart.

"Yes, and Gideon." Nick grimaced a little at the mention of her elder brother. "A daunting but charming parcel of rogues. One could do far worse for a collection of in-laws. In time, I daresay I shall grow quite fond of all of them."

Sara stared at him, wondering if Nick had lost his wits. Or perhaps it was she. She felt a sudden need to sit down, and sank upon the foot of the bed.

"Why didn't you tell me you knew all of this?" she asked. "Why did you let me go on lying to you?"

Nick squirmed and looked a little sheepish. "I discovered all that I did purely by chance, but I was afraid you would think I was spying on you."

"Spying on me!" Sara gave a wild laugh. "Nick, you had every right to do so. I tricked you, lied to you again and again."

"You told me you loved me. Was that untrue?"

"No!" One hot tear escaped to cascade down her cheek. "Those are the truest words I have ever spoken in my whole miserable life."

"Then nothing else matters, my dear," Nick said. He stretched out one hand to her, his eyes soft not with mere forgiveness, but with a loving acceptance of all that she was.

Suppressing a tiny sob, she went to him, allowing him to draw her into the comforting circle of his arm. Stretching out beside him, she buried her face against his chest and wept as she had not allowed herself to do since her days as a small girl.

Nick patted her back, pressing kisses against her hair. "Sara. Sara, my love, whatever is wrong now?"

"N-nothing. Only I never fully appreciated what a remarkable man you are, Nick Drummond."

"Oh. It is most agreeable to hear that, but I wish it would not make you cry. I do not know what I shall do with you if you turn into one of those weepy, sentimental females. Besides, you are getting my bandage wet."

"S-sorry." Sara hiccuped on a laugh and raised up a little, dashing the tears from her eyes, managing to regain some control of herself.

"That is better," Nick said, sweeping one fingertip along the curve of her cheek. "Now I trust there shall be no more foolish talk of divorce. There are other acts that need to be passed in Parliament I would rather devote my energy to."

"I—I know." Sara slowly straightened, easing herself off the bed. "Nick, I don't want there to be any more secrets between us."

"Nor do I, my love."

"Then I think it is time you did a little plain speaking yourself."

When Nick frowned in puzzlement, Sara went over to the tall wardrobe which housed Nick's rainbow array of frock coats. "Do you remember the morning after we were wed?" she asked. "I was attempting to help you dress so that we did not have to be intruded upon so soon by any servants."

Sara eased open the wardrobe door, then reached far back on the top shelf. "I found this when I was looking for a clean stock."

She turned and held up the object that had so unsettled her peace of mind. It was a gauntlet, fashioned to make a man look as though he had no hand, the end curving into a lethal-looking steel hook. She crossed the room and laid the damning evidence upon the bed before him.

Nick fingered the gauntlet and heaved a deep sigh. "I can explain, Sara."

She shook her head, cutting him off. "No explanations are necessary. I don't know what reason compelled you to run about at night, playing at being a footpad, whether you were trying to become a Robin of the Hood, or merely seeking to drive home your point about the need for a better police force."

Nick looked nonplussed. "You appear to have taken this discovery quite calmly, my dear."

Sara shuddered. "I have spent most of my life watching someone I love flirt with the hangman's noose. I never expected I would have to continue the tradition with my husband. But I supposed I am growing resigned to being worried to death."

"Sara—"

"I wish you would not continue on with your activities as the Hook, but I want you to know that I shall support you in this, the same as in any other endeavor, even if we both end up in Newgate."

To her astonishment and indignation, Nick only laughed.

"Sara, Sara! Your devotion overwhelms me. I daresay I will find myself in Newgate someday, most likely because I have written something to annoy those damned Tories who control the government. But I will never be arrested for anything so dashing as being the Hook."

Regarding her with a tender smile, Nick held up the gauntlet. "My dear Sara, I confiscated this infernal thing from your older brother."

The Palmer family gathered around one of the tables in the Running Cat tavern, the murky atmosphere seeming suited to the general mood. Chastity and her youngest son, Davy, sipped at their tankards of ale, both faces as mournful as though attending a wake. Gideon appeared unaffected by their air of discontent. He rocked back on the legs of his chair, listening to his mother's complaints with a kind of lazy amusement.

"I always wished Sary well," Chastity said. "And lord knows I tried to understand the child's mad obsession with becoming a lady and turning respectable. But I neve thought the dire effects of Sary getting married will spill over onto us. Nick Drummond's a pleasant enough fellow, but I could tell at the outset he means to make a thorough pest of himself. Imagine! At our first meeting, telling me he meant to wed my babe, then already hinting that I should not be living over a pawnshop and drinking gin."

Mrs. Palmer took a deep draught of her ale and shuddered. "He even had the boldness to suggest I might like to meet some respectable gentlemen, a—a country curate or a red-faced squire. Mr. Drummond means to saddle me with a second husband. I know he does!"

"You never had a first husband, Mum," Gideon reminded her.

"Don't be impertinent, sir. You know what I mean. I prefer to choose my own admirers."

"I don't know what you are complaining about," Davy said querulously. "What about Drummond's blasted plans for me? He said since I have this interest in handling corpses and picking people's pockets, I might as well do it honestly and become a doctor."

Gideon no longer made any effort to contain his mirth. He laughed hard enough that his chair slammed back down on all fours.

Both his mother and Davy glared at him.

"I don't know what you find so damned amusing," Davy said. "Drummond has already put a crimp in your affairs, hasn't he, my fine sir?"

Davy's sneering remark sobered Gideon a little. His lips twisted at the memory of his grim confrontation with Sara's future husband, listening to Drummond's earnest lecture on the follies of a life of crime.

"I'll never understand how Mr. Drummond figured out you was the Hook, Gideon," Mrs. Palmer lamented. "Sara's husband does not look all that bright, and you did manage to fool all the best Bow Street Runners in London."

Gideon cast a dark glance to where George Nagle was serving up some ale. "Drummond is more clever than he appears, and I have no doubt he was helped along by the gossip and suspicions of a certain tavern host who'd sell out his own mother for a ha'penny."

Davy smirked. "However Drummond found out, he's put a stop to your doings good and proper. He even made you surrender your hook, didn't he?"

"Ah, but that is the wonderful thing about losing a hand made of steel." Gideon's teeth glinted in a feral smile. "One can always have another one made."

Then he raised his glass and proposed a toast to the new bride and groom. "May my dear sister Sara have found her heart's desire, and may she keep her new husband far away from us."

It was a toast Mrs. Palmer and Davy heartily seconded.

Chapter 23

Anne stood on the slope near the willow tree, watching her daughter romp by the pond in St. James's Park. With Pegasus tethered to a tree, the young groom trailed devotedly after Norrie, keeping the child from wading into the waters in her earnest efforts to toss bread to the ducks.

The breeze billowing out the soft folds of Anne's muslin gown, she appeared all that was warm and serene, truly the gentle goddess who had restored spring to the world. As Mandell alighted from his coach to join her, he felt a tightening in his chest, a rush of love and longing for her that was almost painful.

He had not seen Anne since the night at Windermere Palace, had been able to do no more than pen her a note, saying that as soon as he had sorted things out, he would come to her. *Sorting things out*—that had been a mild way to describe the chaos that had surrounded him since his grandfather's death.

Another woman might well not have comprehended his need to be alone after the devastating revelations of that night, to come to terms with the legacy of bitterness and grief that the old duke had left to him. But as Mandell approached across the grass and Anne glanced round, he saw no sign of reproach on her face. Her eyes shone with a silent understanding, a tremulous smile of welcome upon her lips.

Only Anne knew what it cost her to maintain such an aura of restraint. She wanted to run to him, cast herself into his embrace, just as she had been longing to seek him out these past days, offer him her love and consolation. But she

knew from experience that the barriers of Mandell's heart
could not be forced. He had to be willing to allow her in.
He had done so once. She prayed he would be able to
again.

Before Mandell could close the distance between them,
Anne heard Norrie give a glad shout. Hiking up the skirts
of her frock, the little girl rushed pell-mell at Mandell and
flung her arms about his legs.

As Mandell smiled and lifted Norrie high into his arms,
Anne envied the child her spontaneity, her complete freedom from the constraints and doubts that beset adults.
Norrie hugged Mandell and thrust upon him a bedraggled
bouquet of wildflowers and weeds. After a few moments of
whispered conversation, Mandell set the child down and
she went skipping back to the pond.

Mandell came the rest of the way across the grass. He favored Anne with a small bow and presented her with
Norrie's nosegay.

"For you, milady," he said. "Your daughter appears to
think I need some help with my wooing."

"I have never thought so," Anne murmured as she accepted the motley collection of daisies, violets, and blades
of grass.

For a fleeting instant, Mandell smiled and Anne thought
that all was well. But the light vanished from his eyes far
too quickly. She sensed an air of weariness about him that
went as deep as his soul. The first hint of silver had appeared amongst his midnight-dark strands, and fresh lines
of sorrow were carved near that sensitive mouth.

"Your sister told me I would find you here this morning," he said.

"Yes, I know it is early for a walk, but I felt the need to
escape." Anne winced. "Since all that has happened, I find
myself a figure of some notoriety. We are plagued by visitors at all hours, come to offer congratulations upon my
narrow escape. I believe most are just curious to meet a
lady who was once a resident of Newgate."

"That is one nuisance I have not been plagued with,"
Mandell said drily. "Few are presumptuous enough to foist

their curiosity upon the grandson of a murderer. My chief problem has been my servants. They will persist in calling me 'Your Grace' now. Only Hastings seems to understand how it affects me."

Anne wanted to show him how much she also understood, but Mandell turned away from her. He nodded toward where Norrie had coaxed Pegasus to the pond's edge, trying to convince the stubborn pony he needed a drink.

"I trust Eleanor has taken no ill effects through all of this?" he asked.

"She did cling to me for the first day I was returned home," Anne replied. "But children have a way of accepting the most extraordinary events that surprises one. To Norrie, I believe, it all seemed like nothing more than a slightly frightening story of me being held prisoner in a tower. Then you dashed in to rescue me and—and deal with all the ogres. I fear she now expects there to be a happy ending as well."

Anne waited breathlessly, hoping for some sign of concurrence in Mandell. He merely lowered his lashes, veiling his expression, and Anne's heart sank. He was building his walls again. She could sense that, and she did not know how to stop him.

"Norrie and I have both been worried about you," Anne ventured at last. "She—she feared you would be made very sad by the death of your grandfather."

"In truth, Anne, I scarce know what I have been feeling these past few days. Guilt mostly."

When Anne regarded him questioningly, he said, "No matter what the old devil did, the grief and suffering he caused, I would not have wished him such an end. I should never have been so careless, leaving that pistol behind."

"Your grandfather would have but found some other way. What else could he have done? Could you imagine the proud duke of Windermere forced to give an accounting of his actions, even to a jury of his peers?"

"No," Mandell said reluctantly, "I could not."

He swallowed thickly. "That last conversation I had with

my grandfather . . . I have not felt able to speak of it. But I would like to tell you now, Anne."

Anne breathed a tiny sigh. Perhaps the wall this time was not quite so insurmountable as she feared. Norrie's flowers fell from her fingers unheeded as she reached out to take Mandell's hand.

"I am listening," she said quietly.

He seemed to derive great comfort from entwining her fingers with his own. His voice was calm and steady as he related the details of that final interview. Anne could only guess what the duke's horrible revelations had done to Mandell, the ravaging of his spirit reflected in the dark depths of his eyes.

Anne grieved for Lady Celine and her young husband, a couple whose great love had been sacrificed to a revolution and an old man's bitterness. She grieved for the little boy who had thus been deprived of both of his parents. More than anything, she grieved for the man who clung so tightly to her hand as he related these horrors.

"I remembered so little myself of what happened in France," Mandell said. "But yesterday, I found some old letters amongst the duke's private papers that clarified everything. They were from my mother, the last one posted from Calais. She explained that she had decided to defy her husband's wishes that she set sail for England, and instead meant to return with me to Paris."

Mandell gave a wry grimace. "It appears my mother was a true Windermere. Stubborn, arrogant. She simply could not be brought to believe that any French rabble would dare to harm the daughter and grandson of an English duke. Setting that bit of hauteur aside, she wrote as a woman who could not bear the thought of being parted from the man she loved."

"Your mother did not make a wise choice, but a perfectly understandable one."

"That is what I am endeavoring to remember out of the whole senseless tragedy," Mandell said. "How much my parents did love each other, and that they must have been happy for a time."

He bowed his head in silence for a moment before he could continue, "There was a more recent letter amongst my grandfather's effects. This one from the present comte de Valmiere seeking information about myself and my father. God alone only knows why the old man did not destroy it, but I am grateful that he did not.

"I have an uncle living near Caen, and several aunts. It occurs to me that they might be able to tell me a great deal about my father, things that I was never privileged to know. The comte mentioned that he still has some of my father's compositions. It seems that the reason he took my mother to Paris in the first place was that he hoped for an audience at court, a chance to find a patron for his music."

A slight flush of embarrassment stained Mandell's cheeks. "I know this is going to sound absurd, but I feel that if I could learn to play my father's music, I could somehow have a part of him back again, perhaps ... perhaps even regain a part of myself that was taken from me so long ago."

"It does not sound absurd at all," Anne said.

He slipped his hand from her grasp. "I want to go back to France, Anne."

She wondered if he even realized that as he said this he paced several steps away from her. Once more, Anne felt the distance threatening to grow between them. But she forced back the lump in her throat and said, "Of—of course, my lord. If that is what you need to do."

"If circumstances had been different, I would have asked you to go with me. But I no longer have the right to do so, not after these discoveries about my grandfather. He often accused me of having tainted blood, and so I do. Not my father's, but his."

"No, Mandell," Anne protested, seeking to recapture his hand.

But Mandell stepped back, saying in a voice raw with anguish, "There was one dread moment, Anne, when I looked into his eyes and I saw myself reflected there, when I realized there was a danger I could become just like him, cold, ruthless, uncaring."

"No, Mandell, no! There was an evil in him that has never existed in you."

"How can you be so certain of that?" he asked bitterly. "Because you believe that Norrie has this uncanny ability to peer into hearts? Because for some strange reason your little girl loves me?"

"No, because I do."

Her answer stopped his agitated pacing. Every part of him seemed to go still as he stared into her eyes, desperately seeking, wanting to believe.

She cupped his face gently between her hands and said, "I love you, Mandell. Do you think that I could care so much for a man who was as cold and hard as you describe?"

"Then—then despite all that has happened, you would still marry me, Anne?" he asked.

"Yes, my lord."

"You would permit me to be a father to your little girl?"

"Yes, my lord."

"Trust me enough to—to—"

"To surrender my entire life and happiness into your keeping? Yes, my lord," Anne repeated fervently.

A shadow seemed to pass from his features, his eyes shining with such tenderness and humble gratitude that Anne felt tears start to her eyes.

"I have another name, you know," he said almost shyly. "I was christened for my father . . . Dominque."

"Dominque," Anne whispered. "It is a very fine name."

"For so long I tried to forget it."

"I know," she said, caressing back the dark strands of hair from his temple. "Because remembering brought you the nightmare."

"You have banished the nightmares, milady," he said huskily. "For us, I vow there will only be dreams."

Drawing her into his arms, he sealed the promise with his kiss.